ACCLAIM FOR DAVID ANTHONY DURHAM'S

Gabriel's Story

WINNER OF THE AMERICAN LIBRARY
ASSOCIATION BLACK CAUCUS LITERARY AWARD

"Sweeps the reader up into a fascinating, Oz-like whirlwind of language."   —*San Francisco Chronicle*

"Durham captures with exquisite precision the isolation,
loneliness and cruelty of life in the vastness of the
West. . . . The reader turns the last page with regret at
the journey's end."   —*The Times Picayune*

"A bold, sweeping odyssey that tackles big themes. . . . A
thrill to read."   —*The News and Observer*

"Artfully plotted, masterfully written, this is a work of
shimmering intensity and wisdom. . . . *Gabriel's Story*
will easily stand in the first ranks of American literature."
           —Jeffrey Lent, author of *In the Fall*

"A sensational debut . . . lush and atmospheric."
           —*Essence*

DAVID ANTHONY DURHAM

GABRIEL'S STORY

David Anthony Durham was born in 1969 to
parents of Caribbean ancestry. He won the
Zora Neale Hurston/Richard Wright Fiction
Award in 1992 and received an MFA from the
University of Maryland in 1996. He has lived
and traveled widely throughout America and
Europe. Durham, along with his wife and
daughter, now divides his time between the
United States and Scotland.

Gabriel's Story

DAVID ANTHONY DURHAM

Anchor Books • A Division of Random House, Inc. • New York

For Gudrun and Maya

FIRST ANCHOR BOOKS EDITION, APRIL 2002

Copyright © 2001 by David Anthony Durham

The Library of Congress has cataloged the Doubleday edition
as follows:
Durham, David Anthony, 1969–
Gabriel's story / by David Anthony Durham.—1st ed.
     p.   cm.
1. Afro-American families—Fiction. 2. Afro-American
cowboys—Fiction. 3. Young men—Fiction. 4. Kansas—Fiction.
I. Title.
PS3554.U677 G33 2001
813'.6—dc21
00-025291

Anchor ISBN 0-385-72033-5

Book design by Pei Loi Koay

www.anchorbooks.com

Printed in the United States of America

10 9 8 7 6 5 4 3

Gabriel's
Story

T HE BLACK MAN WATCHED THE DOOR. HE STOOD, ONE HAND holding the reins of two horses, the other hand engaged in a sense-less motion, closing and opening, a rock to a board, a rock to a board. His profile against the morning sun was like the chipped edge of a flint arrowhead, carved by the force of stone on stone and left imperfect and therefore best suited to its work.

The horses were beautiful creatures. One was a dun, the other a paint of brown and white, with a faint touch of something like orange. The man sometimes spoke to them in a low whisper, words not of our language and perhaps of none other, but sounds that the horses knew and were comforted by. He watched the door, and as he watched he caught a scent in the air and knew that the cacti on the plains to the east had opened their blooms to the sun. He looked at the horses and could tell by the flare of their nostrils that they smelled it too.

When the door swung open with a bang, he knew something was wrong. A man strode out, a white man, his hat pushed back on his head, the brim of it looking like a halo as it caught the light and illuminated his face. Two strides and he was off the porch, another two and he had reached the dun, taken the reins, stepped into the stirrup, and swung his large frame up into the saddle. He had a young face, tanned and weathered and abused but no older than his years. He set his gaze on the black man, and in that gaze was a shallow anger that was red hot, that burned bright and for a moment obscured the other anger, the slow heat that he carried with him always.

You coming?

The black man didn't ask him where. He slipped on top the paint and sat as if he'd never been off it.

A woman appeared in the door of the house. She was a creature of considerable girth, cloaked in a dress that hung over her like a cover over a piece of furniture, alluding to but rendering mysterious the shapes hidden beneath. She squinted in the sun and called the man by name.

It don't gotta be like this.

The man spat and set his gaze on her. Those were all the words he needed.

You always did have to be a hot-head, she said.

You ain't even seen me warm yet. With that, he spun his horse to the east and rode.

The woman called the black man by name. You ain't gotta go with him, you know? He don't own you. This ain't no slave country anymore, and we don't have no quarrel with you.

If the black man heard her, he gave no indication. He turned and rode away from the ranch and didn't look back and didn't squint, although the sun pierced to the back of his eyes. He fell in behind the other horseman and rode in his wake toward the sun.

Part 1

THE BOY HAD MEASURED THEIR PROGRESS ACROSS THE land through the warped glass of the train's windows. He had seen it all unfurl, from the tidewater up over the broken back of the mountains, out onto rolling hills and into the old frontier, now pacified and peopled and farmed, and further still, through cities and small towns and finally out onto this great expanse, across which they traveled like fleas on a mammoth's back. He had even watched at night, while his younger brother slept against his shoulder and his mother contemplated thoughts of her own. He searched in the land's dark contours for things he dared not name aloud, and he held within himself a rage of voices that to the outside world looked and sounded like silence.

WHEN THEY STEPPED OFF THE TRAIN that afternoon, the boy couldn't help but stare over the crowd and out to the horizon. Looking to the west, he could just make out the geometric shadows that were Crownsville, that cowtown newly bloomed and thriving, connected to the East by a bloodline of iron and steel. To the north and south and back to the east the land rolled away in undulating nothingness. The grass lay heavy and tired from the beating of the previous evening's rain, and the April sky was not a thing of air and gas. Rather, it lay like a solid ceiling of slate, pressing the living down into the prairie.

The train station was made up of several sod-brick buildings. They had crooked roofs out of which sprouted an abundance of green shoots. In front of one of these structures a motley array of men lounged, with expressions of indolent curiosity on their faces. The grass had been trodden down and thinned by the traffic. It was pockmarked with puddles and prints of both feet and hooves, and cut by wagon wheels.

"Gabriel, you and Ben help the men unload," the boy's mother said. "Make sure we get all our crates. There's six of them. Count each one and stack them ready to load on Mr. Johns's wagon." The boys didn't move, but she didn't seem to notice. Instead her gaze rose and roamed through the sparse crowd of people. "Go on and help, like I said," she said, moving away a few steps. The trim of her dress dangled down into the wet grass and mud, but she made no attempt to hold it up.

Gabriel nudged Ben on the shoulder, and the two boys walked toward the freight car, carrying what hand luggage they had with them. Gabriel had just turned fifteen, although he looked two or three years older. He had a strong body, tall and lean, with the long legs of his nomadic ancestors. His wool jacket cramped his shoulders and impeded the swing of his arms. His skin was a dark shade of brown stretched taut across his features, as if the components of his face were growing more rapidly than the shell. His nose was thin-bridged, with a distinctive flair to the nostrils that was wholly African in design.

Ben was his younger by two years. They looked much alike in the rudimentary casts of their appearance, although Ben had a small indentation on his forehead, and his eyebrows were drawn in thin, wispy lines. He also moved with a nervous energy very different from his brother's brooding gait. His gaze bounced from object to object, out toward the fields, from person to person, and back to the enormous iron works of the train that had brought them so far.

The two boys saw to the unloading. Gabriel was quiet and respectful, yet only enough so as to avoid trouble. He counted the crates, inquired about a missing one, and soon had them stacked as his mother had instructed. This done, they climbed onto them, sat, and waited.

The younger boy said, "I reckon we're here."

Gabriel was silent for a long minute. "I reckon we're nowhere."

ELIZA JOHNS REJOINED HER SONS soon after. She had a gaunt face, in which one could trace the origins of her sons' russet eyes, their full lips, and the deep brown hue of their flesh. Her cheekbones curved upward in smooth diagonal lines, unmarked by scar or blemish. She was still beautiful in the eyes of men, perhaps more so now than ever, although years of quiet worry had carved an angular tension into her features. From her erect posture, her civilized clothes, and the demure manner in which she held her hands clasped before her, one might have gathered that she was unaccustomed to the frontier. But there was something determined about the way she set her jaw and surveyed the crowd unflinchingly which seemed well suited for a place such as this.

"You think he's not coming?" Ben asked.

"Don't be silly," Eliza said. "He'll be here." She reached over and straightened Ben's collar with a quick tug, then turned back and faced the crowd. "Don't expect the worst from people until they've shown a history of it."

This answer satisfied the younger boy, but not Gabriel. "He better come. Couldn't pay to go back if we had—"

"There he is now," Eliza said.

Gabriel looked into the crowd. It took him a moment to pick the man out, but he was there, Solomon Johns. He walked toward them with an anxious gait, dodging people and animals and the larger puddles. Gabriel cut his eyes away and studied the ground.

Solomon stood just over six foot three, even with his slightly stooped posture. His size was measured mostly by the width of his shoulders and the weight evenly distributed throughout his torso, a chest as solid as a lifetime of work could make it. His features were a bit irregular, thrown about his face by a casual hand: eyes set far apart, nose wide enough to all but fill the space, and a mouth small by comparison, although what it lacked in size it made up for in enthusiasm: "Eliza! Praise God you made it." He strode toward her as if to lift her off the ground. Only at the last moment did he check himself. Instead of hoisting her into the air, he gripped her by the arms and searched her face, finding her features all and more than he remembered.

Eliza shared his gaze, smiling and nodding. They neither embraced fully nor kissed, but to the two boys watching, the exchange was so intimate as to be embarrassing. They lifted their eyes to meet the man full on only when their mother spoke to them. "Boys, what's the matter with you? Say hello to Mr. Johns."

"Hello, Mr. Johns," Ben intoned.

Gabriel moved his lips.

"Oh, boys! Look at ya!" Solomon reached out and ardently shook each boy's hand. "Lord, you two have grown. And it's only been a year's time? They do grow like weeds, don't they?" He paused and admired them, then turned back to Eliza. "I can hardly believe it. You're all here with me. Y'all came out sooner than I expected, but it sure does me good to see you. Now we can get this thing started for real."

Solomon brought his wagon around, a small, rough-hewn thing of sun-bleached wood, led by a ragged mule with milky eyes. Eliza examined the wagon and the mule with a look of concern, but she voiced no comment. They loaded up quickly, Solomon talking all the time, Eliza and Ben prompting him with questions. Once packed, Solomon pointed out the blankets he had laid across the seat as padding for his wife. The boys had to climb up onto the crates and sit on that awkward perch as the wagon moved off in fits and starts, the wooden wheels sending jolts up through the crates and into the boy's backsides. This was a new reason for Gabriel to scowl, although his brother seemed hardly disturbed, so captured was he by the joy of movement, so amazed at the great open space that was to be their home.

THEY TRAVELED TO THE SOUTH, on a dirt road that was at first wide and newly graded but that devolved quickly into two irregular ruts. They followed these out over the rolling features of the land, passengers on scars that headed straight for the horizon. They passed many a homestead, squat earthen structures like forlorn warts pushed up from the earth, darker versions of the colors and textures of the fields that spread out around them. From a distance, it seemed barely possible that these were the

homes of human beings. They looked more like sheds for mis-
treated and abused animals.

They passed a field where a young boy labored to drive a
plow through the earth. A thin ox aided him in this effort, and
yet their progress was slow. The strain on both showed in the
desperation of their movements, as if each push were the last
they'd be capable of. The boy's arms were bare to the chill air,
his skin so pale it looked lifeless. He paused to stare at the passing family, a smirk on his face that seemed not an invitation to
humor but rather an indication of some joke known only to him.
He continued with his work a moment later, and was still at it as
the wagon crested the next rise and rolled out of sight.

Gabriel turned his eyes to the back of Solomon's head. The
man wore an old hat, narrow-brimmed and weatherbeaten,
stained on the side where his fingers were likely to touch it in
greeting. Gabriel hadn't seen this man in nearly a year, and before
that he had known him for only another nine months. Watching
him now, all the feelings he had nurtured from the start and over
that long absence rose up again. This man had walked in over his
father's freshly dug grave. Ever since, Gabriel had found something offensive in his gestures and smiles, in his words, and in the
very nod of his head. Each kindness seemed a slight disguised,
each touch to his mother's shoulder or back an infidelity.

Solomon drove with a relaxed posture, the reins loose in his
hands, his head bobbing and swaying, seemingly oblivious of the
thoughts of the boy just behind him. "This earth is tough stuff,
I'll tell you," he said. "Break a man's back, break a plow, break an
ox's back for that matter. Sometimes, when you get a good bite
into it, it lets out a ripping sound, like you're tearing the earth's
skin and it don't like it. But there's good soil below it. You just
gotta put in the work to get down to it." He laughed and then fell
silent for a moment. The creaking of the wagon and the turning
of the wheels were the only sounds to be heard.

Eliza watched the backside of the mule, whether entranced or disgusted or just curious, it was hard to tell. She raised her eyes and scanned the horizon before them. "It's a wonder you don't get lost out here. Not a tree to be seen."

"Oh, there's trees around," Solomon said. He waved his hand to indicate their presence nearby. Gabriel followed his gesture with a gaze, but he could find nothing out there except more and more of the thick grass.

The sun set without ever having shone through the clouds. It slipped to the horizon, and the sky dimmed accordingly, with only a mute hint of watery orange to mark the sun's passing the rim of the earth. The family rode on into the night. Solomon assured them that it was not far at all. The mule could even guide them home of its own accord, so familiar was it with the land hereabouts. Ben entwined an arm in the crate lashings and managed to fall asleep, an awkward, rocking slumber, but deep nonetheless. Gabriel's eyes never tired. They stared out at the shadowy land as if challenging it.

An hour or so into the darkness, they broke out of the ruts and turned off to the left, soon settling into new grooves. In another fifteen minutes they pulled to a stop beside a shape of denser darkness than the night. Solomon was cheerful as he called it home and urged the others in and to bed. But all three of the newcomers found it hard to leave the wagon. They stood staring at the shadow before them, each seeking in the others' faces some sign of reassurance, and each finding none.

They stepped down and followed Solomon inside. For a few moments all was blackness, but then the man struck a match and lit a candle. He turned around with it in hand and faced the travelers, silent for a moment. He lit another candle, and the dimensions of the place began to come into view. It was a single room. The walls pushed into and cramped the space, making it feel much smaller on the inside than the shadow had indicated from the outside. It was smoky and moist and earthen all at once, with a smell unpleasant enough to contort Gabriel's face. From what he could make out, the walls flickering and unsteady in the candlelight, the room seemed more like a cave than a house. Beneath his feet, the floor was of hard-packed earth. There was a crooked table, around which sat chairs of the same design. Boxes and crates and undefined objects cluttered the room, barely leaving space for the iron stove that sat central to it, cold now and dead-looking.

"Well, I know it ain't much," Solomon said. "Never did have the touch to make a place look nice. But it's sound, keeps the heat good, and the roof don't leak much." He motioned toward the ceiling with the candle but then drew back as if afraid he might set it aflame, and afraid even more that his words were futile. "It's better you get a view of the place in the daylight. This here candle don't do it justice."

No one responded, but Solomon kept pushing himself through the motions of host. He showed the boys where they'd be sleeping, in a corner, on bedding of straw and hemp. He seemed to find words harder and harder to create. He indicated the space Eliza and he would share, with a nod and an attentive study of her face. Their bed, small for two but made up neatly and displaying an old quilt, was separated from the rest of the room by a curtain.

Eliza asked no questions. She suggested that the boys go to sleep, adding, "We'll get a proper view in the morning." She slipped behind the curtain before the boys could respond.

They stood there, seemingly the only ones shocked by the appearance of things. Gabriel thought back to the brownstone they had left in Baltimore. They had occupied only the upstairs apartment, and it had never seemed so special or spacious before. But now it stood out as infinitely grand: those wide stairs and high ceilings, the bay windows facing a busy street, the kitchen, and the dining room with its inset fireplace and flowered wallpaper. The bedroom that he and Ben had shared had seemed too intimate a space. But that room, with its iron-frame bed and view onto the alley three stories below, was nearly as big as the space they were all to share now. He glanced at his brother, for a rare moment seeking some camaraderie. Indeed, he read similar thoughts written on Ben's troubled features.

Gabriel glanced at the curtain behind which his mother had disappeared. His mouth worked, as if he would call her out and demand some explanation, point out to her the impossibility of what this man had just presented to them. But his tongue couldn't form the words. He moved over to the bed when Solomon offered to get a little fire going to keep the night warm. He sat on the firm pallet and watched the man, his eyes dark and brooding in the candlelight.

THE TWO MEN RODE EAST to San Antonio, where they passed three days in a haze of alcohol and sex. From there they rode on to San Marcus and Mountain City and into Austin, where the white man drew on his bank account and so further fueled their debauchery. They spent time and money in Waco and Fort Graham and Dallas, leaving behind them two men near death, a string of damaged saloons, and three prostitutes who cursed the men by name and description and asked that God do them the one favor of tearing these men from the earth and throwing them to the fires of hell.

The white man harbored a rage that had been newly stirred but that had begun before anything he could name and plagued him in his dreams, both sleeping and awake. He thought up tortures for his enemies, and when they were exhausted, he thought up new enemies and so continued. The black man watched it all with quiet eyes and waited.

Outside of a saloon in Dallas, the white man took the butt of a rifle across his forehead and lay immobile as blood trickled into his eyes, wondering if this was what death felt like, wondering if the fires of hell were actually liquid, and if so, could they be consumed? The black man carried him away and sat him on his horse, and they rode down the Trinity River and camped at one of its forks and sobered up. The white man cursed everything, himself included, and struggled with the demons within, and tried to push them away because they were not his demons but had been planted in him. They need not be his, and this need not be the course of his life. He stared into the flames of their mesquite fire and listened to the coyotes and watched the progress of suckerfish in the river and thereby found a new sanity. He nursed his mind gently and watched it grow calm.

GABRIEL WOKE EARLY THE NEXT MORNING, chilled to the bone and damp. His brother pressed against him, his mouth open, breathing with a peaceful rhythm. Behind the thin screen of cotton Solomon snored, low and nasal, occasionally mumbling some bit of dream conversation. Gabriel listened to the chorus created between them, punctuated by silences that seemed alive with tiny sounds: coyote songs from the prairie, the scurrying of mice, and, fainter still, the burrowing, grinding noise of some creature, whether within the walls or inside the soddy, he could not tell. He lay there for some time, his eyes probing the wall nearest him.

Eventually he sat up and slipped from underneath the woolen blanket he and his brother had shared and emerged fully clothed, even down to his shoes. The room was dimly lit. There was a lone and tiny window, and through it came only the faintest indication of light. In the stove, orange embers pulsed and glowed, warm although they gave no flame.

He stood there like an aged and senile man, looking around him at the foreign world of his own home, until he heard movement beyond the curtain that enclosed the space Eliza and Solomon shared. This spurred him on. He crept over to the door, a wooden thing that neither fully fit the space it occupied nor appeared to have been a door by design. He had to lift it to move it.

Although sunrise had not yet taken place, it was noticeably lighter outside. The sky had all but cleared of clouds, and the last faint traces of stars were still visible in the west. Gabriel walked away from the house with determined steps, across earth touched by frost. He paused only when he got to the top of a hill. There he turned and looked back.

The house was a stark silhouette against the eastern glow. It sat small and inconsequential on the landscape. Next to it lay a plot of turned soil, a tiny brown square he could have held between his fingers. He studied this for a moment, and then his eyes drifted on and stared unfocused at the prairie around and behind the house. He had seen such space yesterday and the day before that, but his eyes were not yet comfortable with it. They roamed across it in search of a boundary, a border, an indication that this land didn't go on forever. No such marker was to be found.

The lonely call of some creature drifted past Gabriel, a cry part canine and part musical. As if summoned by it, a shape emerged from the house: Solomon. He stood for a moment, taking in the morning, then turned to some task on the far side of the house. Gabriel folded his arms across his chest and stood unmoving. A drop of moisture clung to his nostril. He sniffed to halt its progress but otherwise ignored it. How could Solomon call this a home? His letters, although written in another person's hand, had promised so much. They had painted a picture of prosperity that bore no resemblance to what Gabriel now saw before him. He silently named the man a liar, one more slur to add to the list that he'd compiled over the long train ride. He trudged back toward the house, firm in his conviction that his mother would also see this fool's folly. She would look it in the face, turn from it, and flee.

ELIZA DIDN'T DRAW HER CONCLUSIONS as quickly as her son did. Instead, she listened patiently through Solomon's tour of the place. There was little to show, but Solomon managed to stretch the tour out with long, detailed descriptions. For each individual thing he began with a lengthy discourse that proved the nonexistence of the object; then he set about building it with words and gestures before the eyes of his listeners. In such a way, the house began as a flat stretch of grass on which could be found naught but buffalo dung. He told of the grasshopper plow and the yoke of three oxen that had cut the sod into fifty-pound bricks. From there it rose, brick by heavy brick, up from the ground and into the building they now had before them. It was a structure unknown in the East but standard in this treeless habitat. The well beyond the rise was dug with words that sought to convey the full import of the action and the expense of such an endeavor. He indicated the size of the land they owned with gestures that seemed to encompass the earth itself. He pointed out boundaries that no eye but his own could see, and he expounded on their good fortune, by the grace of God, at being able to acquire such a large and promising parcel.

Despite his eloquence, the three newcomers, even Eliza, shared a look of forlorn suspicion as they took in what lay before them. The soddy stood, in the light of day, like an earthen ogre, with the door as its gaping mouth and the dingy window as its one remaining eye. The roof hung low and tired, a bushy mass of hair no different from the fields of grass around them, except dead where the fields were living. Solomon spoke as if the barn existed already, as if there were stables full of thoroughbreds and rows of planted corn, but the three saw none of this. The barn lived only in the man's mind, the stables even more so, and the areas of turned earth were feeble and lifeless in comparison with the untouched expanses around them.

Behind the house and set some thirty yards away was a fenced-in area of mud and filth, at the center of which stood a mid-sized sow. She watched the family approach with a curious gaze, although she didn't let it stop her from her business, which appeared to be nosing around in the mud with her snout. Solomon called her a guarantee against the weather or locusts, a sure profit and a fail-safe so that no one calamity could destroy them. The pig stared back through all of this with a skeptical look that said she was not as impressed with them as they were with her. She grunted, raised her snout in the air, then turned her back to them and moved off toward the far end of the pen.

"I wish I could be showing you the whole place up and running," Solomon said, "but last year was tough, harder than I thought. For everyone, but harder even for the coloreds."

"Here and elsewhere," Eliza said. "That's how it always is."

"True. True. That's how it always is." Solomon nodded at the sad reality of this. "They gave me some trouble about the land, it being such a good piece, but we own it free and clear all the same. Out here, a man ain't so much fighting against white folks as he is fighting against the land. White folks still cause you trouble, but the land . . . Apart from everything else, there were the locusts, a plague of them. Figured you read about it in the papers." Eliza nodded that she had. "They tore through this country, ate everything in sight. Some things I wouldn't have thought you could eat, too. Air was so thick with them you feared to breathe them in. It was a hell of a thing." He looked down at his feet and scuffed the soil with his toe. "But they won't come back this year."

"How do you know?" Ben asked.

"I don't *know*, but that's what I expect. Folks say they never do come back two years consecutive, least not that many. I don't mean to tell the Lord his business, but I figure it's about time for him to smile on us."

Gabriel stood silently for a few moments, apparently meditating on providence and God's role in bestowing it. But when he spoke, his mind showed a different focus. "Thought you said we already had a barn."

"Well . . ." Solomon shrugged like a man caught at some childish prank, embarrassed but smiling. "You would've already had a barn if you'd come out in midsummer. Y'all gotta remember you come out earlier than I expected. It's still in the planning stages right now."

Gabriel acknowledged no humor in the situation. "You didn't write about no planning stage. You wrote a whole lot of things I don't see no sign of."

The man's lips pursed before he spoke, but his voice was calm. "Well, I'm not that good a letter writer. Maubry, the man that wrote the letters out for me, he thought I should keep to the positive side of things. So I wrote things the way I saw them being soon. That's what it's all about out here, looking to the future and making it so. This here is a land and a challenge like God intended."

"This—" Gabriel began, but Eliza silenced him with a glance. She spoke gently, but with a firm back.

"It does beg the imagination a bit, Solomon. You have to grant us that."

Solomon nodded his recognition of this. He looked up at the sky and exhaled a breath so long it might have been pent up the entire day. He seemed to search that blue and tranquil void for some answer that eluded him on earth.

He searched long, and whether he found the answer there or in some other region, Gabriel knew not. But the boy watched with surprise as the man fell to his knees and clenched the turf in his large hands. He stared down at the thick blades of grass that thrust between his fingers, and he asked Eliza to kneel with him. He asked her if she understood what it meant to hold this earth in their hands, to know that it was theirs by right, to do with what they would or could, and that it could be passed down to their children in perpetuity. Did she understand that if there was ever a thing that this nation, which had enslaved them both and so many others as well, could truly give to them, it was land and the right to work it as they would? He begged her to forgive him his folly if she could but asked once more if she understood.

She answered, clasping her hands over his and so doubling his handhold on the earth, "Well, Solomon, I'm listening to you, and I'm trying. I can't see it all clear as you do, but I'm trying."

Gabriel shook his head and turned away, like a man wearied by the ravings of a street-corner prophet.

GABRIEL WAS THE FIRST TO SPOT HIRAM, riding in across the prairie late in the afternoon. His horse, burdened with bags of seed and supplies, plodded with steady steps that brought him on as smoothly as clouds drifting over the land. Hiram was a man in the later years of middle age. His clothes were bedraggled, simple garments of a coarse material like burlap, and his hair was unkempt, a lumpy mass of tight curls. But his face shone with a charisma that held it all together. Gabriel had known him exactly as long as he'd known Solomon. The two had appeared together one day from the fabled South and had left together to plant their dreams in the soil of the West. But this man had an entirely different effect on the boy from his stepfather's. His quiet and unassuming air, his gentle smile, and the humor of his stories made Hiram something like a beloved uncle to both boys.

He dismounted with well-tried movements, although he

walked with a limp, as one leg refused to straighten itself completely, an injury from a distant, southern time. He took in the whole group with a glance, nodded at Gabriel and smiled at Ben. But he walked first toward Eliza, shaking his head and whispering something meant for no ears but his own.

"Hiram." Eliza took his hands in hers and held them firmly. "You got yourself in this mess too? What kind of fools are you two?"

Hiram smiled at this and seemed to find no insult in it. "The kind of fool that is godawful happy to see you. Do you know that you've just become the best-looking woman in a hundred miles? Maybe two hundred?"

"You can't charm me, Hiram. I've been around too long for that." She drew back and looked the man up and down. "And look at yourself! You're dressed as if you're back at South Hill."

"Maybe so," Hiram said, taking a look at his garments, "but here I'm working for no one but myself, and I guess you, now that you're here." Hiram looked her long in the eyes, and something passed between them, a message of both reprimand and forgiveness and a certain pained understanding. But when he looked away and found the boys, his smile returned. "Sweet Jesus, look at you two! Left you boys and find you men. This world moves too fast for me sometimes. Must be getting old." He shook hands with both, bringing them close to him in nearly a full embrace.

Ben's face lit up in the first show of joy this long day. Gabriel tried hard to stand firm but couldn't keep a grin from tugging at his lips. Hiram talked easily with the boys, asking them had they seen any Indians or buffalo, warning them that this land was hard, might be too hard for the likes of them. This got just the expected reaction from Ben, who denied all Hiram said with rough gestures that soon involved the man in a tussling match.

The afternoon passed into twilight. Eliza prepared a supper of

tinned corned beef that they'd brought with them, served alongside some of last year's potatoes, with a measure of lard laid
across it all. To the men's surprise and delight, she also produced a jar of peach preserves, just as soft and sweet as they
remembered from some long-ago time. They ate the fruit in big
dripping spoonfuls that Hiram named "syrup-covered sunlight."
But it was over all too soon, and both men licked the spoons they
ate with and scraped the bottom of the jar as if more of the delicacy might be hidden somewhere in the glass itself.

They soon engaged in a meandering conversation that tended
toward light banter. They talked of people they all knew back
East, about food items and comforts yet to be seen on the plains.
The men told of some of the trials of this land, but did so with
the humor of distance. They made the chill of winter into a joke,
coyotes into playful creatures, and the labors of the land into
things not to be feared but to be proud of. Gabriel sat beside his
brother but seemed to find entertainment only in the dark corners of the room. Each change in the conversation seemed to
annoy him, although he spoke no protest.

Solomon built up a fire and sat tending it like one would a
sick child. For a moment it appeared to have all his attention, and
yet when he spoke, his words came out measured and thought-
ful. "Guess it's easy enough for Hiram and me to laugh. We done
been out here long enough to love the place. I'd ask y'all to give
it some time, if you would. We may look poor, but we got more
than most—this land, the mule, the horse, and the sow out back.
And you and I both farmed the land before, Eliza. I know this
here's different, but we can learn what's to be learned. Think for
a moment how good things maybe could be." He looked at his
wife, his hopes for their future written in the deep lines of his
face. "But I'll tell you what else. Hiram and I talked about it . . .
If you choose to head back East, we'll pay the fare." This got
Gabriel's attention. "There's no cash left to speak of, but we

could sell the horse—sow too, if need be. I'm just saying the choice is yours. Life out here ain't like being a slave, but it's a might harder than the city life y'all been living, might harder than we knew, fore we got here."

Eliza didn't look at Gabriel, but her hand rose in a vague gesture, as if she were reluctantly waving him away. The same hand moved to her lips and quieted some thought there. She walked over and sat down next to Solomon. Gabriel followed her with his eyes, unsure what to read in her face. She leaned forward and spoke close to her husband, although loud enough that the others could still hear her. "Solomon, I been thinking on it all day. When I first saw the house, this house, I just about forgot that we had dreamed this up together. Thought maybe you'd lost your mind and I was about to." She spoke the words plainly, punctuating each one to make sure they were understood. Solomon lowered his eyes and studied the shape and size of his hands. "But Solomon, I tell you what. You my husband, same one I married before God's eyes. I did that cause I thought I could finish this life with you, and that's still what I intend on doing. So what I'm saying is, you have me. All of me. You always have. And I knew that before we boarded the train."

Solomon raised his eyes, which were suddenly moist; his face was flushed and exhausted by the day but timorously joyous at the words his mind was still processing.

Eliza turned to her boys. She still directed her words at Solomon, but her look asked the boys that she be allowed to speak for them too. "I know my boys. I know they're smart enough to wonder what in God's name this is all about. But they're also wise enough, I think, to understand that sometimes you gotta have some faith and put in some hard work to get the things you want. And they're strong too. We'll put them to sod-busting, and they'll have the place turned over in a week's time. They'll do us proud, and make you two men feel like some old somebodies."

Solomon smiled, uneasy. Hiram laughed outright but kept his eyes on the boys.

Gabriel stood with his chin pushed forward, inhaling deeply, as if he might finally speak in something more than a grunt, longer than a sentence. He didn't look at his brother, for he already saw Ben's face in his mind, shy and smiling under the praise and ready to accept anything their mother proposed to them. Gabriel silently cursed the boy, a weaker, feebler version of himself. He held the room in silence for a long moment but in the end spoke only with the breadth of his back. He shoved the door open and stepped into the night air. After striding forward a few steps, he faltered and stopped, witnessing before him a panorama that in no direction promised solace or escape but that led only unto itself, infinitely.

FIVE WEEKS AFTER THEY'D BEGUN THEIR RIDE, the two men ended it, at a ranch north of Fort Griffin. The ranch's main house, near which they stood, sat like a New England estate that had been transplanted by a mischievous whirlwind and set down out of malice upon the wide skillet of the southern plains. It was a building of numerous rooms, smooth planed wood, bay windows, and a wraparound porch that stood a full six feet above the ground. It was painted a bright, pure white, with blue shutters and trim, and it was lined across the front by young apple trees. A little distance away, a buggy stood at the ready, hitched to a thin-muzzled and proud black horse. It watched the two men and their horses with an air of cautious indifference. The white man surveyed the scene with eyes little impressed by the show of grandeur.

Man don't even know where he is, he said.

When the owner appeared, he walked briskly, slightly annoyed, probing with his tongue for some troublesome bit of food that had lodged itself in his teeth. He was dressed in a dinner jacket of a type rarely seen in Texas, with pressed breeches designed for riding in some country where such was done for pleasure rather than out of necessity. He paused at the porch railing, studied the two men, then asked their business.

The white man stated it: the rumor he'd heard and his proposal to remedy it.

The owner had heard rumors of his own where this man was concerned and didn't mind saying so.

The man didn't seem to have an opinion on these rumors. He took off his hat and ran a hand up over his hair, the strands of which were so white they shone like sun-bleached hay. This done, he replaced the hat and all was as before.

You've known me since I was fourteen. You know the places I've worked and the jobs I've done. You want your cattle in Kansas; I want to drive them there. Seems we got a mutual interest, don't it?

The owner agreed to a certain amount of truth in that. He propped one leg up on the railing and wiped the corners of his mouth with his fingertips.

Shame what happened to your father. I can't say he didn't bring it on himself in a godawful way, but it's still a shame. He was a good man in a lot of ways, just couldn't control his excesses.

Can't blame a son for his father.

This seemed to answer some question the owner had yet to state.

No, I don't reckon you should. If I chance it with you, you ain't gonna make me look a fool, are you?

The man smiled and indicated with a shrug that this was an impossibility.

The black man watched it all and waited.

THE MORNING OF THE BOYS' FOURTH DAY IN KANSAS, Solomon and Hiram taught them how to break sod. They yoked the horse, Raleigh, and the mule for the effort and pointed out the features of their plow. It was an old contrivance much used and abused, with wooden handles so dry and worn that their creviced features sliced fast into soft hands. The frame of the thing was some sort of forged metal, ribbed and primitive in design, dented and aged and twisted by its labors, the blade especially so. Solomon wrapped the handles in strips of leather and set to it with the boys and the beasts all full on.

It was awkward work, coordinating the pull of the animals and keeping them to the proper course while the plow bucked and resisted, trying to dig too deeply into the earth or slipping up and out or tipping off to one side. When Gabriel held the plow, it seemed strangely like a living thing, something with a mind of its own and the strength to actualize its intent. It took the exertion of all his muscles, from the wrists up through the shoulders, the wrap of his back and the push of his thighs, right down through his legs to his toes, which dug into the ground in an attempt to find purchase. Every so often the blade bit especially well and sliced forward a foot or so. In an hour they had cut a wavering trough that Solomon deemed long enough for their purposes. They turned the plow and swung the beasts around and labored back. And so the morning passed.

Eliza set a simple lunch for the men and boys, a stew rich with chunks of beef and potatoes, along with cornbread fresh from their Dutch oven. Gabriel was surprised each day that she coped so well with this place, that she seemed to know the primitive tools she found and their use. Her share of the work was exponentially increased by the fact that she was the sole woman of the family, but she fell to it like one returning to an old trade. Every morning and evening she trudged over the rise and down to the well on the other side for water. As their potbellied stove was too misshapen to function otherwise, she cooked over its open flames, with all of the chores related to it: the constant need to feed and monitor the fire; the danger of being burned, singed, or scalded by pots of boiling water that seemed far too large for her thin arms.

Gabriel watched her with anxious eyes, expecting, hoping to see her overwhelmed by it all. But like Solomon and Hiram, she went at these tasks with a satisfied energy. The work was good, and she was happy finally to get at it. She sat next to Solomon, and Gabriel couldn't help noticing each time they touched. Their hands brushed often; their shoulders rubbed together; their laughter always took them toward each other. This too seemed strange to the boy. Try as he might, he could recollect no such closeness between Eliza and his father.

After lunch, the men headed back out to work. Gabriel got up to go but lingered by the door. He turned around and stared at his mother, the light from the open door casting him in silhouette. They occupied the silence for a good few seconds, the only sounds being those of Eliza clearing the table. "What's on your mind?" she asked.

"Daddy didn't raise me to be no farmer."

"It's your daddy you're worried about?" Eliza smiled sadly. She watched him for a moment, then continued collecting the spoons and bowls in one big kettle. "I spent near ten years working in your daddy's funeral parlor. That ain't no work to love either, living off the dead." Gabriel's eyes snapped at her, but Eliza stopped his words before the boy uttered them. "I hear you, Gabriel. I know your father had bigger plans for you than this, but things ain't come to pass quite that way. Just settle your mind to the fact that we're here in Kansas and live with it. I know your father wouldn't've had nothing to do with this, but he's gone."

Gabriel crossed his arms and stood with his legs set wide apart, although there was something nervous even in this defiant stance, something of the child playing the adult. "If you know what he'd've thought, why you spurning him?"

"That was never my intention. Anyway, it's not your place to judge me for your father." She scooped up the last bowl and dropped it in the pot. Her eyes flicked up toward Gabriel, but only for a second. The glance seemed to affect her. She paused in her work, and a melancholy frown wrinkled her brow. She set both her hands on the table and leaned her weight on the unstable boards. "You were special to your father. You know that, don't you? More so than Ben, and don't ask me if that's right. He never could get enough of you, and he always did see all of his hopes and dreams growing in you. That's why you cherish him so. And I'm thankful for it. But Gabriel, there was no great love between him and me. He chose me because he figured I looked good on his arm and was educated enough not to embarrass him and his kin. But he never loved me, and his family never cared for me either. Yes, they're prosperous for black folks, but they got no soul, Gabriel."

"Like Solomon's got soul?" he asked, the words blunt and cold, less a question than an accusation.

"Yes, that's just what I mean. I loved Solomon first, if you have to know. Way back, way back and way south, when I was somebody's property. But I got sold away and found my way to your father and he made his offer and I took it, but I never did forget my soul. I never did forget Solomon. When your father passed I sent for him, wrote him and told him if he wasn't married already he could come up and I'd be his wife."

Gabriel's jaw dropped. "You asked him?"

Eliza nodded. She slipped her hand into an old quilted mitten, lifted a pot of hot water from the fire, and poured it over the dishes.

"He came out with my daddy's money, and this is all he got for it?"

"There's no crime there. What's mine is Solomon's and what was your father's became mine. That's all there is to that. Fact that things here is primitive ain't nobody's fault. We just have to get through it. And the fact that we're here is just a fact, and you can see that plain as anybody else." With that, she made to lift the pot up and move it. "Anyway, this land may be better'n you think. Just give it some time."

"You know what's gonna happen, don't you?"

"I can't say that I do. Never had that gift."

"We gonna work ourselves dumb for nothing. You gonna put me to work out there for nothing. We will go back East, only we'll go back broke and with nothing to show for it."

Eliza rested her hands on her hips and looked at her son with a skeptical grin. "Is that right? That's the way you see it? And that's why you don't aim to do any work to make sure we do succeed? That what you're saying?"

Gabriel rocked forward on the balls of his feet. "Hell, no, that's not what I'm saying. I'll work. I'll work like nobody else here. I'm just saying what I think."

"All right. Now I know. You go on now and help your brother."

Gabriel turned, for a second responding like a dismissed schoolboy. But he paused by the door, blinking in the sunlight. "You won't never be able to say I didn't work the goddamn land." With that, he stepped from her view.

DURING THE AFTERNOON, the two men ventured off to design a new room for Hiram. Gabriel and Ben worked on with the plow, taking turns leading the animals and guiding that rough tool. Gabriel couldn't help cursing under his breath, profanity a necessary feature of the labor. He didn't pause to survey his progress, nor to drink, as Ben often did. He turned himself to the work as if to destroy the land, the tools, the animals, or himself as quickly as possible. As the hours passed, he found none of these things easy to break.

Ben became the silent one. His brow furrowed in worry. It seemed he was slowly coming to grips with the reality of this work and its duration. Several times he seemed on the verge of offering some confidence to his brother, but the other showed only his back, his muscles, and his exertion. As dusk came on, Ben asked if maybe they should quit for the day. Gabriel said the day wasn't over but he could quit if he wanted to. Ben thought this over. "I'll just go get some more water." He walked toward the house with the empty waterskin thrown over his shoulder.

Gabriel called the beasts into motion and found that they listened. Alone with them he struggled forward, but either they were tired or the sod had woven itself into chainmail. He made no progress, though he strained and the animals rolled their eyes and pawed the turf. The blade stuck. The plow overturned. Gabriel stumbled over it and bruised his knees and shouted at Raleigh to stop. He cursed the plow and damned it well and beyond redemption and so thoroughly prayers could not hope to save it. He kicked it, but this he regretted, as the iron cage of the thing lashed back at his foot and sent him hobbling. Raleigh and the mule watched him.

When he had spent his curses, he contemplated the whole sad scene from a distance of twenty paces. With the day's labor they had striated a small section of the prairie with raised lines of sliced turf. There was little sign of the soil beneath, and the lines resembled seams more than furrows, as if the turf had already stitched its wounds and begun to heal. Gabriel wondered who was getting the worst of this day, the ground or his own body. His legs were so tired that they trembled supporting him; his arms ached with a dull soreness, and certain motions sent a swath of pain across his back. He spat and stood waiting for something to come, as if the earth were entitled to the next move and he was content to wait his turn.

But as the earth did nothing, Gabriel strode to the rear of the house and got the ax from the shelter there. He carried it back, dangling from one hand. Standing out before Raleigh, he measured the arc of his swing and sought to find the proposed line of the plow's progress. The ax swung up, cut through the air and down into the earth. It bit. Gabriel released the handle and contemplated the angle at which the shaft projected toward him. He seemed to find a certain satisfaction in this. He cranked the blade out of the earth, took a step back, and swung once more. Without a pause, he worked the blade free and repeated the action, once, twice, and then onward, hammering into the turf a halting, imprecise incision. Each stroke was a new act of increasing fury, stronger and deeper, punctuated by grunts and profanities. The horse and mule watched him with nervous eyes, as if beholding some crazed woodsman who had forgotten the true target of his trade.

Ben returned with the waterskin. "Gabe, what the hell you doing?"

"I'm learning the ground."

"Looks like you gone and lost your sense to me."

Gabriel didn't protest this theory but simply tore into the earth again and again, ignoring his brother and the nervous twitching of the animals. Ben eventually unhitched the plow and led the horse and the mule away. Gabriel stuck to his demented work, hard at it until his mother called him for supper. Only then did he call a truce for the day.

LATE THAT EVENING, Gabriel lay restless and unsleeping. His legs burned. He felt the warm mouth of some creature around his muscles, gnawing on them and pulling them away from the bone. Each inch of him hurt in one way or another, and he kept up a slow, constant movement, trying vainly to find the one posture of comfort which eluded him. The gray highlights of the

ceiling above him became a canvas for the images that pressed in
on him. He remembered the place he had called home, the cob-
bled streets of Baltimore, bustling with carriages and foot traffic,
the harbor full of ships sailing to and from far-flung destinations.
He caught glimpses of his father and of the intentions conjured
between the two of them, schemes from a distant time but all the
more solid for their inaccessibility now. Bits of his earlier conversation with his mother also crept in and nagged at him. He
hadn't known that she and Solomon went that far back, and
somehow this seemed like a betrayal, like a crime done to his
father and still unpunished. He rolled to one side and faced the
wall, hoping this motion might somehow steady his mind and
bring slumber. It did not.

He thought of the long train ride out here, all those miles of
flatlands and rolling prairie and mountains, all the people and
animals and dark spaces and the great sky above. How long
would that journey be on foot? Could he walk back, and if he
did, what would he find, who would he have? He lay planning it
all out, jumping great spaces in his mind, conversing with distant
relatives and creating the kind of life for himself that would make
his father proud. He created plans to the logic of a weary and
troubled young mind in the dead of night, with the breathing of
his sleeping kin surrounding him and the eerie calls of coyotes
roaming the miles of night outside their door. These schemes
became a gateway to slumber and mingled with his dreams and
arose again as questions unanswered in the morn.

*IT WAS THE BLACK MAN who first noticed the Scot. He watched
as the young man cut cattle from the herd for branding. The Scot
moved his horse among the beasts as if he were one of them, as if he
might fool them into complacency. He never attacked too fast, but
maneuvered in such a way that his target always found itself*

standing dumbfounded before him as a lasso dropped around its neck.

But the way he communicated with his horse was what most impressed the black man. He spoke to him, whispered, told him jokes, and asked his opinion of things. The horse would stop on a dime with just the slightest motion from the man's arm. He'd sidle, spin, or squat at some command that observers could hardly detect.

When the blond man rode out to check on their progress, the black man whispered his observations. Together they watched.

What's his name? the blond man asked.

The black man told him, and the other called to him. The Scot rode over and waited, smiling. Sweat hung at the edges of his forehead. He wiped it away with a gloved hand.

They teach you all that back in Scotland?

The man smiled again. When he spoke, his voice betrayed his origins, not in the words he used but in a faint lilt, a soft cadence, and the intentionally playful way he moved words around on his tongue.

Not exactly. We've few cowboys over there, I'm afraid.

Lot of sheepherders, though.

The young man nodded and smiled on. The blond man told the Scot that he had blood of the same origins, a few generations away from their native land but no thinner for it. He told where his people had lived and some of what he knew of the place. The young man nodded and said he remembered the place himself. This pleased the man.

Was it poverty, crime, or boredom that brought you over?

I wouldn't say it was one more than the other. Had my taste of them all, if you'll know the truth.

This pleased the man as well.

I might have a project for you. You up for it?

The Scot asked what it was, but the man offered no further information.

You'd have my answer before I know what I'm agreeing to?

I would. You can know there's money in it, though, extra from your wages for the drive, that is. And you can know you'll be working with Caleb here, taking orders from him instead of me for a little while.

The young man pursed his lips. He looked at the black and found that man's yellow eyes hard on him. He looked back at the white and found his eyes likewise, except flavored with humor.

Fill me in, then.

Good. You'll like this. Just consider it a bit of joke we're planning. A joke on an old friend.

THE MONTH OF MAY PASSED in a dreary haze of endless work. The family was up before the sun. They ate their breakfast as the sky grew pale, and they stepped out into the morning air as the first beams of sunlight touched the landscape, highlighting the tips of the grasses, bringing the soddy out of its dull relief. The myriad tasks to be completed each day dwarfed any chores that Gabriel had ever known before. There was, of course, the constant sod-busting, work that grew no easier with experience. Quite the contrary; to Gabriel's reckoning, the turf grew stronger each day, devised new defenses against the plow point. There were seeds to be sown and the animals to be cared for and tools to be created from makeshift materials.

No day passed during which the boy wasn't stumped by some insurmountable problem. No task was ever completed without a new one presenting itself. Just when a day's work seemed at an end, the harness would break, or Gabriel would slip and gash his knuckles open, or the shovel blade would drop off, or birds would swarm over the fields, devouring the seeds. Just when he lay down to sleep, his pallet would give way, or the wall above him would rain down dirt loosened by the wind, or the dull head of a king snake would appear in the flicker of the candlelight, tongue licking the air in a gesture that seemed a blatant taunt.

Late in the month, Gabriel was put to building the barn next to the pigpen. Day long, he hauled blocks of sod from where they'd been cut and layered them into walls. The sow watched him with her disdainful eyes, as if she respected his efforts but doubted his skills as a mason. Gabriel couldn't help speaking to her under his breath, threats and curses, reminders of the pleasure of bacon and of the short span of her life. He blamed her also for the abundance of flies that swarmed around him. They plagued his eyes, buzzed in his ears, and crawled over any patch of exposed flesh they could find. Half his efforts each day were spent in slapping the insects to death. He barely noticed the days passing into weeks, and yet they did.

IN EARLY JUNE, Gabriel met a person who voiced a similar despair over the circumstances of his life, a boy named James. The two met in town, where James worked doing odd jobs for a white man named Pinkerd, whom he hated with a much-voiced passion. He had been orphaned as an infant outside of Athens, Georgia, and raised on the kindness of the church. He'd happily have stayed there and even continued in that line if the minister's wife hadn't proposed to him a move westward in the care of Pap Singleton, to a Negro community newly spawned on the plains. The boy accepted and found himself transported, mostly by the labor of his own feet, as far as Crownsville, where his entourage disintegrated amid fears of treachery and allegations that all was not as they had been led to believe. "The whole thing fell apart," he said. "Was like every one of them just got the jivers and ran. Left me stuck in Crownsville not knowing a soul in a thousand mile. I'd nary seen a worse day in my life." He managed to find work with Pinkerd and could feed and house himself, but other-

wise he cursed the life that God had given him and wished for
some way out of it.

He came out one Sunday on Gabriel's invitation, for an afternoon of riding and relaxing on the plains. He was a thin-boned
boy, shorter than Gabriel by six inches, with a slim build and a
collarbone that protruded through whatever shirt or jacket he
wore. He arrived talking of cowboys, outlaws, and hangings, with
a dime novel shoved in his rear pocket. It was a gift that a recent
immigrant had given him, as if that man, fresh from Waltham,
Massachusetts, had a manual on the West that had escaped those
already living there. It was called *Richardson of the High Plains*
and promised nonstop action and romance, authentic tales of the
wild and woolly, English-cowboy style.

Gabriel saddled Raleigh and mounted up. The horse pawed
the earth and shook his head once, protesting already. Once he
steadied, Hiram helped Ben up behind his brother. The two
boys just fit into the saddle, perhaps a bit close for comfort but
snug nonetheless. Hiram stepped back and studied them, and
soon concluded that they sat the horse like cavalrymen.

James commented that they looked a little cozy in the saddle
and he'd heard that the cavalry didn't take kindly to such behavior. But a moment later he'd climbed up himself and was trying
his luck at riding behind both Ben and the saddle's cantle.
Gabriel encouraged the horse forward, and they all waved to
Hiram like travelers embarking on a long and noble mission.
Before they had gone twenty yards, however, something about
the precariousness of his position and the hard body of the horse
beneath him discouraged James's riding efforts. He had Gabriel
halt the horse, slid down, and happily walked along next to them.

They moved off, for a while following the tiny creek to the
east of the homestead but then cutting away from it and trotting
through the open prairie. At one point Gabriel kicked Raleigh up
into a canter, about the best the old mount could muster, and he

rode along with the warm southern breeze licking his face. Ben's
arms were cinched tightly around his waist, and Gabriel found
something comforting in this embrace. Looking out at the
prairie, he imagined them to be alone on this great expanse,
explorers heading bravely into the undiscovered heartland of
America. He might have moved on to further visions if he hadn't
heard James shouting after them to "hold up, dang it."

The spot they stopped at was little different from any other
spot on the plains, a slight rise, enough to allow the view to work
its magic or cast its pall, depending on the eye and inclination of
the viewer. This was the first day in many that Gabriel forgot his
loathing of this place. He looked off at the thin ribbons of cloud
to the north and up at the infinite tranquillity of the sky with eyes
that for once saw without judgment, without comment, other
than in the act of vision itself. Ben and James wandered off to
explore a prairie dog city, a megalopolis of sorts, abandoned and
quiet now but impressive nonetheless in its mounds and open-
mouthed tunnels and hidden corridors.

Before long, James came back and sat talking with Gabriel.
Had he had the resources or the inclination, James might have
worn spectacles, as he was often wont to squint at objects in the
distance. He moved with quick, anxious motions and tended to
engage his face in a display of whatever thought process was
going on within him. He spoke of life in town. Things happened
there, he assured Gabriel, things wild and chaotic, things to make
your hair stand on end. He spoke of finding spent slugs in the
street one Sunday morning, described a man who'd nearly killed
another for punching his horse on a drunken wager, and talked of
the time a man he had spoken to personally was hanged by a
posse from a tree just outside town. Children had collected
under the dead man and swung him back and forth by his naked
toes. "Somebody must've stole his boots. Can you imagine that?
Wearing a dead man's boots?"

"What had he done?"

"The dead fella? Ain't got the faintest." James shrugged. "He did something. They always done did something. Cheated or stole, maybe. That's the way cowboys is when they come to town. Don't matter whether they're decent folk or otherwise, they get the stump liquor in them and look to cause a runction."

Gabriel thought on this for a moment. "What do you make of them?"

"Who, cowboys and them? They all right, I guess. Least they free to get on their horses and go out riding wherever they please and can't nobody mess with them cause they mostly do carry a gun." He wrinkled his forehead here and retraced his logic. "Well, I guess some people can mess with them, cause somebody's always shooting or hanging somebody, like I said. I don't know what's better, to live a cowboy life or a town life or a homesteading life. Not one of them's easy."

They both fell silent, as there seemed little more to say. Gabriel offered James the waterskin. He accepted. After he'd drunk, Gabriel took the skin back and squirted some water on his face, washing off the sweat. He sat still after that and watched his brother, who continued to roam the prairie dog city, searching for some living remnant of its community. When Gabriel spoke, it seemed that something about the boy's vain search had inspired him. "I was gonna be a doctor before they brought me out here."

James looked at him incredulously. "A doctor?"

"Yeah."

"A *Negro* doctor?"

"There's Negro doctors."

"I know, but—"

"My daddy was gonna see to it. Told me I could be anything I wanted in this world, now that coloreds were free. Then he died and they brought me out here. That's the stinking way a life can go."

James thought this over for a while. "Well . . ." he said, but he could go no further along those lines. He picked up a piece of grass and ringed his finger with it. "Shit, least you got some kin left. You don't know what it's like working for Pinkerd. It's like being a slave. Worse than that, the things he does . . . I hate him. Honest talking to the Lord above." James tossed away the piece of grass and pulled up another. Again he twined it between his fingers and wove a ribbon of green jewelry. "I ain't nary hated a body more."

A little later the three boys shared a banquet of bacon sandwiches and hardboiled eggs. James pulled out his novel and tried reading aloud. His grasp of the written word was faltering and imperfect at best, slow and downright discordant more often, and Ben took the novel from him and picked up the story. It was a cheaply written tale, vague in its descriptions of place or history but elaborate in its invocation of shady characters, broadbrimmed hats, and six-shooters. The English immigrant rode a white horse. His hair flowed long and blond beneath his Stetson, and his proud Roman nose had a knack for sniffing out young maidens in distress. Ben read of one such encounter, Richardson tracking a band of ten Mexican *banditos* intent on ravishing a young woman, Miss Delilah Day, golden-haired and fair, who was tied to a tree with rough horsehair *reatas,* her dress already ripped to shreds by the brutes' daggers. Coming upon the scene, Richardson didn't pause to ask questions. He blazed in at a full gallop, both pistols aflame as the bullets flew, making fast work of all but two of the *banditos,* leaving them choking on their own blood and filth and vomitus bile—

"It don't say that." James grabbed the corner of the book and took a quick glance at it.

"It do too." Ben made a point of pulling the book away and reading it at an awkward angle, away from James. *"'Richardson held the two remaining* banditos *at bay with his pistol cocked and steady, still smoking from the damage it had already wreaked upon the fiends. With his other hand, he cut the ropes from Miss Day's heaving bosom—'* "

"It don't say that!" James again grabbed for the book.

Ben stretched his arms away. "It do too, you idjit. If you could read, you'd . . ." He tried to start reading again but gave up the effort and fell into a wrestling match with the other boy.

Raleigh watched them with vague and mistrusting eyes, with the air of one who had seen such behavior before and was certain it led to no good. He snorted his judgment on the two. But then something caught his attention. He raised his head and scented the air and looked off to the north.

Gabriel followed the horse's gaze and at first saw nothing but flat prairie. He soon picked out a rider heading toward them at a steady canter. Gabriel watched him for a while in silence. As the man came closer, the boy recognized his clothes, his demeanor on the horse, his firm, forward-facing posture, and his dark face. He knew him not as an individual but as a member of a certain race, a people named in error.

"There's an Indian." He spoke in a voice barely audible, and the boys tussled on. "Ben, I said, there's an Indian. Stop acting the fool and look."

This time the two boys did just that. At first neither was sure why or at what they were supposed to look. They gazed off in different directions, until Ben sighted the rider and let out a low whistle. James squinted and studied the horizon long and hard before he made the rider out. "You say he's an Injun?"

"If I ever saw one," Gabriel said.

"What should we do?" Ben asked, grabbing for Raleigh's hackamore. The action disturbed the horse. He snorted and stepped back, pulling the rope tight in the boy's hand.

"Shhh," Gabriel said, although nobody was making any noise to speak of. "Stop acting the fool. Just wait. He's seen us sure as shit, so let's just wait."

The native rider sat his horse bareback, with only a blanket between himself and the pinto's mottled body. They moved like a single being, united in flesh. They trundled along with a rocking, relaxed motion, the hair of both horse and man flapping up and down with their strides. The man held something in his lap, but other than that, he was unencumbered and traveled light.

Only as the Indian passed alongside them, about fifty yards away, did Gabriel realize that it was a rifle he held cradled across his thighs. It seemed a strangely fixed object, as if it were attached to the man's lap as securely as he to the horse. The man neither slowed nor acknowledged the boys in passing. His eyes were set below a heavy brow. They fixed straight forward on a far distant object, as if his sight could reach beyond the horizon and was little troubled by the curvature of the earth. He moved on in a silence that seemed ghostly. Gabriel entertained the thought that he was witnessing not a man of flesh and blood but an ethereal rider passed from the netherworld into this one on a mission of vengeance for his vanishing people. Before long, the rider had grown small on the horizon and was lost to sight, and all was as before.

The boys stood without speaking for a long while. Eventually Ben asked if all the Indians hadn't been whipped and reserved. James said that most had been, in these parts at least, and he couldn't make no sense of this whatsoever, him riding like he's out for blood and all. Gabriel didn't comment. He swept up their lunch spread and crammed it into the sack Hiram had rigged to the saddle. He climbed aboard the horse and reached down for his brother. Ben swung up behind him.

"Come on," Gabriel said. "Let's go. I don't aim to be here if

he rides back this way." He dug his heels into the horse, and
Raleigh jumped forward into a fast walk.

James called out a protest but quickly fell into step, trotting
along next to them like a servant doing penance. Gabriel spoke
no more, except within himself. For the first time he thought that
while there was still nothing interesting about the toil of his daily
life, at least adventure was skirting the edges of it, offering occasional glimpses that tempted with promises more mythical than
the thin tales of cheap novels.

THE PLOW RESTED ON ITS SIDE like a creature breathing its last.
The blade had finally given in, the greater portion of it bent back
and sheared away from the frame. How the soft earth could have
wreaked such damage on iron was a thing to wonder at, but the
proof was there before them. Gabriel stared at it long and hard
before he went to fetch Solomon, wondering at the malignant
force beneath the turf.

Solomon kneeled before the plow and studied it with calm
eyes. He caressed its rough edges with his fingers, a gentle touch,
as if he feared to do more injury but thought that his fingertips
might ease the metal back into place. They had not this power, as
he conceded with a long breath of air. "Well, this ain't gonna do,"
he said, slowly easing himself up. "You think a smith could mend
her?"

Gabriel stood just behind him, watching his back. He rolled
his eyes at the question. "I doubt God could mend it."

Solomon cut his eyes at the boy, and his words came quick.
"Watch yourself. No need to be profane just yet." He kept his
gaze on Gabriel, but the boy studied the lay of the grass and
made no comment. "What we have to think on is what to do
next. I think we can mend her. We might could buy a second-

hand plow next year from someone who's quitting, but this year we just need to make do with what we got. We could take this down to Maubry's, see what he makes of it."

Gabriel looked toward the southern horizon in time to see a lone rider come over the hill there. The horseman surveyed the land, took in the house and the two standing before it, then disappeared from whence he had come. Gabriel's thoughts flew back to the Indian, although he knew straight away that this was somehow different.

"How about you hitch up the mule and we see about this today?" Solomon asked, not having noticed the horseman. "No use wasting a day over it." He grasped one handle of the plow and looked at the tool from a new angle. But this improved it little, and he let it fall again. "I'll just tell your mother."

He started to move off but paused, first to look at Gabriel, who still stared out at the empty horizon, and then to follow his eyes. As they both stood there, a faint rumbling noise could be heard. It rolled over the landscape like a low-flying flock of birds, a grumble that was both sound and feeling, heard not only through the air but through the soil itself.

The rider appeared again, cresting the hill at a gallop, pausing, and twirling his horse around in a half-circle. He looked back and motioned with his arms, then let his horse fall into a canter down the slope. A second later a section of the horizon began to seethe. It boiled as if a stream swollen with debris had suddenly cut its way through the prairie. This illusion held for a moment only. Then, at either edge of the river, two mounted drovers appeared, and it became clear that the river was one of moving cattle, the first of what promised to be a great herd of livestock.

They came on fast, pouring down into the valley, picking up speed as they approached. They were a sort of cattle that Gabriel had never seen before. They were quick and bony, with low-slung heads and enormous horns that stretched out from either side of their skulls and rose to ominous points. A man could have sat on either horn and ridden the precarious perch. They seemed always on the verge of piercing each other, as if their horns had intentions of their own and the cattle were at their mercy.

Solomon and Gabriel both took a tentative step toward the house, fearing they'd be overrun, but the drovers were hard at their work. They fought to turn the herd from the homestead, whips snapping like gunfire, their horses wheeling and dancing under them. They moved perilously close to those horns, but in so doing managed to turn the tide of the beasts to one side of the house and plowed fields.

A rider emerged out of the throng, a bullwhip in hand. He cut toward the cattle and backed away again, his horse surefooted and light, as if it knew the work as well as the man and reveled in it. The creature looked as though it would reprimand the steers with its teeth if it was allowed to. As his horse spun, the cowboy caught sight of the homesteaders. He paused, reflected on something, then snapped back into motion. The cattle had turned toward him in a surge. He drew the whip up behind him, dark and serpentine, like the tail of some infernal beast. With the full force of his upper body, he snapped it hard and loud at the legs of one of the longhorns. He repeated this three times, till the river corrected its course. Only then did he spur his horse away from the group and ride toward the house.

He drew up before them, reined the horse in, and studied Gabriel and Solomon for a moment. He was a tall man, wide-shouldered and strong, with a square jaw and pale blond highlights for eyebrows. An old Stetson was perched high on his brow, more worn around the rim and ragged than the rider's years could have accomplished. He wore a bright red handkerchief tied loosely around his neck, and a holstered pistol rode his right thigh. The weapon sat quiet and innocuous there, and yet both Gabriel's and Solomon's eyes were quick to note it. Once stopped before them, the rider comfortably, with his whip coiled around the pommel of his saddle.

"Sorry about the trespass," he said, as if all introductions were unnecessary. "Had a stampede day before yesterday. They took us out this way, and now we're just trying to work them back toward Crownsville." He paused and followed the progress of the herd, his eyes seeking out the other drovers and confirming their position.

Gabriel studied the man and horse from head to foot. The horse was long-legged and tall, a dun of stout body, quivering with muscle and energy and a deep-chested strength, a true equine specimen that made old Raleigh look an impostor, a shame to the race. The cowboy's comfort in the saddle projected a complete confidence in himself, in the mount beneath him, in the coil of leather in his hand, and in the pistol at his side. Gabriel's gaze focused on that weapon, his jaw dropping a little at the thought of the power contained therein, such a small thing and so deadly, so much discussed in the lore and legends of this place. Gabriel turned his eyes away when the man looked back at them.

"Anyway, sorry about the inconvenience," he said. "These cattle don't mind property lines. We'll leave you some chips for your troubles, keep your cookfires burning and that." He smiled a half-toothed grin and waited for a response.

Solomon seemed loath to speak to the cowboy. He watched the cattle and was slow in responding. "They stay over thataway and we've got no quarrel."

The man nodded. "Fair enough." His gaze fell on the broken plow. He studied it with an interest that made him lean forward over the horse's neck. The horse cocked its head and pawed the ground. "Shhh," the cowboy whispered, calming it. He looked up as if to speak but paused, looked past them at the sod house and out over the newly tilled fields, as yet devoid of crops. A thought passed over his face, troubled his brow for a second, then vanished. "I guess I'll be getting back at it. I wish you folks the best of luck."

Solomon accepted the wish with a nod but shrugged to question its power. "Thank you much, only it's not luck. We find the Lord provides."

The cowboy found this amusing. "Yeah, that's what they keep telling me. But I've not seen any sign of it yet." Solomon looked up at him with a stony countenance Gabriel had not seen before. The cowboy, whether avoiding his gaze or for some other reason, looked at Gabriel and smiled. With that, he spun his horse and spurred him into a gallop.

They watched him go. As he reached the herd, the man picked up his work where he'd left it, his whip once more snapping like gunfire. The cattle seemed endless in number, pouring over the hill from which they'd appeared and by now topping a distant rise and moving off toward Crownsville.

"Can't say I care for cowboys," Solomon said. "They a rough bunch usually, no courtesy for decent folk. If we'd planted that field instead the othern, they'd have just trampled our crops to naught." He paused, thought it over, and concluded, "Naw, I wouldn't trade places with em for nothing." He turned and walked back toward the house.

Gabriel wasn't so sure. He spoke quietly, so that Solomon wouldn't hear him: "Don't look so bad to me." He watched the cowboy's progress for as long as he could, something in the motion of it drawing him in, the freedom, the control and power of it all, man and horse and beast in a struggle of wills and muscle and horns and gun. Solomon called him to hitch the mule, and the boy turned reluctantly to the work.

IT WENT JUST AS SMOOTHLY AS THEY'D PLANNED. *The night before, the five men had camped beside a shallow river. They kept a small fire and ate quietly before it. A light rain fell, barely a mist, but enough to keep the men hidden beneath the brims of their hats, collars pulled up and heads cradled between shoulderblades.*

The next morning was clear, and the men broke camp and rode out before first light. The horses were just where they'd been told they would be. They spent the morning hours rounding them up, pulling them in from the great basin they occupied, unguarded. They worked fast, as men will whose actions can be viewed by an eye ten miles in the distance. The Scot went at it particularly well, ranging out in a wide periphery of the herd and bringing in the stragglers, sparring with them, taunting them, and then tricking them each time into his chosen direction.

By mid-morning they'd grouped a handsome herd, some thirty head of every description: paints and bays, sorrels and roans. Few of them were branded, and those that were bore brands as varied as their number. By early afternoon, the five men were driving the horses before them at a trot, dead north. The vanguard ate up the miles of grassland as if they were hungry for the motion, in love with it, as if they felt this forced march to be their own dash for freedom and cared little about the ridden beasts that followed them.

The Scot rode up close to the black man and offered a joke about the ease of this venture. If the black man found it amusing, he didn't show. He kicked his horse up and pressed the herd harder.

They were three weeks on the drive north. They passed within sight of Fort Concho, made good time across the flats to Doan's Store, crossed the Red River, and moved on up the Western Trail. They passed more than one herd of cattle along the way, were once blamed for a stampede and nearly shot at, twice lost portions of the herd in the night and had to hunt them, and through the Indian territory they lost five head to ambitious thieves.

But through it all they kept to schedule. They met up with the white man on the outskirts of Crownsville, where he'd arrived a few days earlier with a thousand head of cattle. He walked out to greet them with a smile from ear to ear, shaking his head and pointing his finger from one man to the next. They penned the horses in a corral he'd reserved for them, and then he sat them down in the nearest saloon and plied them with whiskey and asked them their tale. He laughed often as he listened, finding humor in the story that the tellers hadn't intended. He praised them each and all, clapping the black man on the back and tugging the Scot's hat and punching another in the shoulder. And what with the market this weekend . . . Boys, this pig's in heaven.

THE HORSE AND CATTLE MARKETS were at the southern edge of Crownsville, set away from the houses, down a broad slope and in an enormous, shallow bowl. From a distance, one could see a motley conglomeration of fenced-off areas, buildings and parts of buildings, wood structures that jutted up like abandoned scaffolding. What these were or would be was hard to say, but undoubtedly they were the work of some entrepreneurial dreamer, strapped for the moment in want of wood or money.

It was in and about these works that the market in flesh plied its wares. As Gabriel and James walked toward it, they marveled at the mass of life before them. It may have been only a tiny fraction of the great herds of this land's near past, but to their eyes the animals seemed beyond calculation. The herds were such, in fact, that the boys had to choose their way carefully for danger of finding themselves deep within a moaning body of cattle. They twice had to break into a fast jog to avoid such a fate, and they were once shouted at by a cowboy on a sorrel horse, who waved at them with his whip, a gesture directional and threatening at once. They followed his command as best as they could understand it, and before long they had made it through that gauntlet and blended in among human herds of considerably smaller yet no less confusing numbers. It wasn't until they attached themselves to a stationary object, a fence of wood surrounding a ring of some fifty yards squared, that they could again breathe easily.

A bull stood in the center of the ring, eyeing the crowd with belligerent mistrust. It was an enormous thing of solid white, built of muscles. Its horns were adorned with silver caps that caught the sun in blinding flashes. The shaft that hid its member dangled serenely beneath it, conspicuous in its life-giving power. The bull seemed to stand there for no particular purpose that it or the boys could make out, except as a spectacle reminiscent of some pagan culture.

A boy not much older than themselves entered the ring. He wore the hat of a cowboy and walked with a wide-legged swagger, but in fact his arms were so thin as to be diminutive, his chest so narrow as to mark him a child. Gabriel and James watched him closely. The bull spun around when it caught sight of the boy, chucked its head in the air, and flared its nostrils. It hardly looked like a creature that would bow to the whims of man, and it appeared that the boy was about to offer the audience a share of gore at his own expense. But to Gabriel's surprise, the boy just walked over to the beast, stroked it calmly on the nose, and led it away. It walked behind him like a misshapen, obedient sibling.

Soon after, the ring filled with horses. They came in charged with energy, bustling into each corner of the enclosed space, measuring its dimensions. They wheeled and turned, neighed and spoke to each other, shared horse thoughts about this new space and this old event and about the people watching them. Brown was the most prominent color, but a few were black, one was reddish in hue, and many were paints. Some had about them the look of Indian horses, a certain wildness in the eyes and an energy hardly contained in such a small space.

An auctioneer took his post, an elevated platform just high enough that he could see into the crowd, which grew considerably around and behind the boys as the morning's market prepared to begin. He was a small man, long-nosed and balding. He spoke in quick staccato rhythms, his voice a bird that darted with his eyes, reaching back into the audience and catching bids, promoting bids, creating them. Gabriel watched his mouth but could make nothing of the words shaped there. He watched the horses that sold fastest or for the highest price, trying to formulate in his own mind the features that distinguished some from the rest. Several times he deigned to answer James's questions, showing him with a frown the importance of his concentration. Before long, all but three horses were sold. These remainders looked no sorrier than the rest, but for some reason that escaped the boy, these were returned to their masters.

"You got an eye for horses?" Gabriel asked his friend.

James shook his head. "I know you're supposed to check that they have good teeth, like they used to do slaves."

As a new set of horses entered the ring, Gabriel noticed a commotion on the platform. A man had climbed up there and was speaking in animated words with the auctioneer and his assistants. They seemed to know him, were half amused but also wished him to get down. He would not do so, and only grew more passionate in his entreaties. The auctioneer eventually shook his head and grabbed himself a seat, resigning his post for a moment.

The new man smiled heartily at this and took himself out to the edge of the small podium and to the attention of the waiting crowd. He was a tall man, in stature and shape similar to Solomon, except that he stood straight-backed and moved with confidence in himself and his place in the world. He had long arms that stretched beyond the reach of his jacket's sleeves, leaving his pale wrists exposed. His clothing was the usual muted browns, his face well tanned and weathered, but these colors sat strangely on him, as his hair was so blond as to approach white, his eyebrows even more so, and his smile likewise flashed bright in the sunlight.

But it wasn't until the man began speaking that Gabriel recognized him as the cowboy he'd seen the week before, with the herd of cattle back at the homestead. The man introduced himself as Marshall Alexander Hogg, the Marshall being a name only and in no way an indication of profession, the Alexander being his father's notion of a warrior prototype, and Hogg being traditionally Scottish and in no way a suggestion of his character. He spoke in polite and eloquent language edged with humor and somehow slyly common, as if he liked to dazzle the crowd with a certain amount of lyricism but was careful to remind them that he came from the likes of them and was no more or less than a kinsman. He explained his need to speak on behalf of the fine horses the audience could clearly see being led into the corral. He was sure this need not be said, but nevertheless he wished to warn prospective buyers that these were the finest horses likely to be sold in the state in the course of this year. He knew so because he had driven them up from Texas for the express purpose of supplementing the quality of horses in the wonderful state of Kansas.

He went on to say that because of the sad fact that the horses could not demonstrate their full range of abilities in so limited a pen with so limited an amount of time, he wanted to highlight a few of their less obvious qualities. He directed everyone's attention to a certain young bay. This horse, he assured the audience, was smart enough to herd cattle without either rider or instruction. He had a habit of doing just that, managing the herd all day and only calling it quits when his replacement showed up. Another specific horse, he claimed, had mastered several Indian dialects and could happily serve as a translator if the need arose.

Several others had skills in regards to cooking, fishing, and celestial navigation. And quite a few had things to say about animal husbandry.

He had just begun to point out another horse when he called out, "What? Who put my horse in the ring?" His face took on a look of great consternation, lightened by a smile just behind it all. He ranted a few moments, confounded the help he had for their ineptitude or downright treachery, and finally spoke once more to the audience. "That horse, gentlemen, is my own sweet Sophia. She's so smart she once tied up my shoelaces for me. She's so strong she once sent a grizzly to the great beyond with one fell kick. She's so fast she ran from the top to the bottom of a twister in six and half seconds flat. And she's just about pretty enough to marry. But none of you'll have her. She's mine till the good Lord sees to tear us apart, which may happen eventually but surely won't happen today and is likely not to happen in Kansas."

He went on for some time refusing offers that nobody had made as yet, and then he prepared to retire. He said goodbye to the auctioneer, bowed to the audience graciously, and hurried down to the ring with the utmost feigned urgency. Applause followed him from the podium. It turned to laughter when he whispered in his horse's ear and patted her on the rump solicitously. Gabriel laughed with the rest and watched as most of the horses sold high and fast.

GABRIEL WALKED BACK INTO TOWN ALONE, with a casual, loose-legged gait that still had something of the city in it. The hard labor of the past months had carved changes into the boy's body. His hands were callused across the palms and bruised over the knuckles, making them puffed, rugged versions of their former selves. Cords of muscle fanned out across his back like wings growing beneath the skin, and the round curves that joined his chest and arms had twisted into solid balls. The drudgery of farm life, which warped many bodies, broke man-made tools, and took a toll of blood on both the land and its people, seemed only to strengthen this boy and speed his way to manhood. He grew with an intensity beyond that of anything planted in the ground—like a weed, some might say, and with much the same angry intent.

He spotted the wagon from some distance away, parked on a main street near the store. The mule stood with its head hung low, in quiet contemplation of whatever it is that mules are likely to think about. Gabriel walked up to it and stroked the coarse hair of its forelock. He studied the creature for a few moments, then whispered in its ear, "You ever wish you were all horse?" The mule watched him with one rotund eyeball but gave no answer. "Ever think about that? You could have been all a horse or all a donkey, but instead somebody stuck you together a hinny." The mule tossed its head at this and shied away a step, apparently not comfortable with being so characterized.

Gabriel turned and looked at the store. It was a flat-faced wooden building built with a certain practicality of design that highlighted and yet economized on the sturdy timbers trans-ported a thousand miles into this treeless world. It stood out on the street, not in design or size but in the brightness of its fresh white paint, and by the raucous colors of its new sign: HOWE AND SONS GENERAL STORE, yellow letters on a vermilion background, with a border of dark green.

The inside was lit only by the front windows. Gabriel stood for a moment near the door, letting his eyes adjust to the dusty light, trying to make some order of the rows and stacks of mer-chandise, food items, household wares, and building supplies. He eventually located Solomon. He went up behind him, stood for a moment, then cleared his throat. When this brought no motion from Solomon, Gabriel cleared his throat once more and scuffed his foot against a crate. The man turned around, roused out of his thoughts, and smiled at the boy.

"Hey, Gabriel, I was wondering what you were up to. Just looking over some things here. Just dreaming, you know. Just dreaming. What do you think of this here?"

He held out the new plowshare that he'd been contemplating. He ran his fingers over it and checked the blade from different angles in the light, divining a future in its contours. He held it with the delicate fingers of a glassblower as he explained that this blade was some new steel, harder than the old stuff, longer-lived. Perhaps with a blade such as this they could turn up the whole of that south-facing slope and double their tilled land in no time at all. He asked the boy his thoughts and got answers, such as they were, only in shrugs and nods, which seemed neither to confirm nor deny his hopes. Whether disheartened by this response or not, Solomon decided to make the purchase. He took the plowshare and his other supplies up to be tallied by the storekeeper.

Gabriel stood back a little, watching the man calculate their bill. He looked over his features, settling on the man's thick and unpleasant eyebrows and the slightly sinister curl of his mustache. He was cordial in the way of whites to blacks, joking with Solomon and asking after the health of his family, wondering whether they were turning much soil, assuring him that this plow would indeed help their progress, and saying that Solomon was lucky, as this was the last one he had in stock.

This statement, casual as it was, caught the attention of another man, a small fellow with reddish skin and ears that craned forward, rodentlike, as if to pick up just such information. He approached the counter, watched the goings-on for a second, then spoke. "Did I hear you right, Howe? Is that there the last of them new blades?" Howe answered that he had heard right. The man thought this over, his eyes fixed hard and suggestively on the storekeeper's. "Don't you remember I asked you to set one of those aside for me? Just the day before yesterday, came right in here and asked you explicit not to sell the last one except to me."

Howe slowed in his work and drew himself up, his eyes finally meeting the other white man's and joining in some optical discourse. Before long he began to recall just such a conversation. "Hal, damned if I didn't forget all about that."

"I thought you'd remember, though," Hal said, letting a smile tilt his lips. A trickle of tobacco juice escaped the corner of his mouth and blended into the reddish hair of his chin. "I had your word, didn't I?"

"That you did." Howe hung his head for a moment and considered the sad state of these events, then looked up at Solomon. "Sorry, Solomon, looks like this here plow blade was on hold, just like Hal says. I can't sell it to you."

Solomon was slow in answering. Across his face passed many emotions in rapid-fire succession, not the least of which was anger. From where Gabriel stood, he could see the man's fingers grip the gray boards of the counter as if they would pierce through them and rip the wood asunder. The boy waited for what words or deed would come, as surely some must, for this was the man who had so lamented the pain of dreams deferred and cried the virtues of the freedom of honest work.

"You can't?" Solomon asked, as if no other words would come to him.

"Naw, he can't," the customer said. He reached over and took the blade from Solomon's things. As he turned to resume shopping, he murmured, "It'd be wasted on you anyway, damn nigger farmer."

Gabriel followed the man with red-hot eyes. They fixed on the man's ears, on the scrawny tube that was his neck. He looked back at Solomon, his face for once characterized not by a look of loathing but beseeching instead, longing for a wrong to be

righted. Solomon held his gaze for a second but made no com-
munication with the boy, turning instead and settling the bill.

Outside, the two loaded up the wagon in silence. Solomon
patted the boy on the shoulder, turned, and climbed onto the
seat. Gabriel watched him, sour-faced. "That's what you call
being a free man?" He said it quietly, just a whisper, but clearly,
so that his stepfather could hear it.

The man paused before seating himself, thought for a
moment, then let himself down onto the blanket. When he
spoke, his voice was honest, half defeated and far from proud.
"Naw, I don't reckon we're all the way there, but we're on the
way. Things could be a lot worse than somebody taking your
plow. We're still finding the course to better things." He
motioned for the boy to climb aboard.

Gabriel looked around, considering other options and none
too sure that the wagon was the best one. He eventually climbed
in and settled himself, facing the back. He crossed his arms and
sat in silence as the vehicle began its slow, creaking progress
home.

THE SKY THAT SUNDAY EVENING began calm and still. No
breeze blew across the grass, and even the coyotes were silent,
their familiar cacophonous calls absent from the night. Hiram sat
beside a tallow candle, in its warm, flickering light, and read from
the Bible, from the old tales of the pharaohs and the Israelites.
Egypt seemed an incomprehensible land, and Gabriel could
scarcely conjure images of that strange country and the deeds
performed there. Hiram spoke of Moses and Pharaoh, he who
spurned God's wishes, of how Pharaoh was punished with mira-
cles beheld by all, how he became repentant and wished to release the Jews. But each time Moses returned, God would turn
Pharaoh's heart hard and make him refuse and thereby bring

upon his people a new plague. This they repeated time and again. Gabriel couldn't help thinking that God was a cruel God, one who would toy with the souls of men and make them suffer against their wishes, who would choose one race of people over another and so mete out his curses.

Hiram found the words moving to the core and soon turned the evening's reading into a full-blown sermon. He spoke not as Hiram to his close kin but as preacher to a greater audience, with a fervor that made Eliza smile. He began by recollecting their distant homes in the South. He talked of that warm and humid land, of the beauty in its tragic history, and he spoke of the troubles of that place, the hardships they'd all known. They'd come here to escape some of that suffering, hadn't they? They'd come to make a new life for themselves, to prosper, grow, and multiply. Wasn't this so? He paused when they answered in the affirmative, and then said that they might escape many things in this country, but there was one force from which they could never escape. "Do you know what I'm speaking on, all of you?" He looked at the boys, who affirmed that they did. Hiram seemed to doubt this. He closed his eyes and stated, as if to a loved but naughty child for the hundredth time, "Ye cannot escape God's laws, God's sight, God's blessing, and God's judgment."

He went on to tell the story of Jesus' life, summed up and abbreviated, stressing his love for the poor and devotion to the common man. With his own upheld arms he painted a picture of Jesus nailed to the cross, dying once again before their eyes, for their sins, so that man would not be destroyed but could live to be tested further. And later, with quiet words that caused the listeners to crane forward, he told of the man's resurrection. His body became stiff and unwieldy, dead and frozen, and only gradually did he regain life, as the Lord breathed the spirit back into him and Jesus both.

In the end, Hiram turned their eyes back out toward the

fields. He read from the hundred and fifth psalm, verses forty-
two, forty-three, and forty-five, and painted a picture of the
prairie blooming like a giant rose, a sweet-smelling thing of
beauty and delicate refinement. "Are you looking for the
Promised Land?" he asked. Eliza's voice, singsong and light, said
that they were. "Well, behold, you've found its location. Now
farm and reap and thank God for the gift of life." By the time
he'd finished, there was little doubt as to the bounty of this land
or the blessed rightness of their decision to journey here. Gabriel
alone lacked enthusiasm, a fact that he tried hard to demonstrate
with his twisted countenance.

They bedded down a couple of hours later, Hiram wishing all
a fine rest and heading out to his half-completed room. It was
just after the house had fallen into silence that the wind kicked
up. At first it just tickled the prairie, caressed the house as a
benevolent hand pets a loved old dog. But as the night grew
darker, so the wind grew bolder. Before long a tempest howled
against the sides of the house like a Fury intent on utter destruc-
tion. Gusts tore through chinks in the walls and cracks in the
door, creating a whirling dance within the cabin. Gabriel pulled
his cover up over his head and lay listening.

"You hear that?" Ben asked.

"I don't hear nothing. Go to sleep."

But sleep had been blown away by the wind. Both boys lay
with ears alert. The storm soon became a living thing running
across the prairie. Far off they heard the pounding of footsteps,
a steady bass over which the wind played. It grew louder, like a
stampede of cattle, coming on hard and furious. It hit the house
with a force that seemed to rock it. The window shook in its
pane and the door bucked against its hinges. But the pounding
was no herd of maddened beasts, no creatures of the apocalypse.
It was rain.

A few seconds after it began, water started leaking through the roof. It dribbled down at first in a single trickle, then two. Then a section of the ceiling, which had been so faithful in lesser rains, caved in. Water pelted onto the table and floor in a torrent, some liquid, some tiny balls of ice.

"Damn," Ben said. He jumped to his feet. "The roof's broke!"

Gabriel looked over his shoulder but only half took in the scene. He turned away and curled close to the wall. "Who cares?" he mumbled.

Solomon emerged from behind the curtain with a lamp in hand. The light illuminated the downpour and caught the erratic bounces of the hail, like jewels thrown about the table. A second later, Hiram tumbled through the door. The light caught the surprise on his face as he stepped from one downpour into another. "You can't escape the flood!" he yelled, finding sudden humor in the situation.

Solomon was more serious. "Ben, see to Raleigh and the mule. See they don't get too spooked and are tied up properly." Ben jumped into action immediately, reaching for his boots and coat. He was out the door in the space of a few seconds. "Hiram, we gotta mend this roof."

"Directly," Hiram agreed.

"Gabriel, go fetch some of the cut sod. We'll layer it over top as best we can." He and Hiram lifted the table and chairs out of the way. Eliza appeared with the quilt from her bed. She tossed it across the floor, covering the larger part of the rain-soaked area.

Gabriel went so far as to sit up and survey the chaos. He blinked and said, "Let the damn roof leak, for all I care."

Solomon had just set the table down. He swung toward the boy. His hand came up and flew at Gabriel, so fast neither of them seemed to know it was happening. He smacked the boy open-palmed across the cheek, snapping his head around and sending him sprawling back against the pallet. Gabriel was up in a second, chest thrown out and fists at the ready. Solomon met him head on. "What the hell's wrong with you, boy? What kind of creature you got eating at you?"

"Nothing's eating me except being here."

"You're a fool, Gabriel. You're a damn fool child. If you would put away that anger, you'd see we're making a life here." A fresh gust of wind tore through the open door and around the room and fled through the roof, rocking them all where they stood. But Solomon kept his gaze on Gabriel. He spoke just loud enough to be heard over the noise. "I'll accept you into this home like a son. I'll love you like one if you let me, but I ain't gonna tolerate you forever. You can make it with us or not. I don't care. You can be damn sure we can do it without you." He turned and shoved the door aside, Hiram following close on his heels.

Eliza eyed Gabriel angrily. "Get out there and help."

Gabriel pulled on his boots and strode out into the rain without even a jacket to protect him. Ice balls pummeled his back and shoulders, sending his muscles into convulsions that he overcame by turning them into a full-tilt run. He could barely see the ground before him, and he ran with his arms outstretched, feet kicking out in a clumsy, stiff-legged gait. He stumbled over the sod before he knew he'd reached it and landed flat on the slick earth. He jumped up with all the speed of a man who'd tripped over a dead body, but then he stood, gasping, forgetting his mission and staring back at the spectacle that was their home. A jagged line of white lit the sky and a foul, misshapen world flashed into view, outlined in blinding detail. One could have mistaken the soddy for a dinghy afloat in a raging sea. The prairie's contours were suddenly waves, moving with a slow and ominous bulk. The moment passed and all went black. There followed the slow rumble of thunder, a sound that in its breadth and depth overcame all other sounds, like God clearing his throat.

This spurred Gabriel back into motion. He felt for the sod

with his hands and feet, found it, and shimmied his fingers under a block. He hefted it up, sank beneath it, and let the dead weight lie on his shoulder. His footing was loose and sloppy as he struggled toward the house. By the time he reached it, the two men had leaned a ladder against the wall and Solomon had scaled it. He was hard at work on the roof, sorting through the material with some plan that Gabriel could scarcely conceive. Hiram greeted the boy but motioned him to stand back. He began handing short pieces of wood up to Solomon.

Gabriel stood with soil running down one half of his body, rainwater washing down the other. It was only then that he noticed the hail had stopped. But to make up for it, the rain fell much harder. He could just hear the commotion coming from the barn. Raleigh and the mule were anxious. The roar of the wind and rain made it hard to hear what was going on over there, but Gabriel could make out brisk whinnies and hoofbeats, intermingled with Ben's soothing voice, his explanations that all would be well.

Gabriel jumped when Hiram called him. He helped the man push the block of turf onto the roof. Hiram climbed onto the ladder and Gabriel held it as best he could, but the crooked wood shifted and bucked and rocked precariously as the men worked.

Eliza appeared in the open door and stood silhouetted there, her eyes hidden until the sky flashed again. Then Gabriel saw that she was looking at him. Her face went black again before he could read it. Solomon called for another block. This time Gabriel headed off without delay, so consumed in the work, the elements, and the electricity in the air that he didn't even consider any further protest.

THE NEXT MORNING THE FAMILY SURVEYED THE DAMAGE with somber eyes. If the house had once been an ogre, now it

was that ogre's diseased and feeble grandfather. Inside, mud
clogged the floor and seemed to have climbed up objects of its
own accord, staining clothes and beds and even worming its way
into the sealed trunks. The door was propped open to promote
drying, but this succeeded only in merging the mud inside with
the puddles outside. The wildflowers so patiently nurtured by
Eliza had been pummeled to naught, both by the downpour and
by the men's frantic feet. Their patch job cluttered the roof like
rubbish that has collected at the bend in a river—sticks crooked
and cross-hatched, chunks of sod thrown over them every which
way, like finger bandages over a gunshot wound. Looking at it, all
agreed it was a wonder the house had sheltered as well as it had.

The fields were flooded, knee-deep in mud and more like the
rice paddies of the Far East than Kansas wheat fields. It was
impossible to say whether the ground might hold the seeds still
or whether they were likely to float away and sprout in some distant spot, or whether they would just drown outright. Hiram
speculated that the better part of them would be just fine, but
nobody else voiced an opinion on the matter. Raleigh and the
mule seemed largely unaffected, if a bit bedraggled. The sow was
not disturbed at all, slogging about in the mud with obvious
pleasure.

Solomon took it all in impassively. He shook his head but said
not one downhearted word. Once the survey was complete, he
shrugged his shoulders and met the earnest gazes of the others.
"Let's get this place cleaned up," he said.

The others nodded and went silently to work. Gabriel helped
his mother clean out the house, watching her for some sign that
she saw the futility in all this. One storm, he longed to say. One
storm and look at the place. He yearned to name the plagues that
would follow, as if they were Biblical prophecy preordained and
unavoidable. He would have asked her if she'd had enough yet, if
this wasn't proof that the land could wreak upon them any whim

that took its fancy, save that he knew she would not allow him questions. He would have fallen to his knees and begged her to see reason but that he saw no reason himself and was sure that reason no longer played a part in her decisions. So he aided her efforts in silence, watching for any indication that she might be swayed.

Yet again, Eliza gave no sign of regret. She simply went to work, shaking her head in an almost amused manner, as if somebody had played a joke on them all and she couldn't help but acknowledge the humor in it.

GABRIEL WORKED HARD OVER THE NEXT COUPLE OF DAYS. Nobody commented on the outburst of that stormy evening, but it hung over the homestead like a cloud that would neither rain nor blow on. It lingered in Eliza's reproachful eyes, in Hiram's exhaled breaths and in the slow shake of his head at his internal dialogues, and in the polite, distant manner in which Solomon spoke to the boy. Gabriel even saw something different in his brother. It seemed that the younger boy had stepped away, looked back and found his older sibling deficient in his role, no longer one to look up to unquestioningly. Gabriel sometimes wanted to rage at them, to take them on, stir the fire and have at it—anything other than the purgatory of the wary looks and quick sighs. But no one spoke, and the week wore on, uneventful and tiresome, until James arrived.

He found Gabriel and Ben at work around the house. The day was sunny and bright, June's beauty having returned in its blue-skyed glory. The boys had dragged many of the house's contents out into the sun and were spreading them on the ground to dry. James surveyed the damage with wide-eyed wonder. "Damn, you all did get whupped," he said. Once his initial surprise faded, a new look came over his face, an anxious quiver that told Gabriel he had some news to deliver but for some reason dared not do it in front of Ben. He worked with the boys, unfolding sheets and laying out linens with clumsy hands, creating a patchwork of fabric, furniture, and clothing that from above must have looked like a giant, ragged quilt being sewn on the prairie.

It was only when Ben went into the house to fetch the waterskin that James grabbed Gabriel by the wrist. He waited till Ben was inside and then finally exhaled his words close to Gabriel's ear, and loud. "I might have got me a job, and you too if you want it!"

Gabriel pulled away from him and looked over his shoulder toward the house. They were surely out of earshot, but still he silenced James with a hand. A second later he asked, "What're you talking about?"

"I talked to Mr. Hogg."

"Hogg?"

James stamped his foot in exasperation. He explained that Mr. Hogg was the man they had watched hold forth at the auction the other day. James had come upon him out by the stables that morning and considered asking if he had any work. Before he could make up his mind, some other boy had put the same question to him. James had listened to all that was said, most notably that the man was indeed looking to take a few new hands back with him to Texas and that only general skills were required for the particular openings he had to offer.

"He told you this?" Gabriel asked cautiously.

"Naw, not me exactly. He told it to the boy that asked him. He told him to come on back tomorrow afternoon and they could talk about it. What do you think?"

"About what?"

"About getting jobs with Mr. Hogg. Texas, Gabe! Man's got a full ranch, cattle, horses like we seen. You saw the way he ran that show."

"I saw." Gabriel contemplated the sky above him, unable to

share his friend's abounding enthusiasm. "Why would he hire us? Neither of us has ever worked a day on a ranch."

"He didn't tell that other boy no. He was scrawnier than either of us, little sick-looking white boy, but Mr. Hogg told him to come back anyway."

"He probably don't hire coloreds."

"Does too! Had a colored man standing right there with him like his right-hand man."

Gabriel thought this over for some time. "Thought you didn't care for cowboys."

"Shit," James said. "I never said that. They might act a fool sometimes, but I never did say a word against the work. Gabe, two days ago I met a cowboy wasn't fifteen years old. Not fifteen, but had him a horse, a Stetson hat, spurs clanking when he walked, and a six-shooter. Had him a six-shooter like he's ready for a gunfight. Don't that sound sweet?"

Gabriel didn't answer immediately. A hawk rose from a distant field, hung in the air for a moment, then dipped down toward the earth. He stared at the place where it had disappeared, as if it would appear again and award the vigilant. It did not. "Yeah. That sounds all right. I'll see if I can't go in there with you. See what Hogg has to say."

This brought a whoop from James, who talked on without pause, sure that tomorrow was going to be a day that changed their lives for the better. He attributed to Mr. Hogg such characteristics of wealth and benevolence that one would have thought he'd passed a good few years with the man. He asked Gabriel if he could feel it in the air, this force finally come to move their lives toward a greater providence than they'd yet imagined.

Gabriel didn't say whether he could or not. "We'll see" was his laconic answer.

NOBODY PROTESTED WHEN GABRIEL ASKED TO GO TO TOWN.
The previous week's work had tired them all, and the chores left
to be done that morning somehow didn't seem so urgent. The
men walked the grounds, shaking their heads and laughing at
the way God overdoes his bounty sometimes. If Ben had any
interest in going with Gabriel and James, he didn't show it. He
spent the morning tending Raleigh in the barn, something he
had taken to recently. He stroked the horse's nose and spoke to
him softly, telling him things for his ears only. The horse responded by stepping closer to him, as if he would push his
shoulder up against him and rest his weary bones there. Only
Eliza worked on that morning, taking advantage of the empty
house to wash the walls and clean out the corners of the place.
She wished the boys a good day and asked only that Gabriel
make it back for supper.

Gabriel said that he would. He walked to the door and
paused, looking back at his mother. She lifted her eyes and met
his, a curious, loving look. "Hmmn?" she asked. The boy
shrugged that it was nothing, and as an afterthought asked her if
she needed anything from town. She said she didn't. With that
answer, Gabriel walked away, turning his back on her with no
intent of malice but with a nagging feeling that such was somehow the result anyway.

The boys had walked only a half-mile or so before they were
picked up by Mr. Mitchell, the family's nearest neighbor. He was a
kindly Mennonite man who spoke with well-measured words and
long pauses. He asked Gabriel about the progress of their farm and
seemed well pleased to hear that things progressed in accordance
with the Lord's wishes. It was a long ride for Gabriel, but he spoke
with the man in the polite tones he always reserved for white folks.

Outside the general store, Mr. Mitchell bade the boys enjoy
the day, telling Gabriel to meet him no later than four for the

return trip. Gabriel thanked him and turned to survey the streets. There was a busy weekend atmosphere; the streets were filled with cowtown traffic, as new herds were being driven in daily for transport via rail to points east. Wagons full of merchandise and loaded high with baggage rolled by. People strolled: some cowboys and many farmers; some women dressed garishly, whether respectable women or prostitutes, Gabriel wasn't sure. Cowboys patrolled the streets on horseback or on foot, swaggering and proud and a bit louder than necessary. A few people hawked homemade goods, and a row of quiet but poor-looking Indians sold the wares of their people.

James tugged his arm. "Come on. We already done wasted half the day."

They found Marshall Hogg leaning against a fence, half looking over the horses held inside and half talking to the small group of men around him, all cowboys or garbed as such, loose-jointed and weatherworn. Marshall had about him the same confident air he'd had on the podium. Close up, one could see that his hair was not so white as it had first appeared. He had thin, sunburned lips, a square jaw, and a nose slightly crooked in its line of descent, whether by nature's design or because of injury was unclear. He smoked a hand-rolled cigarette, which he perched on his lips so that he could gesture with his hands, talk, and laugh at the same time. His eyes touched on the boys for a second as they approached, but he looked away, hardly noticing them.

James pointed out a boy who stood near Marshall. "That's the boy that asked about work," he said. Indeed, the boy didn't surpass James's earlier description. He was thin around the neck and shoulders and generally sickly-looking, pale enough for the dead of winter and with a nose pink and sore, as if he suffered from that season's illnesses.

"And there's the colored," James whispered.

Again he reached up to point, but Gabriel stopped his arm.

His eyes had already found the man. He stood at the edge of the group, leaning back, both elbows against the fence, one leg bent and resting on a crate of some sort. He was not a man of great stature or girth, but there was something immediately impressive about his body's hard lines. He seemed made entirely of sharp edges: the triangles cut by his limbs, his jutting cheekbones and chin, the narrow slits that were his eyes. The only thing truly rounded about him was the crown of his head, which was clean-shaven and smooth. He returned the boy's attention with his own appraising gaze, but on his face no greeting or kinship could be read.

Gabriel lowered his eyes, and the two approached the men like nervous schoolchildren. They stood waiting for some time before Marshall noticed them. "You two after something?" he asked.

James nodded that they were.

"Well?"

"We . . . Mr. Hogg, we was wondering if you might be needing some hands." It took James a great effort to get the sentence out. Once he had done so, he exhaled a pent-up breath and seemed to relax considerably.

Marshall eyed James briefly, then studied Gabriel. "Is that right?"

Gabriel nodded that it was. He wondered if the man recognized him from the day he'd spoken with him and Solomon. If he did, he gave no sign of it.

"And what can you do?"

"We do everything," James said. "I mean, we'll do anything you put us to."

The white boy looked askance at the two newcomers, his eyes loath to touch on them. He seemed to be preparing some speech in his head but came out with mucus instead, which he sent in the vague direction of Gabriel and James.

Marshall shared a smile with the man next to him. "Here's two young colored boys who figure they can do everything," he repeated for the man's benefit. "They call me Mr. Hogg, too. Polite chiggers." He looked back at the boys. "In my years of ranching, I never have come across a hand that could do *every*-thing. I've found some that can do *something*. A few that could do *this* thing or *that* thing. But the only ones I ever heard try to do everything ended up doing *nothing*. What do you make of that?"

James hesitated. He glanced at Gabriel. "I didn't mean it like that. What I was saying was, Gabe here knows farming, and I been working with—"

"Don't waste your breath, boy. What do they call you two?"

"James and Gabriel."

Marshall feigned surprise at the improbability of this. "The king and the archangel! Very impressive. Well, damned if I could be luckier." He looked at another of his companions. "They look to be two strong ones, don't they? Probably got some fight in them." The man to whom he was speaking smiled a toothless grin and nodded complete agreement. "Tell you what, you boys follow me, all three of you. Got a test for you, if you're up for it." He spun on his heel and started walking off, not looking back.

The boys hesitated. James mouthed some words that Gabriel couldn't make out. He shrugged in answer, and they followed the group of men who had moved off with Marshall. Only the black man remained. He didn't move till the boys did, slowly bringing up the rear.

As the group reformed within the confines of a barn, Gabriel found himself standing close to Marshall. The man raised his arm in a gesture to another, and for a moment the silver glint of a pistol flashed from inside his jacket. The boy craned to see it better but caught only the black handle of the thing, smooth and curving and engraved with some design he couldn't make out.

He straightened up when he realized Marshall was watching him. The man grinned and whispered to the boy, "Don't trust a man with a fancy gun. It may be pretty, but it'll kill you just as dead as a plain shotgun."

He laid a hand on the boy's shoulder for a moment, then walked into the center of the group, creating with his circular path a ring of sorts. He moved a few of the men back with his hands, gesturing, treating the whole thing like some solemn work. When the circle was to his liking, he beckoned Gabriel and James forward and had them stand facing each other. "Now, look into the eyes of your competition." From the position he had put them in, it was clear to each that the other was who he referred to. "You both want a job, but there's room for only one. Question one is whether it's one of you. Question two is which one of you it might be. Figure we got one easy way to settle it—a little boxing match. First boy that bests the other walks away with a dollar. If you impress the jury here, you may walk away with a job. So have at it." He stepped back and motioned for the boys to join in battle.

The boys stared at each other in surprise. Voices around them urged them on, encouraging and coercing at once. The boys still made no move, although James looked at Gabriel with desperation in his eyes. His hands had begun to tremble. He flexed them to steady them, clenching them into fists and then releasing them. He took a few tentative steps from side to side, trying to conjure some solution through movement.

"Boys, you're sorely disappointing me. I won't make you fight if you haven't got it in you. But I will take myself and the job of a lifetime on back to Texas, leave you here in the sorry state I found you in."

These words brought up in James a sudden rage, which he directed at Gabriel. "I'm not going back to Pinkerd's. Let's just do what we've got to," he said.

Gabriel didn't even lift his arms. "James, I ain't fighting you." He'd just turned to leave when James moved forward and punched him on the shoulder, not hard, but enough to bring his attention back. Gabriel wheeled around. "What are you doing? You're gonna let—"

He cut his words as James threw another blow, this time toward his face. His head bobbed out of the way, his feet sure beneath him, sliding him almost imperceptibly away. He would have said something else, but James came at him again. Gabriel had to slip left to avoid yet another whirling fist. A change came over his face. As he looked at James, his scowl returned, his lips drew back from his teeth. When the other boy made another move toward him, Gabriel unleashed an anger quicker even than its genesis. His arm swung up on that well-oiled shoulder joint, fist tight and hard as a rock, and he spun it down toward his friend. It caught the other boy between the lip and the nose, snapping his head back. As James stumbled, Gabriel hit him several more times across the chin, then the neck, dropping one blow into his abdomen.

James pitched over but reached out with one arm and grabbed Gabriel. He drew him in, preferring to receive his blows at close range. The two boys tussled about that way for some time, a moving mass of limbs and grunts. Eventually Gabriel got a grip on James's legs and yanked them into the air. The other boy hit the ground with a force that sent spit from his mouth and churned up a cloud of dust. Gabriel lashed out twice with his heavy foot, catching James in the arms crossed over his chest, this position suddenly his only means of defense.

Gabriel paused in his attack and stood above his newfound foe, his chest thrown out in the attitude of a gladiator considering the kill. He allowed James to rise. The boy's face was bloody and distorted with emotion—anger or desperation, it was hard to say. The boys stared at each other, tired from the effort and seemingly amazed at their own behavior.

Marshall stepped between them, laughing uproariously. "That'll do, boys. Shit-fire! That's what I like to see." He looked back at his companions. "I asked them to fight and they damn well did. As far as I'm concerned, you've both earned work. What about you, you ready to fight one of these?" He turned to the white boy at the edge of the group.

The boy nearly spat when he answered, "I ain't fighting no nigger for a job."

"Figured you wouldn't. We won't be needing your services, then."

"You want the niggers instead?"

"I respect a fighter, is all. I'll always give the best man the job. Ain't that right, Caleb?"

The black man stared back at him, no visible answer on his face. He scrutinized the boys with eyes that seemed to find them a sorry sight, then looked down at his own feet as if they were of equal interest.

Marshall continued undeterred. "Boys, you don't know shit about ranching, do you? Not a thing, I can see that. But if you'll work half as hard as you fight, we'll use you for something. If you want in, be back here tomorrow at sunup. We won't wait for you, so be early." He studied them for a moment, appraising. He wiped a lock of whitish hair from his forehead, then pulled out two cigarettes from his shirt pocket and offered them to the boys. "Have a smoke on it, and remember, there's more where these came from."

Gabriel took the cigarette, holding it out before him as if he was unsure of its purpose. The two boys walked away with the men's best wishes, but they shared none of their enthusiasm. They walked without saying a word to each other, and mumbled their goodbyes without ever asking each other's plans.

~~~~

GABRIEL CLIMBED OUT OF THE MITCHELLS' WAGON at their
turning, a half-mile from the house. He waved goodbye and cut
out across the prairie through the dusky light. The knee-high
grass brushed against his legs with each step. There was an
undertone of insect life in the air, the background hum and chirp
that can be heard and forgotten and thought of as silence. He
walked with a steady progress that soon brought him to one of
the knolls from which he could see the house. It was only here
that he stopped, squatted, and took out the cigarette that
Marshall had given him. He rolled it in his fingers a moment,
then placed it between his lips, where it sat unlit.

To eyes untainted by anger, the house on which the boy looked
was no poorer a beginning than any other in the heart of the continent. It sat lonely on the plain, indeed, but its character was not one
of desolation only. There was in its simple geometry a stoic perse-
verance. The items spread across the grass had been taken inside,
and candlelight flickered in the windowpane like a heart beating,
dim but warm. Plots of turned earth had grown around the house
on three sides, as yet only patches of greater darkness on the plain,
but signs of progress and a testament to months hard spent.

But to this the boy's eyes were blind. His thoughts were bitter.
His gaze focused on the forlorn plow stuck deep in the boggy
field, a sorry tool for such surgery and a fresh reminder that here
too inequity ruled the land. Nothing was truly different here. All
was toil and the flight from racial strife and dreams thrown about
the impartial land like seeds. Where would they take root, if ever,
and who would reap that harvest when the day came? He offered
no answers to these questions. He asked them only as a pretext to
name his one answer, to shape one word into many words, to
make it clear, perhaps only to himself, that *he* would not reap this
harvest and these were not *his* dreams, nor his future, that his
answer had always been and could only be no.

He reached up and touched his chin, felt the bruise there beneath the pressure of his fingers. By the cold vigilance of his stare, one might have thought it was the homestead itself that had so bruised him and not the fists of his friend. He let his fingertips rise higher and massage the balls of his closed eyes. He did this for some time, pausing only to listen to the passage of some birds above him.

With that, he stood up and turned around, not daring the warmth of home and family but choosing instead this dark field in which to make his judgment. As he moved away, he wondered if it could really be this easy. Were decisions made this way, with such silence, in such solitude? He wondered, but even as he asked, he knew that there was nothing easy about this, and he felt within that silence the threat that nothing would ever be easy again, and the fear that solitude might be no more a blessing than it is a curse. He thought so, but still he walked, with hesitant steps that only gradually grew more forceful, away from the light of his home and into the evening's willing embrace.

Part 2

THE CARAVAN MOVED OUT BEFORE NINE. THE BOYS RODE in the cargo wagon, atop crates and satchels of various sizes and descriptions, behind a train of four hitched oxen. Crownsville faded behind them, diminishing in stature and breadth with the passing miles till it was little more than an island mirage in a great, grassy ocean. Eventually even that phantom melted into the sea and was forgotten. James looked back often, a smile across his face that grew with the distance behind them. Gabriel also cast glances back to the north, but his eyes searched the receding horizon as if he feared pursuit. Part of him urged the oxen forward with greater speed, while another part cried out for him to jump ship, run home, and erase this digression before it became a full-blown sin.

James asked Gabriel if this wasn't something, and Gabriel nodded his somber agreement without meeting the boy's eyes. He'd spoken few words to him all morning, afraid that something had changed between them but unable to name it truly. The previous evening's fight had left a sharp taste of betrayal on each bruised portion of his body. He thought that he should still be angry, that James had proved himself a fickle friend. And yet he was not angry, and somehow he felt that it had only drawn them closer.

It was a small company, eight persons including the boys. Marshall led them, riding his horse nearly twice the distance traveled in a day with his constant trips from the front to the rear of the caravan, asking questions, posing observations, and finding things to laugh at. He wore the simple, functional garb of his trade: a thick, sun-bleached cotton shirt, leather chaps, a blue bandanna around his neck, and a Stetson tilted back on the crown of his head so that it framed his face rather than shaded it. He was all fun except when giving orders. Then he spoke in a quiet voice that broached no humor and allowed no questions.

A man named Bill sat just in front of the boys, driving the wagon. He was as slow and strong as the oxen he tended, with features equally wide and bovine. He rarely used his whip, but when he did he threw his whole body into it and snapped it just above the animals' backs, seemingly never touching them but filling the air so full of commotion that they were prompted onward. Early that morning he had overseen the loading, at which the boys had helped, watching them with mistrustful eyes, unsure of their character or motives and fearing some deception.

Another man, Jack, rode with his Stetson low on his head. His nose protruded from underneath the brim as if it were his main feature and the organ through which he sensed the world. His eyes were little more than a notion, hidden in a shadow beneath the brim. He never spoke without first spitting a flume of liquid tobacco. This he achieved with a projectile agility that not only impressed Gabriel but would have impressed even the most hardened aficionado of that activity.

Less appealing still, in Gabriel's eyes, was Rollins, a surly sort with a long torso and short legs. His arms stretched out as if he were an ape astride a horse, and he seemed always ready to explode in some display of anger and status. He looked at Gabriel and James with a certain amount of scorn, which he made clear by riding up next to them and lecturing Bill on the mating proclivities he'd observed in other young colored men, wondering aloud if these two had the same affection for dogs and whores.

Fortunately, there was another man in the group with a more pleasant disposition, a young Scot named Dunlop. He was in his early twenties, thinly built and long-legged. He enjoyed smiling, and when he did so the freckles on his nose danced and wiggled. In his voice was the ring of his homeland, a cadence that Gabriel found poetic. From his handling of horses and his stature in the saddle, however, it seemed he belonged to this country as much as anybody could. It was his job to loose-herd the three riderless horses they had with them, the only ones not sold at auction. He did this with a skill that almost seemed a sixth sense, at times pushing the horses out before him and letting them kick up to a trot, at other times bringing them in so close to the wagon that Gabriel could have reached out and touched them.

But the man who caused Gabriel the greatest concern was the one he saw the least of, the black man, Caleb. He led the way, darker and more silent than ever, on a large painted stallion that had some wildness in it still. It seemed he preferred his own company to that of any other and tolerated the rest only from the solitude of the lead position. Watching him on his horse, Gabriel thought him some dark figure of the apocalypse. It was unclear which of those demons he might incarnate, but when he glanced back at the caravan, Gabriel saw in his gloomy countenance an utter and indescribable loathing for the world and all its creatures. Gabriel had never seen such a face before, black or white, and he couldn't help but hope that his perceptions were wrong. He

knew instinctively that no man should be so twisted, and he knew
further that no man could remain so for long without enacting
some drama upon the world.

THE FIRST EVENING, THEY CAMPED ON THE PRAIRIE several
miles from any settlement, beside a lonely creek that moved
through the land lost and forlorn, switching this way and that in
search of something it seemed destined never to find. They hob-
bled the horses and let them feed and built up a fire of brush and
of what wood they could find along the creek. Above the fire
they suspended a blackened kettle and threw into it the makings
of soup—chunks of smoked meat, lard, and potatoes. With the
utmost concentration, Bill added some herbs that he had bought
in Crownsville, sure that they would flavor it nicely.

Rollins was kind enough to serve the boys their first wooden
bowls, full to the brim, steaming and pooled with oil. He stood
before them, ladle still in hand, urging them to eat. As the first
spoonful passed his lips, Gabriel sensed the heat of it, but he
didn't pause quickly enough. The hot oil bit into his tongue and
the roof of his mouth. He flinched, clamped his lips around the
spoon, and closed his eyes as a wave of pain flooded his senses.
When he looked up again, the first thing he saw was Rollins's
face close to his, smug and smiling with feigned interest and
innocence. "So, what's the verdict?"

Gabriel was trying to figure out how to answer when James
cut him short. The other boy gasped and spewed his food onto
the fire. "Goddamn!" He rose to his feet and danced back a few
steps, as if he'd felt the heat primarily in the seat of his pants and
the soles of his feet. "I near burned my mouth. That's hotter'n
Satan's piss in a frying pan!"

This put Rollins into hysterics. He laughed and joked and
imitated James and Gabriel with his dull features, using gestures

that annoyed Gabriel with their inaccuracy. None of the other men seemed equally amused. "I'll grant you the boy's got a way with words," Marshall said, "but sit yourself, Rollins. Sometimes you act like a damn five-year-old."

Gabriel ate on very carefully after that, staring down at the soup mistrustfully. He blew on it till all semblance of heat was long gone, then tried to slip the food past his tender mouth and straight down into him. No sign or flavor of those herbs could be found, and Gabriel wondered if his enflamed tongue had lost the power to taste. He said nothing, but he couldn't help giving Rollins an occasional angry look.

The men drank coffee and talked and watched the air ripple up from the fire and rise into the milky sky. Jack remembered the hospitality he'd enjoyed in a certain young woman's arms back in Crownsville. He spoke fondly of her, bucktoothed and ignorant though she was. Marshall asked what qualified Jack to call somebody ignorant. Jack answered that the girl was fresh out from Rhode Island, still spoke with that country's nasal tones, and had herself a whole set of ideas on the future of this nation and the role of women in it. Rollins said that he'd no use for buckteeth himself but that a big rump did it for him, that or a schoolgirl just budding or a little Mexican *chica* he could horse-mount and beat up a bit. Jack shook his head and tossed his coffee on the fire and said Rollins was a sick son of a bitch right enough.

Dunlop turned the conversation to other matters. He spoke of the natives and wondered if they'd have troubles passing through the Indian territory. This brought nervous looks from both Gabriel and James. James asked just where was it they were heading, anyway? Laughter all around.

"What kind of fool signed up for a hitch without asking where he was going first?" Rollins asked.

James tried to answer, but his words dribbled away unintelligibly. This brought more laughter.

Dunlop finally enlightened them. "Texas. The New Cornwall Ranch, just the other side of the Red River. We'll be there in three weeks or so. Assuming no troubles." He smiled at the two boys, a crooked smile with a touch of irony in it. "Is that . . . is that what you thought you were getting into?"

James and Gabriel exchanged glances, each looking to the other as if unsure of what he'd expected. It was James who answered. "Yeah, I reckon. We been meaning to get into the cowboy line."

"Well, boys, cheer up, then," Marshall said. "You'll be in it soon enough, soon enough." He glanced around at the other men. "In it up to your ears, I reckon."

IN THE FIRST WEEK FOLLOWING THE BOY'S DISAPPEARANCE, his family scoured the countryside for him. The boy's stepfather and adopted uncle rode out each day in different directions, leaving the chores of home to the mother and the remaining son. They searched the streets of Crownsville and learned quickly that another boy had disappeared also and had inspired great wrath in his former employer. They asked questions of passersby, of persons both white and black, young and old. Yet they found no answers and had to report as much each evening to the boy's mother, who took the news silently.

They widened the search, riding east through Solomon and Junction City and as far as Topeka, and west through Brookville and Ellsworth. The uncle stayed out the longest, returning home via sweeping arcs to Waterville in the north, or south as far as Newton, asking his questions of homesteaders and shopkeepers, cowboys and sheepherders, sometimes passing the night with strangers, once sleeping alone on the open prairie. He knew the boy lived somewhere on this globe and thought that through silence and solitude he could divine where. He listened and searched his past

conversations with the boy for signs and hints, but still he returned
with no news.

At home, the younger son struggled to recreate himself in his
brother's absence. He bowed his head and watched the men ride off
and then went to work. He tried each day to do more and be better
than the day before. If he resented his brother's departure and the
work it cast on him, he never voiced it. He tended the fields as best
he could on his own, mending the things that broke and caring for
the horse and mule in the evenings. At night, his body ached and
stretched and contorted. He awoke in the mornings as if he'd slept
a month instead of a night and had grown accordingly. And
through it all he sought to comfort his mother. He told her that his
brother would return. Of course he would. He was a hothead. He
was anxious and angry and a dang fool sometimes, but he would
return. He's just got to see things for himself for a little. You know
how he is.

When the boy spoke like this, the woman would pull him in
with a one-armed embrace, hugging him to her bosom as if she
would place his words that much closer to her heart. She told him
she believed the same and hoped the same, but she didn't say the
things that troubled her on the inside—the fear, in its overwhelm-
ing girth, of the forces at play in the world. It was a world unfit
for warriors and kings, a world that toppled nations and enslaved
whole races of people, a world one could get lost in and perish in
without so much as a passing glance from God. She hoped and
prayed for the boy's return, but she feared that the world was too
big a thing for this son, too unkind to the young and the old alike,
too indifferent to the follies of youth and the bonds of love.

OVER THE NEXT FEW DAYS THEY MOVED SOUTHWEST. The
land grew flatter and more arid, the farmers poorer and more
desperate. Their homes were often little more than dugouts in

rises of earth, covered over with what wood or sod or bracken
they had scoured from the plains. Dry dirt caked their features
like artificial suntans. And yet their faces said that they were still
proud and free and American, and they were most often white.
Better off than most, in their estimation.

How they could scratch a living out of ground meant only
for the hardiest of grasses was a mystery, on a plain that was
windswept and dry and lonelier still because of the sight of
homesteads separated by miles of nothing but distance. Had they
not heard of the plague of locusts that descend from the skies
and ravish the land? Had they not heard of the fires of late summer, which appear and disappear with the whims of the wind
and lightning and take with them homes and cattle and lives?
Where were the hopes and dreams in a place like this?

But in the passing caravan nobody posed questions such as
these. They nodded their heads when greeted and touched their
hats, and none made conversation. Apart from these greetings,
there was little interaction with the farmers. On some whim that
seemed as inexplicable as it was beneficent, Marshall did make a
gift of one horse each to three homesteads that caught his attention in some way. The homesteaders could make no sense of
such an offer and seemed scarcely willing to accept, but Marshall
insisted and rode on, leaving the farmers with halters in hands,
protests or good wishes on their lips.

As one such homestead passed into the distance, James
nudged Gabriel with an elbow. He whispered a complaint against
Marshall, who could've just as easily given each of them a horse.
But James didn't seem to take the suggestion very seriously. "I
sure as hell wouldn't want to be one of them farmers, though," he
said. "Them people look poor as dirt—poorer than dirt, cause
the dirt ain't got no debt to worry on. Your folks could end up
the same way, and it wouldn't be nobody's fault neither, cept
God's. Don't that make you think we done right?"

It took Gabriel a few moments to answer. He'd looked at the homesteaders with neither kinship nor compassion. His eyes touched little on their faces, and when they did they passed on quickly. It seemed those people were to him sad reminders of things escaped and things to keep moving from. And it seemed also that there was some shame in this. He preferred the sight of his own boots taking bites out of the earth and moving onward toward something he placed faith in still, even though he couldn't clearly define the origins of this faith.

"Yeah, we done right. Farming ain't no way to live," he finally replied.

AT SOME POINT THEY CROSSED INTO THE INDIAN TERRITORY of Oklahoma. Day-long, the view was uniform in its abandoned solemnity. The land stretched out pale and unpeopled, with tufts of grass erupting from the ground like blemishes on the back of some scurvied reprobate. James said this must be the desert, but Jack laughed at this and said maybe one day he'd see real desert and there'd be no mistaking it then. Marshall cautioned all to beware and watch out for Indians, who might protest their passage, ask for payment, or steal what they could. He rode with his rifle ready, sometimes loose across his saddle and other times standing at attention, aimed at the innocent sky. The day passed tense and dry, without a single sighting of another human being, native or otherwise.

It was a somberer evening than most, the desolation of the place having affected the men with melancholia. As Bill tended to the oxen, he sang a song, low and smooth, in a voice that flowed like liquid and seeped out over the land as if to comfort its bare spaces. Gabriel caught hardly a word of the song, but its meaning was more in the sound than in the words, and perhaps it was this that spurred him to pose a question to Dunlop, who sat next to him at the fire.

"Where'd you say you were from—Aberdonia?"

Dunlop laughed. "You've almost got it. Aberdeen's the place, back in Scotland."

"Oh." Gabriel nodded at this as if recollecting the place himself, but then asked, "What's it like over there?"

"Wet and green." Dunlop let this answer lie for a few moments, a complete portrait of the place drawn in two adjectives, but then he mused further, in language both proud and forlorn. He called Scotland an old country and said that in such places the ghosts of the past intermingle with the living. He said it had a beauty that couldn't be described but must be beheld to be truly grasped. He spoke of it as a sad place as well, where inequity had been woven into the fabric so long ago that it seemed the country had crept that way out of the mists of creation and could never change without being destroyed. His father's family had worked the land of Ballater for generations but still couldn't own it outright, as there was a laird, whose ownership took precedence over the rights of common folk. This laird, he said, valued deer hunting more than the lives of his wards. He cleared the land of people so that he and his kind could pursue their sport. It was because of this that Dunlop's family had had to move to the city, where they died fast and furiously from consumption and from the great alcoholic thirst and from sorrows that ate away their spirit. He said it was a place he missed every day.

"Why'd you come over this way?"

"Why?" Dunlop wrinkled his brow. He took a long sip of coffee. "To shoot a grizzly."

"What?"

"To shoot a grizzly." He let this answer sit and watched Gabriel think it over and slowly find acceptance of it. But then, as was his way, he added that he also crossed the ocean to make a life for himself after his family had passed on, one and all, leaving him in a position to choose the trajectory in which his life was to proceed. "How about yourself? You left some family back in Kansas, didn't you?"

Gabriel nodded. He offered no more explanation. He fixed his eyes on a gnarled piece of wood, the rooty workings of some stubborn tree. The flames ate it slowly, afraid of venturing far from their center but impelled outward by the hunger to consume.

Dunlop studied his face in the firelight. He saw the blankness of a troubled heart, not the organ but that other thing with the same name, so necessary to our lives and yet so fickle in its function. Dunlop saw this and proceeded carefully. "Did you fall out with them, then?"

"Maybe you could say that. I had a different mind on some things."

"Different minds are hard to bring together, family or no. Sometimes it's best to find your own mind and follow it." He laughed. "Sometimes—not always."

Gabriel watched him, smiling faintly but showing no joy. He couldn't help wondering how one knew when to follow one's own mind and when not to. James joined them, and the three sat quietly for a few minutes. Eventually Gabriel asked, "You ever shoot that grizzly?"

This brought a new smile from Dunlop. "I haven't—not yet, at least. I saw one once, though, up in Nebraska. Even had my sights on it."

"You miss?" James asked.

"Not exactly." The Scot looked between the two boys, something hidden in his eyes. He shrugged and stood up. "I don't know, lads." He motioned in the air before him, a brief explanation in two sharp twirls of the wrist. He proceeded as if the meaning of this gesture should be clear to all, or clear to none, depending. "Anyway, if I'd bagged the grizzly, I'd have completed my mission. I'd have had to pack up and head home, and I'm not ready to do that just yet. I kind of like this place, strange as it is."

GABRIEL BEDDED DOWN ON THE EDGE OF THE CAMP, placing the wagon between him and the rest of the men. He rolled himself tightly into the worn woolen robe that Marshall had given him and lay with his head hard on the bundle that served as his pillow, his eyes roaming from that strange angle across the horizon. The moon had just risen above the earth's rim, hauling itself up with tired resilience and casting pale light across the plain.

The boy watched the moon's progress for some time, wondering if the same moon might be viewed this evening by his mother or brother, stepfather or adopted uncle. If so, would they wish to share such a sight with him? Or would they turn against him, a unified front that would spurn him just as he had them? What sins against family will be forgiven, and what punished here on earth as in heaven?

He awoke late in the night. The moon was gone now, having progressed its full course across the sky and retired. The landscape was much darker. The fire behind him simmered low and the voices were now silent, turned instead into a chorus of nasal breathing. Gabriel saw nothing new before him and closed his eyes. He held them that way for several seconds, then eased them open again.

His eyes picked out movement in the dim light. A creature emerged from the cover of grass and waddled across a clearing of bare ground into view. An armadillo—a young one, it would seem. Its rotund body caught the dull glow of the starlight and projected an image of monstrous girth in relation to its tiny head and thin snout. It moved clumsily, waddling, and yet somehow it conveyed complete confidence in the correctness of its form. It paused at one point, contemplated a subterranean sound only its

sharp ears could hear, then dug into the soil to reach the delicacy
hidden therein.

Gabriel watched it work at this for some time. After a while,
the creature made its way over to him and brushed up against his
body. The boy didn't move, and neither did the creature retreat
from his foreign smell. It nuzzled into the wool, rustled around
for a few seconds, then lay still. Before long it seemed to sleep.
The boy watched its scaly back rise and fall, rise and fall. He
moved not a muscle, like a father who fears waking his slumber-
ing child. Some time later, while still contemplating this steady
rhythm, Gabriel too drifted into slumber.

He awoke to the early rays of morning light. There was a commotion behind him, Rollins cursing the pain of heat transmitted
through metal. The armadillo was gone, having left no trace,
sign, or footprint. The boy stared at the spot in which the creature had sheltered, then closed his eyes once more and feigned
sleep for as long as the illusion would hold.

GABRIEL AND JAMES WALKED BESIDE THE WAGON, their strides
easily matching the slow rotations of its wooden wheels. They
had risen to a sky clouded over with the threat of rain, but as the
morning passed the clouds did likewise. Gabriel felt the hard-
packed earth through the worn soles of his boots, and he
couldn't help but compare it to dried skin, blistered by so many
days without rain.

Marshall roused the boy from his thoughts. He rode by them
at a canter, tipped his hat, smiled as if addressing polite company,
and moved on up to converse with Caleb.

James leaned close to Gabriel. "What do you make of
Marshall?"

"Don't know. Reckon he knows his job all right."

"Yeah, he does that," James said, although his tone indicated that this answer was not in keeping with the thrust of his question. "Don't he seem strange to you? Like he thinks one thing one minute and then the exact opposite the next."

"How's that make him different from any other white man?"

"Well . . ." James found it hard to argue with this.

"They think what suits them and change their minds when it suits them. That's how come they're white."

James smirked. "Is that why? I thought it had something to do with skin color."

They walked on. Just after eleven o'clock Gabriel noticed that something was happening. Caleb galloped out ahead, and Marshall hefted his rifle and rode with its barrel against his shoulder. Bill motioned to the boys. "Come up, we got us company ahead."

And thus Gabriel rode the wagon into the first settlement of Indians he'd yet seen. It was not the sight he would have imagined. Their homes huddled in the earth like the dens of creatures only half gifted with the knowledge of carpentry, part turf and part skins and part cave. There was only one teepee, massive compared to the other structures but weatherworn, shredded by heat and wind. As the caravan drew near, forms rose up from the hovels and walked out to greet them. Dogs followed the people, more like the protected of this tribe than protectors. In front walked an old man and woman, a couple so aged and wrinkled as to be kin to the first humans. Behind them walked several more of different ages and sizes, all clad in rags and stray garments, one with a cavalry shirt and one sporting a hat of buffalo fur, which seemed strange, as the day was warm.

The old man hailed the wagon in his own language. With a nod from Marshall, they halted and listened to the man's words, sounds thrown together and meaningless to all but Jack. The Indian spoke with gestures that seemed both beseeching and instructional, as if he would ask them for something but must first explain the premise he proposed and provide the background and other salient details.

"They're Kansa," Jack said.

"Are they?" Marshall asked, though he seemed little interested. He took off his hat and worked its shape with his fingers. He looked ahead of them. "What do they have to say?"

Jack and the old man spoke for a few moments. The old woman interrupted twice, punctuating some point of the man's with her own emphasis, nodding her gray head and reaching up toward Marshall with gestures that were difficult to interpret. Jack thought for a minute before translating. He seemed to process the conversation at full length, and he spat before he spoke. "They want food. He says they're starving. They been eating grasshoppers."

"Grasshoppers?" Bill said. "Shit."

The woman nodded.

Marshall stuffed his hat back on his head. "Better than nothing, I guess. They got anything to trade, or they just appealing to our sense of Christian decency?"

Jack shrugged. "You got eyes, Marshall. You figure they got anything to trade?"

A girl stepped forward from the back of the group and touched the side of the wagon. Bill looked down at her, suspicious, but the girl looked around him and studied James. Her hair hung straight and black around her face. Her eyes were black also and large, more like the eyes of a deer than of a person. She might have been as old as sixteen or as young as twelve. It was hard to tell. She reached out and touched James's knee. She caressed it and looked up at him with eyes that were both inviting and curious. James drew back from her and brushed against Gabriel.

"Looks like the squaw fancies coloreds," Bill said, with humor in his voice but a frown on his face. "Never could make sense of Indians."

"Go on and get yourself some if you can," Rollins said. He glanced at Bill and shared a smile with him. "She's clean. You can see that. Clean and sweet, I'll bet ya."

"Get me what?" James asked.

"Get what she'll give you," Rollins said. "Or sell you. She can't cost much out here."

James hesitated. He looked at Gabriel like a man soon to be guilty of some crime seeking forgiveness. He would have asked his friend something, but the urging of the men and the girl made him climb down from the wagon. The girl held his hand in hers and looked him long in the face. She reached out her other hand and touched his chest, slid her fingers over his collarbone and out to the muscles of his shoulder.

James laughed nervously.

The old woman said something and the girl nodded, not taking her eyes off James.

"What'd she say?" Rollins asked.

Jack spat before he answered. "Shit, every redskin's a prophet these days. Said you're not long for this world, James." He shook his head as if it were barely worth going on. "The old dog barks backward and the moon is a piece of cheese with gold inside."

"She said all that?"

"Shit, no, she didn't say that."

"You just said she said it."

Jack looked at Rollins with infinite disgust.

They all lapsed into silence once more. The girl said something that Jack refused to translate. She motioned for James to follow her.

"She wants me to go with her?" He looked beyond her to the structures that passed as homes. "I'm not going over in there. Somebody else go."

"You don't like girls?" Rollins asked. "Or is it squaws you ain't got a taste for? Or . . . Don't tell me you ain't ever wet your

pecker yet. Look, boy, there ain't nothing to it. Just go on with
her and do like she says and come back smiling."

James studied the girl again. "This the way Injuns do?"

"Don't know and don't care. Injuns do or they don't. I can
never tell why and it don't pay to ask. I reckon poverty'll make
a person do near anything. It's gonna cost you, though."

"She ain't asked him for anything yet," Jack said. "Just made
the offer."

James again discovered the humor in the situation and looked
to Gabriel for guidance. Gabriel offered him none.

Marshall had sat quietly through these exchanges but spoke
up now. "Let's go," he said. "They can eat grasshoppers, for all I
care. James, back up in the wagon." He urged his horse forward
twenty feet or so, paused, and wheeled around. Nobody had
moved. "I said let's go. These people are diseased. Look at them.
They're castoffs from their own people. They're the wretched
dregs of a wretched race, and all they want from us is to drag us
down with them. You ain't doing that on my time. Let's go." He
turned again and rode off without looking back.

James stood, unsure what to do, his hand still clasped in the
girl's.

"Come up, boy," Bill said. "I reckon Marshall knows a sick-
ness when he sees it."

With this, James gently withdrew his hand from the girl's. He
climbed up on the wagon and sat next to Gabriel. Bill snapped
the oxen into motion and the cart moved off. James looked back
at the girl, but she didn't watch the cart pull away. She had bent
down and was writing something in the dirt with her finger. The
rest of that motley entourage turned and made their way back to
their hovels, lacking either the energy or the faith to beg more
heartily.

Jack rode up next to the wagon. "You don't know what she
said, do you?"

"I couldn't understand a word," James said.

"She said you had beautiful skin. Called it 'skin the color of the first earth.' " Jack pursed his lips as if he were preparing to spit, then changed his mind and didn't. "They got a funny way of saying things. In the future, you ought best not listen to old Rollins. He got hisself a case of shrivel-dick some time back. Says he's been cured of it, but ever since he's been trying to introduce others to the pleasure of it. Vengeful son of a bitch, he is." With this he kicked his horse into a trot and moved away from the wagon.

THAT EVENING THEY CAMPED beside a thicket of tamarisk trees on the southern bank of the Red River. Rollins prodded James with questions about his sexuality, hypothesizing that the boy suffered from some unnatural disorder. James did his best to keep away from him, going further than necessary to gather wood. The man might have turned his attentions toward Gabriel if Jack hadn't observed that they'd soon be back on much-loved Texan soil. Rollins's mood turned. He smiled and hooted at the thought of that, lauding the virtues of that once free republic and quickly spiraling into a tirade against all things Mexican.

Gabriel ate with little appetite. The wooden spoon felt unwieldy in his fingers, the stew blander than usual. He followed the men's conversation with little more than half-interest, musing on the events of the afternoon, the Indian girl and her family, the mixture of loathing and pity that this conjured in him. Dunlop's voice brought his attention back.

"It's a sad state of affairs with those people, and it's only gonna get worse." The Scot shook his head and prodded a log into the fire with his foot. "They've been done a mighty wrong, if you ask me. It's indecent, is what it is."

"Yeah, there's something sad in it," Marshall said. He spoke absently, the greater part of his attention engaged in rolling a cigarette. He shredded tobacco between his fingers, strung it out upon a brittle sheet of rolling paper, and rolled it closed with one smooth motion of his hand down his pants leg. "It's a sad world and the red man's been given a raw deal in it, but some sad things must come to pass in the betterment of society and mankind in general. You ever given that a thought? Ain't nothing could've been done with the Indians than what has been." He pulled a stick from the fire and lit his cigarette with all seriousness and then tossed the stick back into the flames. "Tell you what. I wish them boys up north speedy progress in dealing with the Sioux and their likes. You may think I'm being coarse, Dunlop, but you weren't born and raised in this country, were you? The story of Rebecca Dary should be enough to prove my point."

"I've heard the story, Marshall," Dunlop said.

This gave the man pause, but only for a second. "You boys ever hear of Rebecca Dary?"

Gabriel and James shook their heads.

"Well, listen here." Marshall didn't begin speaking immediately, however. He waited a few moments to let a suitable silence build, then he reminded everyone that this was no story of the distant past but was little over a decade old. He first painted a picture of the young Rebecca's upbringing in the East, among the cultured society people of Philadelphia. He told of manicured trees and streets paved and daily swept. He told of her long and beautiful auburn hair, of her fair eyes the color of the sky, and of her figure straight and comely. This woman, he said, might have planned nothing more for her life than to reside in that city. She could have married and borne young, watched them tutored and sent on to a fine university. She could have aged gently, feeding her mind on poetry, English novels, and polite conversation.

"Her life could've went that way," Marshall said, "cept then she fell in love, took a fancy to a man of adventure." He was a dashing youth, the young Mr. Dary, with dreams as big as the continent and full faith in his ability to make them happen. They were wed. In a year's time they had quit the East and staked a claim in central Kansas. She bore a child, a baby boy, and with this young one in tow their life progressed.

Marshall paused to look around the fire and challenge each man's eyes to differ with him on any part of his tale as thus far disclosed. Only silence answered him. He went on. In the spring of the Darys' third year, things changed. The previous winter the Kiowas had suffered and starved and died in great numbers. They had seen their food sources destroyed and their lands eaten into by an endless parade of palefaces. They had lived hard and unhappy, and a band of their braves decided to even the score. They began their warpath in southern Kansas and swept north. They killed, scalped, raped, and spread mayhem wherever they could. When they came upon the Dary homestead, they found the husband tilling a field and cleaved open his forehead with a hatchet. They found the baby toddling in the dirt by the front porch and lifted him by the feet and stove in his skull on a fencepost. And Rebecca they found poised in the doorway with a shotgun aimed pointblank at them. She shot two of them dead before they knocked her unconscious and strapped her to the back of a horse and rode off into wild country, about as far from the reach of whites as possible.

Marshall paused again here and looked at his audience. The men sat tensely, as if they thought that this story shouldn't be taken too seriously but were finding that hard to do. Caleb was barely visible, half hidden in the shadows. James had huddled up close to the fire and warmed his hands there, looking at Marshall and waiting. Gabriel too sat listening. There was something in the quality of Marshall's voice that he found intoxicating, something as solid as the written word, and as irrefutable. He kept his eyes on the fire, trying to focus on the flames and the magic of their dance. From the outside, he seemed to have no interest save for the fire's motion, but the man couldn't have held the boy's attention any more completely.

Marshall went on to tell of the early days of Rebecca's capture, when her hair was shorn and handed out to the squaws. She was tied to a post before the teepee of the brave who captured her, and for three weeks she received no food except for what she could steal from the dogs. Each day when the brave returned from his hunts, he would untie her and lead her inside to quench his desire. This done, he lent her to others, who had her one after the other till she was bruised inside and out and numb and could feel no more. This went on for weeks that turned into months and looked to last forever. At some point the brave took a deeper liking to her and stopped sharing her with his companions. He fed her well and took her into his teepee and made her equal to his other wives. They accepted her also, for she was kind and demure and yet showed a strength of character that they admired.

One day the brave killed a buffalo. He cut out its tongue and rode across the miles and brought it to Rebecca and fed her with it, raw and warm from the grip of his palm. Another day they brought in a captured cavalryman and administered to him all forms of degradation. Rebecca was there, watching, with no recognition of a kinship to this man on her face. She was garbed as an Indian and thought as an Indian and spoke the Kiowa language as if she had known no other. She spat on the captured soldier and told him in her foreign tongue that she knew him not except as the bastard child of the creator, a scourge cast by accident into the world and spread like the plague. "And I'm quoting verbatim," Marshall said.

He stopped here and backtracked to make sure all around him

understood the full import of the story thus far. She had seen her husband murdered. Seen her son swung up by his ankles and smashed against a post so hard he was nearly beheaded. She had been raped and raped again and enslaved and had her culture, her decency, and even her hair stripped from her. And yet she spat on that soldier and named his place of origin. Marshall said these things slowly and clearly so that all might hear.

A full year and two months after her capture, she was traded back into civilization as the bounty paid for several chiefs the whites held. She found herself embraced by the white world, drawn into culture and religion and the English language. She was saved from her tormentors and delivered back to her own.

Marshall paused here once more. This time he looked not at his fellows' faces but straight into the fire. When he spoke again, his voice had dropped so low all the men had to lean forward to catch his words.

Later, when she was asked and interviewed over and over again, she said little about her capture or rescue. People said she was ashamed, horrified by it, and didn't care to live the nightmare again for anyone's sake. "But do you know what she said one time when pestered just a little too much by some concerned citizens?" He held the group on the question and looked around as if earnestly expecting one among them to have the answer. "She said, *I wish they'd never found me.* They thought that she was talking about the savages when she said that. But is that how it sounds to you? That's not how it sounds to me. Sounds to me like those redskins had filled her mind so full of their blood logic, pumped her so full of their juices, whispered so long in her ears, that she had become one of them. Worse than one of them, because she had once been one of us. They stripped her of two thousand years of civilization in one year's time, left her nothing but a naked savage. One year, that's all it takes. That's why we've

no choice, never before and still not now, other than to extermi-
nate that beast among us. Tell me I'm wrong if you can."

If Dunlop found any fault in the man's story, he expressed it
silently, by shaking his head and tossing his coffee grounds into
the fire. James raised his hand like a pupil posing a question to
his teacher, but then he changed his mind and made to get up.
Marshall had seen the hand, though, and set on him to speak his
mind.

James was slow to talk, but having been prompted, he did. "I
thought you said you admired them in some ways."

Marshall stared at the boy so long that James was forced to
look away. Only then did he speak. "You don't understand a
damn thing, do you? Yeah, I said I admire them. But I admire
wolves too. You ever seen the way they hunt in packs? They got
their own kings and queens. They cull the herds of the weak and
let the strong prosper. Shit, they're smarter than most people are.
I admire them, but put one in my sights, and I'll shoot it dead
and hang its head on my wall. They may be God's creatures, and
for all I know the reds may be God's lost tribe, but what place do
they have in this world right here, in my world, in the white
man's world?"

James could think of no answer to the question and replied
only with the faintest of shrugs. The others sat still. Marshall
leaned back and lit a cigarette. He seemed content with the
silence he'd created and only broke it once more. "Yeah, some
things are best admired hanging from a nail."

Before long the coyotes swept over the land on patrol, calling
to each other and sharing their ownership of the night with joy
or sorrow, it was hard to tell. Marshall walked off onto the
prairie, rifle in hand, to converse with himself away from human
interference. The tension eased with his absence. Dunlop patted
James on the back and said that Marshall was just the argumenta-

tive type—"Should have been a politician." James smiled timidly at this and looked over at Gabriel, who met his eyes for only a moment.

WITH THE PASSING OF THE FIRST WEEK *of the boy's absence into the second and third, the family dug into their work with a resolve made stronger by their loss. The plots of turned sod stretched ever larger, the planted acres budded and grew, rows of corn took shape, and fields of wheat swayed in the breeze with a texture and motion different from those of the wild grass around them. The buildings grew as well. The new room was completed, making two in their simple dwelling. The barn, much because of the younger son's labor, was roofed, and a chicken coop was built onto one side. Work became so consuming that it seemed the very purpose of life, the meaning of it, a holy act that, in the uncle's words, could be "the prayer of this mortal coil."*

Moments of leisure were few and far between, but when the uncle received a rifle in return for services rendered to a neighbor, he shaved minutes from the evening's rituals to teach the younger son to shoot. The two would walk out some distance on the prairie and spend the last of the evening's light in friendly tutelage. The rifle was a Kentucky long, an old creature born early in the century and well used over the years. The man handled it with care and asked the boy never to disparage its limited capabilities. He taught him how to calculate distance and to think of such things as the lay of the land, whether it rose or fell, the velocity and direction of the wind, and even to consider his own breath and to time his shots in accordance. He noted that with this particular gun you had only one shot at a time, so it was not the weapon of choice against numerous Indians or against even a single grizzly.

Before he let him fire the rifle, the uncle asked the boy never to take life except with reverence, never without a prayer of thanks

and forgiveness. Life is sacred, he said. Above all else, it's a gift
given to each creature by the creator. Us people should never get so
big-headed that we kill without great need. I don't care if it's noth-
ing but a field mouse, you still gotta respect that you undoing
something what God done in the first place. So you better ask his
permission first. He told the boy that he believed all creatures had
souls, just like humans. He said that he knew this to be so because
he'd seen it in their eyes. We all God's creatures, true enough. He
made the boy swear that he understood this and would take it to
heart.

The boy did so with quiet eyes and took the weapon into his
hands. The first time he shot the rifle, he was satisfied to find the
kick not as impressive as he expected, just a nudge against his
shoulder. He welcomed the feeling of power within the barrel, the
force projected outward, the small bullet that ripped through the
air like a scream with teeth. From the first shot the boy showed a
knack for marksmanship. He sent the tin target dancing across
the prairie, and the uncle looked at him with new respect.

But that evening as he tried to sleep, the boy found himself
pained in the shoulder and jaw and, strangely, in the hamstring
of his left leg. He couldn't place the origin of these injuries, and
he didn't mention them to anyone, but he was to suffer from these
ailments ever after, whenever he'd shoot a weapon, either pistol
or rifle, whenever he took a life.

THEY HAD JUST BROKEN CAMP THE NEXT MORNING when a
lone horseman came in from the east. Gabriel watched him tra-
verse the far bank and come to a stop across the river. He hallooed
once and held a hand up in greeting, then let it drop and studied
the water before him. He bent low over his horse's neck and
spoke into its ear. The horse tossed its head and surveyed the
water with mistrust, but stepped forward and took to it gently,

like a bather testing the temperature with a toe. A few steps in
and the horse sank up to its shoulders. It dropped into a swim-
ming rhythm with the rider still leaning forward in the saddle.
When the horse emerged on the near bank, it gleamed and shivered in the morning air.

The rider was wet up half his body, but he did not acknowledge it. In a series of motions strung together so quickly they
seemed only a single movement, he reined the horse to a stop in
the center of camp, flung one leg over the horn of his saddle,
and slid down to the ground. He landed hard but was standing
straight-backed the next moment, chest pushed out and face
anxious. He was just a few years older than Gabriel, thin, with
sharp, almost delicate features and blue eyes that flicked from
man to man uneasily. Rollins and Jack immediately began
joking with him, asking what in Christ's name he was doing up
here, comparing him to a faithful dog that couldn't stand being
parted from its master. The boy's eyes flashed at this, but he
held whatever words he had and directed his gaze toward
Marshall.

"Thank God I found ya! I been riding full chisel since midnight. Marshall, they're fixing to hang you."

The boy spoke with all seriousness, but Marshall smiled. "To
hang me? Well, that's some news, Dallas. Damn if that don't beat
all. To hang *me*? What kind of fool would want to try that? I'm
too big-headed to be hung."

Dallas yanked his hat from his head as if it had suddenly offended him, punched it with one sharp blow, and set it back
in place. "This here's serious, Marshall. It's on account of them
horses y'all stole from Three Bars. Y'all been found out, and
now they're fixing to hang ya sure as shit." He let this sit for a
moment, looking from one man to another with a frank accusation on his face. But he held the expression for only a moment. It
slipped away, to be replaced by a sullen, almost childlike disap-

pointment. "Y'all should have cut me in on it. You know I'd've rode with ya. I ain't afraid of them halfbreeds . . ."

Caleb walked up from the river, wiping his face with his handkerchief in slow, deliberate strokes. His presence seemed to give Dallas pause, although the boy bubbled with things still unsaid. Gabriel watched Marshall, looking to make some sense of this messenger's news. The humor in Marshall's features was undiminished. In fact, he seemed quite amused by the whole thing.

"Which horses was that, Dallas?"

The boy pulled his hat off and punched it again. "The ones y'all stole and drove up in broad daylight past Fort Concho and took up to Crownsville and sold right there at auction for the whole world to see. Jim Rickles from down at Three Bars been making sure every ranch in Texas knows it too. Y'all are being put out of the whole goddamn state of Texas. Word is that Richards might even turn y'all in. He—"

"Wait a minute," Marshall said, waving the boy silent with the palm of his hand. "Are we being put out or hanged or turned in? You're making an awful confusion of it, son. Maybe you should have yourself a cup of coffee or something."

Dallas set his hat back on his head and struggled to control his growing exasperation. "Somebody just might want to listen to what I got to say. I ain't here for my own health, that's for damn sure. Richards has done gone and fired ya, right? I heard the words from his lips myself. And Rickles has been saying he ain't gonna take it sitting down. And since nobody seems to want to hunt you, he's talking about rounding hisself up his own posse and coming after ya. Is that clear enough?"

"Hellfire!" Rollins said, throwing down the canteen he'd been holding and launching one of his instantaneous tirades. "I knew something bad would come of that whole business! I never was a horse thief, and this is exactly why." Dunlop stood still, as if he hadn't taken it all in, and Marshall said nothing, just kept smiling. Caleb had finished his long, slow cleaning of his face. He knotted his handkerchief around his neck and looked as nonplussed as Marshall did amused.

Gabriel cast a quick glance at James, wondering if he too remembered the horses Dallas spoke of. The image of the market came back to him fully, the gaiety and activity of the day, the humor in Marshall's voice, the command he held over the audience. It was that day that had most formed his perception of this man, and even if the days spent in his company had dimmed the image somewhat, it was still, in Gabriel's mind, the moment of introduction to the world he now lived in. But if he'd heard this boy right, if he hadn't misunderstood . . .

Marshall ran his tongue across his front teeth and scented the air. "All right, Dallas, I heard your message. You can go on back to Richards now, if that's what you had in mind."

Dallas was so quick to answer that he sprayed the air before him with spittle. "The hell I will! Richards is the biggest lily-livered dandy in the state of Texas. He's a woman, is what he is. Should've been a sheepherder. And Three Bars, they ain't nothing but a bunch of mixed-breed monkeys and whores. Ain't an honest one among them. I'd've stole the horses myself if you'd asked me to. Hell, I'd ride with ya now and put bullets in the lot of them and hang em from the nearest tree. I'd . . ." He seemed to have more to say, but he faltered. "Shit, you know what I'd do."

Marshall had smiled from the boy's first words. He stepped forward and punched him in the ribs, causing his horse to shy away. "Ain't that perfect?" he asked the others. "Good ole Dallas—never one to shy from runction. Comes up here and volunteers to share the noose with us. That's perfect. You're a piece of work." He thought for a moment, then motioned to Caleb to join him for a private conversation. He paused a few steps on and turned back. "Well, Jack, Bill, you all can head on if you want. Richards'll know you didn't have nothing to do with it. And I reckon he'll be wanting his wagon back." With that, he moved away again.

Dallas stood with a stupefied expression on his face. He called after Marshall, as did Rollins and Dunlop, but Marshall and Caleb went and sat beside the river. Marshall bent to roll a cigarette as they talked. Dallas spat, swung his jaw loose, then spat again. It was only then that he noticed Gabriel and James. Derision curled his lips.

"What's with the coloreds?"

Bill looked at the boys almost sadly. "Marshall hired them."

"For what?"

"Just . . . Well, I don't know. Help out the nigger Enoch, I guess. Make em punchers someday."

"Punchers?" Dallas squinted one eye at Gabriel and seemed to consider the probability of this. "Not a penguin's chance in hell. You boys get on back where you come from."

"They're some good boys. I'll stand for em."

"I don't care if you would stand for them. They ain't about to get no work down there. Marshall should've left them back where they come from." Dallas took a step closer and spoke to the boys in simple tones, loud and clear, as if they were foreigners. "There ain't no work for you down there. If I were you, I'd pull foot before you get yourselves in trouble. That's my advice." Having given it, Dallas turned away and seemed to forget about the boys entirely. "What in tarnation are those two talking about, anyway? Marshall should be talking to me. I'm the one that just about saved his skin."

The young man went on complaining, interrupted often by Rollins's outbursts and Dunlop's questions. Bill and Jack exchanged silent glances. They spoke not a word in council to each other but seemed to be of one mind, as if they'd expected just

such trouble all along and had no interest in hanging around any
longer than they had to. They returned to their preparations to
depart. Gabriel had the feeling that something was slipping away
from him. The earth moved under his feet instead of he over the
earth. He was aware of conversations taking place, but he played
no part in them. He heard Jack express his regrets and say his
goodbyes and watched him ride off, slow and quiet but still
going. He heard the snap of Bill's whip over the oxen and saw
them enter the river. The creatures sank in up to their necks and
surged forward in rhythmic thrusts, like aquatic beasts of burden
harnessed in a fable from some pre-Biblical time. Gabriel
watched them emerge on the other side and move off. He saw
James's face before him, troubled almost to tears and filled with
questions. He turned and sought out Marshall and found only
the man's back, some thirty yards away. He was smoking and
talking quietly with Caleb, oblivious of the shift in the earth and
as calm as any wayward angel whose work is still blessed by
providence. And still the earth rolled beneath the boy's feet, like
a slowly undulating ocean that did not yet drown him but might
at any moment.

FOR THE NEXT HALF-HOUR GABRIEL LISTENED silently to a
tumult of threats and declarations, annoyance and denials. Rollins cursed the fate that would exile him from the land of his
birth. He said it was an absurdity, and further treachery, and
beyond that a blasphemy, that the halfbreed thieves of Three
Bars might accuse them of the same crime they themselves were
guilty of. Dunlop was in less of a temper, but he admitted that the
fact that the law had not been involved did imply some earlier
guilt on the ranch's part. Both of them sought to bring Marshall
and Caleb into the discourse, but those two shared only each
other's council until a decision was made.

At last Marshall approached the group, smiled at them, and set his hands on his hips. His cigarette dangled from the corner of his mouth. "Well, boys, who's for the whorehouse at McKutcheon's Station?"

Gabriel felt James grasp his elbow, but what the touch might mean he didn't turn to see.

"What?" Dunlop asked.

"There ain't no whorehouse at McKutcheon's," Rollins said.

"There's women there, ain't there?"

"Yeah. I reckon. There's them Mexicans he keeps all about the place."

"That's right. If they ain't whores yet, they will be tonight. Come on, I'll buy you all a line of whiskies that'll make your peckers point. First jab's courtesy of yours truly."

He made to turn away, but Dunlop protested. "Marshall, we can't just get pickled. We have to do something. Let's go talk to Richards. He'll see reason."

Marshall responded with a smirk. "I'd say he's seen reason. Good businessman, he is. I never doubted it. Hey, ever had a Mexican, Dunlop?"

"Marshall—"

"They're hotter than one of them habañero chiles. Burn your pecker if you're not in and out quick." He leaned forward and took the cigarette out of his mouth. "You won't have no problem with that, though, will you, Dunlop? You've got the fastest pecker in the West, don't you? Little lovely up in Crownsville told me that. Said she didn't more than touch your thing before you shot your load all over her blouse. She was right well annoyed with you, son." He straightened up and laughed heartily. "Made him pay extra for the laundering."

"Jesus, Marshall, is this a joke?"

Marshall moved toward Dunlop with one enormous step that amazed Gabriel with its suddenness. His hand swung up in a motion overtly threatening, but it was neither a punch nor a slap, just an indication that either could be pulled down from the heavens faster than a lightning strike. Dunlop fell silent, and Marshall completed the motion gently, closing his eyes and bringing his hand up to his own forehead and kneading it. "All things done will be undone, Dunlop. Never question that. But all things in their time." He opened his eyes and spoke with a tension just restrained, a tension totally at odds with his words and thereby more sinister. "Now is not the time. Now is the time for Mexican whores at McKutcheon's. Your horse is saddled—now mount up if you're coming." He turned away and walked off toward his horse.

Dunlop looked at Rollins, who returned the stare. Finally Rollins cursed and gathered up his things to go. Dallas thought the plan over for a second, then yanked on his horse's reins, making the creature spin in a circle, saying, "Let's get us some whores, then." The Scot hesitated longer, walking to his horse only after all the others had mounted. He was on in one fluid motion, and once saddled, he regained his composure.

"What about the boys?" he asked.

Marshall studied the boys as if they'd been rendered visible only by Dunlop's question. His gaze was hard and serious for a moment, this question challenging him more than any thus far in the morning. "Damned if I didn't forget about them two. That is a bit of a pickle, ain't it?" He looked at Caleb when he said this, but Caleb looked off, as if the answer were already settled in his mind and needed no further thought.

As his tone was friendly, James stepped forward and shared with the man some measure of his confusion over the sudden turn of events: their being let go and all, the accusations of theft and other such nonsense. He was confused to the core, though he didn't doubt a wrong was being done and hoped that Marshall would include them in whatever venture he was next to attend to.

Marshall heard him out, head cocked to the side. When the boy had exhausted his words, Marshall spat out his cigarette and said, "Like I said, some pickle." He dug around in his saddlebags and came up with a small object, a coin. He held it between his forefinger and thumb, aimed it at Gabriel, and flipped it out toward him in a high arc, the coin spinning over and over and catching the sun on one side and then the other and coming to rest on Gabriel's palm. "There you go. That's more than a month's wages for your troubles. As for future work and the destiny of your lives, well . . . You all are probably better off quit of me, if I do say so myself. Wish you boys the best." He touched his hat and spun his horse and rode away, kicking up dust, followed close behind by Caleb and Rollins and Dallas.

Dunlop's horse pawed the ground, spurred to motion by the other horses' departure. Dunlop calmed it and lingered with the boys. "Oh, this is so daft. It was a joke almost, those horses . . . Look, I don't know what you'll decide now. Could head straight back home if you wanted. It's an easy path to follow, near dead north. But if you're not ready to quit just yet, walk east here along the river. Just follow it. You'll be at McKutcheon's in two days' time if you're fast. Three at most. You might pick up some work there. Hell, we'll be there ourselves, probably." He looked after the horsemen. They were fast receding. He remembered something, turned round, and checked the bag he kept dangling from one of his rear saddle strings. He handed James a couple of strips of jerky. "I'm sorry, lads. I'd ride with you if I could, but I've got to make Marshall see some sense. Keep your wits about you. You two will be fine." With that, he clucked his horse into motion and was off behind the others.

The two boys watched the men ride into the distance till they blended into the landscape and were lost. Gabriel again felt the earth flex around him. He dropped to one knee and studied the horizon, the ground beneath him, then the horizon again, as if one could give some meaning to the other. He saw his plan for the future slipping away. As his mind sought to hold on to it, he suddenly felt that he'd never had a true notion of his future as a cowboy. He could find no substance to it. It was all like a dream, a treacherous dream that had brought him so far from home and vanished with the passing of riders over the curve of the earth, leaving a world all too real.

"You get the feeling we're in a heap of shit?" James asked.

Gabriel said that was exactly the feeling he had. He couldn't have put it better himself.

ALL THAT DAY THE BOYS FOLLOWED THE RIVERBANK through a landscape of brittle gray grass with patches of soil lying bare to the southern sun. It had taken little under an hour to decide their course. They had first talked through the events of the morning several times, disagreeing about the reality of it, the reasons why, and the results, as if they could argue the facts and so change them. They considered the return route to the north, all those miles on foot, through the Indian territory, past those impover-ished homesteads, and on to what? To questions and accusations and the naming of crimes Gabriel could see no way to deny. He had shoved the coin in his pocket and wondered aloud how far it was to this McKutcheon's. James had needed no further prompt-ing. He figured Pinkerd would near skin him alive for running off, and he didn't favor that. So the two had set to walking.

Although they sighted not a single person that day, they rarely felt truly alone. Longhorns roamed the country in loose herds, seemingly wild. They surveyed the boys with disinterested eyes and kept up a constant movement with their short strides. The only sign of human contact upon them was the brands most of them wore across their hides, scorched acronyms for ranches Gabriel now felt he might never lay his eyes on.

James kept up a nearly constant stream of words: complaints about the state of his feet, descriptions of the warm spots already burning at his toes, questions about the wisdom of their decision, and grumblings about Marshall's fickle nature. Gabriel tried to shut James out. He thought back to the chilly days of March. It was almost shocking to acknowledge the passing of weeks into months, spring into summer. Despite his wishes to the contrary, a portion of his life was slipping by in these western lands. Time did not conform to the whims of humans. It went on, as impartial and unending as the land around them, as callous as Marshall and Caleb and Rollins, men who would abandon them when the tides of their own fortunes changed.

That night they sheltered in a water-carved wash in the riverbank. They divided the jerky evenly and tore into it, washing it down with river water and discovering that this served only to stir their appetites further. Afterward, they sat huddled together like the primitive predecessors of humankind, at the mercy of the night and the creatures that roamed it. It was a strangely active evening, alive with insect calls and bird life, the scurrying of rodents. The river rippled by them, not with a clear sound but more as the indication of an almost silent motion, like an enormous reptile slithering past.

James complained of blisters and condemned walking as a foul invention. He talked about the East, about the hardships there and the troubles, as if he needed to remind himself of the things that had pushed him into this wash. He tried to find joy in these memories but could not. His tale of childhood pranks along the banks of the Chattahoochee River ended in the sighting of a dead body, a former human, bloated, decaying, and swirling gently in the water. He shook the tale off and started again, telling once more of his journey west and the things he saw along the way and the wild excitement that had moved him along. But this tale derailed when he remembered a man he'd met, on a Mississippi riverboat. The man was on his way to Nebraska with his family, but he had not escaped the South unharmed. While still on his home turf, he'd been accosted by whites angry at his pretensions, whites who hated so hard they couldn't stand to be deprived of the target for their hatred and were growing frantic lest too many blacks quit the territory. They asked him was he heading west, and when he answered yes, they beat him soundly and took him up into the hinterlands of that country and sawed off his hands with a bucksaw. They told him he was free to go west if he wanted, but the hands that had picked so many bushels of cotton were gonna stay right where they were conceived, in the grand old South.

"Can you believe that?"

"Yeah."

"I know, but . . . Why would you ever even think of doing that to a person? Just why even think it up? People do some unholy crazy mischief, that's the truth of it."

Gabriel didn't dispute it.

James shook his head; whether at people in general or at himself was not clear. "Why can't I tell a proper story that don't end in somebody dead or maimed?" He posed the question to the night and listened as it went on in its chorus, at no point answering him or even aware that it had been questioned. "You got any stories, Gabe?"

Gabriel said he didn't. He knew only his own life, and none of that deserved retelling. He closed his eyes and told the other boy to do the same. "Let's just go to sleep. Talking ain't gonna help none."

James did agree to try sleep, although he doubted he'd sleep a wink until his feet quit aching and he got some decent food in his belly and could stop worrying about rattlers and had a proper roof over his head, for that matter.

He so spoke, but his breathing had calmed into slumber ten

minutes later, and it was Gabriel who lay awake. He reclined
there in the darkness, listening to the world and thinking of his
mother, touched anew by the shame of the distance between
them. He watched her at the daily chores that she went to with
such devotion, such joy, and eventually realized that when he
thought of her, it was always at the homestead. He no longer
imagined her back in the East, in city clothes or at work in the
funeral parlor or entertaining guests in their home. When he
tried to place her back there now, all he saw was the melancholy
face of a woman walking in a dream of life. He saw eyes shad-
owed by resignation, motions tired from morning till night, a
woman who smiled without smiling, laughed without laughter.
He drifted into sleep on the verge of a realization that his waking
mind had yet to accept.

Gabriel awoke with James shaking him and staring wide-eyed
and fearful into his face. "Listen. You hear that?"

It took Gabriel a second to sort out the sounds, but only a
second. A pack of coyotes had gathered on the bank above them.
They were no more than a few feet away but were out of sight
above the embankment. The boys could hear their breathing and
sense the light touch of their paws on the earth. The coyotes
sniffed and snarled and called to each other, their cries a shrill
cacophony without structure.

Into this came another creature. It moved with greater bulk,
with slower steps, pressing more weight into the ground. Around
it the smaller canines scurried and whined. The images Gabriel
conjured of this beast sent his blood scorching through his veins:
some demon dog, an enormous deity of fur and fangs, with a
snout so long as to be primeval, the saws of its teeth like hungry
demons in their own right. This creature had a greater voice as
well, one that it lifted to the night like the deep and painful music
of all that is carnivorous. It rang in Gabriel's head as if it were the
meaning of sound and the embodiment of life, and for a moment

there was no more to life or death than the howl from that
unseen creature. When it finally faded, an answering call came
back across the night.

James grabbed Gabriel's arm again. Both boys trembled, and
neither could have moved if he had wanted to. So they remained,
awaiting death and afraid to believe their ears as the calls faded
and became a distant chorus. Gabriel listened. James's teeth
chattered. The river moved past them in liquid silence, occasionally gurgling as a rip hit the surface. They were alone once more.
Gabriel's heartbeat seemed the loudest thing on the prairie that
evening, save for the howl of whatever creature had stood above
them. Neither boy spoke, but both prayed for the morning, when
they could get up and walk again.

*THE MOTHER STRUGGLED EACH DAY with the question of when
to be silent and when to speak. She knew that the uncle's intentions
were good and that in this place boys must become men very
quickly. But she never liked the way her youngest son looked
carrying a gun. She watched him walk across the fields and found
something wrong in it, something foreign. She knew that he was
different from other men, softer on the inside, kinder, better. That's
why it seemed so strange that he carried a rifle dangling at his side,
or that he came home with the dead shells of rabbits and prairie
dogs slung over his shoulder. She couldn't help thinking that he was
play-acting. This wasn't him. He was someone different. He was
the boy who had once found a baby bird and fed it milky bread with
a toothpick and slept with it in a box beside his pillow and cried for
days when it gave up its life. That was her second son, so how could
that boy be the one she saw before her now?*

*She asked, and yet she knew the answer. It was the goodness in
him, his need to do right and work hard and take upon his shoulders the burdens he could. She loved him for this, much more than*

she ever told him. And because of this she feared what this life would make of him. She thought how cruel it was for a mother to give part of herself to these boys, how cruel for them to become men just like other men, to leave and disappear and so map the world.

But of these things she didn't speak. She took the carcasses from him and thanked him for his gifts. She set the creatures down on the board, slit them just so with her long knife, and peeled off their hides. She tended the fire, gutted the animals, and stripped the meat from the bones, seasoned the flesh and sewed it into thick cornmeal pies. As she did all this, she prayed. She asked that her oldest son hear her and know the love she felt for him. She asked God to protect him. She challenged him to do better with this son than he had with the boy's father. Let him live. Bring him home. Leave him a boy a little longer. Take him not unto thee, for although thy love is infinite, mine is a mother's. Mine is a mother's love, without judgment, without end.

She looked up from her work, brow dripping, hands spattered with grease and flour. She exhaled deeply and called her men to dinner, each of them, especially the oldest son. She called him home, for he would always be welcome. She called him, although she feared her voice would not carry far enough for him to hear.

AROUND THREE THE NEXT AFTERNOON they came upon a homestead. It was a simple affair, the house situated close to the river and built mostly of sod, except for the facade, at the base of which a few stone slabs had been laid. The building could have contained no more than one room. There was only one visible window, a low roof, and a simple chimney pipe through which a feeble stream of smoke rose.

The two boys squatted and watched it from a distance of a hundred yards. James asked Gabriel what he thought. Should they ask the homesteaders for some food? Gabriel studied their fields, well-turned plots of crops already into a full and prosperous growth, plants he recognized as tomatoes, melons, potatoes, with one long rectangular field of corn. It seemed a farm intended more for subsistence than for any cash crops.

Gabriel was about to say something when a person appeared from inside—a young woman, followed shortly by a boy child, and just after that by a toddler. The woman's hair was dark, long, and black. It trailed down her back in a thick braid. The toddler followed her on bandy legs, teetering with each step. The woman walked out into one of the fields with a basket, knelt, and worked for a few moments. When her basket was full, she went around to the back of the house, returning a moment later with the basket hanging empty in one hand.

Gabriel nudged his friend. "All right, let's give it a try." They walked forward shyly. James held his hat in his hands, and Gabriel set his feet softly on the earth.

As they drew nearer, the woman suddenly straightened and stared at them. The loose dress covering her was little more than a formless bag over her adolescent body, but it couldn't hide the rotund shape of her belly. Gabriel tried to hail her with a wave, instinctively bowing his head as he did so, as if such were a greeting familiar to her people. It was not. She dropped her tools where she stood and went into the house, scooping up the toddler and hissing at the boy to follow. Although James called out to them, they'd disappeared inside within a few seconds.

The boys stood, watching the house and frowning. "Ain't rightly hospitable around here, I guess," James said.

The door to the house swung open again, fast and loud. The first thing to appear was neither woman nor child but the unmistakable profile of a rifle, a thing with barrels more enormous than any Gabriel had seen. Behind it walked a tall skeleton of a man dressed only in worn overalls. His slender arms and protruding collarbone glowed a ghostly white in the shadow of the doorway.

He strode toward the boys like a corpse fresh from the grave and bent on retribution. His face was gaunt, his flesh a striated leathery substance that barely disguised the bones of his skull. His eyes, if he had any, were shaded under the cornice of his brows and hidden behind a curtain of limp and graying hair. If this impaired his vision any, it did not show in his actions. With his rifle pointed at the boys from twenty paces, he said, "State your business directly, or you're two dead niggers."

The boys exchanged glances, as if conferring on just what their business was. James ventured to answer. "Pardon, sir, we don't mean no trespass. We's just walking past your place, and . . ." He paused when the man brushed the hair out of his eyes and studied the boys more closely, squinting one eye shut in the process. ". . . Just wondering might we trouble you for—"

"No."

"I mean . . ." James looked at Gabriel for help. "A bite to eat? That's all."

"I done said no. We don't feed niggers here. Go on about your business or you're dead, sure as Lincoln's a dead son of a bitch. Deadest son of a bitch rotting in hell." He stepped a little closer. "You think I'd feed a nigger? You come to the wrong man. Had my way, we'd send the whole horde of you back to the filth you slunk out of." He thrust the rifle toward James's groin. "I'd cut off your nutsacks with my own knife and make oysters, you scum-sucking sons a bitches in heat. Why would I feed you? Shit, I'd rather shoot you dead."

Gabriel had had enough. His face screwed itself into all the apology he could muster, and he tugged James to get him moving. But James said, "We could pay."

The man paused. "Pay?"

"Yeah. Show him the coin, Gabe."

Gabriel cut the boy with his eyes and cursed him under his breath.

The man stepped closer still.

"Show him the coin, Gabe," James repeated.

Gabriel still hesitated. He took a half step away but froze as the barrels of the gun anticipated further movement. Behind the man, the young woman appeared in the doorway. She watched them with frightened eyes, whether for them or because of them Gabriel couldn't tell. He reached into his pocket, brought the coin forth, and held it up at eye level.

The man resumed his one-eyed squint. "Where'd you get that?"

"What?"

"Where'd you get that?" Without waiting for an answer, the man let his rifle fall from vigilance and strode forward. "Give it to me." He stretched out his hand and beckoned, like a father about to reprimand a wayward child.

Gabriel snapped his hand into a fist around the coin. He stepped back but thrust his chin forward and looked as hard as he could at the man. "No. I think we'll keep it and move on."

The man's jaw dropped open. "You'll what?" He swung the rifle back on the job, at chest level. It trembled slightly in his grip. "You trying to give me a reason? That coin's worth more than the both of you. You gonna give it?"

"No."

"Why shouldn't I pull, then?"

Gabriel held his squinting gaze, all his effort directed. In the man's creased eyes and in the ragged lines that were his eyebrows and in the sour twisted flesh there was an unreasoning and consuming hatred. Gabriel knew that he'd not seen such a hopeless creature yet, for in this man's hatred his life was unredeemable: his procreation a curse, his seed poison, his intentions tainted far back into his past. He saw all this, and he didn't doubt for a moment that the man could shoot them dead. But still, with a calm entirely at odds with the tumult in his head, Gabriel answered the man's question. "Might frighten them." He nudged his chin toward something behind the man.

"Huh?" The man turned around and, seeing the woman and children, began ranting at them to get back into the house.

Neither boy hesitated for a moment. They both spun and ran upriver as fast as they could. Gabriel waited to hear the gunshot, waited for the impact that must come with it. But only the man's curses followed them, warnings never to show themselves again, damnation brought down upon their kin and their forefathers' kin, promises that he'd shoot on sight next time and make nigger sausage with the remains. All of his words came strangely clear to Gabriel's ears, full, complete sentences that rang in his head even after he'd dropped down beside the river and put the man far behind them.

They moved on a half-mile or so before collapsing on the riverbank, panting and rolling in the dust like two fish fresh from the water, struggling for life. It was some time before James spoke. "I thought homesteaders were supposed to be neighborly. You reckon that old man's the one got that girl knocked up?"

"Probably."

"He's an evil son of a bitch, ain't he? He'd put Pinkerd to shame. We told him no, though. Didn't we? Old bastard asked and we told him no." He grinned and nudged Gabriel on the shoulder playfully.

"Yeah, *I* told him no. Fat lot of good it did us." Gabriel didn't seem as impressed by this fact as James was, although there was an odd, almost satisfied calm in his voice. He opened his fist and studied the coin still held there, moist and shining against his skin. "James, if you ever open your fool trap like that again, I'll wring your neck. I swear to God I will. We ain't gonna spend it unless we have to. I mean *have* to. You hear me?" James reminded him that half the coin was his, but Gabriel slipped it into his trouser pocket and looked back toward the homestead, which was out of sight. "Anyway, what now?"

AROUND DUSK THE TWO BOYS ENTERED THE RIVER fully clothed. The water was shaded just enough to have gone black and was colder than Gabriel expected. He felt his skin tighten as the current wrapped around him and swirled him downstream, gently, slowly, yet with a power conspicuous in its ease. His feet dangled beneath him, and the plains slipped by from this strangest of angles, as if he'd become part of the vein of the world and could look out at the passing skin of it.

They held a tense silence, and as they neared the house, both boys sank up to their chins in the water. At the house, all was as it had been on their initial approach. It was quiet, save for the occasional clink and clatter of dinnertime activities. The front door, while they still had a view of it, was closed, and it appeared that the man and the children were at supper. The stream of smoke had thickened, and with it came the scent of frying meat. This scent alone was enough to firm their plan.

"You ready?" James whispered.

Gabriel nodded, and together they scrambled up the clay bank, slipping and dripping and cursing the slick surface. A few steps from the water, they crouched and listened. All was as before. They slunk forward again, sticking to the worn path by the river, coming up around the back of the house. Gabriel thanked God twice: first when he saw that this side of the house had no window and again when they reached the barrels set against the wall, on which lay several bundles of carrots, tomatoes, turnips, and, most mouthwateringly beautiful, three large melons.

The boys set to stuffing their pockets. This was done in a few seconds. They continued to grab more, wedging carrots into armpits, cradling turnips as delicately as if they were babies, each holding a melon on top of it all. Only when neither could conceive of balancing more did the boys turn and tiptoe away, following the riverbank and keeping to the windowless side of the house. James looked over at Gabriel, a grin splitting his face. He looked as if he wanted to talk, but Gabriel shook his head. A few steps further on, though, and James couldn't help himself. "We did it," he whispered. "Easy as—"

"Nigger boys, freeze!"

The call came from behind them. Both boys halted in midstride. Before they had time to confer, the man yelled again, instructing them to turn. They did so, rotating slowly. The man had his rifle aimed dead at them. He held it there for the longest few seconds that Gabriel had yet experienced, those two barrels, the two holes therein, as clear to the boy's eyes as if the space of seventy yards didn't separate him from them.

The man lowered the rifle a moment. He pursed his lips and seemed to consider the possibilities. He looked as though he might talk, then decided not to. He shrugged, said something that Gabriel couldn't make out, then swung the gun up again and shot. Gabriel saw the buck of the gun and the stirring of air at its barrel. The next instant, James whirled as if some force had snatched him up by the head and spun him like a top. The vegetables in his hands flew out in every direction, and he landed spread-eagled on the ground. Before Gabriel could even think what this meant, the boy was back on his feet and flying away.

Gabriel tore out behind him, his booty thrown to the wind. With his runner's stride, he was soon abreast of James, then past him. He didn't question the boy's defiance of death at that moment, but felt only the frantic need for motion, each second, each fraction thereof, too long a space of time, his strides too slow for the workings of his mind. He heard the rifle once more.

He thought he sensed the slug's passage above his head, and then he saw the scuff of dust that marked a bullet's impact rise before them. He ran on, unaware of the pounding in his chest or the pain in his legs.

They didn't stop moving until the house had fallen well behind them. This time they were on the far side of it, and they came to rest relieved at this and breathing heavily. James took some time to find his voice. When he did, he showed Gabriel the nick in his left ear, which, despite his worries, was no more than a bruised redness on his earlobe. He replayed the scene, swearing on the body of Jesus that he'd never heard anything as loud as that bullet. It was the force of its sound that had lifted him from the ground that way. He looked at his friend with all seriousness. "These people don't play, Gabe. If he'd've aimed two inches to the left, I'd be a dead nigger, just like he said."

Gabriel put a hand on the boy's shoulder. He felt awkward over this tenderness, but he let it lie there. "He didn't get you, though. We got him." He rummaged through his pockets and displayed his findings on the ground before them. "Look, we got something—near a dozen carrots, some turnips too."

"Shit. I can't eat no raw turnip. Anyway, I ain't even hungry no more."

"You will be. Give it a few minutes."

"Near lost it all for twelve carrots." James shook his head at the thought of it.

"Not even gold ones, either," Gabriel said.

It took James a few seconds to look at Gabriel. His jaw dropped with shock when he saw the smile on Gabriel's face. "You think that's funny? Now you're suddenly gonna have yourself a laugh?" Gabriel couldn't help nodding. "That's not even a slight bit funny."

Gabriel went on smiling, almost chuckling. "It is, a slight bit, ain't it?"

"No, I'm not gonna laugh. Don't smile." He pulled a stern face but couldn't hold it. All jokes aside, life, and the continuation of it, tickled them both with playful fingers, and they felt the mirth of those who have felt the passing breath of death but not its sting.

They washed the carrots in the river and divided them. Their mouths were watering before the first bite, and James said he'd never thought a carrot looked so good. They crunched into them, one bite after the next, and in the space of twenty minutes the boys were left contemplating the turnips. "You gonna try it?" James asked. Gabriel said he would if James would, and James said the same. They passed another twenty minutes at a standstill, then they both went at it. The turnips were hard to bite and difficult to chew and sour. They left a knot in the boys' stomachs and the next morning a taste in their mouths that they'd never forget.

ALL THE NEXT DAY THE BOYS WALKED on through the unchanging landscape. They reached no settlement and met no people, and all passed in monotony. By noon Gabriel's head was throbbing with a thick wrap of pain that went from his eyeballs up onto his forehead, out over the temples, and all the way around to the nape of his neck. He begged silence of James, and they walked like two mute and impoverished monks. Only once during the day did they see a human, a horseman across the river and a good few miles off. If he saw them, he showed no sign. He simply traversed the horizon like a silhouette puppet on a distant stage and moved on.

They camped that night on a flat slab of rock that allowed no sleep, and they were walking again before dawn, under a light rain that disappeared as the sun rose. They drank often from the river, slurping the surface, sinking their faces into the water and

coming up gasping and dripping and luxuriating in the refresh-
ing chill of it. When they peed, they did so facing away from
each other, the splash of their urine the only sound save for the
wind. Emptied, they were slow to move on, each boy watching
the play of the heat on the horizon. The pain in Gabriel's head
grew deeper, like an infection entering the bones of his skull. He
felt as though his body were shutting down, his bowels constrict-
ing from lack of use, his muscles growing weak under the constant strain of work without fuel. James no longer talked of his
feet, or of the journey west, or of much of anything. The two
boys conserved their energy for the chore of movement, the task
of steadying their dizzy heads and squinting in the white light of
midday.

A little before dusk they came in sight of a settlement, which
they took to be McKutcheon's Station. James pointed it out, then
fell to his knees and whispered a quick and heartfelt prayer.
Gabriel's body also went limp, as if the sight might be too much
for his strained resources. He caught himself and shook his head.
He immediately regretted doing so and stood blinded by a long
contraction of pain. When it passed, he opened his eyes and
nudged James into movement, saying, "Come on. You can't walk
on your knees."

McKutcheon's Station was a small conglomeration of buildings
built of a white wood, weathered and parched but a far cry from
the sod homes of the homesteaders. No more than a half-dozen
in number, they faced each other along what might have been the
main street in a large town but was little more than a central open
space in this one. An extensive, although entirely empty, corral
system stretched out from the eastern side of the settlement.
Fences cut out onto the prairie in chaotic dimensions, rounded
pens with thin shoots connecting them, like an equation writ
large for celestial observers.

At the edge of the settlement they came upon Dunlop. He was

sitting on a tree stump, rolling a cigarette with the utmost concentration. Beneath the trees nearby, the men's horses grazed.
They looked up as the boys walked in, studied them, then lowered their heads and fell to cropping the grass. Dunlop didn't
notice the boys until they were a few feet away. His head snapped
up. He eyed them wearily, recognition only slowly taking hold of
his features. "All right, lads? I wasn't sure if I'd set eyes on you
again," he said. There was something a bit thick about his voice,
a dryness in his throat, and more than the usual lilt of Scotland.
His eyes were tainted a faint shade of red, and his cheeks were
alive with a fur of reddish brown stubble. "You two are in a bit
of a state," he added.

Gabriel stood looking at him for some time, thinking that
much the same could be said about him. But it was James who
remembered the reason for their state. "You know where we
could get some vittles?"

"Aye, aye, some food'll do you good." Dunlop started to rise
but found the motion awkward, as he still held the half-rolled
cigarette in his hands. He tossed it away and led the boys into
McKutcheon's Station proper. It was even smaller than it had
seemed from a distance. In fact, it was not a town at all. It was
more of a way station for cattlemen on their journey north or
south, dominated by McKutcheon's General Store, with its adja-
cent McKutcheon's Livery, which sat across the street from
McK's Watering Hole. There were a few other buildings, but all
had an air of abandonment about them.

Dunlop led the boys across the main street and around to
what appeared to be the back of a small building. He called out
and was soon answered by an elderly Hispanic woman. She was
dark-faced and wrinkled, with a bulging mass of oil-black hair
trailing down her back. She eyed the boys with something like
distrust but waved them toward a rough-hewn table set against
a tree for support.

The boys sat slouch-shouldered on a bench, lacking the energy to swat at the flies that plagued their arms and faces. As Dunlop began the long chore of rolling another cigarette, he filled them in on the events of the last few days. Apparently Marshall had convinced neither the Mexican girls themselves nor McKutcheon on their behalf that they should go into prostitution. Marshall raised a bit of a fuss, but McKutcheon locked the girls away in his barnlike abode and would hear no more about it. Dunlop had seen no sign of them since the first night. Marshall and the others had then turned their full resources to drink. Thereafter, the time had passed in a sort of drunken haze of card games and shooting contests, in arguments and laughter, and occasionally in retching. It was this last activity that had taken Dunlop to the spot where the boys had found him, where he was fast deciding that he preferred the company of horses to that of men.

The Hispanic woman returned with two plates of refried beans and a platter of steaming corn tortillas. The boys eyed the food with silent awe. Both were slow in trying it, as if they doubted their ability to consume such fare and thought they were better off taking it in with their eyes. The woman seemed pleased by their reaction but wouldn't leave until they began eating, scooping up big helpings of the beans with the tortillas and chewing with slow relish. Dunlop watched them for a moment, then turned away as the previous evening's drink threatened to well up once more.

The food held James's full attention for only a few moments. He kept chewing but managed to speak between mouthfuls. "Dunlop, what the heck happened back there? What was that Dallas talking about, with them horses and all? Y'all weren't horse-thieving for real, were you?"

Dunlop shook his head, a sad gesture more like a nod than a denial. "For Christ's sake, lads, it was just a wee joke—just a laugh, really. An expensive joke, aye, but . . ." He explained that the butt of the joke was the ranch called Three Bars. He'd never seen the place properly himself, but he more than knew it by reputation. It was run by the dubious couple of Jim Rickles and Ugly Mary. Rickles was an Indian fighter and Civil War veteran who wore the wounds of those professions with distinction: a ragged scar across his forehead, from where his skull had been loosened by an Apache hatchet, and a left hand of three digits only, the other two severed by a Union bayonet. Ugly Mary was a former prostitute. It was said that she'd thrice had bottles broken over her head in barroom brawls. The first had knocked her cold, the second had only stunned her, and the third had just made her mad enough to shoot the man who had injured her. She was also famed for having once emasculated an unpleasant customer with her bare teeth.

"She did what?" Gabriel asked.

Dunlop nodded his head in answer. "Took away the very thing that God gave Adam."

Rickles and Ugly Mary had retired from their lines and taken up ranching a few years ago, joining their holdings in a state of unsanctified matrimony. They scrounged together a motley crew of punchers from the far corners of the state and had been suspects in horse- and cattle-rustling debates ever since. Nothing had ever been pinned on them, but no honest ranch in Texas had any kind words for them, and Marshall seemed to have a particular loathing for them. Indeed, Dunlop suspected that Marshall had once been in some sort of partnership with them, a deal that had gone sour and left Marshall vengeful. "But who would've thought they'd have us turned out? It's injustice all over again. I still can't believe it. Aye, we stole a few head from them, but they stole them in the first place and everybody knows it." He fell quiet, shaking his head at the whole thing and holding his cigarette out before him as if he were offering it to some invisible person. "Something has to be done, if Marshall ever sobers up long enough. He'll make us all drunkards before he's through."

IT HADN'T STARTED AS A HUNTING TRIP. The younger son and his uncle hitched the wagon to the mule and rode out on the prairie to gather cow chips. They spent the afternoon at this, talking as they did so, the man telling tales of home, things that made the boy wonder whether the souls of white men were different from those of other beings and if they were measured by the same scales in heaven. They were just preparing to leave when the boy spotted a herd of antelope. They were nearly a mile away, but the sighting excited both man and boy and the two set out toward them at a fast walk. The man grabbed his rifle, almost as an afterthought, and told the mule to stay put.

They were lucky enough to be downwind, and they approached the creatures slyly and quietly. They moved forward in fits and starts and before long came to a slight rise above a long dry wash. The man's hand shot up to steady the boy. The antelope grazed on the other side, spread in a loose herd, alert and relaxed at the same time, ears and eyes never halting long in their diligence. This is the best we're gonna get, the man said. It's a shot.

It is that, the boy said, but only then did the possible purpose of this venture become clear to him. He felt a thickness in his throat and suddenly became aware of the pulse in his palms. He found the rifle in his hands and was unsure how it got there.

Give it a go, the man said. You've got a steady arm already, and your eyesight's damn sure better'n mine. But mind the wind, and take your shot before they scent us.

The boy took the rifle and looked out at the antelope. Which one should I shoot?

The man chuckled at his optimism. There's a hunter what

means business. He pointed out one of the older bucks and asked if the boy saw the one he meant.

Yeah. The boy lifted the rifle up and sighted the animal and held it in view for the space of many breaths. There was no wind where he stood, but the grass at the antelope's feet switched and swayed with it. He accounted for this as best he could and waited longer still. When he pulled the trigger, he had the sensation that part of him flew out of the barrel of the gun behind the bullet. It was as if he touched the animal over all that distance, and with his touch the antelope stumbled backward and fell down. It got up again, dazed by its own clumsiness, walked a few steps, considered the horizon, on which the silhouettes of its kind stood out, then crumpled. The others watched it fall, then darted off like dry leaves scattering before a breeze.

The boy felt his uncle's hand on his shoulder. Dead on.

When they reached the antelope, it lay staring wide-eyed at the sky. The clouds passing overhead were reflected there but were no longer seen by those eyes or thought of by the beast behind them.

The bullet had entered its skull but had not left it. The man speculated that it had ricocheted around in the skull, shredding the brain. Looking at the boy's expression, he added that this was a most humane way to die. Couldn't be more painless.

The boy stood nearby as the man skinned and gutted the animal. He didn't offer to help, and the man didn't ask. That night the boy dreamed of the sky reflected in the orb of an antelope's eye. He woke up wondering what that meant, and for the first time he knew that the world was a tableau laden with signs.

GABRIEL REALIZED THERE WAS SOMETHING IN HIS MOUTH, a ball of some sort, a rough object that threatened to choke him. He became aware of it only gradually, as his eyes fluttered open and tried to make sense of what turned out to be the thin,

crooked branches of a honey mesquite tree. Having grasped that
he was lying on his back, with his neck twisted around at an awkward angle, he rolled over and in so doing launched himself off
the porch on which he had been lying. He lay sprawled in the
dust a moment, as if this position were as good as any, until he
remembered the ball in his throat. He rose as far as his hands
and knees and tried to spit the object out. It wouldn't come, and
his mouth was so parched that he could hardly produce any liquid at all. He stayed at this strange heaving for a few moments,
slowly awakening to the fact that the ball was nothing more than
his tongue, inflamed and dry and as limp as if it were a salt-tor-
tured slug. His head ached as it had on his forced march, but
worse now, for it seemed that his brain was afloat in alcohol.
With the slightest movement it bumped up against the confines
of his skull and clouded his eyes with pain.

He stood up and began stumbling toward the saloon, but he
stopped and thought better of it. He remembered another source
of water, one that seemed to have had some dim part in the
events of the previous night. Retracing a thin thread of memory,
he found the water trough at the back of the saloon. The water
was tepid and murky, with bits of debris floating on it, but
Gabriel drank from it deep and long. It seemed he might do so
indefinitely, except that he jerked upright suddenly and began
patting his trousers with his palms, calming down only when he
found the coin and touched it once more.

As he stared into his reflection in the trough, events of the
previous evening floated back to him bit by fragmented bit. He
remembered being patted on the back by heavy hands, com-
mended on his safe passage, his "trial by trail," as Marshall put it.
It seemed that their abandonment had been nothing more than
an unfortunate circumstance, a small, impromptu test that, once
passed, could be laughed off and drunk away and forgotten. He
saw Marshall's face close to his own, smiling and sweaty and

speaking to him in a flow of words that had no beginning, no ending, and no meaning that he could now discern. He heard again the chorus of songs sung with thick voices and saw the grins that devolved into frowns that became harsh words thrown about the room and made physical. Then he remembered the world twirling and the sky bright with stars, creatures of light that were not still as they should have been but that moved and trembled above him as if God's fingers had made the earth a top and set it spinning. The boy closed his eyes, cringed at a whiskey-flavored belch in his mouth, and vowed never to drink again.

GABRIEL FOUND JAMES IN MUCH THE SAME STATE. The two boys attempted to eat breakfast but didn't get much further than a few mouthfuls. They returned to the porch upon which Gabriel had spent the night. The building seemed to be abandoned, and they lounged about through the rest of the morning and on into the afternoon, watching the occasional foot traffic from one building to another, nodding at two passing horsemen who rode, quiet and deliberate, through town from one end to the other and on. It wasn't until the sun had passed its zenith and begun to relent that any real activity started. A group of men gathered a little way down the street. They entertained themselves with tarantula fights, a sport enlivened by the appearance of a bottle and the easy flow of money.

Gabriel first noticed the man because of his black Stetson, something he hadn't seen before, since most cowboys wore neutral shades of tan and brown, a reflection more of the color of the soil in the country they worked than any design of the hat-makers. This man's hat was a dark, dark gray, with a hatband of rattlesnake skin with the rattle still attached. He sauntered over to the boys with an air of mischief, a crooked grin tilting his thin lips. Several others followed just behind him, nondescript and poor-looking with whiskey slowing their steps and shaping their faces into grimaces of mirth.

"Hey, boys, how the hell are ya?" the man in the black hat asked. He set one boot up on the porch and smiled at the boys. He had a long, thin nose that pointed up slightly at the end, and his eyes crowded in on either side of it. There was a thin scar down his left cheek, as if the point of a knifeblade had traced the line of the jawbone beneath. "You boys are punchers, aren't ya?"

"Well . . ." James began, but shrugged to convey that that was not exactly the case.

"Who do you work for?"

Again James started to mumble a response, but Gabriel spoke more forcefully. "We don't work for nobody. Looking, though."

This seemed to entertain the man. He glanced back at his companions. "These boys are just looking, is all. And I'd've sworn they were punchers. Guess they had me." He watched them for a moment, then said, "You're wondering how I got my scar, aren't ya?" He turned his head to let them see it better. "You should've seen the other guy." He chuckled at this and again cast glances behind him. When he looked back at them, he grew a little more serious. "We was wondering if you boys could help settle a bet for us. We been arguing like you wouldn't believe and just need us an impartial party like yourselves. See, we've been talking about which one of us is the better shot, that is, whether it's me or any of the rest of these scoundrels. I don't trust them as far as I can throw them, so how's about one of you two judge for us?"

Gabriel studied the man. "I don't know nothing about judging nothing. One of y'all could do it better. I'd just as soon not get mixed up in it."

"Mixed up in it?" The man looked back at his friends. "He thinks one of y'all could do it better. Shit. Boy, you're giving these fellas more credit than they're worth. Truth is, each and every one of these fellas is as crooked as a diamondback. Come on, help us out. I'm just asking a favor." He said the last sentence with particular emphasis, his voice cast a bit lower than before and laced with threat.

James stepped forward. "All right. I'll judge y'all."

The man glanced at him. "Thanks, boy, but I'd prefer your friend here. He seems the right critical type, and that's what I'm looking for. Come on, you, I ain't asking anymore." The man turned and walked slowly away. Some of his entourage followed, but others lingered near Gabriel, encouraging him on with hard glances.

James began to say something, but Gabriel silenced him and rose. He followed the man out into the street and down it a little way, to the side of a barnlike building. The man stopped before a pole that must have been sunk into the ground as the start of a project that was never completed. He motioned Gabriel over and moved him into position by the shoulders. By the time he'd turned around and faced the street, two others had appeared, holding a rope between them. One was no older than Gabriel, and when Gabriel's eyes touched on him, he looked away shyly.

"You ever hear of William Tell?" the man asked. "He was Swiss, I think. Did a little trick with a bow and arrow that I always fancied giving a try. Okay boys, show him how to be the judge."

Something in the man's narrow eyes unnerved Gabriel enough that he started to move. But he'd hardly taken a step to the side when the two men with the rope had leapt beyond him. The rope hit his chest and smashed him back into the pole, pinning both arms to his sides. He wriggled hard and might have gotten free, except that the two men were quick in their work, one laying the rope low so that the other could jump over it and continue around. In the space of a few seconds they had wound

the rope around him twice and had him bound so tightly that
the rope bit into his skin and constricted his breathing.

"Now we got us some sport!" the man said. "And you boys
wanted to set a rattler against a king snake. That ain't nothing
like what you're about to see." He paced back and forth in front
of Gabriel like a hunter before some long-desired and dangerous
prey. "Now, look here, boy. All you gotta do is stand there looking as dumb as you please, right? You can do that, can't you?
Just stand there, and what I'm gonna do is show these boys how
a marksman tests his skills. Don't think I got anything against
you. I like you well enough, even if you do got a bit of an attitude
for a nigger. If I'm as good as I think I am, you'll keep all your
parts and I'll buy you a drink afterward. Who's got something
for me to shoot?"

James had backed away a good distance, casually first. But
once the man started debating with the others on what should
serve as a target, he fell into a full run toward the saloon. Gabriel
watched him while he could, but his attention was soon drawn to
other matters. One of the men approached him with an earthen
jug, an old thing with a chip in the rim. He lifted it up to eye
level. Gabriel flinched, but the man was gentle. He set the jug
on the boy's head and tried to balance it there. He let go several
times, but each time the jug began to fall. Eventually he pressed
Gabriel's head back against the pole and leaned the jug against
it. This worked. He backed away, leaving Gabriel tied there in
an awkward, straight-backed posture, chin pointing forward like
a gesture of defiance.

The man in the black hat paced away a few steps, turned, and
examined his prospects. He seemed pleased by the target and by
the thin crowd watching him. He lifted his hat from his head,
held it aloft for a second, then set it back in place, as if allowing
his scalp to breathe. Then he said, "All right, boy, now hold still.
Just smile, stupid-like, and close your eyes if you need to. This

won't hurt a bit." He drew his pistol and spun the chamber in his palm, commenting to the others about how beautiful the sound was. He held the weapon with his wrist cocked at a slight angle, his legs set together tightly, and his chest held high, like a Spanish bullfighter. He lifted the pistol and sighted on Gabriel.

The boy hadn't spoken since he'd been tied. He hadn't fought or even protested, but he did so now, in one simple motion. He tilted his head to the side. The jug teetered, shifted, and fell to the ground, where it shattered into large, chunky pieces.

The man lowered his pistol and stared at him. A few in the crowd laughed: one complimented the boy's gumption. The man was not similarly amused. "You'd make a fool of me?" He shifted his jaw from side to side, his gun hand hanging limp. "You'd make me a fool?" In one quick motion, less formal than his former posture and more like a child mimicking a gunfighter, he lifted his pistol, aimed, and pulled the trigger.

As with the old man's rifle a few days before, Gabriel saw a commotion of air and spark around the gun's barrel. He saw the jerk of the man's hand and how it translated up through his forearm and shoulder. He never heard the pistol's report, because the next sensation he felt was that of something scorching across his scalp. It was just a split second of feeling, but it was as if a rod of red-hot metal had been laid on his head. The wood behind his head splintered, and the whole pole shivered with a vibration that Gabriel felt right down to his toes. All went black.

He was still feeling the trembling of the pole and the world was still black when he began to hear voices around him, laughing and joking. Rough hands clasped his head, and with their touch, Gabriel opened his eyes. The world returned, in the shape of the man's smiling face, so close to his that he could smell the scent of him, a sweet-smelling scent like that of a baby. "There, that wasn't so bad, just a little haircut," the man said. "But it didn't count for shit, did it? A man can't shoot without a

target, right?" He moved in even closer. "You move your head
again, and I'll put a bullet through your forehead." With that, he
spun away and called for another jug.

Gabriel stood in a daze as another object was balanced on his
head, this time just a piece of wood about the size of a pint glass.
He only half noticed the people walking toward them from the
saloon. He didn't really take them in, but part of him was aware,
if only by shape and movement, that one of them was Marshall.

The man checked his pistol with a certain formality, made
jokes with the others, and asked for bets. He lifted the pistol up,
sighted on Gabriel, then chuckled and looked at one of his companions, who instantly fell into hysterics. "Ain't this better'n
watching a king kill a rattler?" he said. By the time he focused on
Gabriel again, Marshall was closing in fast. Neither the man nor
the others noticed, and the man turned his pistol toward Gabriel
once more.

Marshall walked toward the man with steps temporarily
unswayed by alcohol. He slid his hand down to his gun, drew it
out, and gripped the handle tightly. As he approached, he first
pointed the pistol at the back of the man's head, held it there
through the space of several steps, but then decided otherwise.
He lifted his arm high above his head, strode forward in two
stunningly fast paces, and just as the man began to turn brought
the pistol down on the crown of his head with the full force of his
arm, his torso, and the weight of his body.

Gabriel would have thought the blow would make some
sound, some concussion, crack, or slap. It made none. The man
reeled beneath the impact, stumbling on legs suddenly gone to
jelly. His hand convulsed and the pistol shot off, the bullet hitting
the ground beneath him. With that, he fell into a crumpled ball
and lay motionless.

Marshall looked down at him with a curious smile. A drunken
grin creased his face, but only for a second. Then he snapped to

attention and looked hard at the man's companions. "Any one of you close enough to this one to get offended, you might as well say so now." His eyes drifted from one to the next, unflinching, heated, almost cajoling something out of them. They held their tongues. "Anybody have problems with me? Tell me now, cause I plan to go on drinking and I like to get this kind of stuff taken care of first."

A thin, nervous man spoke from the shelter of the porch, half hidden by the railing. "You might damn near have killed a man for a nigger? We was just funnin."

"That's right. I damn near killed him. He's lucky I didn't put a bullet through his head, acting the fool the way he was. If I'd've known I could get it back, I'd've shot him dead. No use wasting a bullet when you don't have to." Marshall waved his gun at them in disgust. "What are you all staring like a bunch of monkeys for? The whole lot of you—" He cut himself off and snapped back to the man who'd spoken. "We got a problem, you and I?"

The man hesitated, looked from Marshall to the others, and held out just long enough to look like he'd given it some thought. "I ain't knowed the fella from Adam. Ain't none of my kin to worry about."

Marshall nodded at the wisdom of this, a grin again pushing up his cheeks. "Yeah. We should look out for our kin, shouldn't we? That boy ain't my kin neither, but he's a good one. Got gumption, ain't he?" He glanced over at Gabriel, squinted, and studied him like something newly discovered. When he spoke, it was with the last vestiges of sobriety. "Take that thing off your head, boy. You look like an idjit." He turned and holstered his gun and walked unsteadily over to Caleb, who had to reach out and steady him at the last minute. They walked arm in arm back to the saloon, leaving the crowd in an uneasy silence.

Gabriel nodded his head and let the board fall. He hissed at James, who ran to untie him. He did so with nervous hands and eyes darting out to study the men. "You think that's how he got that first scar?" James asked. Gabriel didn't answer, and neither did he speak when the two boys circumnavigated the unconscious man and walked fast toward the saloon.

GABRIEL AND JAMES HUNG TO THE WALL OF THE SALOON that evening, turning down offers of alcohol and watching both the men and the door anxiously. Marshall seemed intent on pounding down whiskey with ever increasing vigor, with no concern whatever for the man who lay unconscious outside. Every so often, James crept out and checked on the man's status. Each time he returned shaking his head: "Man's out cold."

Both Rollins and Dallas did their best to keep pace with Marshall, but the alcohol took hold of them more quickly. Rollins slurred his speech and grew argumentative, his large body seeming ever more apelike. Dallas, in contrast, felt more sublime with each mouthful, finding some music within his head and moving to it, rocking slightly and moving more and more into a world of his own. Dunlop declined the drink for an hour or so but finally gave in, turning to the boys and shrugging and throwing down a glass of whiskey like a man born to it. Caleb sat straight in his chair, his red eyes filmed over and glassy. While there was no demonstrative joy on the man's dark face, the alcohol did soften something within him. Once or twice he even smiled at some remark of Marshall's, a strange action for his sharp features, as if his lips meant to turn down but in their drunkenness got the motion backward.

McKutcheon stood with arms crossed and face stern, his assistant trying his best to hold the same posture with authority. Before long, some of the men who'd watched Gabriel being tied up and shot at entered the bar. They were shy at first, walking in with heads down and moving quickly to the counter. But when they saw Marshall's mood and realized that all was forgotten, they joined in the revelry. A pack of cards appeared and then another, and the men fell to more serious play.

Gabriel was just wondering if it would be safe to go out and find someplace to sleep when Marshall remembered him and ordered, "Come here, boy, have a drink with your savior." He stood and motioned the boy to an empty table in the corner. He settled himself there with a bottle and two glasses. Gabriel joined him, leaving James to the work of holding up the wall.

"How's it feel to be alive? That man'd probably have shot you dead if I hadn't walloped him. You ever seen a bigger idiot? Makes me ashamed to be a white man. Have a drink." Marshall pushed a half-full glass toward him. "I once saw a man jump out a second-story window on a dare. These two fools got in an argument over something or other. One told the other he had a mind to break his legs; other said he wouldn't give him the plea-sure, said if he knew it would come down to that he'd just as soon jump out the window and do himself in. Other one dared him, and that was that." Marshall kicked back another glass and shook his head at the foolishness of people.

"What happened?" Gabriel asked.

Marshall seemed surprised by the question. "Man jumped. Broke both legs and did something to his spine to boot. That was Alabama, though. No accounting for what them folks'll do on a dare." He waved his empty shot glass beneath his nose, inhaling the scent with flaring nostrils. "The elixir of life right here. It'll kill you one day, but until then you're loving the very notion of it. Ain't that the truth?"

Gabriel nodded and sat listening as the man held forth in a rambling flow of words. Marshall's thoughts connected with little transition, little order, creating a web of theories and conjectures that he draped across the boy piece by piece. He spoke of topics as varied as the value of a human life, the debt owed to great thinkers, the sins committed in the name of God, and the nature of the retribution that might follow. He asked the boy what he made of all this, and when the boy answered that he didn't rightly know, Marshall nodded and moved in closer to him and looked him long and steadily in the eye.

"You ever hate somebody so much as to want to kill em?" he asked.

Again the boy answered that he didn't know, and once more Marshall nodded and seemed satisfied with the answer.

"I've hated three people in my life. First one's already dead. I didn't have anything to do with it, but that wasn't cause I didn't think about it. See, I used to be afraid of my own shadow, afraid of living and, worse yet, afraid of dying. It was that man, that first one I hated, that made me that way. You wouldn't want to know how he done that to me, but he sure enough did."

Marshall paused and concentrated on pouring himself another whiskey. He only half filled the glass, spilling some on the table. Gabriel tried to avoid his eyes, focusing instead on the grain of the wood table. When Marshall spoke again, he leaned in close enough for the boy to smell his breath.

"Then one day I watched him die. I was right beside his bed, watching him breathe his last breaths, his body full of knife wounds from a bunch of fool Mexicans. He closed his eyes and lay there like a log, and I would've sworn he'd've passed on already, but then he opened his eyes and set them on me and said one last thing. You know what he said? He said, 'This ain't the end of it.' He said, 'Get you to hell, boy, and don't worry, I'll be waiting for ya." Marshall stared hard at Gabriel, his eyes wavering in the effort, bloodshot but inescapable. "I didn't mourn for the man, not for one minute. But it did get me think-ing. If a bunch of poor-as-dirt ignorant Mexicans could do that to my father . . . then what kind of world is it we're living in? What's the reason in it? And if you can't find no reason, then what? How do you make your way in the world? You hear what I'm asking?" Marshall motioned with his hand, as if he would hold the answers between his fingers. He studied the shape of his fingers and the empty air clasped between them. Gabriel watched him for a long moment, wondering what the man saw there and fearing that if he looked long enough, he might see it too.

Marshall roused himself and flicked away the invisible object. He made to rise, but faltered in the effort and found one last thought to share.

"I told you once before that this here world is a white man's world, but that's a lie and I know it. It ain't a white man's world. It ain't a Christian world. It's none of our world. And that's a troubling thing to think on. That's a real troubling thought." With that, he turned and rejoined the others.

GABRIEL AWOKE WITH A HEAVY GLOVED HAND across his mouth, to the scent of leather and sweat, and to a shadowy face pressed close to his own. He reached out and pushed against the shape below the face, finding it hard and warm and entirely too real to the touch. He tried to call out, but the hand cinched down further.

"Shhh," the face hissed close to his ear, in a voice he immediately recognized. "Goddamn, boy! Hold your tongue." Gabriel held still, but Marshall was slow to release him. There was just enough light in the abandoned barn to make out the man's features. They were drawn with jagged, sleepless lines, somehow numb and tired and fated all at once. The hand lifted off his mouth. "Get up, boy. We're going for a ride. Looks like that scrawny-assed idiot I walloped has gone and died on us. Must've been soft in the head."

It took Gabriel a moment to process the man's words. He

tried to speak but found it hard to move his lips. As his mind cleared, it focused on one word and tried to make sense of it.

"He . . . he died?"

"Don't act so goddamn surprised. Remember, the poor fool died for you. I traded a white soul for a black one, and don't you forget it. Now get up. Meet us out by the horses, and bring the other boy with ya." With that he was gone.

They rode out fifteen minutes later, Gabriel behind Dunlop and James behind Rollins. They forded the Red River, and Gabriel came out shivering and wide awake. They kept a steady pace through the early morning, riding for two hours in darkness, then on through the semidarkness and into the light. They lunched at a creek and watered the horses and rode on again till nightfall, when they camped in a mesquite grove beside a watering hole.

The men didn't drink that night. The evening passed, slow and solemn. Somewhere out on the plains a cow lowed, long and mournful and insistent. Rollins threatened to hunt her down and shoot her dead, but he seemed reluctant to leave the fireside, as did the others. Dunlop broke a long silence when he said that it seemed like things were going from bad to worse with each passing day. He asked Marshall just what he had in mind. He wondered aloud if maybe this wasn't the best idea, running away like this. Maybe things could be explained back at McKutcheon's, smoothed over and made right.

"It just seems different now, my head being clear and that," he said. "Are you sure the man died?"

Marshall spoke plainly when he answered, casually, as if the sobering influence of the day's riding had put him in a better mood. "He's dead all right." He said he'd felt it all along, and that he would've known it was so even if he hadn't heard it reported with his own ears.

"Whatcha mean, you felt it?" Dallas asked. "You mean him

dying and all, like his spirit moving on? My granma used to say—"

But Marshall answered that that was not what he'd meant at all. "I meant I could feel the man's skull give when I whacked him. I knew I'd gotten through to the soft stuff." His lips crinkled in a gesture that wasn't exactly a smile but was hard to interpret as anything else. The men watched him in silence, questions still alive, unspoken but held on anxious lips. Marshall rose and scratched his chin and looked around the group as if enticing something out of them. Still none spoke, and at this Marshall smiled. "Well, let me go shoot that cow." He walked off chuckling, rifle in hand, and was a long time in returning.

THE SECOND DAY PASSED IN MUCH THE SAME WAY. They moved steadily to the southwest, spelling the horses only when they had to, shifting the boys from mount to mount throughout the day and never once, within Gabriel's hearing, discussing the destination to which they rode with such haste. Gabriel told himself this was simply flight, simply the passage of mile after mile between themselves and a man's death. He told himself that this was the way of the West. This was life and death by a code much admired in the minds of men, written of in books and newspapers. And these were men who would prosper still, for how could a man like Marshall not prosper when he seemed to hold the fate of other men so completely in his grasp? So he thought as he rode, as he lay waiting for sleep, and so the days passed into a third, a fourth, and onward.

On the fifth day Caleb roused the men in the dead of night. Gabriel heard a low whisper of sound while still deep within his dreams, but he woke only at the touch of the man's fingers against his shoulder. He was instantly alert, heart beating, blood alive in his veins, and ears pricked. Caleb's dark shadow, barely visible in the dim starlight but unmistakable in its stealth, moved off to the next man.

The sky was a heavy, velvety black. A moist wind blew into their faces from the west, and they rode into it for several hours. As their shapes began to emerge into the yellow shadows and highlights of dawn, Caleb left the group, riding silently off to the south. Gabriel watched him go. He turned to James and saw that he too followed the man with his eyes, but neither boy spoke his questions aloud.

They rode on for another fifteen minutes, then dismounted and led the horses forward for another ten, until the blocky silhouettes of a few ranch buildings came into view. Gabriel stood with the rest and studied them. The men stared long and spoke little, watching the threadlike smoke that drifted up from the chimney of one of the buildings and danced off with the prodding of the wind.

"What do you reckon?" Marshall asked.

Rollins didn't hesitate to answer. "That's last night's fire."

"I figure the same," Marshall said. "They're in there dreaming the dreams of angels, no doubt."

"How many you figure there are in the bunkhouse?" Dallas asked. "You say they got a dog?"

"It don't matter. Caleb'll see to that."

Rollins guffawed. "I bet he will. What about the nigger boys?"

Marshall looked at Gabriel and James. "You boys ain't asked me word one, have you?" He watched them a moment, but when James prepared to speak, he continued. "That's smart. It don't pay to ask too many questions. What'll happen will happen. Let's stake the horses. Dunlop and . . . James, you two watch them. Rest of us, let's get to walking. Caleb's probably finished by now."

Gabriel walked across the plains with Marshall and Rollins and Dallas, the other three well armed and tense and moving in a way that chilled Gabriel to the bone. As they went, Marshall explained to Gabriel that they were about to pay a social call, a little visit to his old friends at Three Bars. It was gonna be a surprise, but he was sure they'd be glad to see him. He said also that Gabriel had a part to play in this surprise and that all would be made clear to him soon. It would be simple. It would just require a little nerve, was all, and Marshall said he knew the boy had nerve. He knew that for sure, and now was the time to test it.

THE DOG SAW THE BLACK MAN COMING *from a half-mile out, walking through the first light of dawn. He came forward from the bunkhouse porch, and as was his job and his duty and a calling only he among all that lived in these parts was any good at, he set to barking. He had a rhythm he liked to use and fell right into it: three sharp yelps and then a howl, three sharp, then howl. He repeated this refrain four times before he caught the scent of the man and checked himself, finding in it something familiar. He sat on his haunches and watched the man, cocking his head to one side as he favored his left eye and seemed to see better this way. He knew the man's stride, knew the set of his shoulders, and recognized the gesture he made, a motion as if he were shaking dice at hip level. He wondered vaguely at the man's long absence, and then forgot about that and wondered if the man had brought him anything. He trotted out to meet him.*

The black man knelt as the dog approached. He let the creature cuddle up to him, a mangy thing with a tender foot, twice kicked by horses and once shot at in some long-ago time. The man scratched behind the dog's ears and spoke to him in tones the creature remembered. The man apologized for what was about to happen and said that there was a part of him that was saddened by it, but only a part, and that the rest of him had long ago been consumed. He said a dog's life was a difficult one anyway and things would be better for him soon. So saying, the man clamped the dog's jaw shut in one gloved hand, placed the creature between his knees, and slit its throat in a motion so complete that the dog's head flopped straight back onto its shoulders.

The man watched the blood pour out in spurts. He felt the life the animal was kicking for and heard it when the dog began to pee. He was holding it still when the creature gave up its fight and grew calm, calmer than it had ever been. The man let it drop and looked down on his work.

There, isn't that better? he asked.

As he expected no answer, he walked on, knife held out to the side and dripping, toward the bunkhouse where two men slept, soundly and soon forever.

GABRIEL RAPPED ON THE DOOR TO THE RANCH HOUSE with his fist. The wood was hard and grainy. It hurt his knuckles and allowed little sound to escape. There was a window beside the door, but he could see little through it, as it mirrored the dawn behind him. He knocked again. Still no one came. A dry wind blew across from the south, bringing a cloud of dust that tickled Gabriel's skin and made a tinkling sound against the weathered boards. Other than that, all was silence. Gabriel turned around and looked out over the yard. He saw no sign of the others, and he wondered with a whisper what the hell he was doing here.

He heard her first, heavy footsteps like those of a man in workboots. Then he saw her through the reflection on the glass pane. She emerged there through the rising sun, her face red with the heat of it, round, and quite discernibly angry. She pressed her stout nose against the glass, stared at the boy with hard eyes, then kicked the door open. It swung out toward Gabriel, making him jump back to avoid its arc. She stood framed in the doorway, her body more than filling the space. She held a rifle at thigh level, tilted up in such a way that Gabriel could see down the barrels of the thing.

"There's few white men can get me out of bed this early, and no black boys that I know," she said. "What the hell you want, nigger? And it better be good."

In the strange way of a troubled mind, Gabriel found himself thinking two thoughts that surely were not the most necessary at the moment. First, he thought that Ugly Mary was not truly ugly, although she was so large that he was amazed at the notion that men had paid for her favors. And second, he couldn't help but feel a certain amazement at the number of times he'd had guns pointed at him in the last few days.

"Are you a goddamn idjit or what? I asked you your business."

"I . . . I just . . ." Gabriel drew a blank. He searched for some possible answer to the woman's question, but there seemed none. The absurdity of it astounded him. He gave the only answer he could. "They just told me to knock."

"They what?" Mary asked, stunned enough by the answer to let the rifle sag.

Another set of footsteps pounded through the house, and a man appeared. "What in God's name's going on here?" he demanded. He pushed Mary out of the way, set his hands on his hips, and stared at Gabriel as if he'd never heard or conceived of such a thing. He was a lanky man of considerable height, gaunt-featured and treelike. He opened his mouth to say something else, but then a very strange thing happened. In an instant, a moment frozen in Gabriel's mind then and forever after, a dimple of red no larger than a dime appeared on the man's forehead, above his left eye. At the same instant, the doorjamb behind him splintered. And also in the same instant, a fan of liquid sprayed the doorjamb, the nearby wall, and the left side of Ugly Mary's face. And then the instant was gone, and others followed it.

A rifle's report echoed in the air, a small thing, a noise no louder than a person clapping. The man's face went blank, his eyes careened up in their sockets, and he stumbled forward, grabbing Gabriel's shoulder with his enormous hand. His grip was so strong that the boy didn't even think of moving, but the man did. His head began to shudder, his neck loosened, and his body leaned over backward, pulling Gabriel part of the way with him but letting go as he hit the dry boards of the floor.

Ugly Mary took only a second to recover. Her rifle fanned past Gabriel and beyond him toward the prairie. She shot, her bulk quivering with the force of it, and Gabriel finally moved. He hit the deck, felt two bullets pass above him, and thought better of his position. He crawled off the far end of the porch in a second and looked back to see the carnage behind him.

Mary stood wide-legged, with her repeating rifle spraying bullets before her. Her reign of terror didn't last long, though. She quickly spent her cartridges, and just as quickly the unseen foe's bullets found her. They entered her flesh like concussions delivered to bone and muscle and flesh. She stumbled forward, dropped to her knees with a weight that must have crushed her kneecaps. Of this injury she showed no sign. She held the gun as if she might kill her attackers with the instrument and her will alone. She began to yell, a wail that started low and unintelligible but slowly became something of English speech. She invoked the wrath of her God and asked that she meet her murderers in hell. She began another curse but was cut short when a bullet smashed her lower jaw and blew out a portion of her skull. She fell backward and cursed no more.

Gabriel stared at the two fallen forms and didn't move until he heard the other men approaching. They collected around the porch and surveyed the scene in silence. Marshall looked down on the two bodies with eyes that seemed almost sad. Kneeling before Mary, he touched her cheek, testing it for warmth as if the

flu might have been what ailed her, staining his hand with her
blood in the process. He didn't seem to notice or care. He was
silent for some time, and Gabriel thought he read in his eyes a
kind of passion that made this all seem meaningful. But when
he spoke, his voice was without remorse.

"Guess they had it coming."

Marshall sent Dallas back for Dunlop and James, and when
they arrived, he instructed the three boys to go inside with
Rollins and take anything useful. James surveyed the scene with
trembling features, his face a pale reflection of its usual rich
color. Gabriel felt he could scarcely move himself, but when
Marshall repeated the order, he pulled James by the wrist to get
him going. They followed Rollins inside, stepping gingerly
around Mary's body to do so.

For the next twenty minutes they ransacked the place. Rollins
yelled out instructions, demonstrating the proper way to throw
open drawers and overturn furniture. Dallas proved more than
proficient at this, punctuating each action with hoots and curses.
Gabriel and James went through the motions of searching but
seemed oblivious of the motives of their work. James found a rifle
cabinet, opened it, and stared at its contents as if he'd never seen
such weapons before. He had just turned away from it when
Rollins noted his discovery and told James to carry the weapons
outside.

Gabriel found nothing of value. Left alone for a moment in
the upstairs bedroom, he sat on the bed and stared at the photographs lining the dresser, daguerreotypes of an array of people.
He found himself remembering his home in Baltimore, remembering a dresser much like this one on which photographs of his
own family sat. He felt his eyes go watery. The world before him
blurred, and for a moment he felt that he'd forgotten how to
breathe. A new round of shouting from downstairs brought him
back.

Rollins called Marshall inside. "There's a safe here."

It was a small thing, solid and nondescript and no bigger than a breadbox, so plain that neither Gabriel nor James had even noticed it. The men quickly discovered that it was locked but could be opened with a key, if one could be found. The next half-hour passed in a hasty search for the key. It was eventually found, on a hunch of Marshall's, on a chain around Mary's neck, hidden in the folds of her bosom.

From where Gabriel stood, he couldn't see the safe as the men huddled around it. He looked out the front door at the limp torso of the woman, at the great plain and the yellowing sun behind it. Rollins let out a low whistle, which brought back Gabriel's attention. Marshall turned slowly, holding something in his hand, something heavy. It looked like a block of wood in the shadow where Marshall held it. But when he stepped into the sunlight, it threw back the light like a thing afire. Gabriel realized what it was, a long, brownish yellow piece of metal—gold, a brick so dense that Marshall had to support it against his abdomen.

"My friends," Marshall said, "justice never got any better."

Another twenty minutes found Gabriel and James standing outside as the men prepared to leave. Marshall was in a fine mood, seemingly untroubled by thoughts of escape or capture, or by any remorse. He spoke to the boys as he checked his saddle and rigged it to carry an extra saddlebag.

"So here's the way things lie, boys. We got ourselves these two dead bodies here, two in the bunkhouse, and we got that other guy back at McKutcheon's. That's a whole lot of killing for a few days' work. You boys got two choices. You sit here and wait for the law to show. You tell them the best story you can and then get yourselves hanged. Cause that's what would happen. Two niggers sitting on the porch with a string of dead bodies around and an open safe. You know you're hanged already. That's option number one. Number two is you take a hold of one of them guns and come along with us and quit this country and try your luck elsewhere. Which is it?"

Gabriel was stumped by the question.

It was James who spoke. "I . . . I don't aim to be no killer."

"Oh, shit. You ain't gotta do no killing. These two here, they were just an old score. That man back at McKutcheon's . . . Well, I reckon I just did that to save you boys' lives. Not that you ever did say thank you. Myself, I don't give a good damn. I'm going to California." He looked at Rollins as if he'd just discovered their windfall and was still processing the possibilities. "Shit. What do you say, Rollins? How bout we spend the rest of our lives drinking tequila by the beach and sticking Mexican whores? That ain't a bad way to go. My daddy would roll in his grave, but he never did know a good thing when he saw it. Anyway, boys, I don't give a good shit what you two do—"

"Marshall?" Rollins interrupted him. "We can't leave them boys here. First sheriff asks them a question, they'll spill their guts quicker than a pig at slaughter. That ain't no clean getaway. Same goes for Dunlop." He motioned with his head. "He's looking a little spooked."

Gabriel remembered Dunlop and turned in the direction Rollins had indicated. The young Scot stood beside his horse, holding the creature by the reins and staring around him like a man totally lost.

Marshall pondered all this for a troubled moment but quickly reached a decision. "All right, I take it back. You two saddle up. California's waiting." He strode away, seemingly unconcerned as to whether the boys would obey or not. He went and spoke to Dunlop, and whatever he said proved most convincing.

Rollins watched the two boys as if he'd had another alternative in mind, but he didn't state it. "Come on, then," he said, and he followed them till they were saddled and ready. Gabriel's horse, a rust-colored mare with timid eyes, shied and shimmied.

The boy sat her with a concerned face that seemed only half there. The horse sensed this and was uneasy about it, and only quieted when actually under way. The party rode out to the northwest, Gabriel toward the back of the line but followed by Caleb. They left behind four dead, the two in the bunkhouse, whom Gabriel never saw, and the two on the porch, whom he'd seen all too closely. On some whim, Marshall propped Mary and Rickles up against the wall, their empty eyes staring unblinking into the morning sun, an image that Gabriel never managed to clean from his mind completely—the first true sign of the things to come.

Part 3

THE FIRST TIME THE BOY SAW THE CREATURE, HE KNEW where the tales of monsters sprang from. He was awakened from a long, meandering dream by the sow's anxious squeals and Raleigh's deep-throated neigh. He had his trousers on in a few seconds, boots just after. He ran for the door without lacing them, shoved it open, strode out into the night, and circled the house toward the barn. He wasn't ready for what he saw there and knew so immediately.

A beast stood poised on the sod fence of the pigpen. It was outlined in the starlight, rendered unreal and ghostly and more fearsome than it might have appeared in the reasoning light of day. The boy tried to name the beast, but he couldn't create the word in his mind. Its legs were spread wide, its neck was low, and its ears lay flat against its head. The hair along the crest of its shoulders and down its back stood at attention. It had been gazing down at *the frantic sow, but when the boy appeared it snapped its head around. It stared at him, head slinking from side to side, paws kneading the turf beneath it. It seemed to consider the boy first to discover if he was to be feared, and then, having decided that he wasn't, to decide whether it might dine doubly tonight.*

The boy read all this in the creature's eyes, for the beast concealed nothing of its thoughts, or the hunger within it and the need, above all else, to quench it. But only when its lips drew back from its jaws and exposed the white glint of its fangs did the boy remember its name: wolf. He tried to step back, but his feet were stuck to the ground. He tried to call out, but he'd lost his voice. The boy grasped at his thigh as if somehow the action might produce a weapon, or suffice as a call of alarm that he couldn't otherwise muster. It did neither.

The wolf let out a growl, sank low, and prepared to dive for the boy. It might have, except that the boy's uncle came bounding around the side of the house, rifle in hand. The man aimed and fired before the wolf had fully taken in his presence.

What happened next neither the man nor the boy could fully say later. It was as if the rifle's blast took the wolf away with the speed of the bullet. The animal simply vanished, leaving nothing but empty space before them and ringing silence and the question as to whether it had been an illusion. They might have thought so, except that the wolf let up a howl of protest from the safety of the black fields, a cry ringing with indignation and resentment and with the pent-up lusts of a lifetime. When it began to fade, lesser creatures picked up the call and added to it. The night came alive with cries of canine camaraderie, from all directions and distances, leaving the boy with the feeling that they were hopelessly outnumbered, surrounded by and deep within a legion of carnivorous life.

The next morning, the boy searched the ground with his stepfather and uncle. They found the wolf's tracks in the soil beside the

*sod fence and on the fence itself and around the back of the house
and at the door to the stables. They kept the pig in the barn from
then on, but two days later they awoke to find four of their five
hens dead and feathers strewn about. Again they found the beast's
tracks.*

Looks like we got a little problem, the stepfather said.

The uncle and the boy agreed.

GABRIEL AND THE OTHERS RODE HARD through the next week,
hitting the Pecos River late on the second day, turning and following its course northwest. Most of each day was spent in riding. Although they stopped regularly to water the horses and rest
them, they never broke for long. The constant motion atop a living being of hard contours, sinew, and muscle wreaked havoc on
Gabriel's body. Each stride sent jolts of pain through his backside and into his lower back and straight up the chain of his
spine. His hands clenched the reins with a white-knuckled passion that left his fingers twisted like claws. When he dismounted
each evening, he walked on bowed, clumsy versions of his former
legs.

They passed from Texas into New Mexico at some unmarked
boundary, and as the week wore on, they kept the Pecos to their
left. Across it Gabriel spied the foothills of the southern Rockies,
sharp, sand-colored ridges out of which grew buttresses of reddish stone and beyond which the ground rose to greater heights.
To their right lay the great expanse of the Llano Estacado, a land
so barren that Gabriel could imagine no creature living there by
choice. The plains stretched to the horizon, spotted by occasional prickly pear and tree cholla, all sharing muted colors that
varied little except with the rising and setting of the sun, when
that orb played tricks of light across the land and set colors moving in ribbons.

At night they huddled around a tiny fire. Sometimes they laid up in dry areas of the riverbed, finding shelter within the water-carved features. Although days were passing, pushing in between themselves and the horror of Three Bars, neither Gabriel, James, nor Dunlop had found his voice again. None ate more than his first plateful of food, and none joined in the nightly discourse held between Marshall and Rollins and Dallas, all of whom seemed like actors finally realized, finally given their moment in the light and loving every second of it. As the two boys sat staring at the fire and Dunlop sat staring into the night, the other three threw out plans for their future in California. Rollins talked only of whores and a life of leisure; Dallas considered trading in his spurs and sailing to Hawaii; Marshall cast webs of schemes, business ventures and building projects and even plans for a career in politics. Gabriel would have said they looked and sounded more like children at play than fugitives and murderers, except he knew that wasn't true. They looked like all of these.

Caleb rarely joined them in these sessions. He developed a habit of nightly reconnaissance. He'd backtrack their trail during the early evening and return in the black hours, emerging suddenly as a shape beside the fire. He walked with such stealth that nobody saw him arrive. Rather, they just realized at some moment that he was among them once more. Each evening, by his silence, he assured the men that they were not yet being followed. Gabriel thought many a time that if Caleb were tracking them instead of with them, they'd all be dead before the next sunrise. He wondered when Caleb found time to sleep, and whether he went on his nightly searches as the hunted or the hunter.

Marshall spoke to the boys as if he hadn't noticed their silence. In his orations they had been partners from the beginning and shared any guilt equally with the rest. It seemed that all knew and none needed to hear again of the boys' obligations to the group. But Gabriel felt the other men's watchful eyes on them day-long, saw in their glances a constant scrutiny, especially from Dallas and Rollins. These two watched them as if they longed to be provoked and were just waiting for the digression that would give them the excuse.

On the fourth night out, they camped in a protected arroyo with a view toward the setting sun. They supped on frying-pan bread and thick strips of bacon. For the first time since Three Bars, Marshall retrieved the gold from his saddlebag and set the brick on a blanket. The men studied it from several angles. None touched the bullion, as this seemed a luxury meant only for Marshall, but they commented on the glint of the stuff in the set-ting sun and whistled at the prospects the soft metal conjured in their minds. Gabriel, from the edge of the group, couldn't help but find the display somehow wrong. He couldn't get the images of Ugly Mary and Rickles from his mind. The bar of gold seemed a strange, dead thing, like a coffin set out in state or the mound of an unmarked grave.

"What do ya think it's worth?" Dallas asked.

The men debated this question for some time. Rollins was convinced it would fetch a thousand dollars. He called it a "thousand-dollar bar" and said the logic of it was clear to anyone with a lick of sense. Dallas thought it might go for more. As gold-hungry as people were out in California, they'd probably fall over themselves offering hard currency for the stuff, until each of the men would be as rich as the king of Siam. This comparison drew some interest from Marshall, who couldn't imagine what a skinny-necked Alabama boy like Dallas knew of the riches of the Far East.

"I tell you boys the God-honest truth," Marshall said at last. "This here gold ain't worth what it used to be, not anymore. There was a time you could've wiped out a whole nation of red-skins for what we got laying here. There was a time you could've

hung a thousand Jews from crosses and beat the living shit out of
your slaves and nobody've batted an eyelash." He looked around
at the group, pausing on Gabriel and James and then shaking his
head sharply to bring back his wandering mind. "But them days
are long gone. Sad truth is, the world is changing and ain't one of
us knows what it's gonna end up looking like. That's why I don't
mind us staking ourselves to a little insurance." He picked up the
brick with reverent hands and held it up for the others to see. "I
can't say exactly, cause I wasn't there when they picked this fella
up, but you're looking at more than a couple thousand here. Old
Mary never cared for banks. There were too many Easterners
involved for her liking, too many Yankees. I remember her saying
she'd look after her own cash, thank you very much. Nobody'd
get hers except over her dead body. And those were her words,
not mine." He paused and weighed the brick in his hand. "Yessir,
this here's the weight of justice done. No fat bitch's gonna outfox
the man who taught her all she knew."

"Hell no she ain't," Dallas agreed, "not when she's full of lead
and twenty pounds heavier for it." He couldn't help breaking
into a little dance, a sort of a heel-to-toe jig to the music of his
own whistling. Rollins knelt close to the gold and repeated its
worth several times, until interrupted by Dunlop's forlorn voice.

"It's not worth the lives you took to get it," he mumbled, just
loudly enough to be heard. He looked off into the distance,
toward the East, as he had done since they arrived at camp. His
expression was so vague and distant that one might have
doubted he'd even spoken, except that he spoke again. "And it's
sure not worth the time we'll all spend burning."

All eyes turned to him, then cautiously moved back to Marshall, who found no insult in the statement but in fact seemed glad
to hear it, saying, "That's an interesting point, Dunlop, the whole
question of God and Satan and punishment and that. Problem for
me is that if I'm damned as a sinner, then I'm damned as a sinner

and that's that. If I'm damned, I was damned a long time ago. I've been living a damned life now for thirty-some years, and I can't do a thing about it. If I was to drop down on my knees and pray, I'd be making God out a fool. I'd be trying to pull the wool over his eyes, so to speak. I'd be kowtowing to the Almighty just to get a bit of the good stuff in the hereafter. Now, wouldn't that make me bout the biggest hypocrite you ever seen? If there's one thing I hate, it's a hypocrite. I'd rather share a mescal with an honest man in hell than drink wine with some brown-nose saint in heaven." He seemed annoyed for a moment, bitter, as if he knew exactly whom he spoke of when he mentioned this saint. "Anyway, the world's too damn complicated for any one son of a bitch to have made it up." He stood up and heaved the brick onto Dunlop's lap. "Here, feel the weight of a man's soul."

Dunlop convulsed away from it, scrambling to his feet and looking back at it as if the metal were a living creature capable of great harm. He looked ready to lash out, but he didn't find his voice again, and any words he might have uttered would've been drowned out by the men's laughter. Dunlop sat again, turned his back, and continued his contemplation of the east.

Marshall bounded over and snatched up the brick. He held it close to the back of Dunlop's head, and for a moment Gabriel thought he was going to hit him with it. But instead he knelt behind the man and spoke close to his ear, with the soft voice of a friend.

"Careful there, Dunlop, you gotta keep control of that temper of yours. Don't go all soft on me and get yourself in trouble, you hear? I like you. We've blood of Scots, you and I. But don't think I'd hesitate. I'd take you out of the world faster than your daddy shot you into it, and I'd enjoy it just as much."

Dunlop didn't move. He showed no sign of even having heard, but Marshall backed off, satisfied. Gabriel felt James's gaze hard on him, but he avoided the other boy's eyes.

Dallas spat in Dunlop's general direction, accurately enough that a few flecks of the spit touched the man's boots. "Never knew you were such a damn twat anyway," he said. "Should've known, though, seeing's how the so-called Scotchmen don't even wear trousers." He turned back to the group, having suddenly found humor in his loathing. "Did y'all know that? Dunlop told me so himself. Said they used to go to battle the whole lot of them half naked, nothing but a piece a cloth wrapped around their jewels."

Dallas amused the others for some time by dancing about in imitation of warriors in ball gowns, doing his best to mimic a Scottish accent. Something in it sent Rollins into hysterics. But when things died down again and Marshall began to hide the brick away, Rollins asked him seriously, "So you knew all along they had the gold there? I figured you were just being a vengeful son of a bitch. But you had a plan, didn't you?"

Marshall finished cinching up his saddlebags before answering. He looked up at Rollins and said, "You don't think I'd kill them just for the pleasure of it, do you?"

Something in the question seemed like a threat. At least, Rollins took it so. He backed away a step and shook his head. "Hell, no. I know you're always up to something or other. I went along with it, didn't I?" He looked down at the fire, dismissing the conversation with a wave. "I was just saying . . . just pulling your chain a little."

Marshall didn't seem truly satisfied with this answer, but he let it sit. He found a bottle of whiskey and proposed a little drink, just a ration to ease the evening's tensions. The others agreed readily enough. Gabriel watched them, Marshall's question still loud and unanswered in his mind.

NEAR THE END OF THE WEEK THEY TURNED toward the mountains of the Sangre de Cristo range. Throughout days of riding, they rarely spotted other people. Twice they saw Indians in the distance, Navajos according to Marshall, quiet travelers who appeared and disappeared with the stealth of coyotes. They only once passed within shouting distance of another group of white men. But neither group hailed the other, and they rode on without comment, into a land more and more remote.

They wove their way through changing surroundings, finding cooler mornings and chilly evenings in the shadows of the mountains. The air thinned, becoming crisper and more variously scented. They were now in a country where each wood had its own distinct smell, where creosote and sage, mesquite and juniper and piñon, wafted on the breeze along with the drifting sands. The dry soil took on a reddish hue, somehow more earthen and richer than that of the plains, deep umber tones that clothed the mountains in shades as varied as that of human skin.

Gabriel rode into the landscape only vaguely aware of its beauty. He looked at the rocks and cliffs and shrubs as if he feared that they had some malignant life hidden within them. In its various shapes and forms, the land seemed to be composed of living beings trapped in stone buttresses, frozen faces that would have whispered to him had not the land held them prisoner. With each look he found movement dancing just out of his vision's reach. And although the movement was always explained by something—the play of the wind, the trickle of sand, the spiny back of a horned toad, or the grotesque progress of a scorpion— Gabriel couldn't shake the suspicion that the world was no longer as he believed. The land was alive in a way he'd not known before, in a way made all the greater for the images of the dead, which still served as a screen upon which the world was cast.

These feelings were made more concrete on the evening of their seventh day of flight. Having gone a little distance from camp to relieve himself, Gabriel came upon the half-decayed corpse of a mule deer entangled in the twisted branches of an old juniper tree. The smell of it hit him at once, entering his nose and pouring down into his guts like a foul liquid. At first it looked as though the deer had been captured where it stood, as if the tree had grown up around it and lifted it from the ground. It seemed somehow Biblical, some amalgamation of a burning bush and a living crucifix. What kind of land was this, he wondered, where trees set traps?

As he stood staring, it became clear from the bloody and scuffed ground that something had dragged the deer into the tree by brute force, a creature with the strength, with the guile, and perhaps even with the artistry to build a statue of rotting flesh. The corpse had been gutted and cleaned of internals. Its two hind legs were broken at their midpoint and shredded, whether by teeth or claws was unclear. But most horrible to Gabriel's mind were the deer's eye sockets, empty depressions that crawled with insect life. Once more this journey had given him an image he'd carry ever after.

He didn't sleep that night, nor the next. And it was with weary, thankful eyes that he first beheld Santa Fe, nine days after leaving Three Bars.

THE YOUNGER BROTHER BUILT AN ENCLOSURE in the barn to house the remaining chicken and protect it from the wolf. Three days later the beast returned. It was propelled by a hunger born deep within and of strange origins. It clawed at the door and sniffed around it and tested each chink and crack to see if it could pass through. It couldn't, but it kept at it until the man appeared and shot at it once more. The wolf felt the bullet scorch past its left flank, so close it could smell the hot metal against its fur later that evening. Its hunger was unabated, but it quit the scene and retreated to the darkness and howled and planned its return.

The boy asked his uncle if he had ever heard of a wolf behaving so. The man answered that he had not, although he figured this meant little, as beasts will always surprise you when you least expect it. He thought maybe the wolf was an old one, maybe it was injured or sick and couldn't hunt properly and so was seeking out a stationary food source. The boy responded that the animal he'd seen looked neither elderly nor sickly. The man nodded his head and said that was rightly so. Truth is, I ain't got the faintest what to make of it.

The boy asked his uncle if he might sleep with his rifle beside his bed. The man considered this and conferred with the boy's mother and then agreed. Guess I done missed it twice. Maybe your luck'll be better.

The boy didn't tell the others what he planned, but that evening he waited anxiously till his stepfather's breathing fell into the familiar pattern of sleep. Then he waited longer, knowing his mother was slow to sleep and he must be patient. Eventually he rose and walked barefoot to the door, gun in one hand, boots in the other. He opened the door carefully, although he found that the slightest movement caused sound louder than reason would have thought possible.

Once outside, he high-stepped around to the side of the house, pulled on his boots, and made his way to the barn. He had to speak to the animals as he fumbled with the door, as any motion in the dark now made them nervous. He soothed them and, once inside, stroked Raleigh and patted the mule and explained his plans to them all, asked for their blessing and strength to aid him. The pig alone seemed skeptical, grunting and watching him askance and making low, throaty sounds, a discourse the boy was fated never to understand.

He sat opposite the door on a three-legged stool and laid the gun across his lap. He waited. Several times he checked the chamber. Several times he checked his pockets for more bullets, and each time

he doubted he had done so and repeated the action. So passed the
night, in silence save for the noises of the animals and the scurry-
ing of mice and the friction of the sky rubbing past the world.

  As the sky lightened with the first signs of the approaching
dawn, the boy crept back into the house and to bed.

THE SCENT OF PIÑON HUNG IN THE OVERCAST AIR like a
transparent blanket. Gabriel breathed it in through his nose,
rolling the scent around on his palate and tasting it. There was
something sweet in it, something clean and earthy. He had never
seen a town like Santa Fe. The muted shapes and colors of the
adobe buildings blended with the landscape as if they were a natural part of the earth's architecture. The place bustled with people, mestizos mostly, brown people, some with modest faces and
others with proud ones, many showing the features of empire,
the clash of cultures betrayed in the shapes of eyes and noses, in
speech and clothing.

Once the horses were tied to a hitching post, Marshall proposed a quick drink. This was met with enthusiasm. "But we're
not here to get swizzled," he added. "A drink or two is all I'm
suggesting. No whoring. No fighting. Let's just keep our wits
about us." With little more than a gesture, he assigned the boys
to watch the horses. With his saddlebag in one hand, he threw
the other arm around Dunlop and led him away, although the
man seemed to sink under the pressure of the limb. Dallas cast a
glance back at Gabriel and James before he entered the bar, some
seventy yards away. He caught their attention, nodded, and pretended to shoot them with his finger.

The second he was through the door, James grabbed
Gabriel's arm and said urgently, "C'mon, let's make a run for it.
Let's do it now. This could be our only chance."

Gabriel looked at him sadly. There was little spite left in his countenance, but he could offer no confidence in such a plan. He leaned against the post and looked at the horses. The creatures' eyes touched on the boys with the same indifference with which they looked upon the ground or the board to which they were bound.

"There ain't no use. They'd track us down just for the pleasure of it."

James seemed to know this was the truth, but he argued anyway, pointing out all the foot and horse and wagon traffic of the roads. He doubted anybody could track them through all that. "Study on it. They wouldn't even know where to start. We could ride off in the wrong direction or something. Or ride straight back the way we came. Think of all the places to hide out there."

"I don't know. You heard what he said. They won't be long."

"Yeah, they will. You seen the way they drink." James stared hard at the cantina. He squinted his eyes and looked as though he were trying to peer through the adobe at the men inside. "They're probably drinking already." He turned the same intense vision on his friend. "I see that dead woman all over the place, Gabe. Don't matter if I'm sleeping or awake—all I can do is see her. Last night she came after me and got on me and started touching me all over. It wasn't even no dream. I could've sworn she was on me for real, though. She was all bloody . . . Jesus Christ. This ain't what I was thinking when I ran off from Pinkerd's, and they'll probably kill us anyway. Gabe, what else can we do? We gotta go."

Gabriel tried not to look at James, but the passion of his friend's plea tugged at him. He met his gaze, saw the quivering hope and fear there, saw the horizon reflected in his eyes and his own distorted reflection. For the first time, a tingling sense of possibility crept into him. It was a big world, full of hiding places, full of vast spaces, and he was small, so small in compari-

son. He could be lost and never found. He could find his way
home.

Gabriel looked at his horse, her sleek muzzle and oily brown
coat. His gaze moved down the reins to the hitching post. They
weren't even tied to it. They were only thrown over the board
and wrapped around it twice. He could have them undone in
less than a second. He slid his fingers around the reins and felt
the dry texture of the leather.

As if in answer to this touch, a man emerged from the cantina.
The boy's gaze shot to him faster than a bullet would have.
Caleb. He stood in the doorway with his head tilted back ever so
slightly, as if he were scenting the air. His face was nothing but a
dark shadow beneath his hat, his eyes only the faintest points of
substance against that black void. His head turned, and small
and distant as his eyes were, Gabriel felt their touch as if they
had a physical force, as if the man had reached out and grasped
his chin between his fingers.

Gabriel pulled his hand away from the reins. He held it out
beside him for a moment, flexing his fingers, and then he passed
the palm across his lips, exhaling a breath onto it as he did so. It
was a strange gesture, and the boy wasn't exactly sure why he did
it. But only then did Caleb lean back against the adobe wall. He
pulled a cigarette from his shirt pocket and lit it. The flare of the
match illuminated the contours of his face for a second and
proved that he was a man of flesh and bone, not a phantom in dis-
guise. But if this was any comfort, it didn't show on either boy's
face. They both stood tense and stiff, and try as he might, Gabriel
could not get rid of the pressure that seemed to grip his jaw.

THEIR STAY IN SANTA FE WAS SHORT, two nights and only one
full day, which they spent supplying themselves for the journey
west. They camped behind a livery that boarded the horses,

shod, fed, and rested them. They set to the work of stocking up
on things they'd found themselves in want of on their ride from
Three Bars. They bought several boxes of matches, extra water
bottles, and, at Rollins's request, a new coffeepot. Gabriel was
sent out with Rollins and Dallas to buy food. They returned
with their horses laden with blocks of bacon, canned tomatoes,
sacks of beans, flour, baking powder, bricks of lard, and, again at
the Texan's urging, more coffee than Gabriel could have imagined consuming. Marshall came back with a map, some sort of
geological survey commissioned by the government. The men
looked it over carefully, studied it from different angles, and
even held it up to the light. All agreed they could make little
sense of it.

By the time they rode out of Santa Fe, something had changed
in the group's demeanor. The accumulation of days and miles in
travel and their undisturbed passage through the city had lifted
the men's spirits. It seemed that some unstated boundary had
been crossed and put behind them. The tension eased. Indeed,
even Gabriel found it impossible to conceive of somebody tracking them through the wilderness. He took little joy in this fact,
however, for it had never seemed to him that the true danger
would come from without. It was right here in the company of
the men that he felt most ill at ease, and watching Marshall relax
and joke with the others, listening to him spin schemes for a
future lived in wealthy debauchery, he felt the rules and norms of
society slipping further away. But still he rode in silence, still he
and James shared long glances, searched each other without
words, still the days passed and they moved ever deeper into the
West, into a land that swallowed them without end.

IT CAME ON THE THIRD NIGHT OF THE BOY'S VIGIL. *He had*
fallen asleep, although he knew so only because when he opened his

eyes the world was different from what he remembered. It was still just as dark. The animals were still near at hand. The gun still sat cradled in his lap. But something was different. He swallowed and was surprised at how loud the sound was. He'd never heard the world more clearly. It was as if he had woken as some new sort of being, one with ears that could float away from him and speed out into the night.

He would have shaken his head to rid himself of the sensation, except it was thus that he heard the beast's footfalls when they were still far away. Raleigh heard them too and lifted his head and neighed and watched the boy. But the boy just listened to the swish of paws through the grass, to the breathing of the life out there. He could even hear the saliva as it fell from the creature's lips and splashed against the earth. He knew just when the wolf loped in from the cultivated fields, crossed the space between house and barn, and set its eyes on the barn door. There it paused. The boy's fingers gripped the rifle so tightly they were white against it, but he didn't notice. He noticed nothing save the presence on the other side of the door.

When the wolf moved, it did so suddenly, as if all reserve had been cast away. It shoved its head into the crack of the door and tried to squirm through. The boy forgot the rifle and fell back against the wall and stared at it. The wood bucked and shimmied against the rope latch, then gave with a crack. The wolf stepped forward. The boy couldn't believe the size of its head. It was a monster of a head, a disembodied thing with enormous eyes. Its snout was longer than his forearm, with flaps of skin that pulled back from its teeth in exertion and hunger and anger. Behind this came a body somehow small by comparison, bony and barely capable of bearing the weight of its skull and all the more grotesque for it. The creature paused in the door and surveyed the barn with quick jerks of its head, taking in the frantic horse and mule and

the crazed pig, which was trying to burrow through the wall of the
barn. Then it looked at the boy.

The boy saw the hairs on the creature's back rise up. He saw its
teeth standing like so many ivory phantoms in the dim light. And
he saw into its skull through the sockets of its eyes. That's when he
remembered the gun. As the beast leapt toward him, he brought
the rifle up to his chin and pulled, aiming into the blur of motion
before him. He fell back with the kick of the gun and bounced off
the wall and landed on his knees. He came up lashing out with
the butt of the rifle, pulling the trigger again and again, although
there was nothing left to fire. Only slowly did he realize that he
was still alive and that the wolf was not upon him. He spun
around, searching out the corners of the barn. But there was noth-
ing, only Raleigh and the mule and the pig and the nervous cluck-
ing of the one remaining hen.

He could never truly believe that the kick of the gun had been so
great. In his dreams for many nights to follow, the kick was actu-
ally the force of the wolf's chest butting against the rifle and ac-
cepting his bullet. But in real life there was no sign that the wolf
had been shot. No body, no blood, nothing except the tracks that
proved it had actually been there. How he could have missed it he
would never understand. The wolf didn't come back again, but
the victory left the boy with a deep sense of something unfulfilled.

ON A MORNING TWO DAYS OUT OF SANTA FE, the group came
to the top of a sandstone ridge and looked down upon a farm. It
was a complex of three structures, a main house and two barns,
which sat next to a shallow river. Behind the house and lining the
river ran well-tended rows of corn, among which a man and a
woman worked, heads down and moving slowly up the lanes,
oblivious of the watchers above. At the back of the house, two

teenage girls washed clothes, occasionally laughing and flicking soapy water at each other. The whole valley was lightly dotted with firs, which shimmered in the morning breeze and sent their green smell wafting up the ridge. A goat munched on the sparse grass at the far edge of the field, and a single mule grazed from a long tether on the spit of land within the river's fork. The place conveyed a sense of idyllic tranquillity. Gabriel couldn't help but think of his own family, the green grass, the sod house, the people and the quiet warmth therein.

Marshall led them forward. He hailed the family from a hundred yards. The two heads in the field snapped up. They exchanged some words. The woman circled quickly around the house, gathered the two girls, and disappeared inside. The man walked forward to welcome them. He looked to be a mestizo, mostly of Spanish descent but with features that also betrayed Indian ancestry. His legs were slightly bowed, his arms somehow short for his body, but his face had a strength to it, a quiet, polite calm, which instantly seemed both a greeting and a warning. His nose was prominent and sharply hooked, and his beard was carefully kept. He stood before the horsemen, wiping his hands with a handkerchief, and greeted them in Spanish.

Marshall looked at Rollins as if something in the greeting would amuse him, then back at the man. "Howdy," he said. "This here's a beautiful spread you got. I never would've thought it, all this desert around the place. Little Eden. Hope you don't mind us passing through."

The man watched Marshall, looked over the other men, and answered, switching into English without comment, "Thank you. You're welcome to pass."

Marshall nodded. An awkward moment followed, a tense silence as the man waited for a response or movement from the travelers. Marshall seemed too enraptured by the tranquillity of the place to notice. He inhaled deeply and tilted his head to the side. "Listen to that creek. Ain't that nice? Just gurgling like that." Dallas affirmed that it was nice—right pretty-sounding, he thought. Marshall wondered out loud how far it was to the next creek, wondered if they'd find as nice a place as this to take some lunch and water the horses. He let the question hang in the air until the man made his offer, the offer he must make in that land of few homes and unwritten hospitality. Marshall accepted.

The man called to his wife. Almost instantly she appeared. She cracked the door open, paused, then slipped through and pulled the door closed behind her. The man asked her to prepare a lunch for the visitors. She went back into the house and returned with a cutting board at her waist, holding a large knife in the other hand. She set them down on a wooden table. A moment later the two girls emerged from the house, one carrying a plate of corn tortillas and the other a slab of bacon. They looked to be in their early teens, one slightly older than the other, both slim and tall, taller already than their father. Despite their demure manner, their down-turned faces, the short steps with which they walked, and the plain dresses they wore, or perhaps because of these, the girls betrayed a budding, youthful sensuality. Rollins let out a low whistle. The mother's eyes cut him, but she made no comment.

Marshall instructed the others to water the horses and stake them out. Once this was done, the men gathered under the firs and listened as Marshall and the man spoke.

"This is a hell of a lonely country, ain't it?" Marshall began.

The man agreed that it was, but he said it suited them well. They were prospering here and enjoying the quiet toil of the earth and the solitude.

"What about Indians, bandits and that? You feel safe, what with the womenfolk and all?"

The man said that he enjoyed good relations with the nearby Indians. They traded often, and he'd found them to be nothing save peace-loving, curious folk, simple in the way of God's first children and thus beautiful. He said also that he had a son, a strong young man who was away just now but who was a comfort to them all in their solitude. He was a soldier, a *vaquero*, a son and brother, all at once.

"He's talented, your son. Jack of all trades."

The man agreed. He stroked the dark hair of his mustache with his fingers. "He is good at many things."

Marshall smiled and turned to his companions. "These here are good folk, living a good life. You hear that, Dallas? You should learn something from this."

Dallas nodded, although his attention was on the girls.

"Hey, Dallas, you hearing me?" The boy nodded. Marshall turned to the man. "Think Dallas there's much impressed with your daughters. Fine family you've got. Makes me a little envious, tell you the truth."

Once the women had set out the food, the wife led the girls off a little distance to eat by themselves. Rollins stood and asked them back to the table. They would not come, and the man said that was the way it should be. Marshall told Rollins to sit down and act like he had some sense.

As they ate, Marshall probed the man further with questions about his life. The man answered him politely, thoroughly, as if it were his duty, one that he didn't take lightly. Yes, it was a joy to father a family and see the children grow. No, he wouldn't give it up for anything. Yes, his family had come north from Mexico several generations ago, from the Guadalajara region. And yes, it was difficult to say where his heart and loyalties lay, being part of a conquered territory, beaten, but not truly accepted into this socalled union. While there were few in Nuevo Mexico who bore his familial name, there were many who did in Viejo Mexico. This he would never forget.

Despite his cordial responses, the man watched the group

with slight disdain, which he did not give voice to but which he couldn't help showing all the same. His eyes said that it was rude to ask such questions and that only his good manners prevented him from pointing this out. If Marshall noticed this, he gave not the slightest sign. He chatted on between mouthfuls of food, so completely engrossed by the man's words and so unaware of what his body was saying that Gabriel felt a tingling low in his back. He didn't know what was going to happen here, but he feared that the peace of the afternoon was too much like a blank page and these men were too anxious to write their history on all things pure.

After lunch the men lounged around, showing no signs of haste. Their postures were relaxed enough, but their eyes moved with quick, nervous shifts, landing often on the man, the girls, the wife, and then sliding to Marshall. The woman went inside. Shortly after, Dallas sidled off to where the girls were back at the washing. He moved casually, as if taking in the air over there and enjoying the view of the river without a clear thought in his head. When he finally turned to face the two, he seemed almost surprised to discover that the girls were so near at hand. Gabriel heard the beginning of his conversation: "Hey, y'all girls speak American?" He moved a little closer and looked to be helping them with the laundering.

Marshall told the Mexican that their destination was California. He asked him about the country to the west of here, and the man told him what he knew of it. He said it was high desert country, that they were at the edge of a plateau that stretched for two hundred miles, that beyond that there were more mountains. A bad country, he called it, many scorpions and few people. They should conserve their water, for there would be little this time of the year. Beyond that, he said, the land leveled again and was desert until you reached more mountains. Somewhere beyond that was the Colorado River, and beyond that California, but he could not speak with detail, for he had never been that far. He said it would be a long trip, but he wished them a good voyage.

"Oh, it'll be a good one," Marshall said.

"Why do you make this trip?" the man asked.

"Well . . ." Marshall waved the question away. "Hey, here we've shared your table and all that and had this nice talk, but I don't even know your name."

The man smiled. "I find travelers are often slow to speak of names. I am Diego Maria Fuentes."

Rollins guffawed. "Maria?"

The man looked at him without apology. "Yes. It's not as it sounds, though. My—"

There was a shout. They all turned in time to see one of the girls shove Dallas with such force that he stumbled backward down the shallow slope and fell into the river. He stood up cursing, and the things that happened next followed each other so fast that Gabriel could hardly keep the string of events in order. The door to the house flew open and the woman emerged, brandishing a long slaughter knife. She flew toward her girls and beyond, toward Dallas. The boy drew his pistol in a flourish that sent a spray of water into the air and sighted on her. The father stood to move, but Rollins stopped his progress with one of his long, stiff arms.

"What, you think I won't shoot a woman?" Dallas yelled. "Goddamn, what the hell you thinking, pulling a knife on me? I'll shoot you dead just as soon as look at ya." His gun hand jerked with his words, impassioned and yet unsteady. The boy cast a quick look at Marshall. "I wasn't even doing nothing. Just told the girl she smelled like strawberries."

The Mexican, still trapped behind Rollins's arm, whispered God's name quietly and spoke Marshall's aloud. He pushed the arm away and began to move forward. His body seemed divided between two disparate inclinations. His hands gestured for appeasement, drew calming circles in the air, and tried to wave the tension away. But his eyes and lips betrayed him, respectively cutting the boy with all the venom they had and muttering a quick string of Spanish expletives.

Whether Dallas would have understood the man's words was doubtful, but Marshall seemed to grasp them clearly enough. He swung on the man, drew his pistol, and stopped him with the butt of it. The impact across his mouth knocked out four of his front teeth. He stumbled backward and fell flat on his back. He struggled to his feet, but Marshall hit him again with the pistol, across the forehead this time. As the man stood, dazed, Marshall swung the full force of his kick to the man's groin. He went down.

Marshall stared at him a moment. "I can't stand to hear my men talked about that way, leastways not by yourself. Dallas may be the son of a whore and a mongrel dog, but it ain't your place to say it." He turned to the others. "Damn! Just when I was enjoying the afternoon, too. Dallas, you damn horny toad, what are you playing at? Now look what you've gotten us into. Look at this fella. Just a minute ago we were doing a little polite conversating. But you had to act a fool, and he had to go and get uppity."

Rollins, so excited that he sprayed moisture with his words, stood before the man with his fist swinging low before his face, waiting for the slightest provocation to lash out. "Damn right, he got uppity! Mexicans are the uppitiest sons of bitches next to niggers! But now look at him."

The man's eyes rolled. He tried to stand, even reached out toward Marshall, for support or to do him injury. Marshall slipped away from his fingers and pushed Rollins back in the same motion. All his attention was focused on the man's movements, on the gurgling sound his throat was making and the blood that poured freely from his forehead and the corners of his mouth. Dunlop walked toward the man with outstretched arms, but before he reached him, Marshall tossed his gun to his left hand and punched the man with his right. The blow snapped the man's head around and sent flying a froth of blood and spit. The man fell on his face and groveled in the dirt.

Dunlop stooped over him as if he would help but feared to touch him. Marshall looked at the Scot with revelation in his face.

"Look at him, Dunlop. The worm does turn, doesn't it?"

Shouts from Dallas redirected their attention. He had the woman on her knees, with his pistol aimed dead at her forehead. He was yelling at her, and she was trying to respond but could scarcely utter a word for his cursing. Caleb slipped behind the woman, took the knife from her, threw her down, and bound her hands and legs as he would bind a calf for branding. Dallas turned his gun on the two girls, who stood in such complete shock that they seemed to understand nothing, not even the function of the weapon aimed at them.

A moment passed in stillness, each person frozen in a posture of crime or torture, each stunned at the prospect of what the next moment might bring. The tinkling of the river played in the silence; a crow called in the distance; the horses watched the human antics with apprehension. Gabriel felt he could scarcely breathe. He stood trapped by the stretched moment in time.

It was Dallas who broke the stillness. He smiled. Whether the smile was enough to change the direction of the men's actions or whether they had shared a plan from the outset, Gabriel couldn't say. But he watched it unfold, an almost silent chain of actions that couldn't have been smoother if choreographed. Caleb dragged the woman across the ground and set her beside her husband. Marshall waved his hand toward the girls, and Rollins and Dallas took them inside. The girls walked like numb crea-tures to be directed, with no fight, just eyes hungering for their

parents, seeing their state and then following the men's directions. Dallas broke the silence by asking if the other men figured
the girls were virgins. Marshall said he figured they were. Yes, he
figured they were. Then they were gone into the house.

Gabriel looked at James, and he back. They both looked at
Dunlop, who pulled his eyes slowly from the man at his feet. His
gaze passed over the boys and fell on the house. He stared at it
with an emotion that grew as the silent seconds passed. His
cheeks trembled; his jaw worked up and down as if he would
speak. He mumbled something, shook his head, and stumbled
forward. He moved in a trancelike state, carried forward by
something beneath his conscious mind. His steps were wild and
clumsy and barely kept him upright. And they were short-lived.

Caleb was up and over the picnic table and to Dunlop in a few
strides. He kicked the man's feet from under him, drew his gun
as he fell, and landed on top of him, his knee digging into
Dunlop's back, the muzzle of his pistol pressed into his neck.
Dunlop cried out, sounds that were not words, that were not
even protests of pain but howls of a torment that language
couldn't explain. His feet thrashed in the dirt and his fingertips
gripped the earth, but Caleb held him down.

Gabriel took a step toward them, but he was stopped before
he could even form a clear thought. Caleb didn't change his grip
on Dunlop, but his eyes flashed a threat at the boy. Gabriel froze,
and the man went to work binding Dunlop's hands. He didn't
feel the need to check the power of his threat. And indeed, there
was no need.

Gabriel stood immobile, James at his side, watching. Caleb
tied the parents together, back to back, with efficient, silent
motions. He then sat biting his fingernails, listening to the stony
silence that came from the house, watching the couple and the
boys with his coal-black, narrow eyes. When the men emerged
from the house, they did so triumphantly, throwing about jokes

and laughter, pushing one of the girls before them, the one who had shoved Dallas. She was bound at the wrists and blindfolded. There followed an argument that Gabriel caught very little of, as he was staring at the girl. She stood as still as he, head straight, chin raised, and jaw set tight. Her blouse was ripped open down the front and her skirt was crumpled and soiled. She stood until Rollins grabbed her by the wrist and led her toward the horses. She walked with a limping, pained progress, but she did not fight.

The argument, which Gabriel had missed, had been won for the moment by the baser demons of the men's nature. The whole group mounted and rode, the girl on one of her father's horses, a long-legged gelding that was strung by the halter behind Rollins. Dallas led a paint mare away in a similar fashion, loading her up with various objects that he took a fancy to. Only Caleb stayed behind. As Gabriel reached the rise on the far side of the house, he cast one last glance back. Caleb sat a few feet away from the couple, seeming from the distance like a friend sharing the afternoon. A form stepped from the house: the other girl. With that last glimpse, the land pushed its elbow in between them and the homestead was no more.

THEY CARRIED ON THROUGH THE TANGERINE HIGHLIGHTS of dusk and for several hours into the night. The group's mood sombered as the darkness deepened. Dunlop rode with his hands tied behind his back, silent, eyes distant, letting the horse tag along behind the others of its own accord. The girl was similarly bound, although blindfolded as well. Gabriel watched her from his position several horses behind, trying to read her body and gain some understanding of her thoughts. But she gave few signs to decipher. She sat on her horse with an erect back, with a balance she maintained with her legs alone, with a calm that was

somehow defiant and defeated at once. The bright red handkerchief that was fastened around her eyes remained until they
stopped and made camp, until they'd built up a fire and broken
out the mescal stolen from the girl's home. Only when the tone
of revelry had been reestablished did Rollins yank the scarf from
her eyes, with the air of a magician.

The rapists toasted their deeds and talked of penetration and
blood and the joy of total power as if there were no such thing as
remorse, as if the louder their voices were, the less shame they
felt, as if they would shout it up to God and see him blush.
Rollins proposed that the girls had enjoyed it, that all women
have something in them that likes it that way, that there is a little
she-cat in them who may scream and fight but needs it like all the
rest. He tried to get the girl to answer this claim, but she stared
stonily into the air above the fire. Marshall said he figured that
theory was based on some faulty logic, but Rollins stuck to it,
saying he could tell she'd liked it and would soon be liking it
again.

But despite their words, none of the men touched the girl
that night. They grew quieter. They sat, one and all, beneath a
canopy of low-hung stars. The night was so clear and the air so
delicate that Gabriel found himself wishing he could breathe in
the stars and so take on their light, wishing he could touch them
and be pulled up toward them, away from this place and these
men. Before long, Rollins slept, snoring, his head thrown back.
Dallas sat out on a ridge nearby and seemed for once to wrestle
with his thoughts. Marshall lay on his back and talked to himself
in a low murmur. James lay on his side next to Gabriel, head
clasped firmly in his hands, silent.

Gabriel watched them all, especially the girl, who sat cross-
legged, bound, and still. She neither moved nor stretched nor
slept, but just stared. She didn't return his gaze. He looked back
at the small fire of mesquite before him. The flames were like

spirits captured within the wood, beings stretching up their arms into the night and tasting the air of freedom. They made him think back to the girl's parents. What had happened to them? He tried to convince himself that Caleb had stayed behind only to make sure they were properly bound and could not give chase or run for help. That must have been it. That had to have been it, for they must not die. At least, if they lived, nothing was irrevocable yet. There was still hope. He went to sleep arguing with himself, painfully aware of how hollow his words sounded.

Late that night Gabriel awoke. His eyes first took in the stars, which looked strange to him. They had rotated their positions, the familiar ones slipping from the sky while new ones came to take their place. He thought he had woken for no reason, until he realized that somebody was standing at the edge of the firepit, not more than ten feet away from him. The fire had died down to embers, but its faint red glow and the bone-white highlights cast by the stars illuminated the shape enough to give it form. He felt his pulse quicken. A tingling surged through his body, as if his blood had just come alive with tiny bubbles.

The man was hatless, his shoulders stooped. He teetered a little, cleared his throat, and lifted a bottle. The moonlight sparkled on the glass. There followed a sound that at first Gabriel couldn't place. It was a dry rasp, a gurgle, an expulsion of air just ordered enough to resemble speech. He listened, but it wasn't until the silence after the sound that he knew what it was. Caleb had spoken. Gabriel held so still that even his breathing ceased. He waited, and the voice came again. This time, with effort, he made sense of the sound.

"I could have you all." The man tilted the bottle again. After he'd drunk, he stood teetering once more. "All of you, right now."

Gabriel could just make out his eyes, thin crescents in highlight, but he couldn't tell where his gaze was directed. He tried to guess but was stunned by a realization that chilled him to the core. If he could see Caleb's eyes, then . . . He slammed his eyes shut. A moment later he heard an expulsion of air, a guttural noise, and two soft grunts. It took him a second to realize that the sounds put together made laughter. The bottle fell to the ground. There was a rustling of boots on earth, and then he knew that the man had moved away a few feet and collapsed.

Gabriel listened for any sounds to follow, but there was nothing except the whisper of a high wind and the men's snores. It was only after several minutes of tense awareness that he realized he was not the only one awake. He could just make out the outline of the girl, still upright, still staring before her, eyes and ears as alert as Gabriel's.

THE MORNING BEGAN WITH ARGUMENTS. Marshall protested the kidnapping of the girl. He said he cared not a lick for her well-being and liked the taste of her himself, but he figured they'd had her already and ought to just get moving. No use slowing themselves and giving some greasers an excuse to track them. Dallas and Rollins put up a united front, calling forth all possible strands of logic, from the improbability that anybody would even come upon the farm within the next month to lessons on the biological necessity of the relief the girl could offer. They'd already seen she could ride. Hell, in a day or two they'd probably have her cooking and doing the washing for them. Dallas even suggested that they could sell her once they got to California, thus earning hard cash to boot.

But in the end, Rollins responded with action rather than words. He strode over to the girl, reached around her shoulders, and yanked open the torn front of her dress, exposing her chest. His rough hands cupped the small orbs that were her breasts, and this brought a smile to his face. He squeezed them, measured the weight of them, looked up at Marshall, and said, "Tell me you don't want these along with us." He slid one hand down and cupped the spot between her legs. The girl twisted her head to the side and spat. She set her jaw, and that was all. "And this down here, sweet as a Georgia peach and you know it. Come on, Marshall, my yanker's been one swollen-up lonely son of a bitch for too long now. If we're going to hell, let's do it right, let's take a little pussy with us."

Marshall looked at the man with disgust. "I guess thinking with your head don't have anything to do with your outlook, does it?" Rollins didn't feel he needed to answer. Marshall's eyes drifted over to Caleb. He exchanged a long look with the man, then sighed. "I guess she ain't got much to live for anyway . . . But if some son-of-a-bitch Mexican comes hunting her, I'll serve you both up on a platter for him. Can't stand a man who takes a little twat that seriously. Makes me wonder if your mother loved you proper."

So decided, they broke camp and moved on, inconvenienced only briefly by Dunlop, who launched into a vitriolic tirade against the men and their actions. Marshall stripped off one of his own socks, stuffed it in the man's mouth, and bound it tight, saying, "There. Now don't eat it, Dunlop."

THE NIGHTS WERE COOL ON THE COLORADO PLATEAU. They rode across a rutted, butted, and sand-washed landscape five thousand feet above the sea. They were in a country open to sky, moving vulnerably beneath it, closer to God and more insignificant for it. The land they traveled through was thick with chaparral and creosote bushes. They stirred up pigeons and quail, which lifted into the air with raucous cries and, more often than not, flew in line with the riders. Dallas shot five of them before Marshall told him that he should think about saving his ammunition. He did for a few hours, until some jackrabbits proved too large a temptation for him. He shot three in the space of an hour.

For the first few days the girl did manage to slow their progress. She sat unresponsive in camp, had to be pulled to her feet and set in the saddle bodily. She was no longer blindfolded, and her hands were tied in front of her instead of behind her back, but she still refused to give her horse any direction. It would dawdle along at the end of its tether, following reluctantly. Every so often it would sink on its haunches and fight forward progress, once jerking Dallas, who was leading it, completely from the saddle. This happened so often on the second day, and so often at precarious moments for the lead rider—just mounting a ridge of slippery rock, just about to descend a slope—that Rollins finally deduced that the horse was acting on signals from the girl. From then on she rode James's horse and he hers. Thus they picked up the pace.

Gabriel kept his eye on James, who seemed less and less of this world. He no longer responded to comments thrown his way, no longer even met Gabriel's gaze. Instead, he stared blankly at the passing land and the creatures in it. It seemed he'd forgotten the most basic actions of life. Marshall had to shout at him to get him to move; more than twice Rollins slapped him across the back of his head in an attempt to get a response from him. Gabriel did what he could to help him along, hitching and unhitching his saddle, fetching him food at supper, and rolling out his blanket in the evening. But he could tell that the boy's being was somewhere else entirely, and he knew that he must bring him back, that James must come back and face the here-and-now if he was ever to escape it. He whispered this to his friend in their rare moments of solitude, but if the boy heard, he gave no sign. His eyes stayed wide and quivering and nervous, like those of a mouse beneath the canopy of the night sky.

Gabriel never actually saw what the men did with the girl.

They'd lead her away one by one during the evening. At first they'd return cheerful and boastful, teasing Gabriel and James about not being invited to the party. Dallas couldn't help but demonstrate for the boys the way he'd "given it to her," thrusting into the air as if to damage it. Even Caleb led the girl away occasionally. Rollins bubbled in protest at this but couldn't muster the courage to voice it and shrugged it off instead, saying she was just a brownskin anyway.

But as the days passed, the mood changed. Rollins began to return from his sessions with the girl with a strange look in his eyes, a bewilderment that he gave no voice to and that he tried to soothe with whiskey. By the third day Dallas stopped his boasting, and by the fourth he even passed up his nightly indulgence. Always the girl returned to the fire as stony-faced as before, stiff-backed, expressionless, and distant.

WHEN THE SON LOOKED DOWN UPON HIS HOME with his companion, his heart was light. He turned to his friend and spoke, telling him how he would now meet his sisters and he'd see that they were the most beautiful girls in all of the Spanish-speaking world. There was something of the flavor of Mexico in him, and of Spain and that country's ancient vaquero traditions. He wore Chihuahua spurs and dark pantalones and a low-brimmed black hat with crimson needlework decorating the band. His face was tan and handsome and warm still from the touch of a young woman in Santa Fe, a woman he decided he loved, although he'd yet to tell her this.

As he descended toward the house, a strange feeling came over him. The stillness of the place made no sense, as it was midday. He checked his horse and angled slightly, moving around toward the front of the house. Then he saw them. He thundered down at a gallop, calling out for his family members by name and relation. The buzzards around his father's body took flight with cries of protest, like avian undertakers disturbed at their rightful work. The son was off his horse before he'd even stopped it, slipping over its shoulder and hitting the ground at a full run. He bent to his father and just as quickly drew back from him. The man lay on his stomach, with his cheek resting on the ground, but even so the son could see that he had no eyes. He could see from the shredded material of his clothing where the birds had stuck their grotesque heads into his body.

Just then another bird plodded out of the house, stood teetering in the doorway like a drunken glutton, and took flight. The son was inside in four great bounds. What he saw there sent up a howl of pain like none that either his companion or the horses had heard before. The son's friend tried to enter the house, but the son pushed him out, saying it was not for his eyes to see them so. He asked him to ride back to Santa Fe. He didn't tell him why, and the man didn't ask, because he knew already.

Through the afternoon, the son worked on the bodies of his mother and sister. He bathed them as best he could, laid them out upon their beds, and pulled their blankets up to their chins, as most of the damage done to their bodies began below the neck. He brought his father inside also, and he burned candles for them all, praying as if he still believed in God. After that, he walked out to the river and sank into its water on all fours. He purged himself into the flowing current and knelt there long after in silence. In this silence was a misery too loud to pronounce, and within that misery was a chaos of thoughts such as a man should never have. He wished to quiet them.

Before the sun set that evening he had found the riders' tracks. He knew the direction they rode and their number and guessed that they had only three days on him. He recognized the shoes of the gelding and understood then that it was not only for the dead that he must mourn. While he awaited his companions, he shot three

buzzards from their circular flight and set their bodies aflame,
asking God to do the same with their souls.

IN FOUR DAYS THEY COVERED ALMOST TWO HUNDRED MILES
and saw no other human beings. On the afternoon of the fifth
day they bisected a wide expanse of open mesa, the soil clothed
almost uniformly with short fat shrubs, small plants abloom with
pale white flowers. That evening they stopped early and set the
horses to graze. Rollins blindfolded the girl again, and the men
slipped naked into the creek near camp and washed the filth off
their bodies. Gabriel had to be instructed to do so by Marshall,
but once in the chilly, forgiving water, he felt some of the tension
within him slip away. He imagined the water could wash him
clean, could not just soothe his skin but enter into him and ease
away the stains, the pain, the guilt that wrapped around his heart
and slowed its beating. He closed his eyes and tried to quiet his
thoughts.

When he opened his eyes the sun was setting. From where he
sat, in a small bowl of water, it seemed to be dropping directly
into the pool with him. He wondered if this was what the sunset
looked like in California, wondered if he'd ever see that place, or
see his family again, or ever again feel that his life was in his own
hands.

As if in answer to some of these questions, Marshall came into
view. He spotted Gabriel and walked toward him, barechested
and seeming larger than usual. He carried a metal canteen in one
hand. The skin of his chest was thin and opaque, pink and,
despite the girth of his torso and the muscles clearly outlined
there, somehow fragile. Gabriel realized he'd never seen the man
shirtless, and something about it struck him as obscene. He
turned his gaze down to the dark water in which he sat.

Marshall sat down at the edge of the pool. He slipped one

bare foot into the water. Dirt and debris floated away from it. He
fingered the canteen, then lifted it absently to his mouth and took
several large gulps. The wince that ran across his face and the
way it eased into a sort of relaxed pleasure indicated to the boy
that the canteen was full of whiskey. Marshall wiped the back of
his hand across his mouth and sat contemplating the reflection of
the sky in the water's surface.

"You think killing's wrong, don't you? That's what's got you
acting so damn high and mighty. You gonna tell me you never
thought of killing someone yourself?" Gabriel didn't answer, but
the man didn't seem to expect him to. "What if somebody raped
your mother? What if some lanky, no-toothed son-of-a-bitch
Confederate tied you to a pole and made you watch while he did
it to her? Had her get on her knees like a dog." Marshall paused
and allowed the boy to form the image. He met the boy's eyes
this time and waited for an answer. "Wouldn't you track the bastard down and put a bullet through him?"

"I might—"

"You might?" He offered the boy a drink. Gabriel started to
refuse, but his hand seemed to rise from the water of its own
accord and grasp the metal canteen. "Shit, I know you better'n
that. You wouldn't even need a gun. You'd beat the living shit out
of him with your bare hands. You got an anger in you just like all
your race. Rightly so. All it takes is enough anger. Put the right
person through the right ordeal, and they'll kill faster than they
can think."

Gabriel took a drink. He surprised himself, not actually knowing he was going to do so until he felt the thick liquid sliding
down his throat.

Marshall looked up at a thin line of birds passing above them,
then continued. "Yeah, I reckon anybody's been born out of a
woman can understand that. But if you're gonna say that killing
somebody is wrong, then it's got to always be wrong. It don't get

right just cause they deserve it, does it? And it don't get wrong just cause they don't deserve it. You following me?" The man motioned for the whiskey and took another swallow. "Shit. You ain't following me. I ain't even following myself. That's a problem I developed lately. When I was your age, I used to have notions that made some sense, but then I grew up, and I saw more than my share of things, and then sense got plain thrown out the window, along with God and all his lick-spittle little angels. I'll tell you something. Listen here. We'll see if I can't add a little more clarifying confusion to your thoughts." He motioned Gabriel closer and told him a tale he said was of his youth, a thing he'd seen with his own eyes and knew to be truer than most things he'd seen since.

While a boy, he'd worked on a ranch outside Austin owned by a man named Clemmins. This Clemmins was a strange man in Marshall's eyes, was then and always would be. He had an avowed faith in Christianity, something that he pressed on his men, so losing many of them to less religious operations. One spring a traveling preacher came through, calling himself a missionary and intent on continuing the work the Spaniards had begun with the natives to the south. He stayed a fortnight, drank with Clemmins, and talked of religion and God and the destiny of mankind. When he left, he was full of zeal; two months later he was dead, scalped and robbed of everything on him.

When Clemmins heard this news, he went into a murderous fury. He hunted the lands of the murder with his men, never tiring, hungry to avenge the man of God. It so happened that he and Marshall were out alone one afternoon when they came upon the camp of a stray Indian, burning a low fire that let off almost no smoke. There was perhaps nothing unusual about this, but to Clemmins it was a hint of guilt. The two rode in. The Indian jumped up and started to run, stopped and came back and began talking to them in Spanish. Clemmins leveled his

shotgun at the man and asked him if he knew the padre who had
been killed. The man took a moment to answer, and in this hesitation Clemmins saw guilt. He drove the man to his knees, then
had him lie spread-eagled on the ground, and before long he had
him tied and bound to a tree. "Bit like you were back at
McKutcheon's," Marshall added. He nudged Gabriel playfully
on the shoulder.

Gabriel looked away and caught sight of Dunlop, who had
just climbed up from the hollow in which he'd bathed, hands
still tied behind his back. He met the boy's gaze from a distance
of a hundred yards, then walked on to camp. Gabriel lost the
thread of Marshall's story for a moment, but when he picked it
up again, it had turned worse than he could have imagined.

"He made a slit about four inches long in the red's belly. Cut
right through to the insides." Marshall demonstrated where on
his own body, then went on to tell how Clemmins reached in and
probed the man's insides with his fingers, watching his face the
whole time, poking him, watching the pain writhe across his features in spasms, his living hand within the man's living body. He
asked him did he remember it now, was it coming back to him,
was he a filthy red murderer and was he regretting it now? That
hand found what it was looking for, paused for a moment; then,
with one tremendous effort, he yanked from the man's body a
loop of his small intestine. He got a bit of the stuff out into the
open air, with the Indian screaming and convulsing and watching
Clemmins tug his life out of him. Clemmins stopped when a
good portion of the man's insides had been pulled through the
incision. He stepped back, pleased by his actions, looking from
the Indian to Marshall with a grin of pure joy. But he was not finished yet.

"He told me to pull the man's trousers down. I thought I
couldn't do that, wouldn't do that, but when a man like that tells
you to pull, you pull."

Marshall did as he was told, an awkward job what with the man's dangling, bloody intestines. In the end he used the knife to cut the cord that held the Indian's trousers up, and he pulled them to the ground. He returned the knife to Clemmins and watched as the man handled the Indian's privates, measuring their weight and texture and length. Gripping the Indian's penis in one hand and pulling it taut, Clemmins cut it from his body. The Indian flinched but could no longer cry out. It wasn't even obvious that he still knew what was happening to him. Clemmins held the member up in his bare hand, commented on the size and shape of it, then threw it away, losing it in a landscape of stone and sand. Clemmins nearly split himself laughing. They left the man that way, food for the scavengers of the night. Justice done.

"All this for a minister who should've left them people alone in the first place. What's worse is, they found the man who really killed the minister a week later. He wasn't even an Indian, was a halfbreed Mexican-American. Still had the minister's Bible with him. It had gold leaf, see, and that fool got it in his head that must be worth something, figured gold was gold." Marshall leaned back and contemplated the boy from a distance that suddenly seemed great. "What do you make of that? Don't that just seem like a right mistake on God's part?"

"I reckon."

"Damn right, you reckon. Clemmins claimed he was doing it all in God's name, and God never said a word against him, never said, 'Clemmins you're a right demented son of a bitch, and I don't want you cutting people up in my name.' Never said a thing like that. True enough, the man did come to a bloody end himself, but that ain't no surprise. He didn't die half as slow as some that he'd killed, or half as early." Marshall raised the canteen and smelled the liquor. He frowned, but whether at the smell of the whiskey or at his own thoughts was unclear.

"Anyway, what we done at Three Bars wasn't a big thing—wasn't no big thing at the Mexican's either. That's my point, even if I didn't make it properly. Truth is, God don't give a good goddamn who we kill here on earth. Never did and never will. So you shouldn't worry about it either. I'm not saying to go and make a habit outta gutting people. I'm just saying if you're gonna be anything in this world other than a dirt-poor nigger, you're gonna have to take a few things from some other people. There ain't enough of the good stuff to go around. So you take it—some gold from this one, some pussy from that one, a life from another. That's all there is to it. The devil's an iron horse, my boy. You either get aboard or you eat the lead."

The man rose, his foot stirring the water, and drank once more. "As far as the girl goes, hell, she's just in training. She'll make more as a whore in San Francisco than she ever would've otherwise. She's a lot better off than her parents, that's for sure. You just gotta learn how to look at things the right way." With that he turned and moved off, leaving Gabriel with a mind full of new images to crowd out the old.

ON THE MORNING OF THE EIGHTH DAY out of Santa Fe, Caleb walked into camp as the others were sipping coffee. He sat down next to Marshall, took off his hat, and set it on his knee. He leaned close to the man and spoke his words directly into his ear. The others all went about their business, drinking coffee, picking bits of food from their teeth, looking over their saddles, but they watched the two men from the corners of their eyes.

Gabriel knew that Caleb had been out since before sunset. There was nothing new about that, but something in the man's movements made him uneasy immediately. He had just finished cutting James's bacon into bite-sized pieces, a chore he'd taken to over the last few days as the boy seemed weary of using the implements himself. He pushed a bowl toward him and told him to eat, then bent to his own meal.

He'd taken a few bites when Marshall tossed his coffee into the fire. "If that ain't perfect, I don't know what is. Get up, y'all. We're being tracked. And they're making time on us."

"Son of a sodomite!" Dallas said. "Are you kidding me?"

Marshall stood up and waved his coffee cup in the air, drying it. "Dallas, you ever heard Caleb kid?"

The boy thought about this for a moment and answered candidly. "No, I ain't never heard Caleb say nothing, to tell the truth."

"Well, I have. He figures we've got a day and a half on em."

"Day and a half?" Rollins asked.

"No more than two, but seeing as how they're closing in faster than a hungry coyote chasing a plump hen, we best make our plans fast and quick."

Marshall began to gather up his things, but the others were perplexed, Rollins more so than any. "Now, hang on a second. That don't sound right. Not by a jugful, it don't," he said. "If they've been tracking us all the way from Texas, how come we've just now noticed them? We done put in hundreds of miles without no sign of anybody. And nobody would track us this far into the territory just for killing Rickles and that whore. That's for damn sure."

This seemed to give the men pause. Marshall pursed his lips and mumbled something that sounded like agreement, then fell silent, contemplating the situation at a different angle. Gabriel was more surprised than anyone to hear James's voice, cracked and raspy but loud enough to be heard by all. "Could be the Mexicans. Cause of what you done to them and the girl." He didn't raise his eyes from the food in his lap, and after speaking these words, he began eating again.

Gabriel noticed the girl's eyes flick toward James. She took him in in one quick glance, as if it was the first time she'd done so, then she looked back down into her lap, letting her black hair fall before her face.

"Well, I'll be damned! The Lazarus speaks. I feel honored." Marshall smiled and looked around the group in amazement. His gaze settled on Dunlop. "Maybe next we'll hear from Jesus Christ himself. You got anything to say, Messiah?"

Dunlop's gag hung around his neck, but traces of it were clearly to be seen in the indentations running across his cheeks. He looked at Marshall directly when he answered. "Yes, I have something to say. I hope they hang you."

Again Gabriel saw the girl look up, at Dunlop this time. She looked down again before anybody else noticed.

"If it comes to that, they might hang you too."

"That's fine, so long as they hang you first, so I can watch."

Dallas stepped toward the Scot as if to strike him, but Marshall discouraged him with a wave. "Don't get riled, Alabama. I like a man who speaks his mind. And, yeah, a pack of greasers could be trailing us. The man did say he had a son. For that matter, it could be on account of that damn fool at McKutcheon's. There's more than one son of a bitch out there with a grudge against us."

Dallas pushed his hat up high over his brow, a position Marshall often favored. "I'm not even thinking bout who the hell it might be—I'm thinking, how can Caleb see them if they're two days away?" He looked at Caleb and cast his voice a bit lower than usual. "You see somebody's fire? And if you did, how you know they're after us?"

Again it was Marshall who answered. "He didn't see them."

"What?" This was too much for Dallas. "I don't mean no disrespect, Caleb, but damn. Shit. You had me worried. I don't know what planet you from, but right here on earth we don't say someone's after us till we got good reason. Shit."

Caleb stared at him.

"Hold your shits, Dallas," Marshall said. "I don't reckon Caleb's wrong. You don't have to understand it, just have sense enough to believe it. So let's say some son of a bitch is trailing us." He waved away Dallas's protests. "Let's just say that's so. We still got a decision to make. We gonna hightail it away? We gonna set ourselves up and ambush em?" He paused and looked around the group.

Dallas cast his vote: "I'll ambush em, if they ever existed anyhow." He drew his pistol and pointed it in the air and almost fired. He checked himself at the last minute and burst into laughter. "That's right. That's right. Gotta save them bullets. Might be somebody following us." He pretended to look around cautiously, then fell to laughing again.

But the other men voted to ride. Marshall ordered the boys to their horses and nudged Dunlop with his boot, saying, "Get up, Scotland. You're an outlaw too." But the man didn't move immediately. The Scot's eyes were turned to the horizon once more, with a different sort of hunger this time. Try as he might, Gabriel couldn't figure out how to read this gaze.

THEY CROSSED THE UPPER REACHES OF A BRANCH of the Colorado River that morning and rode into a landscape that changed again. The mountains before them rose like sand blankets draped around skeletons of rock. As they came closer, Gabriel could almost believe they were the ancient carcasses of some giant creatures—backbones, ribs, limbs, and digits stretched out and decaying beneath a godawful sun that followed them and beat down as if to warn them off.

They rode fueled by fear of the unseen hunters behind them. No man save Caleb was sure of their presence, but all pushed onward just the same. They didn't gallop for fear of overheating the horses, but they pushed them at a speed that sorely tested their endurance. The pursuers might have been little more than a notion at first, but after a day they all woke up with this notion woven into the fabric of their dreams, making it much realer during their waking hours. Gabriel noticed that each member of the party had his own way of looking behind him. Marshall tugged the brim of his hat down on his forehead and stared back at the land with humorless candor. Rollins rode with his body almost sidesaddle, eyes probing the land. Dallas would canter along, conversing loudly and casually, then wheel his horse around as if he could surprise their pursuers. James and Dunlop and the girl shared a silence on the subject, but each of them could be seen taking in the land with wide sweeping gazes that seemed as hungry as they were desperate. Caleb ignored their pursuers altogether during the waking hours, disappearing only at night on his solitary missions. As for Gabriel, he tried not to look back, but he couldn't help doing just that, searching with hope or fear—he was never sure which—and finding nothing save land and more land.

The chaparral became sparser. Saguaros grew up instead, strange, multilimbed figures standing in the distance. Prickly pears, yuccas, and cushion cacti all dotted the landscape. After two days in the mountains, Gabriel felt his body had become a pincushion. Everything in this country, it seemed, came armed with thorns and stingers. Each rock seemed to hide something venomous. He twice found scorpions in his boots and once woke eye to eye with a spiny lizard. And more times than he could count, their horses stirred up the now familiar whir that was a rattler.

He fought to keep James with him, but the boy showed little improvement. The emotional toll was starting to show on his body. His thin frame grew gaunter each day, his cheeks hollower, nose thinner, each of his features more and more measured by its

simple geometry—skin on bone, flesh over muscle. His lips had
long ago chapped beneath the sun, and one of his only movements over the long days became the frequent probing of them
with his tongue, wetting them again and again, like a lizard testing the air. But his saliva simply sped the drying process.
Sometimes when Gabriel prompted him to eat, he noticed
creases of blood as the boy chewed. James showed no sign that
this caused him any pain, or that he was even aware of why he
was eating. Only Gabriel's efforts made him eat at all, and
Gabriel knew things couldn't continue like this for long. It
seemed the boy wouldn't last another week, much less survive
this trek turned flight across desert, mesa, and mountain.

ONE EVENING THEY CAMPED IN A WEST-FACING CAVE beneath
a tall shelf of rock. Dallas spotted a herd of peccaries, small
piglike creatures, grazing in a ravine. Against Marshall's advice,
he climbed down the rocky slope and disappeared. Gabriel
heard the echo of five shots, and a half-hour later Dallas
returned, scuffed and scratched and sweaty but dragging two of
the creatures at a rope's length behind him. For the first time in
several days they built a large fire and sat around it to enjoy the
smell of fresh-killed meat.

Rollins complained that the peccary meat was coarse and hard
to chew, and furthermore a little hairy for his liking, but he ate a
fair share of it. Marshall said he liked it fine: "Puts me in mind of
dog." Dallas challenged him to name the place and date when
he'd eaten dog meat, but Marshall just smiled, said he'd eaten
worse things than dog in his time, and would proceed no further
on the subject.

Gabriel cut a plate of meat for James, but neither boy had the
hunger to consume it. Gabriel's eyes nervously flicked over the
walls of the cave around him. He saw shapes within the sand-

stone contours, creatures and spirits and other things, but he
couldn't tell if it was just the play of the firelight against the
wavering stone or if they were images conjured out of his own
mind. It was Marshall who provided the answer.

"Those are Injun drawings. I see you thinking about it,
Archangel. Your mind ain't playing tricks on ya." He stood up and
pointed with a half-consumed leg. He traced over the lines only
partially there, giving them shape as he spoke. "This here's a deer.
That's something looks like a buffalo, although I doubt there were
ever buffalo in this territory. And see that, you know what that is?"
He motioned toward a creature on the far wall. "You ever heard
the word *conquistador*? I don't figure you have, cause that's not in
the average black boy's education. But that there is a conquistador.
One of the first so-called white men to enter this country. Bunch of
damn fools, the whole lot of them. Thought they'd find themselves
a mountain of gold around here and save their souls at the same
time. Spent years hunting for the stuff, making good Christian
slaves out of all the redskins they didn't kill straight away. They got
themselves a good many pieces of Indian pussy while they were at
it." He looked at Rollins and smiled. "Fucked em so hard and long
they damn near wiped out the race."

"That's the way I'd do it."

The two men talked on, occasionally interrupted by questions
from Dallas, who seemed to take quite an interest in the conquis-
tadors. Gabriel only half listened, still studying the image and
finding in it nothing human. It was a creature with four legs, with
a stout, amorphous circle of a body and two protrusions that
might have been heads. Around it were rings of wavering red, as
if the creature were encased in circles of fire. Gabriel could make
no sense of it, and he saw nothing in it to match Marshall's
words, only a chaos that began in a time that he couldn't even
fathom. He turned from it uneasily and again picked up the
men's conversation.

"I say we're carrying too much dead weight," Rollins said. He didn't look at the boys when he spoke, but Gabriel understood immediately the turn the conversation had taken. "Can't expect to make time when half the group ain't up to it."

"I second that," Dallas said. He took a quick swig of mescal and tossed the canteen toward Rollins. "I second that, for damn sure."

Marshall turned this over in his mind. "Could be you got something there," he said at last. "We ain't exactly shoveling coal up the devil's ass, if you know what I mean." He waited, but none of the others indicated whether they did or not. "But you could look at it another way. You could figure the larger the force, the stronger. Maybe give these two coloreds some arms and let them fight along with us. Y'all would like that, wouldn't ya?"

Rollins didn't give the boys time to answer. "You must've lost the little bit of sense you was born with. One of them boys is as useless as a lame horse, other one'd probably put the bullet in you himself."

"Rightly so," Marshall said. "Wouldn't blame him if he did. But I don't think the Archangel's that type of nigger. I think he's more the faithful dog type." He turned and scrutinized Gabriel for a long moment, then rose with the energy of sudden inspiration. "I'll prove it, too," he said. He strode over to his saddlebags, rummaged around while the others waited in silence, and finally came back into the light of the fire. Upheld for all to see was a tiny nickel-plated gun, barely large enough to fill his palm. "This here belonged to the old heifer herself. Some say it's a whore's weapon, but I figure a derringer will kill a man as quick as anything else. Here you go, boy, arm yourself." He tossed the gun toward Gabriel, who snatched it out of the air with a defensive motion, then set it down just as quickly on the sand before him. "Keep it," Marshall said. "Just remember not to shoot your load too soon. Hear? Wait till you see the whites of their eyes."

This set Dallas to laughing. He clapped his hands as if somebody had suddenly struck up a tune, repeating "the whites of their eyes, whites of their eyes" as if the phrase were a song in itself. Rollins was none too sure about it. He began to caution Marshall, but then he gave up in disgust and stalked away.

Gabriel felt someone's eyes on him. He looked up into the frank stare of the Mexican girl. It was the first time she'd looked directly at him, and it made his heart beat faster. There was an openness in those sad, beautiful eyes that he'd never glimpsed, as if they were two small portals into a world as yet unimagined. He saw that there was also a question, a whole host of questions, etched in the lines that creased her forehead. And further, as his eyes began to water from an unblinking stare, he read a challenge written in her tight lips. Then she lay down on her side, eyes blank once more.

Before long Marshall moved away from the fire. He settled himself against the wall of the cave and whispered a song just under his breath. He sang just softly enough that Gabriel couldn't hear the words, and just loudly enough that he couldn't escape them. Gabriel looked down at the pistol before him, a tiny thing, inanimate although lit by moving firelight. He could still feel it in his hand, the coolness, the weight, the corrugated roughness of its handle. He didn't pick it up, but neither did he move away from it.

The boy pushed a half-burned log further into the fire, slowly regaining his calm, easing his heart. His eyes fell on Dunlop, who lay on the other side of the fire, on his side, hands still tied behind his back. His head rested at an odd angle, as if he were relaxed in an awkward sleep, but his eyes met Gabriel's as if they'd been waiting. He mouthed a word.

Gabriel craned forward, feeling the heat of the fire on his chin. The man repeated the word and added a few more. Gabriel shook his head. His eyes darted over to Marshall, but he was turned the other way. "What?" Gabriel whispered, but Dunlop still didn't speak aloud. He watched the boy with a face of complete sorrow. It was sadder, Gabriel thought, than the face of a dying man. Dunlop nodded, as if he heard the boy's thoughts. He turned away from the fire and curled into himself and spoke no more.

As Gabriel stretched out to sleep, he slid his hand over the derringer. He didn't pick it up, but he cupped it within his palm, between his flesh and the sand, and slept holding it in partnership with the earth.

THE SCOT LED HIS HORSE AWAY in the quiet, dead hours of deep night. He held the reins twined tight in the fingers of his bound hands, taking small steps and placing his feet lightly on the earth. He asked the horse for silence, but the creature seemed to know already that this was called for. It made no noise but looked with round, anxious eyes back toward the sleeping men.

Thirty minutes later, the man found a ridge of rock about waist high. He led the horse beside it and asked it to stand still. He scrambled up unto the shelf. A second later, he was astride the horse. He gripped it with his knees and urged it forward. He did his best to head to the east, galloping across the flats and letting the horse pick its way through the chaparral groves. He spoke to his horse, asking it to help him have strength, telling it that he had feared for so long his head was clouded with the stuff and he couldn't think straight. He asked it to help him think, to give him speed, and he promised it that this was not flight. That it could not be flight, because he had too many cords binding him to others, too many things incomplete.

He rode on through the dawn, hatless, his brown hair flapping with the breeze against him, up and down with the motion of the horse. His face was red in the sun's light, stern, coppered by it as if

he were made of that metal. Never before had the world looked so
bleak to him, so crimson and aflame and pockmarked and lonely,
so much like hell. He thought of things he hadn't thought of in a
long time, of family dead and buried, of days spent in another
land, and of times when the burdens on his soul had been but the
yearnings of a child. Those times seemed filled with sadness, and
he wondered why he hadn't realized it then.

He clucked to his horse and urged it to greater speed.

GABRIEL AWOKE TO A COMMOTION IN CAMP. Rollins was cursing and Dallas was looking around with sleepy eyes and Marshall
was laughing. "That cheeky bastard," he said. "Everybody up.
We got us a runaway."

The men sought out Dunlop's tracks from where his horse
had been staked and saw that he had led it away on foot, only
mounting up about a mile away, with the help of a shelf of rock.
It was obvious that he was still hand-tied. But it didn't matter.
He was away.

Marshall seemed more amused than angered by the whole
thing. Dallas wanted to ride out immediately, but Marshall said it
could wait a bit. Rollins said he didn't give two shits what happened to Dunlop anymore. He figured he'd end up dead anyway,
a hand-tied idjit out in the wilderness, maybe heading straight for
a posse that was out to kill him. "To my mind, he's as dead as if I
shot him myself," Rollins said.

Marshall heard him out but seemed less sure of Dunlop's
demise. He said he'd hired the Scot himself, and he didn't hire
fools. "But still. Some things can't be helped. Dallas, that idea of
yours about Hawaii's sounding better by the minute."

It had taken James the entire length of the conversation to
process the most fundamental aspect of the news. "He's gone?"
He spoke through cracked lips, looking from one person to the

next as if seeing them for the first time, checking each one to confirm what he'd thought he heard. "He's gone?" His eyes settled on Gabriel. "Gabe, he gone and left us? He didn't do that. Did he? He . . . He . . ." The boy struggled to his feet, a wide-eyed and crazed intensity suddenly taking him over. "He's leaving us to die?"

Rollins strode over to him, saying, "Shut your mouth, boy. We got things to think about." With one movement he kicked James's legs from under him, sending him sprawling. He turned and resumed his conversation.

James was up in a second. Faster than Gabriel had ever seen him move, he ran toward the man's receding back, jumped, and landed with his hands like claws in Rollins's neck. He tore at the man's flesh with his fingers, dug his heels into his sides, and pounded him with the full force of his body.

But only for a few seconds. Rollins spun with the boy on his back, grabbed him with one hand across his collar, and threw him to the ground with a force that completely knocked the air out of him. He lashed into the boy's face with his boot, kicking like a man possessed as James writhed in a cloud of dust.

Gabriel rose to his feet unsteadily, for the first time able to grasp the possibility of his own death. It grew as suddenly within him as James's anger had. If he had to watch this in order to live, life was not something he wanted anymore. Let him die and let this end. So he thought, and with this thought he asked his legs to carry him forward. But something happened before he'd even taken a step.

He didn't see the girl move, but somehow she slipped like mercury into the whirlwind of violence. She placed herself between the man and the boy and looked up at Rollins with a defiance that gave the man pause. She yelled something at him in Spanish. Rollins backed away, but only long enough to draw. His gun appeared in his hand as if it had always been there, and he aimed it pointblank at the boy's head and told the girl to get the hell out of the way or she'd die on the spot. Only then did Marshall caution him to stop.

"Why can't I kill him? Kill them both, for fuck's sake. Marshall, he done scratched my neck. Not to mention that he's a damn fool nigger that never should've been with us in the first place and will probably get us killed."

"One could say the same about you—the damn fool part, I mean," Marshall replied. "Leave him for now, Rollins. Just do it, cause I said so. You already kicked the tar out of him, and it's your fault the girl's here in the first place."

"And I wish we had never brought her. She ain't even a decent fuck no more. She just lies there hating ya, looking away like yer not even doing it to her. Goddamn, she makes ya feel . . ."

"Dickless? Makes you feel like you ain't even got a pecker and are no more a man than one of them Chihuahua rats is a dog? I know the feeling. And it's a neat trick. But put your fucking gun away and let's talk."

Rollins did reholster his pistol, but he only managed to control his anger by venting it on an unburned log. He stamped the thing till it broke in half and then kicked one section of it till it rolled down the ravine and out of sight.

The girl helped Gabriel tend to James. His trembling face was bloody and smeared with dirt. Rollins's boot had bruised and sliced the flesh open in several places, and the boy's lip had been cut so deeply that blood ran down his chin. The girl said something to him in Spanish, got him to meet her eyes, and so convinced him to let his face be cleaned. She touched him gently, her bound hands still skillful enough to know the proper motions to clean his wounds best. Gabriel watched her, following the directions she gave with her eyes, fetching water when she asked, scrounging up a plate of food. Together they calmed James and made him eat. James's eyes were wary, but beneath the girl's care he grew less anxious than he'd been for some time.

Before long the men decided to damn Dunlop and just ride.
Marshall ordered the boys and the girl to mount up, but he
stopped Gabriel as he prepared to saddle his horse. He held him
at arm's length and stared him down. The boy held his gaze for
as long as he could, then lowered it.

"You need to be tied too? I see you sulking and thinking and
plotting things out. But you ain't gonna give me any trouble, are
you?"

Gabriel tried not to answer, but eventually he moved his head,
a motion that might have been a nervous tic but that passed as
a no.

"Good. You boys don't need to give us no trouble. You all
ride on with us like you're doing and you'll be rich men soon.
You hear?" He shook Gabriel by the shoulder and moved his
face into the boy's line of vision. "Some of that gold's yours. You
can do with it what you want, but try and do us like Dunlop's
done, and you're as dead as he is. Deader, I suppose. Where I
come from, niggers die slower than whites and in a hell of a lot
more pain. I'm a camel's hair from shooting the whole lot of you
and doing this on my own. Believe me." He released the boy's
arm and called to the others to mount up.

THE MEXICAN SAW THE LONE HORSEMAN *from a half-mile out.*
He stopped his men, and together they watched him. He asked the
man beside him what he saw, and the man told him, confirming
that his own eyes were not in error. He led his men forward slowly.

The horseman stood on a sandstone ridge as the Mexicans rode
up. They paused before him. No greetings passed, but the men
watched each other and waited.

You were with them?

The man answered that he was.

Have you come to me to die?

That was not my intention.

Were you part of their crime?

The man answered that he felt some guilt because he had been there and had been unable to stop them but that no, he had not taken part in the crime. He wished with all his heart that it had not happened, and he prayed for the family's forgiveness.

The son cocked an eyebrow. He studied the man closely: his honest, sun-reddened face, the deep hurt in his blue eyes, the slope of his shoulders. He had not expected one of them to look like this.

Why are your hands tied?

The man told him. The others sat silent, looking between the stranger and their friend.

The son listened. He touched his mustache with his fingers, felt the give of the hairs against his skin.

You don't know what happened, do you?

The son helped the bound man dismount from his horse. He sat with him on the ground a little distance from the others, who watched with mistrustful eyes. The son told him the truth of his family, of their fate, and the other man, the Scot, dropped his head and cried and tried to speak but couldn't find the words. The son looked away and waited.

The Scot tried to find the words to share his grief over the other's loss, but again words failed him. The son nodded, but he said, *This thing that was done to my family was not God's work. It was not in the plan of his universe. It was something that God had no hand in. Sometimes man forgets himself and thinks he is God, but he is not, and nothing good can come of this. Sometimes the acts of man rip open wounds in the world that cry to be healed but that can't be. Perhaps they can only be bandaged. Maybe not even that.*

But you'll try?

I will. What would I be if I didn't?

They were silent for some time. The horses nearby cropped the

grass. The men watched them and watched the horizon and
smoked. Eventually the son rose and pulled a knife from his boot.
He asked the Scot about his missing sister; the man told what he
knew. The son breathed in the news, closed his eyes for a second to
control it, then knelt and cut the ropes that bound the man's hands.

Go with God.

He met the man's eyes and studied them, checking once more
that he was not making an error, then he turned and signaled
with his hand for the others to mount up. They did so, although
they cast glances at the young man and seemed to think that all
was not as it should be.

The son was astride his horse and had turned it to the west
before the Scot called to him. He turned. The Scot asked his ques-
tion. The Mexican nodded his answer and waited as the other
mounted up.

THE NEXT TWO DAYS PASSED IN A BLUR OF MOTION that
halted only late in the evenings. They'd come into a high, dry land,
baked by the unrelenting Arizona sun, through which only the
barren ghosts of rivers ran. Water had grown increasingly scarce
for some time, but now they found themselves eating up miles of
desert without the slightest sign of moisture. The horses had little forage. They all showed signs of fatigue. The girl's gelding
walked with tender-footed steps, and Rollins's black mare grew
too weak to ride. She was let loose in the wilderness, and Rollins
mounted the spare horse taken from the Mexicans. He rode away
without a backward glance. The horse watched them go, seemed
for a moment to consider following, and then decided against it.

Early that evening the group shared a few cans of tomatoes,
their juice more delicious than Gabriel had ever imagined. His
share was so small, however, that when they finally stopped, just
after midnight, he sat with a dry mouth, sucking what moisture

he could from the grease of bacon fat. The men had grown increasingly surly and taciturn. Rollins complained of a "stomping" headache. Dallas was a silent ghost of his normal self, although this had only partially to do with his fatigue and dehydration. Marshall had found out that Dallas had dumped some of their tinned tomatoes back at the Mexican homestead so he could use the space for mescal. He'd hit the boy hard enough to lay him out, then threatened to make him drink the foul liquid till he puked the stuff up and then make him drink it again.

None of the men showed any interest in the girl, and neither did they stop her from sitting with James and Gabriel, the only two with whom she voluntarily shared space. Once the men were all asleep, she roused the two boys, produced a tin of tomatoes, and shared it with them. She made sure that each drank slowly, and made it clear through gestures that James should let the moisture soothe his lips.

Gabriel thanked her, the first words he had actually spoken to her, but she shook away his thanks and hid the empty can. She slept between the two boys, again speaking with gestures that made it clear she would do so as long as neither of them touched her. They didn't, but as the night grew cool Gabriel swore he could feel heat coming off her body. He looked at her outline in the starlight and felt something for her that was not desire, something that was deeper, as if he saw in her all that he had ever seen of things kind, of things beautiful and feminine, and of God and mother. He felt no desire, save for the bone-deep longing for the world to be set right once more.

THE ENTIRETY OF THE NEXT DAY WAS SPENT EXPLORING a canyon that roughly followed their course west. The group dropped down into it with the hope of finding the stream that had carved it. But they found a dry creekbed choked with house-sized boulders. For much of the way the canyon was so narrow and jumbled that they couldn't even ride their horses but had to lead them instead. They climbed out of the canyon around dusk, seared and hollow versions of the people they had been that morning. The horses hung their heads low and sniffed the soil for moisture and shook their heads at the folly that had brought them here. James's horse threw a shoe coming out of the canyon. Gabriel had to hold her hind leg cupped in his armpit as Rollins chiseled away at the horse's hoof wall and then banged a new shoe in place with a fury that seemed a punishment. Dallas's pony watched the procedure, then stamped the ground with her right hoof as if demanding an end to this madness that very instant. But it didn't end.

That night the three adolescents again shared the evening's space. Again the girl made it clear she was not to be touched, and again she produced a can of tomatoes and shared it equally among them. James broke down crying as she fed him, the tears slowly progressing down his cheeks and into the corners of his lips. The girl smiled when she saw this and said something to him that she found humorous. But later she whispered to calm him, words of no lullaby and words that neither boy could understand but that brought some semblance of peace nonetheless.

AROUND NOON THE NEXT DAY they came upon three bowls carved by nature into a large, bare shelf of rock. They were each a couple of yards in diameter, a couple of feet in depth, and half filled with green, putrid water. The men thanked God and Satan both and drank it down like animals. They calmed the horses and let them cool off and allowed them to drink slowly. Once their canteens were full and each of them had drunk all he could take in, the men set out to destroy the water source. Dallas splashed around in the bowls, kicking the water into the wind, spraying it out across the parched granite and so exposing it to the heat of the sun. Before he left, he wrote his name in urine. They rode on, Dallas spitting into the wind and challenging their pursuers to follow them now to their own parched deaths.

That evening the girl indicated that she had no more tomatoes. She lay down as on the previous nights and Gabriel felt the closeness of her once more. As she whispered between the two boys, Gabriel stared out at the firmament, a canopy of stars brighter now than he'd ever seen before. Before long James fell asleep, his breathing a dry rasp that was painful just to listen to. Gabriel tried to listen to the girl instead and was surprised to discover that she'd begun to speak in English. The shock of it lasted only a second. He realized he'd always known she could understand them. Of course she could.

At first her whispers seemed strewn together in a meaningless string of recognizable words. It was only gradually that Gabriel began to understand her fully. She was telling them goodbye. She said that she believed in them, that she understood them. She said that they both wore their hearts on their faces and that their hearts were good. "I know that you are afraid and that you are good. You thank me for helping your friend, but it is not him I help. It is me. I help my soul. You must do the same. I help him now, yes, but when my time comes, I will go and not look back. You should do the same." She paused and lay still for some time. "You have a gun. One day . . . use it."

Gabriel turned over and looked at her. "I'm sorry . . . for what they did to you."

But the girl shook off his sorrow. She motioned with her hand that she didn't need this from him, then she stretched out a thin finger and touched his chest. "Your name is Gabriel, yes?" The boy nodded. "Then don't forget who you're named after. I have the name of the first woman that God created. Understand? They are the ones who will be sorry. They will all die."

Gabriel began to say something else, but she silenced him

with a finger. She touched it to his lips. "Sleep. My brother
comes for me tomorrow. Rest, Gabriel."

THE NEXT AFTERNOON THEY DESCENDED through a pass in
the hills and rode out across a wide plateau of scoured land that
stretched for miles in each direction. It was already late in the
day. The sky to the north had darkened with ominous roils of
gray clouds that seethed southward with a Biblical bulk. There
was a wavering line of darkness on the land far ahead, perhaps
twenty miles or so, which Gabriel knew to be a river. Beyond that
the land stretched out in all its barrenness to the horizon, where
there was only the faintest yellow hint of more mountains.
Gabriel knew that once out on that flat expanse, they'd be in
clear view through a full day of riding. If he knew this, the others
must too. But none commented or even slowed their horses.
They rode into this new terrain in silence.

    Two hours later they caught their first glimpse of their track-
ers, and for the first time the whole group understood the reality
of their situation. The trackers were no myth of Caleb's, nor were
they their own fears, no phantoms haunting their conscience.
They were a band of twelve, riding down into the basin and
across the plateau like a military phalanx. There was something
uncanny in their progress. They took chunks out of the land with
each passing minute, as if mounted on ever-fresh horses. They
rode with bold and undisguised vigor, like preordained mission-
aries who did not fear their own death for the glory of their cause
and were propelled onward to destiny with a knowledge unknown to the heathen. As they came on, so did the clouds,
laying a blanket of darkness across the plains and bringing with
them deep rolls of thunder as if the belly of the earth were hungry.

    "For fuck's sake!" Rollins said. "Can you believe this? Who
the hell are they?"

Marshall wheeled his horse and studied them, bringing the group to a sudden halt. "They ain't Texans, that's for sure. No Texan has that kind of religion." He spat, then looked down at the circle in the dust as if he regretted it. "Tell you what. Let's give them the girl. If it's her they're after, maybe that'll satisfy them."

"And if they ain't after her?" Dallas asked.

"Maybe she'll satisfy them anyway. Leastways, distract them a bit." He turned and looked at the girl. "It was a pleasure, miss. Consider yourself free to go. I think we'll be doing the same. Let's go. And that means you too, boys. If I were you, I wouldn't want to meet up with that bunch anyway. Off we go." He spurred his horse forward a few steps. The others started forward as well, but paused when Marshall did. He turned his eyes hard on the boys. "Come on."

Gabriel's and James's horses whinnied and moved forward a few steps, but still the boys didn't ride. Gabriel met the girl's eyes. She was calm, calmer now than ever. She sat almost serenely in the saddle, as wind whipped her garments about her and the clouds billowed. She held the hair that was blowing about her face with one hand and gestured with the other, a motion somewhere between a dismissal and an absolution.

"Go. I cannot say they wouldn't kill you."

Marshall looked at her wide-eyed. He cracked a smile and said, "I'll be damned. But you heard her, boys. They got killing on the mind. Let's not make it too easy for them." A moment later he was off, the others fast behind him.

"Go," she repeated.

This time the boys did as she instructed. Gabriel looked back often as he galloped. The girl never changed her position. She sat on the horse, growing smaller with distance, waiting.

The boys caught up with the group when they paused to study a canyon. It began as a small depression in the plateau but soon

narrowed and deepened and dropped out of sight. They rode
along its rim for another half-mile, then came abruptly to the river
that Gabriel had seen from the hills. But it was not as he imagined.
It was not a river to be forded but a canyon that dropped down a
hundred feet or more, with sheer sandstone walls that dizzied
Gabriel with their muted colors and fine, wavering designs.

Caleb rode out to the left, paused and studied the canyon, and
returned. He believed there was no way across and would be
none for many miles. They could ride along the rim and hope
that somehow this would lead them to something before the
horses died of thirst. Or they could drop down into the canyon
via the smaller one they'd ridden past. If they were held up there,
they could fight, perhaps, or find some route out.

Marshall looked from one to the other among the group, his
eyes for once not full of answers. There was a quivering tension
in his face, and he cast his vote for the canyon. For Gabriel, the
smell of fear from Marshall was more frightening even than the
sight of the riders behind them.

As the storm broke and rain fell from the sky in quarter-sized
drops, the group dropped down into the canyon. They had to
dismount and lead their horses, cooing to them and humming
and trying to keep them calm as they skittered and fought for
footing. The men slipped and bashed their shins on the loose
flakes of stone, and lightning lit the sky and thunder rolled across
the prairie like someone tossing out a blanket of stones. Gabriel
could barely keep his footing. His horse supported him as he
dangled and stumbled at the end of its reins and followed him
down out of a sense of obligation that had nothing in common
with its own wishes.

Soon the descent eased to a more gradual slope, but as it did,
the walls on either side grew higher, narrow and carved by the
workings of water into smooth organic shapes, so it seemed as
if they were descending into a living creature. The walls played

tricks with the already mysterious flashes of light, each bolt creating around them a moving landscape of contours. The horses didn't like it. James's horse began to buck. Gabriel saw it in brilliant, electric detail, the horse dancing from side to side, fighting against the walls, then kicking out behind it and lunging forward. The canyon darkened for a long moment of commotion, and when Gabriel could see again, James's horse was gone, having somehow bolted past the boy and pushed through the line ahead. James rose from the ground, sore, groaning, and cursing. He set out after the horse.

Feeling as though he were alone for a moment, Gabriel turned and looked past his own horse. Caleb stood only a few feet away, watching him, with his horse so close behind him that the creature's muzzle nearly rested on his shoulder. Gabriel moved forward again. A few hundred yards in and the walls gradually widened, enough that they could walk two abreast. The rain still fell steadily, and Gabriel noticed for the first time the water through which he sloshed. It was only ankle deep, but it rushed by him in a stream that seemed to increase in volume even as he watched. It was as if the earth, parched for so long beneath the sun, had forgotten how to absorb the moisture and was trying to shed it instead. He stumbled through it with careless feet, kicking them forward and trusting his boots to find their footing of their own accord.

Then they reached a dead end. The walls around them curved into a sort of bowl, twenty feet wide, facing a branch of the river, which rolled by in swirls of boiling current, mud-laden and brown like the walls around them. It seemed a different form of the same substance: rock turned to water, sand to flowing current. The horses shied and brushed against each other and looked around with wild eyes. The men let loose their headstalls and the horses bent to drink, only in this activity finding a moment of calm.

Dallas scrambled back up the canyon to keep lookout, and the men huddled in the rain and tried to think. None of them stated it, but they seemed of a single mind on one point. They had no wish to do battle with those twelve, not here, not like this, not with the rain pelting them and the horses wild and their hearts trembling with a terror they couldn't fully name. James stood close to the others, his eyes hard on each of the men as they spoke. He seemed to have forgotten his fear of these men and his loathing for their deeds. For a moment, he was united with them by a greater fear. Gabriel stood a little away from the others, watching the horses, the current of the river before them, and the walls of the canyon up to their brim, above which the sky had darkened almost to night. He thought of the girl as he'd last seen her. From where did her serenity come?

Dallas returned at a dead run, stumbling and tripping, moving forward more like a rolling boulder than a two-legged creature. "They're coming," he cried. The men were in motion instantly. They moved toward the horses, and as they did so, a clap of thunder brought its hand down on the canyon, sending a jarring rumble of echoes through the place. The horses grew frantic. One reached for another with its teeth; two others passed a few blurred seconds exchanging kicks. The men tried to separate them, to soothe them so that they could be ridden. But in the end Marshall yelled to just grab a horse and mount up, damn it, or die here. He was on a horse the next second, apparently having jumped from the ground and landed dead in the saddle.

In the flickering light, Gabriel watched him spur the horse into the water. The horse fought and neighed and would have balked, but Marshall's will was stronger. Horse and man entered the water, sank into it, and were swept away. Gabriel stood without moving, and it was only by accident that he caught a horse. The creature was running past him, up the canyon, and its reins brushed his hand. He grabbed them. The horse stopped, and

Gabriel mounted. He watched Dallas and Rollins go into the water, and it was only then, as they were swept downstream, that he knew what he could do.

As James entered the river, Gabriel felt a sudden desire to yell to him, to call him back. He didn't have the plan formulated clearly in his mind. It was only a vague notion of a possibility, and he needed extra seconds to think. But James's mount kicked free of the shore. The boy turned and shot a glance back over his shoulder. Gabriel didn't move. He met James's eyes, but he didn't beckon. He didn't call to him. He didn't gesture. It was too late for any of these things. He simply met his eyes and watched him slip away.

Caleb followed James's gaze back to Gabriel. It was just a momentary glimpse, and the next second he was in the current and moving. Gabriel almost followed, so strong had the touch of the man's eyes been, but when he heard a sound behind him he found his resolve once more. He moved the horse to the water, talking to it, asking for its strength and for its faith in him, and also calling silently to James to forgive him. They entered the water, and he turned the horse upstream.

At first Gabriel had to fight to keep the horse pointed into the current. It tried every few seconds to turn, but he yanked it back on course each time. To his surprise, the horse found some foot- ing. It strove forward a few good strides, water billowing off its chest, then it fell into deeper water. Gabriel shot glances behind him but could see nothing. It seemed they had already put a cor- nice of stone between him and the beach, although he scarcely thought this was possible.

His attention was drawn back to the horse as he almost pitched from the saddle. The creature had swum into a swirling eddy that sent the confused horse and boy circling in a strange flow of gurgling, recirculating water. Gabriel felt the horse fight- ing panic beneath him, trying desperately to sort out the currents and make sense of it all. In a moment between swells, it slipped forward again and crossed the main current. Gabriel thought for a moment that all was lost and that the horse was retreating. But the creature never turned the side of its body to the current. Instead, it ferried across the current at a slight angle, touched land, and a second later was up on a shore that Gabriel hadn't even noticed.

The horse didn't await further command. It bounded up a shallow wash, paused, and went on, slipping where it got steeper. Gabriel pitched forward in the saddle. The horn twisted into his abdomen, and as he called out in pain, he fell from the saddle, his foot tangled in the stirrup and his body dangerously close to the horse's frantic hooves. He rolled away, sprang to his feet, and was back with the horse in a second. He tried to stroke its muzzle, but the horse snapped its head up and bared its teeth. Gabriel gave it the full length of the reins and then led it forward until the ground sloped more gradually. He mounted again, and the horse pushed forward in a frantic set of strides.

Horse and boy burst into the open air of the prairie like creatures expelled from the earth by force. The horse paused, shocked by the sudden change. For a second, Gabriel thought that all was silence, but then he realized it was just the opposite—all was sound, the steady beating of the rain on the earth, of the wind across it. He shot a glance behind him but wasn't even sure he could see the wash through which they had traveled. He was sure of one thing: there was not a living person left on God's earth, not a living creature to be seen at all, save for the horse and himself.

A sputter of sheet lightning afforded a quick illumination of the land. Under its light, the boy realized for the first time why he'd felt so little control over the horse. It wasn't his horse. He looked down on the long silver withers and sharp ears of Marshall's dun. He spurred her forward and was off, fighting through motion the deep sense of foreboding that this realization left within him.

Part 4

FOR THE FIRST HALF-MILE THEY CLUNG TO THEIR EX-
hausted horses with little semblance of control. They bobbed and
swirled with the current, both men and horses fighting to keep
their heads above the waves. The torrent pushed them onward.
The walls rushed past on either side, adding to the chaos of speed
and amplifying the roar of the river, which was now the only
sound save for the muffled shouts of one man to another.

The blond man held the lead by a good forty yards. His eyes
were riveted downstream, but he realized too late that the flood of
water in which they flowed was not this river's main stem. He saw
the sky open before him, and as he rose on the crest of a wave, he
saw the junction of the two currents, this one and the larger one it
fed. When the rivers merged, the two currents tore into each other.
Both he and his horse were sucked under. He felt the horse slip
away from him, though he tried with all his strength to hold the

reins. *The current was a hand that pushed him down and twisted his limbs and rolled him over. It held him down long enough that he feared for his life, and then thrust him up to the surface. He turned and would have shouted to the rest, but he spat water instead of words.*

Each of the others hit the boil line and overturned just as quickly. Feet and hooves gashed the air, and then all went under. They were tumbled about like straw figures and came up gasping and as white as their skin tones would allow. The large man breached the surface with both hands raised above him as in supplication to God; the young man lashed out toward the air and broke into it cursing; the thin-chested black boy came up stroking toward one shore with all his might; the dark man in the rear only lost his horse for the space of a few seconds. Alone of them all, he seemed to find purchase on top of the water.

The horses swam for shore, but the current was swifter now and even more chaotic. The black horse reached a sieve of boulders and tried to mount them. It scrabbled against the stone with its shins but could find no footing. The water pushed against it, and its body buckled between two rocks and stuck fast. Another horse, the glossy-hued sorrel, scrambled onto a shelf of rock, but it was so crazed that it ran into the wall and slipped. Its hind legs twisted, and it came down against the edge of the shelf with a force that broke its back.

Having witnessed most of this, the blond man turned his gaze back downstream. He breathed deeply, and rode impassively through a train of twenty-foot waves, finding a rhythm within them and breathing each time he broke the surface, resting when he went under. Breathing and resting. So he rode them out. A half-mile further down, he crossed an eddy line. He swirled downward, but once more the depths found him distasteful. When he breathed again, it was in quiet water behind a jutting shelf of rock. He pulled himself halfway out of the river and collapsed. The black man and his horse joined him sometime later. They sat beside him and shared the dripping night in silence.

Neither of them knew the fate of the other three. They didn't see them swim around the bend and onward. The young man made it to shore by the sheer force of his cursing efforts. The other white man tried but could gain no control of his squat body. His long arms lashed out in a chaos of motion, and in the end he simply watched with wide eyes as he slid down a flume of water and into a wall of foaming backwash. It hit him in the face with a force beyond anything he would have thought possible. The down-rushing current flipped him over and pushed him to the bottom of the river. When he surfaced, he was blue and nearly dead and so exhausted he could not move his limbs. It wouldn't have helped if he could. He came up in water bubbling upstream. He was pushed back into the same flume. When he next hit the surface, he didn't try to breathe but only looked at the sky for a few seconds. The current pushed him down and let him up again and again, like a rag doll, like a toy meant to look human but that had never had, and would never have, a beating heart.

It was the black boy who swam the farthest. He slid along the canyon wall, his fingers searching vainly for a hold. He had just about given up in body and mind when the river calmed into a long pool of slow-moving water. He floated on his back, buoyant now that he'd stopped fighting. The evening's light dimmed; the clouds above him rolled on and spent their fury. He cried. Finally, after so many days under the weight of his own mind, he floated free of it. He felt himself wrapped within a deep, somber embrace that was beyond reason or conscious thought but was emotion wrung to its core, to its length and breadth, and left exhausted.

It was strange, he thought, floating like this, letting go like this. Strange that everything now seemed so clear. Stars appeared, and the boy watched the dancing play of their light across the river's surface. He found a beauty in this that was akin to no portion of *his soul. He knew now that he would not swim for shore. He thought of his friend and almost formed his name on his lips. If his friend could only feel what he now felt coming . . . If he could only know what it feels like to swim into the heavens.*

GABRIEL RODE AT A GALLOP as long as the light held. He slowed to a canter when he could no longer see the land before him or make any sense of directions, then eventually eased into a dull, halting plod. He could barely make out the highlights that were the horse's gray ears, and he could feel the animal's fatigue in her labored breathing and reluctant steps. But he wouldn't let her stop. All he thought of was movement. It seemed the only thing that could save him, and he rode the entire night, his eyes open and his mind alert. More than once he believed he heard pursuers. More than once he asked the horse to tread less heavily on the ground and to keep to herself her complaints and neighs.

By morning he had put fifteen miles between himself and the others. As the sun rose, he realized he'd crossed the great bowl and risen into a rugged, rust-colored wilderness of decaying hills and cacti. He was amazed that the horse had managed to pick her way through the thorny landscape, but he didn't pause to commend the creature. He didn't trust the distance. He didn't trust his own eyes. The coast was clear, not a soul to be seen, yet still, each time he turned his gaze forward, he felt riders at his back—which ones, why, and with what motive didn't matter. He must flee them all.

He kept it up all day, pausing only to water the horse at another fork of the Colorado River, a shallow canyon that proved not difficult to cross. The horse would have stayed by its waters, but Gabriel pushed her on. The afternoon took them into a landscape dotted with buttes and strewn with rocks. Water pooled in sulfurous depressions that made their progress a winding, uncertain one. The air was a rank substance, thick in the nostrils and more like a liquid than the thin gas it was meant to be. It attacked the boy's eyes and stung the back of his throat. But he pushed on, forgetting the land behind him and not even pausing to consider the land to come.

Gabriel remembered late in the afternoon that a horse could be ridden to death. He dismounted, suddenly aware that the creature had been pushed to the limit of her endurance and teetered at the edge of oblivion. She walked delicately on her left forehoof, and judging by the way she shook her head, she seemed to have trouble seeing. Gabriel led her on patiently, slowly, and yet unrelentingly. He wished her to live, but life meant movement.

The two camped that evening beside a shallow creek that held water only in stagnant pools between the rocks. It took Gabriel some time to find an opening deep enough to scoop up water with his hands. His fingers stirred up muck from the rocks, but he drank anyway, till he was bloated and exhausted from the effort of it. Only then, lying on his back and staring into the sky of early evening, with the horse still lapping at the water a few feet away, did he pause long enough to wonder what had happened to the others. Yes, he'd seen them drive their horses into a raging river. He'd seen the phalanx of riders closing in behind them, he'd felt the palpable fear in each man, and he'd cringed beneath the pressure of the downpour that sought to drown them all where they stood. But what had happened next? It seemed impossible that they could live through the moments to follow, and yet he could believe only so much as he'd seen. And he hadn't seen Marshall die, or Caleb. Those two might never die, at least not through an act of man.

Nonetheless, he believed quite completely that James was now dead. It had been written on his face for some time. He saw

James's face before him with a clarity beyond that of the actual moment, and he asked himself questions whose answers he already knew by heart. Had his eyes really been so torn by betrayal? Had he been so painfully aware of all that came before and all that would come to him in the next few moments? Was it death written there?

The horse raised its head and exhaled a long breath. Gabriel knew the creature was still saddled and waited to be tended to. But still he didn't rise. It seemed too great an action beneath the weight of the stars. He remembered once hearing a tale in which stars were the souls of men after death and the earliest stars to appear were the most recently passed. Looking at them now, he could believe this to be so. His eyes followed the appearance of one star, then another, the faint trace of a third, then a bloom in which the purple velvet of the night seemed alive with points of light. So many souls. He said a prayer for them all, knowing with a certainty beyond reason that one of those points was the soul of his companion.

He didn't fully mourn that night, but he knew he would some-day. That night, the future lay before him like an enormous ques-tion, a puzzle that he looked at from a distance that grew greater and greater as his fatigue overcame him. When he finally slept, he did so with a stony heaviness that was broken neither by the calls of the coyotes that swarmed around him to drink at the pool nor by the enormous rush of sound and movement that was the awakening of desert bats. They surged up from a cave mouth less than a half-mile from where he slept, circled in ascending spirals of thousands upon thousands of separate beings, then shot into the night air in a fury of hunger. When he rose the next morning, he would feel that during his sleep he had traveled very far in the company of a great host of beings.

THEY FOUND THE WHITE BOY SITTING on a rock at the edge of the water, shirtless, weaponless, horseless, and dejected. He turned as they approached. He spat.

Well, shit, if this ain't just perfect. You hombres know where a man can get a shirt around here?

The men didn't speak to him, other than to have him rise and climb out of the canyon at gunpoint.

Didn't figure you did.

The trek out took three hours. At the rim, the boy looked back down upon the river. Damn. He let his eyes follow its course as it meandered away in a bizarre, circuitous route, the canyon walls layering in on each other in dozens of colors and shapes, growing deeper with the passing miles and so stretching to the horizon like a disease eating into the land. The men prodded him to movement.

They walked another twenty minutes before they came to a simple camp. The son was there. He rose when he saw the boy and set down his coffee and walked to him. The son's face had aged in the past week. Lines furrowed his forehead, and the weight of mourning sat at the back of his eyes. His lips were parched and peeling. He touched them before he spoke.

Were you party to the murder of Diego Maria Fuentes?

Who?

My father. Mi padre y mi familia. Did you kill them?

Hell, no, I didn't kill nobody.

The son asked him who did, but the boy said he had no goddamn idea. The man did not believe him. The other men beat the boy for several minutes, and the man asked him again. He still had no goddamn idea, but he figured it might have been the nigger.

He's a murdering son of bitch if ever there was one. I ain't had nothing to do with that, though.

You believe it was the Negro?

The boy told him yes. He named the man and called him a stinking nigger.

Now can I go? He's probably dead down in that canyon anyhow.

The son asked him if he had defiled the girl along with the others. The boy was slow in answering. He said that he might've had a little poke but that it wasn't what the man thought.

The girl liked it when I did it to her. It was that hairy son of a bitch and the nigger that she didn't like. I always gave it to her gentle-like. Don't tell me you ain't never done the same.

But the son gave a signal, and one of the men knocked the boy unconscious with the butt of his rifle. When the boy awoke, it was to a stinging pain in his groin. His head heaved, and the world seemed skewed, and before he was conscious of anything else he was conscious of his own nudity. He was tied down on the desert floor, with his arms and legs pulled taut toward the world's four quarters by horsehair ropes that bit into his skin. The ropes were held in place by boulders, on each of which a Mexican sat watching. Between his legs was the conspicuous mound of an anthill. It was these creatures that had begun to attack the flesh between his legs.

The boy screamed out, first with pain, then with curses, then with pleas for mercy. He twisted and yanked at the ropes and thrashed his legs, but it was no use. He asked if he was to die this way, and they told him yes. He asked how long it would take, and they told him only a day or two. They watched him with cold black eyes, and not one of them seemed to feel the boy's pain, or care. They looked at him, then off at the horizon, with the indifference of men who had seen much worse. Two of them smoked; one bit his nails and spat the splinters to the wind.

The insects rose from the mound in great numbers, but they went to their work with a single mind, their pincers slicing into his flesh like the knives of so many whalers into a huge beast. The boy lay back, writhing in pain. He begged, but none moved; he

cried, but none even flinched; he cursed, but the men only watched.
Only when he whispered a woman's name did the son decide it was
enough. He rode up to him and, from horseback, placed the barrels
of his shotgun on the right portion of the boy's chest. The boy was
silenced with one blast, and mercy was awarded. The other men
looked at the son, but the son turned without comment. He caught
sight of the Scot and the girl coming toward them and rode out to
intercept them.

WHEN GABRIEL AWOKE FROM HIS FIRST LONG SLEEP, it was
midday and the horse was nowhere to be found. The boy viewed
this fact with quiet eyes and set out to find her. As she had made
no attempt to conceal her movements, he soon found her settled
down in the shade of a large boulder. The horse registered the
boy's presence with a nicker, then slowly rose and came out of
the shade to greet him, clanking and sore beneath the saddle.

Gabriel apologized to her silently for the mistreatment, then
thought again and spoke aloud. The horse's ears pricked up.
She eyed the boy, then turned broadside to him and stood as
he unfastened the saddle and its accounterments. The saddlebags were heavier than he'd anticipated. He dropped the first
one hard on his toe. He laid them out on the ground and
sorted through the supplies provided to him by providence—or
accident, he wasn't sure which. There were ample matches, a
large sack of flour, half a block of bacon, a lump of lard, several
twists of tobacco, and a frying pan lid. No pan was to be found,
but Gabriel only half registered this fact. His attention was
drawn to a jar of preserves, a rich, sugary jam of a fruit similar
to strawberries but somehow different. He ate it straight from
the jar, shoveling it into his mouth with his fingers and soon
feeling an exhilarated lightheadedness. He let the horse lick his
fingers.

Marshall's Winchester was still loaded and heavy. Gabriel studied it carefully, afraid to shift any of its levers or to fire it but staring at each section of the thing as if its function could be divined through sight alone. He set it away from the rest of the supplies. He did likewise with the two Smith and Wesson thirty-two-caliber revolvers, along with the cartridges for both makes of weapon and even his tiny derringer.

Only after his arsenal had been so displayed did the boy turn his attention to the remaining sack. He slipped the gold brick out of it carefully, cradling its soft, dense weight with all the care he'd give an infant. He set it down, remembering how it had once looked like a coffin. It didn't look so anymore. Coffins were for beings who had given up their lives and so moved on. But this square of gold was not of the same make at all. It had never lived, never breathed. It was simply a bit of metal that, through no fault of its own, drove men to acts of passion. What should he do with it? What could he do with it? He stood above the display trying to think it out, to answer the question right there and have it over with. But no option that he mulled over seemed quite right. It made no sense to leave it where it lay, or to hide it, or to give it away, or to take it home and fall prey to the dreams and schemes such things lead men to. Men like Marshall . . .

The thought sent chills through the boy. He looked anxiously around him, for fear that his thoughts might instantly become reality. Then he packed hastily. Because he could not answer his own questions, he would try to conquer them through motion. He would ride; he would walk if the horse was tired; he would keep up a steady movement for as long as it took to find his way home. He threw the saddle over one shoulder and carried the bags dangling from his other arm. As he led the horse away, Gabriel had the feeling that he was just now beginning his real journey.

FOR THREE DAYS THE MEXICAN, his companions, and the Scot patrolled the rim of the canyon. They ranged down its edge some thirty miles, stationed at different points, searching for signs of the living or the dead. They spotted the bodies of two horses, one floating in a section of flat water twenty miles downstream, another where the waters of the storm receded, wedged between several rocks, its legs splayed out in bizarre directions. It looked like thrown-together pieces of a horse. Its muzzle pointed up toward the canyon walls, so that the man who found it thought the creature was looking at him. They found a few pieces of debris, some saddlebags, and a waterskin.

It wasn't until the second day, at the full extension of their search, that they found the black boy. He had washed ashore on a narrow strip of beach lining a sheer cliff face. To get to him, the Scot led several of the men down a ravine and into the river upstream of the body. They floated a quarter-mile down to him in the slack water. The boy was lying face down, and the Scot rolled him over most gently. The boy's eyes were closed, something remarked upon by one of the men. His clothes were all in order except for his boots, which had been sucked off by the current. The Scot probed various portions of his body, as if he might find the source of the injury that ailed the boy, but there was none. His body was completely intact, whole and undamaged. He was simply dead. They considered the trek back to the rim with this dead one carried between them, and as it scarcely seemed possible, they agreed to bury him where he lay. The one who knew the proper words spoke only Spanish. The Scot shrugged and asked him to proceed, and the man did, intoning solemn foreign words that the Scot couldn't understand but that he trusted would lead the boy to heaven as surely as any others.

In the evenings the son sat with his sister. They talked little about what had happened. They spoke as if they were not sitting

*on a bowled scoop of the high desert, as if they had not lost the
things they had lost and not seen the things they had seen. Only
once did the brother speak to his sister of the future they must now
share. He said he didn't see it yet, didn't understand how there
could be such a thing, although he knew there must be, because the
world did not stop to notice the pain of any one person, no matter
how deep it was. He promised her that they would find a way, a
path in life that would honor those they'd left behind. He promised
her that one day she would be whole again and he would be whole
again. Everything that was Papi lives on in us, everything that
was Mama and that was Cristina. They all live on in us. The girl
nodded and said that she believed this. Perhaps more even than
you do, she said.*

*Late on the third day, the son thanked the men for their help.
He called them brothers now and forever and praised their bravery
and let them know that he would lay down his life for theirs at a
moment's notice. Then he told them to go home. It was over. They
drank together that evening, although they did so with the most
somber reverence. The son's first companion asked what he would
do, and the son said he would stay away a few more days; he
needed the solitude if he was to find a reason to live on. He con-
fessed to this one that it was not as he'd told his sister. He did not
believe his own words. I should have killed them with my own
hands. I should have eaten their hearts and dragged them into hell
by their entrails.*

*The companion offered to stay with him, but the son would not
let him. The next morning the men rode home, taking the girl with
them. The son watched them to the eastern horizon, then mounted
his horse and sat. The Scot had stayed as well, saying that he too
needed solitude to find a future. He sat on a rock. The son thanked
him for all he had done and called him a brother like the others
and assured him that his guilt had vanished as his heart was*

*good. He bade the man to go once more with God, and with that he
moved off. He gave his horse no direction but let it graze where it
would. As there was little that could be thought of as food, the horse
wandered upstream. The man eventually dismounted and followed
behind the horse, like a shepherd with a flock of one.*

*He spent the day like this, and it was in this way that he came
upon the narrow ravine upriver from where the fugitives had
entered, beyond the area searched by his men. It was little more
than a crack in the earth, and it stretched down toward the river
at such a sharp angle that he doubted the possibility of the tracks
he saw within it. But they were there. He saw where the tracks
ascended, where they reached the surface, and how the lone horse
had risen out of the earth. He saw that it had pawed the ground
and twisted in a half-circle. And then he saw it move off to the
north. He followed the tracks to the horizon. He asked for God's
presence, and then he whistled for his horse.*

*He found the Scot sitting in the same place he had left him,
in the same posture. I think this is not over, he said.*

*The Scot looked up at him and searched his features for the
meaning behind his words. He found it. He rose.*

Good. It didn't feel quite like it was.

GABRIEL HAD LITTLE KNOWLEDGE OF THE GEOGRAPHY of the
western portions of his country. He simply knew that with the
men he had traveled south to Texas and then west through the
New Mexico territory and into Arizona, all the way to the river
canyon where he'd made his escape. As he would not retrace that
route, his course seemed obvious. First north, then east. Somehow,
he hoped, that simple elbow of direction would lead him home.
It would, but it would also take him over territory he had never
conceived of before.

For the first few days on his own, Gabriel headed to the northeast through a landscape that he'd become familiar with over the recent weeks. He intersected once more with a main stem of the Colorado River and followed its scarred banks. When the river forked off either due east or in a more northerly direction, Gabriel opted for the east, feeling comforted by the notion that he was moving closer to the rising sun with each step. It was a deserted country, nowhere marked by boundary or fence line, roadless and empty save for the animal life, for birds, for shadscale, sagebrush, and the wind in all of its various moods.

Through the days of silent travel he developed a routine, a discipline almost, enforced by nobody but himself and therefore that much more natural. He tried to eat frugally. In the mornings, he collected the fruit of the prickly pear cactus, as he'd seen Dunlop do once. He skinned each one carefully and took small bites of it, finding it sweet and good, although it stained his fingertips a deep maroon and left a strange sensation in his mouth, the unshakable feeling that his gums and tongue were being stuck by tiny pins. At midday he'd pause long enough to roll a cigarette and sit with one leg thrown over the horn of his saddle, inhaling the smoke and taking in the country. He'd never smoked before, but now, with his solitude close around him, it seemed a natural thing to do. He made only the smallest of fires in the evenings. Huddled beside it, with the horse just a few steps away, he fried strips of bacon and baked bread, a hard, greasy loaf shaped decidedly like the frying pan lid. He followed this with coffee, an oily syrup that he drank straight from the all-purpose lid. It was a foul mixture, and yet somehow it seemed right, just the stuff to fill his stomach and fuel his imaginings as he stared up at the night sky.

His mind during the first few nights was uneasy, anxious, barely able to dream of the future, alert to any noise not of his own making. A tumble of rolling stones, the crackle of dry brush

on the ground, an unexpected movement behind a greasewood
plant: all these sent adrenaline reeling through his body. It wasn't
any natural creature that he feared. He'd learned to avoid rattle-
snakes, to check his blanket and boots carefully for scorpions.
He'd heard coyotes so often and so nearby that they were necessary features of the land, and unexpectedly sighting a gray fox
caused him more embarrassment than alarm. The canine paused
not more than twenty yards from the boy and watched curiously
as he squatted above a shallow depression to relieve himself,
pants around his knees, flat rock held in one hand. But no, it was
man that Gabriel feared. And he was aware of the irony of being
so alone in a wilderness yet so troubled by the notion of other
people.

When the river turned south, Gabriel abandoned it and kept
heading east toward the San Juan range of the Rocky Mountains.
With the growing elevation, the air grew cooler. Though the days
were still warmed by the sun, the nights dropped quickly in temperature. Gabriel found water sources more varied than in the
south. The blue skies of morning gave way on a daily basis to a
host of billowing clouds which sometimes actually rained but
more often than not just threatened.

By the second week of his solitary journey, Gabriel realized
he'd come to know his horse as he'd never known another animal. He'd grown accustomed to the feel of her, the swell and
release of her breathing. Her earthy scent was around him always,
in the fibers of his clothes, on his hands, in his very skin. He came
to know her temperament, her gestures, the manner in which she
raised her head at a certain angle to scent the air, the way she
sidestepped on being brought to a halt, as if she agreed to stop
but could never quite agree to do so on his chosen spot. Through
the daily chore of saddling and unsaddling her, he'd come to
know the feel of her coat, to find a beauty in the play of the light
over her creamy gray hair. He'd run his fingers over her ribs in the

evening, up over her rump and down her thigh, thinking of the parts that made her all and completely a horse, so perfect for her function, a tool in but no true accomplice to the crimes of man.

Late one morning Gabriel picked his way through a juniper woodland. He led the horse by the reins, listening to the progress of his feet and the horse's hooves across the earth, inhaling the rich scent of the massive trees, and watching the leaping of squirrels from ground to air, branch to branch. He told the horse the history that he had never told James. He spoke of his childhood in the distant east, of his father, now more a notion than a true memory, of his brother, whom he longed to see again, and of his stepfather and uncle, two men who'd grown in stature and wisdom in his eyes, such kind, strong men, so rare in the world. Of his mother he spoke haltingly, as if the horse might judge him. He said that it would be the hardest to see her again. He couldn't imagine explaining to her. It was as if he not only owned the guilt of having abandoned them but also owned the crimes of the men he'd traveled with. How could he deny that? He'd never fought them. He'd never voiced his beliefs, like Dunlop, or even like James. He'd done nothing to be proud of since his first days in Kansas, and he'd only managed to escape Marshall because he'd abandoned a friend who needed him. How could he tell his mother this and expect her to take him back? For that was what he realized he most wanted now. Just to be let back. To be a child, a son, and a brother.

He came to the lip of a sandstone canyon without even noticing. He stepped right up to its edge and paused only when he felt a rush of air catch against his face and realized that the land dropped away before him into a bowl a couple of hundred feet deep. He was dizzied by the realization, and still holding the horse's reins, he fell to one knee. For a moment the earth tilted before him, so expansive was the scale compared to the closed greenness of the forest. But when the ground steadied and settled into proportion, another surprise followed. The cliff wall on the opposite side of the canyon was carved with geometric lines, dotted with black squares, fenced with looping circles and corridors of stone. Gabriel blinked, shook his head, and inched closer to the edge.

An eagle flew over the canyon, again throwing off his perceptions, placing a distance of a half-mile between him and the far wall. It was a city, a palace built in stone, carved into a cliff face that stretched above it for several hundred feet. The windows and doors of the place gaped black and empty, strangely like the eyes and mouths of people mourning. And it was still, so still. Not a living thing moved in the city; no one walked the streets. There were no fires, no children at play.

When next a gust of air brushed his face and shoulders, he couldn't help but feel something ghostly in the touch, as if spirits had flown up from the hollow rooms to inspect him. A breeze swirled around him, and he knew it was no breeze but really the force that remains after death, at least on consecrated ground. The horse felt it too. She backed a step and snorted, clicked her teeth and urged the boy away from this place.

Gabriel stood and slowly turned, taking in as much of the deserted city as he could in one far-reaching gaze. As he led the horse away, he felt sure that as beautiful as the city was, it was not for him to look upon too closely. It belonged to another time, to another people, whose ancient joys and miseries and passing from the earth had very little to do with him. He almost felt he should say a prayer, but he couldn't imagine the words to use and didn't wish to offend whatever gods ruled that place. A few hundred yards away from the canyon, he slipped aboard the dun and rode steadily through the afternoon, away from the cliff dwellings of Mesa Verde.

THE TWO HAD COVERED THEIR TRACKS UP *and out of the canyon meticulously. They traveled through the cover of night for* the first few days, as the land was so flat and scoured that they might be seen from many miles away. They shared the black man's horse, and they left no waste behind. With a dry bundle of snakeweed, they brushed away any footprint or scuffmark that could be read. It was slow progress, but the desert gave way beneath them and they moved steadily to freedom. After four days they came upon a mining town. The place had seen a short-lived boom and bust, and the streets were empty save for a three-legged dog that watched them through blurred, suspicious eyes. They found no people, but the blond man did manage to rope a burro that had been living wild on the outskirts of town, and so he had a mount once more.

Outside of Prescott, Arizona, the two came upon a lawman who didn't like the look of them. He rode alone, upon a large bay horse, and he spoke to them with a smirk verging on belligerence. He asked them their business, their destination, their intentions. He laughed at the burro beneath the white man. It was short-lived laughter, however. The blond pulled his silver-inlaid twenty-two from his shoulder holster and shot the lawman through the neck. He shot him again through the chest and slipped off his burro and yanked the man from his horse. He asked the black man for his rifle. He put the barrel of the Winchester against the deputy's face and shot out both his eyes, shot out the space that made his nose, shot till he had emptied the chamber and the man's head was a lumpy jumble of flesh and bone, brain matter and hair.

The black man watched the white from on horseback, ready to ride, but the other was not so inclined. He took a seat beside the lawman and rolled a cigarette. He spoke to him, asked him his name, and apologized for the inconvenience regarding his face. He explained that he'd been feeling a bit out of sorts the last few weeks. It seemed that aspects of his destiny had been taken out of his own hands and manipulated by others, and this was one thing he couldn't happily put up with. He now wanted to get some of

*that control back, and the lawman had just been in the wrong
place, asking the wrong man questions at a trying time in his life.*

I apologize. I'm sure Saint Peter will understand.

*Against the black man's wishes, they camped right there next to
the dead man. The black listened to the white as he talked on, but
he thought of other things, of the past they had shared, of the
things done between them that no other knew of. They each contained an anger, but it came out in such different ways. The black
man would have taken no joy from the lawman's death. It was a
death with a function, yes, but it lacked meaning. He preferred to
kill in a different way, quietly, slowly, with more time for both him
and the other to realize the significance of the act.*

*When the blond man finally talked himself to sleep, the black sat
watching his profile. He had a desire, a momentary, fleeting urge
that he'd felt more than once before, to wake that man into pain.
But it passed as quickly as it came, and he just watched. There
were features the two had in common: the wide, high reach of their
foreheads, the lines cut by their eyebrows, and the heavy set of their
jaws. The black sometimes wondered if anyone had ever noted these
similarities, but he thought not. This was a world that saw only
difference, and there was as much at odds about their features as
there was in common: pale skin to dark brown, thin nose to wide,
white-blond hair on one, loose curls of black on the other. No, there
was nobody alive to comment on their bond. Not even the blond
man knew that the same man had fathered them both.*

*The black remembered this man now, saw his weathered face
and heard again his vitriolic tirades in the name of God. To the
blond man, he'd bequeathed a tortured bloodline; to the black, he'd
given blood but denied it and so planted the seeds of rage. The
black man did something then that he never did before the eyes of
men. He reached up and touched his fingers to his lips. He parted
them and let his fingertips caress the scar tissue that had once been
his tongue. He tried to remember the last clear words he had spo-*

ken with it, words that were somehow so vile as to rile that weathered holy man to anger. He had been only a boy, perhaps twelve, when he had named the white man as his father. The father had cursed the very thought of it and with his knife silenced the boy forever after. Silenced his speech, at least, but never silenced the anger within, or the questions.

Rarely did the black man think of his mother, but he did so that evening. He remembered her only from the fragmented view of a child, as an emotion, as a few images pasted together without logical connection. She was the being who defined words that otherwise had no definition for him. She, with blue-black skin, with white-white teeth, with giving flesh to her arms and a smell to her sweat that was like fruit. She was the warm glow of his beginning. She had once been life stripped of all other trappings. And yet . . .

There he was, staring in through the cracks in their shack as the white man mounted her, rode her in a way the boy had thought was meant only for four-legged creatures. And there she was after the holy man departed, hugging her child to her breast, humming and asking him to forget that which mattered not. But he hadn't forgotten, and he couldn't imagine that he ever would. He knew that it was this, at least partly, that made him ask the things he did of other people's flesh.

When the blond man rose in the early hours of the morning, the black made no mention of his thoughts. The two saddled up silently and left the dead man stripped of weapons, tobacco, and horse, with the burro grazing nearby to keep him company. They had no need for words, for they both knew their destination. There could be only one way for this now. Once released, chaos must run its course, and these brothers would see it to completion.

THE SAN JUANS ROSE BEFORE GABRIEL like a great receding barricade conceived by the gods and built of the earth itself. He knew he would have to learn mountain travel through trial and error. He could construct an image of what was to come from dimly remembered descriptions, but he felt surer each day that he could complete this journey—if not the whole of it, at least that day's portion. He wove his way into the foothills, seeking passage through small gaps in the hillsides, over mounds of wind-scoured sandstone, around tilted slabs of granite. Each ridge gave way to another and another, each higher than the one before. He learned to gauge the scale of the peaks only slowly, with his weary progress from base to peak and down again. He felt minuscule below the mountains, like an ant, a tiny thief crawling over the toes of giants. Thus he rode or led the horse with hushed respect, as if he feared to wake the mountains, and he listened—at first for signs of other people, but increasingly to the many voices around him.

There was a pattern to the world, a meaning modeled by the land itself, that he began to divine through his silent journey. When did he begin to recognize the feel of the sun on south-facing slopes and the smell of the large pines that grew there? When did he first come to expect the moist feel of the valley floors, or to know the call of that shy bird with the forward-leaning plume above its eyes? And when did he become the person who would spend an entire afternoon standing in a knee-deep stream, watching the progress of a rainbow trout against the current, feeling that he couldn't possibly move on because moments of pure connection were so rare?

More and more it seemed that creatures without language were speaking to him. For one full day a magpie stalked him. The black-and-white bird leapt from tree to tree, watching the boy with cagy sidelong glances, calling out in a sharp, rising call that sounded like a question. Another time he found himself dining with a family of skunks. The creatures plodded into camp like formally dressed dinner guests. They helped themselves to several slices of bacon, most of the lard, and a chunk of bread. Gabriel knew enough of these creatures to keep his distance. He thought a few well-placed rifle blasts might discourage them, but he had neither the heart for killing nor the desire to attract attention to himself. He spent the night watching the banquet from a nearby hollow.

And there were more frightening dialogues as well. Once the night was interrupted by eerie, tortured screams that seemed to echo across the mountains, gaining breadth and scale with each reverberation. The boy held the rifle tightly, staring into the dark. He could hear a beast moving through the trees, circling his camp in a close circuit that put terror into the horse. It seemed that the cries were those of a troubled soul, a creature part human, part animal, and part demon. He believed it was coming for him and he awaited it. But it never did come, just circled and cried, circled and cried.

The next morning Gabriel found a mountain lion's tracks less than fifty yards from where he'd slept. The cat had indeed paced round and round the camp. The large pawprints layered over each other. There were no claw marks, as the boy expected, just soft, padded orbs so numerous that he might have been surrounded by a pack of the cats. Gabriel knew that lions traveled alone. Hiram had told him that long ago. He didn't doubt the man for a moment, didn't question how he came to the knowledge, but still he saddled up with haste and rode the anxious horse into the dawn.

Mid-morning of his sixteenth day alone, Gabriel emerged from the treeline onto a long sloping scree. He gazed up at the pure skeleton of the earth, the ivory itself in naked and dizzying height. The granite peaks cut jagged lines against the sky. Enormous slabs of rock lay about the incline like the wreckage of demolished buildings. Brilliant white snowfields filled in the shaded northern slopes, and the sky loomed above it all, as infinite in ether as the mountains were in stone. Gabriel stood in awe for several minutes, then urged the mare forward.

That night he camped above the treeline, and it turned bitterly cold. A wind blew up from the valley and spread a dusting of ice crystals across his camp. He huddled beneath his blanket, shivering and fireless, wondering how long this could continue. Do these mountains end, or do they stairstep all the way to God's throne? That night he thought anything was possible, so near was he to the roof of the sky and so great was the friction of the clouds across the world's backbone.

Two days later, he saw a mining camp from a distance of perhaps five miles. He stopped in a windswept pass and looked down upon the wound. For some time he watched the activity of the antlike things that moved around the mouth of the mine. They seemed little more than curiosities to him, tiny creatures to be neither loved nor despised, just watched from a distance. Later, when he would try to describe his time in the mountains, the images would crowd in one on another, each clamoring for attention, each adding to the collage of memory that seemed thick enough to represent a complete lifetime of its own. If this were so, it was a life of earth and sky, rock and wind. It was spent in the company of mountain goats and bighorn sheep, picas and marmots and beavers. It was a life lived leanly, beneath pine trees and along riversides, growing thin in the saddle and yet stronger for it, a bone-deep strength that would never leave him. And it was a life that marked its maturity when he looked down upon that mine. From that day on, his journey changed. He'd crossed the Continental Divide without knowing it, and he'd begun the descent that would eventually lead him back onto the Great Plains, back into the world of men. He clucked to the dun and proceeded, looping off to the north and so avoiding the mine by a good few miles.

GABRIEL KEPT TO HIMSELF as he passed the settlements along
the Arkansas River. He gave the homes a wide berth and spent
the nights in secluded spots away from the homesteads. Those
who did see him pass looked at him with a strange mixture of
curiosity and respect. There was something old and trailworn
about him, despite his young face. He was comfortable with his
mount's movements beneath him, and it showed in the way he
sat the horse. It seemed to a stranger's eyes that he was at ease
with his place in the world. People's gazes noted the quality of
the horse, the value of the saddle, and always the holstered rifle
and the thirty-two he'd begun to wear on his hip. If they questioned a young black boy's right to these things, they did not do
so within Gabriel's hearing.

When his supplies dwindled, Gabriel ventured into a town
that sat cradled in a bend of the river. He could discern no
name for the place, but it was easy enough to find the general
store, as the building bore the traits of all such establishments.
He bought a few supplies with the coin he'd earned in that
long-ago time with Marshall: a small sack of potatoes, some
more bacon and cornmeal and matches. He didn't see the need
for a proper frying pan, but as the coin was worth more than the
food, the boy also purchased a hat. It was neither newly made
nor of a current style. It was of an older make, more like an old
Mexican poblano. The shopkeeper kept it on display above the
counter, and he happily traded it to the boy, although he
still claimed he couldn't make change for the coin. A small
crowd of scrawny youths gathered around and watched, as if
this boy's shopping was the best amusement to be had that day.
A few yards of calico balanced the sums, and Gabriel walked
from the store with the fabric under his arm like a man shopping for his sweetheart. The boys walked out behind him,
silently watched him mount the dun, and watched him ride

away, the hush broken only by a mumbled phrase that Gabriel didn't catch.

He had his first and only real trouble that evening. He camped on the southern bank of the Arkansas, in a grove of low-slung trees. The evening had been alive with song: crickets in the tall grass nearby, swallows from somewhere along the far bank. He lay on his back with his head propped against the saddle, listening to the night music and recalling that Native Americans could communicate by birdcalls. As he drifted off to sleep, the avian music had so captured his mind that his dreams began as a string of melodies and only slowly took visible shape.

When he opened his eyes sometime later, the first thing he noticed was the absence of song. He listened to the silence and then realized why he'd woken. The dun snorted a protest and stamped its foot once more. Gabriel turned on his side and took in the moonlit scene in one glance. Three boys stood in a loose line along the riverbank. A fourth had ventured near enough to throw a hackamore over the horse.

He knew they had seen him move, but he didn't let that stop him. Before he'd fully thought out the action, Gabriel unholstered the thirty-two and trained it on the boy holding the hackamore. He didn't speak. He couldn't imagine the appropriate words. Neither could he imagine what would follow, what he would do with the gun if events didn't somehow turn the right way. But despite his inner hesitation, his arm held the pistol steadily, pointed dead on the other boy's chest. Time passed very slowly, but nobody moved.

The boy beside the horse eventually looked to the others for support. "His hand's shaking. Ain't it, y'all?" His voice quavered when he spoke, nearly cracking with each word, and Gabriel couldn't help noticing how childlike it sounded. His nose was a hooked bill outlined in gray. His eyes were tiny black specks beside it. The others kept their distance, and the boy eventually had to turn back to Gabriel. "You wouldn't kill a man for a horse, would ya?" He spoke with a clear intention of sounding calm and confident, but his voice betrayed him again.

Gabriel knew that his hand was not shaking, but he felt an almost irresistible urge to clasp his other hand over it. That hand even went so far as to rise from his side. He fought it back, redirected it to his chin, where it stroked the thin traces of hair like an intellectual giving the question a full breadth and depth of thought. It was a hard stance to hold, and Gabriel was aware that it verged on the ridiculous. He cocked the gun, a noise that was absurdly loud in the night. His hand still held his chin. But once the gun was cocked, feeling that he needed to do something more, he let his hand fall from his chin and float away from his side. It was a gesture without reason, stranger than the one that preceded it, but somehow it was just the thing to break the other boy's resolve.

The boy cleared his throat. "I wasn't . . . I mean, I ain't meant nothing . . . It was Whittle said we should do it." He pointed a thin finger toward the others. "I never did . . ." The boy lost his flow of words, paused, then was struck dumb by the realization that he was holding the hackamore. He dropped the rope. All three of the others had been inching back throughout the conversation. One of them called to the boy with the horse, but still he didn't move.

Gabriel held his stance. His arm was just as steady as when he'd begun, his eyes just as attentively focused on the boy, but it still took all his effort just to state one word with authority.

"Go."

That was all the boy needed. He whispered something under his breath and gestured to the others, who were already moving away before him. There was the motion of them dispersing in the moonlight, the sound of their feet thudding on the earth, an occasional twig breaking, and then they were gone into the night from which they'd come. Only when the distance between them was great enough did the boys find voice, naming Gabriel's race and threatening him with words that had escaped them only a moment before.

Gabriel saddled the horse by the same gray light and rode out twenty minutes later, aware that he had just avoided considerable danger, and even more aware that he'd just drawn a gun on another person for the first time.

WHEN HE ENTERED WESTERN KANSAS, Gabriel found a troubled land. The dry heat of summer had left the plains a tinderbox. Clouds gathered, thunder rumbled, and rain loomed imminent, but time and again the heavens withheld their moisture and threw down bolts of lightning instead. By the time of Gabriel's passage, in the second week of September, wide swaths of prairie lay charred and brittle.

He traveled for three days through such territory. The first day the turf crackled beneath him. Gabriel rode carefully, as if the horse's hooves were actually his own and he could feel the heat of the ground through them. On the second day, he often dismounted and touched the earth with his hand to test its warmth. In some places the fires were so recent that the heat of them still rippled the air. Eerie phantoms of smoke crept up from the ground and flew away before the wind. He saw more than one wheat field ruined, more than one home destroyed, and many white faces rendered far blacker than his by soot. The third day was one long and weary progress through a land of damned souls. The towns had swollen with people in search of aid or rest or friendship. The roads to and from them were strung their full length with a sad procession of the beleaguered. He watched one man hurl bits of wood and tools into the ravished hull of his home, fueling the fire within it. And he passed within fifty yards of a soot-covered family dressed in their Sunday best, standing with heads bowed before a miniature grave.

In some long-ago time, it seemed, Gabriel had called such curses on all who were fool enough to tempt the land. But now he rode back among them with mumbled prayers on his lips, both for those around him and for his own wayward soul. Despite their hardships, the people were still proud. Three times thirsty men refused his offer of water; once a mother turned her back on him as he nodded his condolences. He managed to make only one present. As he passed a young girl walking barefoot behind her mother, he sank low in the saddle and handed her the folded square of calico. He silenced the girl's thanks with a finger to his lips and rode on before his gift might be refused. Hiram used to say something about pride coming before a fall, but Gabriel hoped that no further fall need follow for these people.

THE SCOT WAS SURE THAT HE RECOGNIZED THE TRACKS of the dun horse. He said as much to the Mexican, and they followed, each with the hope that this trail would lead him to a final act of vengeance. But with each passing day the Scot grew less sure. Yes, it was the dun, but why did its rider choose such a circuitous course? Why did he not cover his tracks, and why leave such clear markers at his campsites? Why did he cross rivers so directly, never using the opportunity for deception? It was a lone rider, yes, a certain horse, yes, but this was all they could be sure of. That, and that the rider rode with an unrelenting pace that they gained on only slowly.

They lost the trail many times as it changed terrain. Through the scrubland it was easy enough, and in the mesa land of juniper and pine they rode silently, sharing each other's company with the trail clear before them. It wasn't until the mountains proper that they felt the trail become truly difficult. They lost it on scree and tallus slopes, found it in the slow progress of horse and man across a glacier, then lost it again in an area of chaotic felsenmeers, a jagged plain of jumbled rock thrust upward like geometric offspring growing from their mother rock. They continued to move east, but spent a week with no clear sign to follow.

Camped one evening in the foothills of the Front range, the Scot and the Mexican decided to descend onto the flatlands to resupply themselves and determine their course, which way it would take them, and if it would take them together. The Scot did not fancy the notion of what the future held. He had grown close to this man in their days together. He had talked to him the way men should, but rarely do, talk to one another. They told the tales that were their lives and so conveyed the meanings they had found or that had escaped them, the fears they had conquered and those left unvanquished. The Scot came to know what this man's family had meant to him. He heard the father's words through the son's mouth and learned of a mother's kindness, and he closed his eyes at the thought of the dreams two girls had conjured for themselves but could now never have.

They bought food and supplies beside the Arkansas River, and it was there that they asked if any had noted the passing of a rider on a dun horse. It was there that they got their answer, from a hook-nosed adolescent. Yes. Less than a week ago. They asked who the rider was, and the Scot couldn't help hiding his surprise at the answer.

A black boy.

A Negro? A man or a boy?

I said he was a boy. Younger than me, anyhow. I remember cause he had a right uppity look about him.

This story was confirmed in the next town, and once more by a wagon train carrying supplies west. The two men talked it out. The Scot told what he knew of this boy, and the Mexican nodded,

saying that his sister had said much the same. He wasn't the one
they wanted, but they should be sure. And perhaps he would know
something more of the fate of the others. They decided to stay the
course a little longer.

GABRIEL RECOGNIZED THE LAND: the slow undulations and
sweeping breadth of it, the creek that snaked its way to the south,
the shallow depression that framed his family's homestead,
and the squat building itself, a little larger, yet mostly unchanged
by the passing months. But this was all that he recognized. He
sat on a rise that he'd walked many a time the previous spring
and surveyed the farm. There was not the faintest sign of the fires
that troubled the western plains, no swarm of locusts and no
withering hot wind. The corn crop stood tall and erect, cut in
wavering lines and yet all the more beautiful for the imprecision.
To the east the sloping field devoted to wheat had grown into a
sun-tanned, golden expanse. The family plot showed an array of
life. There were crops short and tall, gray-brown to deep green,
plants that Gabriel knew and some that he didn't. Melons sat in
the fields like giant seeds; pumpkins grew in ground that had
been uncut sod when he'd left. Raleigh stood staked near the
barn, and the pig was just visible in its pen. There were no people to be seen.

It had all changed so much. At first Gabriel felt a nagging
desire to retreat. He could turn away now before anybody saw
him and fade into the plains. It seemed that might be better for
them all. Look, there before him was the proof that they didn't
need him, the clear and irrefutable evidence that all he'd said had
been wrong. The land had prospered through the hard work of
others. A family he had deserted had persevered. How could he
return now?

So he thought, but he didn't turn away. Without consciously

deciding to, he urged the horse forward. He rode down toward the house, shy and respectful, a tight lump in his throat and tension ringing his eyes. He gripped the reins firmly, and he was no more relaxed when he finally stopped in the clearing before the house. Raleigh looked up at him and studied the new horse. The sow's grunts floated into the air. Other than that, all was quiet, still.

It was Ben who first emerged. He stepped out into the bright midday light and paused dead in his tracks. His jaw dropped, and his face was fogged by an expression of utter confusion. He was much changed—a full inch taller, Gabriel would have guessed, and a few pounds heavier around the shoulders and chest. He was shirtless beneath his overalls, and his tight torso was cast in much the same dark material as Gabriel's. But there was no mistaking him. Here was Ben, wholly and completely and undeniably this horseman's kin but a young man in his own right.

"Gabe?"

Before Gabriel had time to answer, another shape appeared in the doorway—Solomon, followed shortly after by Hiram and finally by Eliza. They were all as he remembered them. It was strange for them to be flesh and blood and standing before him, but they were unchanged from the images of his dreams and hopes. They looked up at him and took him in with disbelieving eyes—Gabriel, saddled and sitting on a silver horse, rifle and pistol at hand, hatted and tall. For the first time, the boy fully imagined the image he must cut. He felt a wave of shame wash over him. They would think . . . They would see him as . . . But he didn't even have time to shape the thoughts fully.

Eliza pushed between the others and stepped forward. She stared up at her son with a face that was guarded in its recognition, as if she saw and hoped but couldn't believe just yet. As she came closer, the sun brought out the sharp contours of her features. There were lines, not so fine anymore, around her eyes, and ribbons of gray touched her thick black hair. She ran a hand

up over her forehead and tried to smooth down some of the
unruly strands.

"Gabriel, I done gone hoarse from praying for you."

Her voice was instantly familiar, although the boy wasn't sure
how to read it, as frank a declaration as it was. He made to speak,
but he didn't yet have the words. Only a few seconds had passed,
but he wasn't even sure that he had heard her right, or that she
had spoken at all.

The woman seemed to understand this. "We've just started
eating," she said. "There's a place at the table for you if you're
inclined." She let this sit in the air between them, but this was
not enough either, and she knew it. She waited a second longer,
then she stretched her arms out to him as if her feet were rooted
to the ground but her arms could reach however far they had to.
"Come here."

It took the boy a moment to recognize her posture, so long
had it been since he'd seen it. She stood thus as he slipped from
the dun. His feet touched the earth, and his legs instantly went
wobbly. In three strides he covered a lifetime of distance. With
the first step he forgot that he was Gabriel the hunted. With the
second he knew nothing but the nearness of his mother. And by
that third step he was a child who'd just learned to stand. He fell
into her embrace with a force that almost knocked the woman
down. She wrapped her arms around him and whispered to him
and soothed him as she would a baby. He didn't know when he
began to cry, but at some point he realized his body was shaking
with sobs. He felt the tears squeezing through his tight-shut eyelids and falling onto the warm shoulder of his mother, felt her
hand brush his hat off and stroke his head, and heard her words
soft and soothing in his ears. In the space of a few seconds, he
was her child again.

THAT EVENING THEY SAT AROUND THE KITCHEN TABLE as Gabriel told his tale. He began with halting phrases and apologetic glances. The others prompted him cautiously. Eliza sat next to him, rubbing his hand and affirming his words with faint murmurs of understanding. Solomon made a pot of coffee. He fumbled with the small cups in his large hands. Hiram sat silent and attentive, an expression of troubled joy written on his face. And Ben stood near at hand, with undisguised awe in his large eyes.

Gabriel stumbled forward as if it were not only the tale but the words themselves that he needed to recall from the past. He told of the ride south in the wagon, of the men he rode with and the homesteads they passed. He told of the chain of events that broke the group up, of the long walk he and James made together, of the things that came to pass at McKutcheon's, of being twice shot at. He told of the wonder of the land across which he'd traveled, losing himself in the unpeopled landscape of his mind, creating a panorama of desolate expanses and flesh-covered mountains and temples carved in stone. He told of the gold. He let it be known that he had seen things he wished he never had and that people had been wronged greatly, some even to death, but he did not give details.

It was difficult, but manageable, to tell of those things. It was another thing altogether to find the right words to form the images that haunted him still. Ugly Mary and Rickles staring out at the rising sun, a deer impaled upon a living tree, smoke hanging in the air above Santa Fe, the sight of a homestead and a river glistening in the morning sun: of these things he didn't speak. Of friendships made and lost; of James and how he was betrayed; of Dunlop, whom he'd last seen bound and tied in the light of campfire; and of the girl, so abused, robbed of blood and history and kin: of these he did not speak, only bowed his head and prayed for the images to pass in silence.

Eliza watched him, both as he spoke and through his silences, and she never took her hand from his. By the time he finished, more than one pot of coffee had been consumed. He had told his tale incompletely, with great chunks left yawning with questions, but Gabriel felt more exhausted than ever before. It seemed the toil of all those days in fear had been relived in one evening, and he sat with his head heavy between his shoulders. The night had grown thick about them, and each member of the family was alive with questions. Most of these they held to themselves, either to keep safely unspoken or to ask at some later, gentler time. But some questions were too urgent to wait.

Ben swallowed before he spoke, a sound loud enough to warn the room of his intention. "Gabe? What's happened to James?"

Gabriel seemed pained by the question. He closed his eyes and his lips and then inhaled through his nose and exhaled his words. "I don't know. I couldn't bring him with me." He opened his eyes. His gaze met his mother's, and something in the contact brought forth a flow of words, one fast upon another. He repeated that he hadn't been able to bring him. He had tried and he had wanted to, but James wouldn't have made it. He was in the water already. He was floating away, and Gabriel had only a second to make his choice. As quickly as his words came out, he lost composure. His lips worked and his forehead wrinkled into jagged lines and tears burst from his eyes. His words were twirling away, snapshots of thoughts and images that none in the room could follow.

Eliza pulled the boy close to her once more and held his head under her chin. She told him to let it go. "These things are past. Don't hold them too tight." With her eyes she cautioned Ben to question his brother no further. "You just let them go and pray for the souls of the departed," she said.

She held Gabriel until he pulled back and wiped the moisture from his face. He seemed to want to speak more, but he didn't.

They sat in solemn thought for some time. Attempts at conversation went nowhere, and it wasn't until Eliza suggested bed for them all that Gabriel again found he had something that needed saying. He got up from the table and stepped outside and returned with a saddlebag. He unbuckled the bag and set it on the table.

"I've got more I should tell you," he said. "I will, but . . . I can't say it all just yet. But you should maybe look at this."

The others sat a moment looking at it, as if the worn leather somehow spoke volumes all by itself. Eventually Solomon reached out and emptied the contents onto the table. The gold bar made a strangely muted sound against the wood. It was less than spectacular in appearance, but still it took the collective breath out of the room.

Solomon gripped his jaw in his hands and massaged the tension there. This done, he whistled. "You rode off on the man's horse . . ."

Gabriel dropped his eyes to a dark space on the floor. "I didn't mean to. It was crazy that night. The horse just came to me."

"A blessing and a curse both," Hiram said. He seemed to have trouble controlling the lump in his throat. "I'll be damned."

Ben stepped closer, the tip of his tongue protruding through his teeth as if he might touch it to the metal. "Man alive. That's gold? It don't even look that nice." He reached a tentative hand toward the bar.

Eliza stopped him, saying, "You leave that where it lies, Ben." Her gaze flicked up to Solomon, who seemed to have one eye on her and one on the gold at the same time. She again placed her hand on her son's and squeezed it. "Let's not forget what's happened today. We done got Gabriel back. He's walked along the valley of death, but he's come home."

She allowed no more conversation. She said it was time for

them all to sleep, and she carefully put the gold back into the
saddlebag. They left it there on the table and went off to their
troubled sleep, each trying to work out through dreams the questions that the morrow would bring.

GABRIEL WAS AWAKE BEFORE SUNRISE. He lay listening to the
room around him. It seemed that the sounds of his sleeping kin
were the most comforting noises in the world. He tried to remember a time when this had not been so, but it seemed impossible.
How could he ever have wanted to be anyplace else? What's better than waking to the touch of your brother at your elbow? Or
the sound of your stepfather's snoring? Or the rustle of the linen
when your mother rolls over in her sleep? All of the closeness
that had once seemed suffocating and wrong now seemed life-
giving and so fundamentally right as to be unquestionable.

He heard Solomon rise before any of the others. He listened
as the man dressed, following each motion betrayed by sound,
from pulling on his thick overalls to sliding his feet into his boots
and doing up the laces. The leather creaked as the boots grew
tight, and Gabriel almost thought he could hear the protests of
the man's gnarled fingers. Just after Solomon had slipped quietly
through the door, Gabriel rose, dressed, and followed him out.

Although the western horizon lay gray and slatelike, the east
was already growing light. The very rim of the eastern sky was
tinted a tranquil turquoise. A lone bird called its greeting to the
morning from the roof of the house, then darted for cover when
Gabriel turned toward it. He couldn't see Solomon, and it took
him a minute of listening to the prairie silence to locate the man.
He found him hefting the slop bucket up onto the fence of the
sow's enclosure.

Solomon paused when he saw the boy and said, "Morning."
Gabriel nodded his greeting and indicated that he would like to

help. Solomon made it clear that he didn't have to. Actually, he said, it was normally Ben's job to feed the animals. He had just figured they could all use some rest, what with staying up late the previous night. Gabriel wasn't sure, but he thought he heard a backhanded bite to these words, as if Solomon would offer his generosity while reminding the boy of the disruption he had caused. His face betrayed no such double meaning, but the boy heard it all the same. Gabriel took the bucket from him and climbed into the pigpen.

They worked slowly, the two of them. After tending the sow, Solomon led Gabriel around to the newly constructed chicken coop. It was a thing hardly resembling a manmade structure, a motley conglomeration of posts and sticks and curving loops of wire that held the chickens only as long as they consented. Solomon looked at the structure sadly but cautioned Gabriel against disparaging it. "Ben built it hisself, and he right proud of it," he said. He tried a smile, but Gabriel nodded and considered the coop without a hint of humor. They let the nervous birds loose and tossed out feed to them.

As Gabriel showed no inclination to speak, Solomon filled the silence with his own halting string of words. He told of the work of the summer, what crops they had planted, where and why, which things grew well and which didn't grow at all. There had been a scare in late July with the appearance of cinchbugs in some of the corn, and later, in early August, they'd watched the crops bake under a cloudless sky. But the Lord protects, as Hiram said. Nothing truly came of the insects, and rain did fall in time to save most of the crops. While those to the west were ravaged by fires, some to the south by drought, and many pockets all around the plains by locusts, they had fared well. "I been telling them we need to harvest what we got fore we lose it," Solomon said, "but Hiram and your mother are the most patient-est types you'd come across. Almost seems like they were waiting

for you to show up. Myself, I told them they best not wait." The
man bent to examine a piece of wire that stuck out in a ragged
loop from the chicken coop. He studied it intently. "I don't mean
to sound coarse, Gabriel. I'm happy to have you home, and I
thank God you're safe. But I do wonder . . . I wonder how long
you're staying for, whether you come to work or whether you just
passing through."

The boy's eyes tried to hold on to the man's face, but as
Solomon spoke, they grew wearier and wearier, until they eventually floated away and settled on the dry earth. There was a
cringing tension in Gabriel's face that both accepted and sought
to deny the man's questions. He felt a whole host of words tum-
bling around within him. He wanted to let them out. He wanted
to shout and make it clear how much he wanted to stay, how he'd
learned from this journey and come back different and would
prove it with time. He wanted them all to understand him completely, to read him like a slate before them so they could know
the things he'd been through while permitting him never to say
them out loud. But each claim seemed anchored to a refuting
fact, denied by his own words, damned forever by actions taken
and untaken, choked to silence by them all.

Solomon straightened and watched him for a few moments,
giving him time to speak. But when the hush went unbroken, he
sucked his lips and patted the boy on the shoulder. "Come on,
let's get us some breakfast. Figure your mother will make her
best for you."

IT WASN'T UNTIL THAT EVENING that Gabriel found himself
alone with his mother for more than a few minutes. He sat across
the table from her, both of them shucking corn. The green rich-
ness of the husks was thick in the room, temporarily covering the
damp smell that had so disturbed Gabriel in the early days

out here. He wrapped his fingers around the cornhusks, pulling them away with a satisfying ripping sound. He ran his fingers down the firm white kernels, finding a pleasure just in the touch of them, in their neat near-uniformity, in the way they fit so tightly together. He tried to think about them only, to feel the pleasure of this work, the close comfort of the soddy, and the nearness of his mother. But from one moment to the next, his mind would wander. He would find himself staring blankly at a space on the wall. He was not sure how long these lapses lasted, and he was not sure just what images were tugging at his mind's eye. But one came up time and again.

"Sometimes it helps to talk, Gabriel." The boy was suddenly aware that his mother had been staring at him for some time. "I see you got a confusion in you. Sometimes it helps just to say it out loud. I don't know what it is, son, but spit it out to the world. Having a tortured rememoration ain't no different from taking a bit of some spoiled fruit. You spit it out fore you swallow it. Cause if you swallow it down, it'll be a long time fore it passes."

The boy looked as though he would disdain the comparison, but instead he said, "There was a girl."

Eliza waited, but the boy stared at his hands. "Yes? Tell me about her."

Gabriel shook his head. It didn't seem possible. He turned from her as if he would rise from the table and move away. Somehow this motion helped him. The slight angle at which he'd turned away gave him strength, although it looked as though he were ready to flee. "There was a girl," he repeated, and slowly, haltingly, this segment of his untold story emerged. He spoke of the family, describing their homestead with a certain pained detail: the fir trees shimmering in the breeze, the tiny creek, and the fields that lined it. As he began to speak of the father, he paused. He retraced something in his mind and met his mother's eyes. He dropped them and moved on, skipping forward and leaving things unsaid but thereby conveying the substance of the events clearly enough. He had known all along what the men were doing. He had watched them beat down the father and mother, bind them, and defile their daughters. He had seen them lead the girl off each evening and heard the lewd words with which they bragged. And yet he'd done nothing.

Lines of frustration furrowed his brow, crept down the bridge of his nose, and tightened around his eyes as he continued. "She fed us. When we was on the run and didn't have any water . . . She had some canned tomatoes, and she would feed them to me and James. Even after all of that." He looked at his mother as if she might understand this act and render some meaning back to him. She smiled sadly and simply waited. The boy finished his story, leaving the girl once more astride her horse in the desert.

Eliza listened through it all, watching her son and sometimes closing her eyes. In the end she walked around the table and hugged him. She told him he was a good boy, a good man, and he shouldn't take the guilt for other men's crimes too much to his heart. She said that such things can rarely be explained, even using the lessons of the church, and that sometimes things must simply be lived with. "Men will do awful things without laws to bind them. Even with laws to bind them. They say that all men are good at heart until Satan gets within them. But I don't know if I believe that. It's awful hard for me to separate the sinner from the sin. So what do you do? You go on. You be the person that you are, but be stronger for the things you seen. Know that the Lord let you live for a reason, and don't let him down."

She loosened her grip and studied her son from a different angle. "Us mothers, we always want to save our children from the awful things we seen, and we want to give them a future better than anything we seen. Looks like I ain't more than half accomplished it on the first count. The things you seen are part of my life too. You hear? There are things that happen in a life that

aren't fit for a mother to tell a son. I got my own share of rememoration, and some of it awful bad. That's as plain as I can make
it." She paused when the door opened. Ben peeked in, hesitated
a moment, then smiled. Eliza motioned for him to enter, then
said, "I haven't saved you from seeing evil at work, but I'm still
here with you. And I'll be here as long as you need me. You
gonna get to see them good things I never did. You gonna find
this life is a good thing, a gift that just humbles you to think on.
Maybe that girl knew the same thing."

Later that evening a number of things were decided. The gold
and the pistols were to be buried deep in the earth on the far side
of the cornfield. The family voted with one voice that they could
see fit neither to spend nor to discard the bullion, so let it be
buried and see if time couldn't make something of it. They'd see
if they couldn't trade Marshall's saddle at market next weekend,
along with any saddlebags and accouterments that had adorned
the mount. The rifle they'd keep in the soddy for security, and
the dun horse would remain, for the time being, in the barn with
Raleigh. This was the hardest decision. They knew the horse
might bring unwelcome attention, but it was the horse that had
brought Gabriel home to them, a beautiful creature with no guilt
for her master's crimes and with nobody in the world with more
claim to her than the boy.

GABRIEL WAS HOME, and there was work to be done. Before he
knew it, he was adjusting once more to the patterns of farm life.
He was up in the morning with Ben, tending the animals and
walking from the chill of the night into the first rays of sun. It
was harvest time, and the corn needed to be cut by hand. The
brothers took turns swinging the long knife that served as har-
vester. It blistered his hands, as did the rough stalks that they
piled into bundles to dry, but he welcomed these blisters. They

were so different in their feel and function from the worn
patches of skin he'd developed from holding the reins.

After supper, Hiram still read from the Bible. To Gabriel, listening now with an attention he had never given before, the stories were vividly evocative of his life-and-death struggles. He
understood the words now in a way he never had before. Yes, the
hand of God was in it all, but he acted only through the deeds of
humans. The boy couldn't help wondering if that hand directed
or followed. Was it there to guide, or was it there simply to wit-
ness with shame the beings God had created? And also he
thought it strange that the crimes of man had never really
changed. These were stories of murder and betrayal, of avarice
and lust, and of lives lived with and without faith. Those Biblical
times were not so different after all.

One Saturday afternoon the two boys saddled the horses and
rode along the creek together, Ben on the dun and Gabriel once
more on calm old Raleigh. At first they talked of simple things:
the weather and the coming of fall, horses and saddles and the
colored church that had sprung up on the prairie north of
Crownsville. It was a long way to go, and the congregation was
little more than a handful of families, but there was something
special to it all the same. Ben spoke of new friends he'd made
there: a boy named Kip, his brother, Eustace, and a girl named
Jessica, about whom Ben had more than a few words to say. It
was only after this flow of conversation slowed and the horses
drew to a halt and munched the grass beneath them that Ben
asked his brother more about his travels.

Gabriel spoke without looking at Ben much. His gaze studied
the rippling water of the creek next to them or watched the
clouds that were floating in from the north, high and silent. Ben
didn't push him too long or too hard. He let up when tension
showed on his brother's face, and he found other things to talk
about. He told of his experience with the wolf, how it had scared

him to the very core and yet he'd felt a need, a destiny almost, to hunt the beast. And he described the first time he'd shot an antelope, hinting at the emotions he felt and watching Gabriel to read his reaction.

"You ever kill anything while you was out there?" he asked. "That's a couple times now I've shot something. Least I think I shot the wolf—never did find it, though."

Gabriel threw his leg over the saddlehorn and slipped to the ground. Raleigh shied to the side, surprised by the sudden movement, but Gabriel tugged his reins just enough to reassure him. Then he kneeled down beside the shallow stream and answered. "Naw, I didn't really need to hunt. Had supplies . . . bacon and that."

"Oh." Ben nodded. He looked down and wrapped the dun's coarse hair around his fingers. "This a fine horse, Gabe. Damn. I didn't think I'd ever ride a horse like this. You think we could breed her? That's a good business, don't you think?" He laid out a plan of breeding and horse-rearing. His scheme tumbled out so quickly it must have been long held and mulled over. He spoke of a hundred head of horses, all bred for particular purposes, trained by himself and Gabe, if he was up to it. He said he'd seen a book about it in Howe's shop, and when he saved up some money he was gonna . . . He stopped in mid-sentence, staring at his brother as if he'd just been struck dumb by a thought.

Gabriel noticed the look and had some inkling of the boy's thoughts. "I don't know," he said. "Truth is, I don't really think she's my horse."

"Whose is she, then? I'll claim her. Slap a brand on her, gentle-like, but—"

Gabriel cupped a handful of the cool water in his palm, raised it, then let the moisture slip through his fingers. "Ben, I was lucky to get away. I could've died out there. Wouldn't've been the only one."

"You seen people killed?"

Gabriel nodded.

"Bad folks or good?"

Gabriel looked at his brother and then away. "They were just people. Don't know what good or bad had to do with it."

"Well . . . Hiram says that's all there really is in the world. Good, bad, and runction they cause fighting each other."

"I don't know. Maybe in Bible times it was like that." Gabriel stood and pulled Raleigh close to him. He looked into the horse's eyes and touched his muzzle. "Nowadays the devil's an iron horse."

This raised Ben's eyebrows. It was obvious he wanted to ask more, but Gabriel mounted and squeezed Raleigh with his ankles. Gabriel knew a statement like that would only fuel his brother's questions, but he couldn't help uttering portions of the thoughts that plagued him, just as he couldn't help keeping other things hidden. He hoped—he believed—that time would bring it all out. This story needed time to unfold, and Gabriel wished nothing more than a long lifetime to tell it slowly, to heal himself among these people.

Behind him, Ben let the dun follow of her own accord, watching the sway of his brother's back before him.

IT WAS A TUESDAY MORNING. The family was just up and beginning breakfast when Ben burst through the door, slops bucket splashing his leg and spilling onto the floor. "Two riders," he said.

The room was a blur of motion. Gabriel was up and moving toward the door before Ben's words had faded from the room. Solomon reached for the Kentucky long and tossed it to Hiram, who breached it on his knee and checked the load. Solomon yanked the Winchester from the wall. "It's okay, Eliza," he said,

his words overtly at odds with his actions. "We'll see who it is."
He strode into the morning, with Hiram fast beside him.

Gabriel was five paces out into the yard before he saw them.
They were closer than he expected, moving in along the edge of
the cornfield. At first he saw only the men's bobbing torsos and
their horses' heads, but it was enough to send a chill reeling
through his body. He recognized the man in front, and it was
recognition that he feared. He began to spin around, ready to
shout at the others, but something caught in his mind and made
him falter. It wasn't a clear thought at first, just a hesitation that
he tried to fight against but that kept him still and silent. He recognized the rider, but . . .

Solomon and Hiram were standing beside him by the time the
horsemen rode clear of the corn and turned toward the house,
and it was only then that Gabriel understood his own mind. The
way the rider sat his horse, the loose comfort of his dangling legs,
the supple to-and-fro of his torso . . . He fell to his knees with
the relief of the recognition.

Solomon, not knowing how to read the boy, grasped his
shoulder and said something about standing together. "We all
here, Gabriel."

But the boy smiled and shook his head, saying, "It's okay.
He's a friend."

DUNLOP AND THE MEXICAN SHARED THE BREAKFAST that
morning. The family watched the transaction between them and
Gabriel with cautious eyes. They didn't speak of the events that
had brought them together and the trials that had forged their
relationship. While this was in the back of their eyes and was
clear for all to see, the Scot kept the conversation on simple
things. He asked the men about the summer's work and commented on Eliza's cooking and praised the homestead as a fine

product of such a short time's labor. Gabriel nodded and listened and looked around at his family to see how these words
affected them.

Dunlop's face betrayed the fatigue of his torments. Tiny lines
sprang from the corners of his eyes. His lips had a thin, slack
quality while they were at rest. Only when he smiled did they
spring to full life. Indeed, that was just how he was—saddened
during the quiet moments but as likely as ever to move the conversation to things of joy, to state for all to remember the simple
things for which one might give thanks.

The Mexican sat, silent and polite. He was not a tall man but
was proportioned in such a way that he gave that impression. His
posture was erect, almost formal, and his features were composed
of strong lines. His eyes were two black stones; his nose was
prominent and bent at its midpoint. A scar above his left eyebrow cut diagonally across his forehead, and his mustache was
trimmed in a style Gabriel had seen only on the streets of Santa
Fe. The olive skin of his cheeks had been shaved recently.
Dunlop introduced him as Ludovico, Ludovico Maria Fuentes.
He looked at Gabriel when he said this name, and it was clear
that the boy listened carefully and grasped its import. But no
more was said of it just then.

It was not a day that could be spent idly, but the two visitors
insisted that they share the day's labor. Solomon looked at them
doubtfully and at first wouldn't hear of it. But Ludovico was firm
on the point. He said he was not a stranger to this work, and he
considered it only proper that hospitality should flow two ways.
He walked out to the field beside Ben, looking oddly attired for
farm life but falling into it with a vigor that impressed all.

It was Dunlop who needed direction. He was awkward with
the corn knife, seemed both afraid of damaging the stalks and at
risk of damaging himself. Gabriel asked if his family had not been
farmers, and the Scot answered, aye, they, but not he. Some skills

were not hereditary, it seemed. He carried the bundles of corn in a full embrace, finding some humor in this and turning the work into a comic dance with cornsheaf partners. He had Gabriel laughing from the outset, something that Eliza didn't fail to notice, even from a considerable distance.

The morning passed quickly into afternoon. Eliza made lunch and brought it out to them, then asked Ben for his assistance back at the house, leaving Gabriel with his two companions. The three, as if aware of the import of the moment, fell quiet. They ate studiously, chunks of rough-cut bread and slices of ham, with some greenish jelly that Gabriel had never taken to. The day was fair and breezy, with high wisps of clouds far to the north. A cowbird landed on a patch of trodden grass nearby, hopped around in curious circles, then flew off to join a company of passing blackbirds.

Eventually Ludovico sighed. He wiped his lips and smoothed his fingers over his mustache. He praised Eliza's preparation of the meal, as simple as it was, then began to speak in earnest.

"You know my family?"

Gabriel nodded that he did.

"I think you may not know what happened to them." Gabriel glanced at Dunlop and waited. And so the Mexican told him all, filling in that further portion of the nightmare.

As he spoke, Gabriel realized that he had known it all along. He hadn't let himself state it clearly. How could he? But he had known. He remembered the very night, being awakened by that form in the darkness, the mumbling voice and the sound that must have been laughter but was no kin to joy. Of course he had known. But the equally shocking revelation was that the girl must have known too. It was in her eyes the whole time. Full, complete knowledge, beyond his. Had she simply known of her own accord, or had she been told? He knew the answer right away. Caleb, who so rarely shaped words but could do it occasionally . . . Caleb had whispered it in her ear.

"My sister spoke of you," Ludovico said.

Gabriel's thoughts snapped back to the present. "She did?"

"Yes. She said you were kind to her, that you were a good person, honorable. She said that you did what you could to help her and have no guilt like the others. She said this of your friend too, the one we found."

Dunlop had been tugging absently at the stitching of his trouser leg, but his head snapped up. His eyes went straight to Gabriel, who stared at the man as if his words had made no sense whatsoever.

"I'm sorry. Perhaps you didn't know what became of him. Is that so?"

"I didn't know for sure," Gabriel said.

Ludovico pursed his lips and looked at Dunlop. "I see."

The Scot adjusted his hat, shifting the angle of it, then finding it not to his liking. He took it off and held it in his lap as he explained. "We found James, Gabe. Found him downstream a good few miles from where Marshall and them went in. I . . . I don't know, Gabe, but I don't think he had a hard time of it. He had his eyes closed. I'm no doctor, but most people I've seen die haven't been happy about it, and they all pretty much had their eyes open. Not James. Looked more like he just went to sleep." Ludovico watched him through all of this and didn't comment. "That's how it looked, at least." Dunlop didn't mention that the force of the water had sucked off the boy's boots. He went on to tell of Dallas, that he was found alive and unrepentant in his views but had not remained so for long, and of the horses and what gear they'd found. But this was all he could speak of with certainty.

"We had hoped you might tell us more," Ludovico said.

Gabriel said that he couldn't. He told the man of his escape, and the Mexican listened gravely. He began to nod when the boy spoke of the mountains and his journey there. Before long the boy stopped.

The man didn't ask him to continue but said, "Strange, when the acts of one man upon another so call out for justice, but nobody hears. This is hard for me to understand." He stood up, stretched his legs, and scented the air blowing in from the west. "I think this is the end of it. It's not the end I would have written, but . . ." Still looking off to the west, he motioned like one throwing out seeds. "I've been too long away. Thank you, Gabriel. Tomorrow I should leave."

Gabriel seemed to be seeking those seeds where they might lie in the grass. "What are you going to do now?" he asked.

Ludovico looked at Dunlop to see if he would answer first. He didn't. "Well," the Mexican said, "I'll return to my sister. We'll sell my family's land. I'll go to Santa Fe and speak to a lady I know. I'll ask her if she will have me for a husband. If she will, I'll ask her and my sister to go with me to Mexico. There is a man there, back in my father's father's country, in Guadalajara, who will employ me. We'll try to live without forgetting. I don't know if all these things will come, but I owe it to my parents to try. That's what I'll do."

To the same question Dunlop shrugged. "I don't know, Gabe. I've fair lost sense of myself." He looked as if he might speak on, but he couldn't state it any more clearly.

THE FAMILY CAME TO THE DECISION THAT EVENING. They spoke in the solitude of the soddy. Hiram said the choice was obvious. God had brought these two men here to help cleanse them of sin. Think of them not as men, he said, but as the instruments of our Lord. This was one time when God was showing them the way clearly; the least they could do was acknowledge it and do the right thing.

Solomon raised the question of a new plow, but he did so

with a quiet voice that faded, saying, "That and some more sows. Could buy Franklin's wagon off him, and next year . . ."

Hiram watched him. "You know I can't tell you what to do with your own family, but you and me both been trying to build this place with hard work and good faith. That gold's got blood on it, Solomon. You can't build a life on blood. That's what they tried to do down South, with our blood, and look how they paid for it. If we gonna do this, we gotta do it clean."

Solomon sighed. "I know. Just wanted to say it, cause I know we was all thinking it. Just wanted to say it is all, so we know what we're giving up."

"And what we're gaining."

Solomon sighed again. "Truth is, I don't know what we'd do with a gold brick anyway. Can you imagine me marching into Howe's and throwing down that hunk of metal?" This finally brought out some of the man's humor. "They'd lock me up faster than I could ask for change. And they'd keep the gold anyhow. A white man could get away with that, but naw, this land ain't gonna give us nothing we don't work for. Might not even give us that."

Eliza said only that she wanted no part of any stolen property. "Let them have it."

But before the decision was made final, they all looked at Gabriel. It was a long time before he answered. He saw something in Solomon's eyes that belied his words. Not that the man didn't agree, but there was a piece of him whose faith had been challenged too far, a piece of him that was of this world and willing to play by the rules of this world. Ben had hung his head low from the start of the conversation, but Gabriel remembered his dream of that hundred head of horses. In Eliza and Hiram he saw a firmer resolve, although he knew it was for different reasons. But they had asked for his voice, and for him the decision was easy: "Let them have it."

Before the sun had lifted itself from the night, Gabriel and Ben strode off, shovel in hand, to the turned earth on the far side of the cornfield. They went to digging with a vigor that warmed their bodies and brought moisture to their foreheads. They made quick work of it, drawing out the saddlebags and tossing them to the side and filling the hole once more. They'd put the guns in a rough wooden crate, and this they buried again, shovelful by shovelful. The boys were careful to replace the block of sod neatly, smoothing out the edges and mussing the grass so that no sign of the treasure remained. Ben asked if Gabriel wanted to take one last look at the gold, but his brother declined, saying, "I've studied it enough."

They presented the gold to the two men after they had mounted. Solomon laid it over Ludovico's saddlehorn. The man tried to refuse it, but Solomon insisted. Ludovico looked at Dunlop, and together they denied their right to such treasure. "Keep it," Dunlop said. "We wouldn't know what to do with it."

But Solomon would not allow the Mexican to give it back. He tried to form the words to explain the gift, but in the end he just stepped away and would have nothing more to do with it. "Take it. It's a gift given, and that's that," he said.

Gabriel watched the two ride away quietly. They seemed ill at ease with the gold, unsure of what to do with it and completely surprised by its appearance. The boy couldn't help feeling that something had been lost with their leavetaking. A moment had been thrown out of balance and couldn't be retrieved. But it was all right. The right thing had been done. Perhaps, Gabriel thought, someday he'd see them again. Perhaps they'd return, having prospered and turned the gold to good use. If any could erase the sins that tarnished it and make of it something good, those two could.

The men went to work as usual that morning, although a hush pervaded the group. A farmer whom Gabriel hadn't met, a Mr. March, appeared after lunch. He spoke to the men about helping

with the wheat harvest, he having newly acquired a reaper that
would speed the process.

Gabriel and Ben worked away at the last corner of the cornfield, moving more slowly as the uncut corner grew into a smaller
and smaller triangle.

"We could go get Mr. Mitchell to bring out his stallion. Get
him together with the dun," Gabriel suddenly said.

Ben paused. He stood upright, knife in hand, and gazed away
toward the south, the direction of the Mitchells' farm. "You
think?"

"Yeah. He's a good horse, ain't he?"

The boy thought this over. "Yeah. I reckon he is." His eyes
drifted over to his brother, but Gabriel turned away and continued working, the hint of a smile creasing his lips.

THE SCOT AND THE MEXICAN RODE WEST TOGETHER toward
*Crownsville, talking little, surveying the cloud-choked sky above
them, each thinking through his private dialogues. Each man's
heart beat with sadness, and to this they wished to give no voice.
The Mexican did not say that Gabriel's family reminded him of
his own, but this was so. The Scot did not voice his fear of the
yawning loneliness he felt might soon engulf him, but he saw it
coming just as clearly as he did the clouds.*

*They didn't discuss the plan that they had conceived until they
were actually before the general store. It seemed obvious. Inside the
store, they asked if the shopkeeper knew the boy's stepfather by
name and description. The shopkeeper looked between the two
men. He squinted in such a way that his eyebrows creased together
and joined in one thick black line.*

Course I do. Count him as one of my regulars.

*The Scot nodded, and the Mexican brought forth a drawstring
purse. He held it up for the man to see, then emptied it on the*

countertop. Gold coins, a few silver, several crumpled banknotes.
He told the man the money's worth and his intention. The two
men went shopping. In the next half-hour they picked out a new
plow with riggings, a wide, multipurpose woodstove, china plates
and cutlery, a bolt of gingham and a wall clock, feed for the horses
and, on a notion of the Scot's, panes of glass for windows that did
not yet exist. They requested that the goods be delivered within the
week, and did so in public hearing, so that the small crowd that
had gathered might serve as witnesses. They had the man swear to
carry out the deal exactly as requested and made it known that if
for any reason, he didn't like the nature of this transaction, they
would find somebody who did.

The shopkeeper told them to smooth their hackles over: I'm hap-
pier than a pig in shit. He said he liked the colored man well
enough himself and would see that everything was carried out to
their satisfaction. Only question he had was just what made them
folks so popular these days?

The Scot asked him what he meant.

Well, damned if you're not the second posse of cowboys through
here on the day. Two other fellas came through this morning, ask-
ing directions out to their place.

The Scot looked at his companion, but the Mexican had already
spun for the door.

THE CLOUDS STAYED HEAVY IN THE SKY as dusk approached,
but Hiram doubted they'd actually let loose before the next
morning. He and Ben hitched the mule to the wagon and rode
off to the Mitchells' with an offering of corn, payment that had
never been requested but that was well deserved for services of
friendship throughout the summer. Eliza made them swear to be
back for suppertime, and the two joked that no such swearing
was necessary. They'd be back.

The mood was light in the soddy. Eliza baked cornbread and prepared a stew thick with chicken and onion. Solomon sat across from Gabriel at the table. The man trimmed his nails with a pair of scissors and explained to the boy the state of the farm as he saw it and the profits that might be seen in the coming weeks. All told, their future looked promising, and despite his earlier reluctance over the gold, Solomon seemed content with their decision. Gabriel found this more of a relief than he could have imagined. Without realizing it, he fell into an easy flow of conversation with the man. Eliza didn't turn from her cooking, but she did pause and listen for a while, her face more at ease than it had been in many months.

They heard the horses first: the clop of their hooves against the packed earth in front of the house, a high-pitched whinny, and then a silence different from the one that had preceded it. Gabriel looked at his mother and then at Solomon. A moment passed between them, and that was all they had. The door nearly came off its hinges with the pressure of the man's kick. The first thing the boy saw was the man's boot, and then his silhouette framed against the evening sky, and then he was inside. Marshall, followed by the black angel on his shoulder. It took the man a moment to take in the room, and in this time Solomon flew toward the rifle above the window, Eliza stood and gripped Gabriel by the elbow, and the boy faced them head on. All motion stopped there, however, as Marshall's hands rose up, long-barreled forty-fours pointed at both man and boy. Caleb's rifle made one sweeping scan that seemed to leave all vulnerable.

"Well," Marshall said, "if this ain't cozy. Nigger, go head and touch that. See if I don't make your boy a bastard and your wife a whore."

Solomon's arm was extended toward the rifle, but he held it steady. His fingers trembled, his eyes shifted from man to man, and his lips were pressed so tightly together that it looked painful. He didn't lower his hand; neither did he complete the motion.

"Look, you heard me, didn't you? I wouldn't hesitate, but before you go and do something stupid, I'll just tell you I'm here on business. Simple as that. Business between me and the boy. Once completed, we'll be on our way. Think about that fore you ruin your family's life."

In the space of these few sentences, Gabriel had heard and remembered all that was Marshall. The explosion of profanity, so quickly followed by his reasonable voice, his smooth cadence and confident eyes and that smile, which tickled one side of his lips and then the other as he spoke. Gabriel turned to speak to Solomon, but the man had already lowered his arm. The boy wanted to cry out, but again the room was in motion.

Caleb slipped from behind Marshall and in two strides covered the distance between him and Solomon. He hit Solomon hard with the flat of his rifle's stock, snapping the man's head to one side and leaving him dazed. Gabriel moved toward Caleb, but Marshall caught his foot and sent him sprawling. He rose in an instant, but by then Marshall had his arms around Eliza, one pistoled hand tight against her breast, the other aimed point-blank at her cheek. Solomon fell below Caleb's weight.

Marshall smiled and for the first time addressed himself to Gabriel. He spoke slowly and courteously. "Left us for dead, didn't you? Well, I can't blame you. Things were getting a bit out of hand. But should have had more faith, my boy, should have had more faith."

Caleb finished binding Solomon. He threw him facedown on the floor, bound his legs and hands together, and pulled them taut, so that he lay like a cradle against the matting. This done, Caleb proceeded to do the same to Gabriel, then to tie up Eliza.

Marshall talked throughout, telling of what had befallen himself and Caleb after they'd entered the river. He spoke not as one wielding a gun and binding prisoners but as an old companion to a friend who had, sadly, let him down. He told of his swim in the Colorado, the nights spent sharing a horse and sneaking across the desert, the mule that he had had to ride and the lawman who had found humor in this and so sealed his fate in this life. He said the whole affair had made for a pathetic show—"Nothing to be proud of, I'll tell you that much." He speculated that Gabriel had fared much better, on a stout horse like the dun mare, what with a little armory and a load of something special to boot.

Caleb's fingers were as hard as wood. They were bony and long, yet so powerful that they cinched Gabriel's wrists together in the grip of one hand. The man carried lengths of rope draped around his neck, as a tailor would a tape measure. And he went about his work with a similar crispness, snapping a few coils of the rope around the boy's wrists, passing one piece over and under the other, then twisting the knot and threading the rope back through. Gabriel could feel the man's breath on him, so close were their faces, and just as Caleb drew the knot taut, he met the boy's gaze. His eyes were as jaundiced and coal-black as ever, but for once they looked at the boy with an expression he could read.

Gabriel slammed his eyes shut, for the man's eyes projected a version of the future that threatened to crowd out all semblance of sanity. It was not that the boy had read Caleb's thoughts. Rather, it seemed that the man had thrust them upon the boy, using an almost physical force to push against his eyelids and try to enter his being. Images clamored before him like spirits calling to be made flesh. They were so close, so strong. They were nearly everything, but Gabriel fought them off, knowing he had to think more clearly than ever before. The look in Caleb's eyes had told him that completely. The end was written there, and it would be a very bad end. It would be unthinkable, unless he could find a way. He must find a way. He opened his eyes again.

Caleb had stepped away and turned his attention to Eliza. Marshall had been rolling a cigarette as he spoke. He didn't light it, just rolled it between his fingers. He sat down with his legs spread wide. "Now what do you reckon? Should we have ourselves a little something to eat, or should we get right to business?" he said. The room answered with silence. Marshall looked at Caleb, smiled, and shrugged. "They ain't got much to say, do they?" He looked over the table, working his mouth casually, a bit like an elderly man might with his dentures. He pulled off a chunk of bread, dipped it in the stew, and lifted it, dripping, to his mouth.

Eliza was tied to a chair beside the table. Caleb pushed it to the side and sat just before her. He folded back her dress, exposing the naked flesh of her legs. Solomon craned his head to see, muttering a curse, but Caleb kept his full attention on the woman's face. He ran one thin finger up her inner thigh. He went just so far, lifted his finger away, and touched it to the other thigh. He did this mechanically, slowly, looking only into the woman's eyes and never wavering in his gaze.

Speaking through a full mouth, Marshall complimented Eliza on her cooking. "That's a fine, fine meal. You know, this kind of thing half puts me in the mind to find myself a wife. That might be just the thing I need. Course, a woman's expensive. My kind of woman, anyway." He glanced at Caleb as if he'd just remembered him. "What's going on here?" he asked, cracking a smile that said he knew the answer well enough. He stood up and looked over Caleb's shoulder, taking in the view. "Nice. Altogether a nice piece, for a colored. You'd like a little poke, wouldn't you? That's what you're thinking about. You see the look on ole Caleb's face?" He turned to Gabriel. "See that look? That's a man thinking about getting himself up to some unholy, barbaric doings. The kind of stuff Clemmins used to get up to. Makes me wish we had the time for it."

Marshall sat back down and crossed his legs. "But alas, time is not a thing to waste. And ya know, I may look a wealthy man, but I've nothing but my good name and misappropriated horse. That and a couple of guns. Couldn't hardly go courting, could I? And that's what's brought me to you people. Your boy here rode off with a fair chunk of my property. A horse I loved like a . . . well, like a horse. My guns and ammo and a little something else. I don't suppose he told you about that little extra something, did he?"

"We buried it," Gabriel said.

Marshall had directed his question to Eliza, but he turned and looked at Gabriel. "You don't say? You buried it?"

The boy nodded.

"You sure, now? I won't be sore if you bought yourself something sweet along the way. Just make sure you're not lying to me."

"I'm not. It's just outside a ways."

Marshall pulled Gabriel up by his shoulder. "Come on. I'll leave you folks in Caleb's hands." He shoved Gabriel toward the door.

Eliza met her son's eyes. It was just a second of connection, a brief glance that asked him a whole host of questions. But then the boy was gone, the questions left unanswered.

MARSHALL UNTIED THE BOY'S HANDS and had him walk a few paces before him, carrying the spade. Gabriel led him to the spot beside the creek, the same spot he'd dug up and filled in that same morning. Marshall inspected the ground with suspicious eyes until he got his fingers into a crease in the turf and pulled up the flap as smoothly as one would a rug. He gestured to the boy to work.

With each stroke it seemed the spade dug farther into the soil than Gabriel would have liked. His muscles shoved the tool into the earth but recoiled as the iron blade bit. It was a strange

motion, made even more awkward by the fact that Marshall sat
watching him. Gabriel tried to ignore him, digging as if alone in
the world and on a mission of his own accord. But he couldn't
help glancing at the man.

Marshall rested an elbow on one knee, drawing quietly on his
cigarette and watching Gabriel dig. When he exhaled smoke, he
tended to look off to the horizon, his eyes exploring it for only
the length of the breath, then coming back to the boy. As casual
as he seemed, Gabriel didn't for a moment forget the pistol that
he held cradled between his legs. He occasionally took his hand
from it, to touch his hat brim or smooth over the coarse hair of
his unshaven face. Each time he did this, Gabriel's heart quick-
ened. His mind surged. How quickly could he cover the three
paces to the man? Could he drive the spade point first into his
neck? Could he swing it up and smash the back of it across his
face? Would he get an extra second if the man was looking into
the distance?

Marshall chuckled, and Gabriel realized that he'd been staring
at the gun and his digging had slowed. He bent to the work
again.

"Don't you wish?" Marshall said. "You'd like to kill me,
wouldn't you? Boy, you are a piece of work. I did a better job on
you than I knew. You know what I said that first day I saw you
and the other one? I said, 'Hell, this here boy's greener than a
blade of bluegrass.' That's exactly what I said. But I saw you had
the potential. You had an anger I thought I might could redirect
in a more useful direction, if you know what I mean. You can't
say I was all wrong, either. You did turn out to be a doublecross-
ing, thieving little chigger. Cept you stole from the wrong person.
That, and you turned out to be a self-righteous son of a bitch to
boot. I couldn't've predicted all that. You got brains a
dimwit like Dallas or Rollins never even thought of, you know
that? My personal opinion is that you shouldn't've used them

brains to buck me. Most white folks think a boy like you is nothing but a hairless gorilla. You could've used that. Could've had the last laugh on all of them." He shook his head and spat. "Well, fuck it. What am I wasting my words for? You done fucked yourself, Archangel. Fucked yourself and your whole damn family." The man got up and stretched his legs.

Gabriel dug on, averting his eyes so completely from Marshall that he wasn't actually looking at his work. He could barely control the chill that passed through his body when the shovel hit the trunk. He paused despite himself, and Marshall smiled.

"That's the sound I was waiting for. Go on."

Gabriel uncovered the top, brushed it off with his fingers, and worked the edges free of dirt. He used the shovel to pry the box loose, rocking it with his weight, and finally managed to get his fingers around either side of it and hoist it out. He fell to the side as he did so, and the weight landed hard on the soil next to him. Again Gabriel's head reeled with fear, but the box made nothing more than an innocuous shifting sound. Marshall didn't seem to notice.

"Okay, get up. Boy, you don't how lucky you are. I've half a mind to call off my grudge and ride out of here unbloodied." He knelt down and touched the lid of the box, finding its latch and tugging it with his fingers. "Yessir, but that's only half my mind. Other half's a different matter. Where the hell's the key for this thing?"

"Inside."

A flicker of annoyance passed over the man's face. "We best go get it then," he said, motioning with the gun, and Gabriel fell into step before him, crate in hand.

Gabriel's boots swished through the grass. Behind him, Marshall's spurs produced a slight jingling with each step. The boy tried to block out the sounds and plan what he would do next. He had set this in motion, and now he'd have to see it through. If he could just get the guns in his hands . . . He'd have to try to get the key himself, to open the box himself and hope that he'd have the chance to do what came next. There was no other way now.

Marshall started talking as they headed back along the cornfield, saying something about the strange behavior of people with a gun pointed at them, but Gabriel suddenly ceased listening. His eyes shot up at some inclination of their own, and there he saw the first ripple of movement coming over the hill. It was Hiram and Ben returning in the wagon. He wasn't sure whether Marshall saw them, but the sight sent his mind reeling. It seemed that with this development, all notion of a plan was gone. He wanted to rise on the balls of his feet and shout for them to flee. He wished he could drop the box right there and have the revolvers in his hand. He would shoot this time. He would shoot with everything he had. He could—

Marshall clucked his tongue. "If that ain't a hassle. Who's that?"

Gabriel didn't answer.

Marshall shoved him on the shoulder. "Who is it? They family?"

Gabriel listened to himself speak but barely felt that he was creating the words.

"That's just dandy. Don't get any ideas, Archangel. You know who you're dealing with, don't you? You know you only live as long as I say." With that, Marshall urged the boy forward. "Keep it casual."

They walked on, and the wagon rolled in. Gabriel tried to focus once more, to calm his mind and bring it back. He couldn't signal to them. He knew that much. If he did, and if they somehow understood the signal and fled for help, they'd find the others dead on their return.

They closed to within two hundred yards. Before long, the

squeaking of the wagon's wheels carried over the distance.
Hiram and Ben exchanged glances. They said something to each
other, but they kept coming.

Marshall and Gabriel passed in front of the barn and moved
across the trampled earth toward the house. "Just don't do nothing stupid," Marshall said. "Let them come on in."

A hundred yards. The wheels moved slowly, wobbling.
Gabriel could just make out the features of Hiram's and Ben's
faces. He stared for a long moment and tried to pull Ben's eyes
to him. What he might say or how, he didn't know, but he must
make the contact. He did, and whether he had a message to convey or not, Ben read something there. He turned, spoke to
Hiram, and reached for something behind him.

This was enough for Marshall. He lifted one of his pistols and
fired. The shot missed Hiram but passed close enough that he
cocked his head and listened to the bullet's passage. He yanked
the reins and turned toward Ben. In the time this took, Marshall
backhanded Gabriel across the face, sending him sprawling and
loosing the box from his hands. The man was on the boy in a
moment. He pushed his face into the ground and planted the
weight of his knee against Gabriel's forearm and pressed the barrel of one of the pistols against the back of his hand.

Marshall resumed shooting with his free hand. This time
Hiram fell back. He tried to get off the wagon, clutching his side
as he did, then changed his mind and urged the horse to speed
up. He yelled something to Ben, who jumped from the wagon
and ran, rifle in hand. Marshall fired the pistol, hitting Hiram
once more and leaving him sprawled across the seat of the moving wagon.

Gabriel tried to wrench his hand free. He punched at
Marshall with his other hand, but the man's eyes stayed on the
field, following Ben.

He had spent the bullets of one gun. He let it drop and pulled the trigger of the other pistol, the one pressed against Gabriel's flesh. The boy felt an explosion of pain that began in his hand but ripped through the rest of his body like an electric shock. He collapsed beneath it, rolling on his back and holding his hand by the wrist before him, staring at its trembling, blood-red image against the gray sky. He was aware that Marshall was standing up and emptying the second pistol, but he knew of Ben's escape because of the man's response.

"Goddamn the little chigger! He's fast as a monkey, he is." He yanked Gabriel to his feet. "Get up, you, and stop your wailing." He pushed Gabriel forward and stepped toward the box.

Only then did Gabriel get some sense of purpose back. He circled around the man and motioned that he would still carry the box. He got the fingers of his good hand under it and, using his foot and then his elbow, hefted it up. Marshall commented that he mustn't be hurt too bad, then walked behind him the rest of the way to the house, reloading the pistols along the way. Caleb was standing in the doorway to greet them.

THE YOUNGER BROTHER RAN OVER THE RISE and on to the west. Before long his lungs were scorched by the effort, his legs numb and exhausted. His breathing came in deep, labored gasps, and his ears rang with the sounds his body made as he flew into the wind. But it was none of these things that finally stopped him. It was the recollection, sudden and complete, of why he was running, and what that meant for those he loved. He slowed, stumbled over something, then sprawled on the grass, still clutching the rifle.

At first the boy just lay in the grass, so shocked that he could form no clear thought but felt only a jumble of emotions that he fought not to believe. He didn't know these men. He'd never spoken to them or heard their voices or looked closely into their eyes. How could he know what was the right thing to do? He didn't even know how many of them there were. He'd seen two horses, but . . . Maybe they just wanted the money. They might ride off at any second . . . But there was no money. They weren't riding anywhere. They had already shot his uncle. They had shown themselves for what they were. He knew his brother had not yet told him the full extent of their evil, and now they had come to show them all.

He had to speak to himself in simple words, clearly, silently, to steady his mind. Think. Turn and go back. He must do something, for he couldn't wait for them to do what they would. He tried to tell himself that his actions would not open a window to chaos. That window was already open. All he could do was try to close it. He had a glimpse of a world without those he loved, and the wave of anguish it sent through him was enough to send him to his feet. He would have to find a way, and he could run no farther than this very spot on the plains.

As he turned, his eyes fell on the thing that had tripped him. There in the tall grass were the sun-weathered bones of some creature's skeleton. His mind immediately conjured up morbid images of a dead human, but almost as quickly his eyes noticed the ragged fur that cloaked some of the mass, the curves of an animal rib cage, and the long muzzle that could only be canine. Rows of incisors still clung to the jaw, but the flesh all about them and the rest of the bones had been cleaned almost completely, pulled at, no doubt, by vultures, and eaten by maggots, and attacked by various other creatures seen and unseen by the human eye.

His eyes rose and combed the grass nearby as if he expected to see burial markers. There was nothing, only the dry grass and the warm wind from the south and the cloudy sky. He turned his gaze toward the rise that separated him from his home. He didn't ask what providence had brought this sign to him. He just started walking, cracking the gun open as he did so and checking that it was loaded. He steadied his mind around the fact that he had only

one shot with this old Kentucky long. Only one. He had only the
shot already primed in the rifle. The rest of his ammo lay in the
back of the wagon.

The boy closed his eyes for the space of several breaths. He
walked on, feeling the grass brush against his legs. Steady. Steady
the mind. Hide in the trees along the creek. There would be a clear
shot from there. Steady. This was the biggest thing he'd ever been
asked to do. He pushed the questions away and filled their spaces
with the words the uncle had taught him to say before killing.

MARSHALL INSTRUCTED CALEB TO BRING THE OTHERS OUT,
and the key along with them. Caleb slipped back inside without
comment. On a nod from Marshall, Gabriel set the box down
beside the men's horses. His hand gushed blood. He didn't
know whether to clench it or to let it hang limp, so he did
both, alternately. Each time he flexed it, a searing pain shot up
his arm. When he relaxed it, he could feel the painful pulse
through his palm. His shirt and pants were soon stained a thick
red.

When Solomon and Eliza stepped outside, their eyes flew
straight to Gabriel. Eliza gasped and tried to go to him. Marshall
stepped in her way and explained, "He's all right. Just hand-
shot. It's painful, and it's a bitch to heal, but it won't be the thing
that kills him."

In answer to his mother's questioning gaze, Gabriel muttered
something. Marshall silenced him with a forceful blow to his
abdomen, but the couple seemed to understand well enough.
Within seconds they saw the wagon and the dim shape half hidden within it. Solomon called for the presence of God, and Eliza
asked if she could go tend to Hiram. But Marshall told her to
shut her trap. He figured the old fella was dead meat right
enough, and there was nothing she could do about it.

She hung her head. "I guess we can't expect a moment's worth of decency from you."

"No, don't expect nothing from him," Solomon said. His voice was tight. It was an exertion just to form the words, but he spat them out with vehemence. "The fool walketh in darkness, and so too shall he be damned to darkness."

Marshall found this very amusing, but he chose not to answer either of them directly. "Another time I'd discourse with you. Unfortunately, we ain't got much time, not with the way that monkey was running. We better keep ourselves to business. What do you say, Caleb? We gonna get this over with and pull foot?"

Caleb went on staring at Eliza.

"There's time to finish this off, but that's about it."

Caleb turned his head toward Marshall. He didn't speak but shared a moment in vision with the white man. There was a statement on his face, and Gabriel read it as clearly as Marshall did.

"Okay," Marshall said, "you do what you want once I leave, but I'm getting the gold and going. The rest is up to yourself."

Caleb nodded.

Marshall motioned with his hand, and Caleb nudged the couple in the back of the legs so they fell to their knees. "Now," Marshall said, "open that crate, and let's see what we got." He tossed the boy the key. "I'll tell you what. I'll even give you one way out. All you gotta do is send a prayer to heaven asking for a miracle, and this is it. You're gonna open up that crate now and pull out my rightful plunder. You're gonna count out the bricks, and if they come to two—two solid bricks of gold bullion—I'll consider it a divine intervention, and the lot of you will win yourselves a pardon. But if God don't see fit to intervene in this way . . . then you can name the spot where you take the bullet. I won't even take no joy from it. You just name your spot. We'll take care of each of you the same way."

Gabriel looked down at the box. He didn't raise his eyes when he spoke. His voice was dry, forlorn, and older than ever before. "Marshall, there never were two bars."

"Exactly. You sure do cut to the quick of things when you want to. That's why I'm looking for an act of God. You people have faith, don't ya? Let's put it to the test."

"We don't test our God," Solomon said. He kneeled beside his wife, both with their hands bound behind them, but he held himself straight, chin high and bruised face jutting up into the air. "He tests us. All else is vanity." He didn't look at Marshall directly but added, almost as an afterthought, "And you're about the vainest man that ever walked the earth."

Marshall thought this over for a second, seemed to consider ignoring it, but then walked over and leaned close to Solomon's face. "Don't quote Scripture to me. You think I can't spit it back at ya, don't ya? Well, 'Vanity of vanities. All is vanity.' Ecclesiastes. Same book that says, 'If the clouds be full of rain, they empty themselves upon the earth, and if the tree fall toward the south, or toward the north, in the place where the tree falleth, there it shall be.' Now what the hell does that mean? Ain't that the biggest piece of nonsense you ever heard? And I'll tell you another thing. I grew up listening to this shit, and the man who taught it to me was my father. Called himself Clemmins, and that's all I really ever called him myself, cause I wasn't about to call him Papa. This man used to spout the gospel like nobody's business. You woulda thought he had the spirit in him for sure, cept he was the evilest bastard I've ever known. Worse than Caleb here."

He straightened up, looking as though he might conclude the matter with that, but he caught Eliza's eye and remembered something. He moved over to her, pushing Caleb out of the way to get near her face.

"There were a few good things Clemmins did for me when I was a boy," he said. "One of them was, he set me up with my first screw. She was a black woman, much like yourself." Behind Marshall, Caleb shifted his eyes. He looked away from Eliza and focused on the back of Marshall's head. "Pretty thing she was, in her way. She was dark, like she'd just got off the boat from Guinea. She knew how to be ridden, too." He turned away and gestured at Gabriel with his gun. "Open that thing."

Gabriel turned the key, and the padlock fell open silently, as if it had died in his hands and gone limp. The boy moved slowly, for he had seen the shift in Caleb's gaze. He moved the lock away from the crate and set it on the ground, then brought his fingers to the rusted iron of the latch. Caleb's eyes had been steel-cold upon his mother, until something Marshall said . . . He lifted the latch free and released it. Caleb's face had undergone a slow recoiling, as if he'd been slapped by a hand moving in slow motion . . . The latch stayed exactly where he left it, pointing toward him. Gabriel half opened it. He tried to read Caleb's expression, and still he could not. The man took a step toward Marshall; his lips moved; his eyes blinked; but he was wholly unreadable.

Gabriel slipped his hand inside the crate, and for a few frantic seconds he felt nothing but the dusty grain of the wood. Then his fingers brushed something. He grasped it in the palm of his hand. It was cool against his flesh, hard and small. His finger touched the trigger. It seemed so tiny in his hand. He held out a second longer, but that was all he had. His hand rose, and with it the top of the box swung open and up came the gun, tight in his grip. The boy fully realized what he'd done only when he saw the short muzzle of the derringer before him. He knew in a flash of clarity that with this gun he'd have only one shot, a small shot at that, one that would have to be taken at close range.

Before he had time to act, a shot came from the trees along the creek. Beyond Marshall, Caleb jerked suddenly. He turned to the left, and as he did so, a spray of moisture sprang from his shoulder and hung for a second in the air. A snap followed, a dull, muted sound that Gabriel recognized as rifle fire. Marshall might have seen the gun in Gabriel's hand, but he moved before he'd fully comprehended it. In the second it took the man to call to Caleb, Gabriel sprang to his feet, leapt over the box, and laid the muzzle of the derringer against Marshall's neck. The man's eyes snapped toward him, full recognition there for the first time, and the boy pulled the trigger.

At first it seemed as if nothing had changed. Marshall stood with a look on his face that was not much different from his familiar smirk. He didn't raise his gun. He didn't move. Then all at once his eyes flushed red, deeply and darkly red, a crimson like that which suddenly poured forth from his nose and tinted his teeth. He opened his mouth and stepped toward the boy. Gabriel thought he was falling, but instead Marshall grabbed him by the neck and brought him to his chest with one all-powerful arm. He jerked his body in one direction and another, using Gabriel as a shield against any more bullets. But he could not find the source of the shot that hit Caleb, and he turned the boy to face his parents.

Caleb held his rifle in one hand, but the other arm dangled, limp. When Marshall tried to speak, his voice was muffled and altogether unintelligible. He twice tried to form words but came out with a rasping, gurgling chaos of sound. Instead he gestured his instructions to Caleb with his gun hand, then brought the barrel of his pistol to rest on Gabriel's cheek. He turned the boy's face toward his parents so that he would see them die.

Caleb looked slowly from Marshall to the bound couple, then back to Marshall again. If he felt the pain of his shoulder wound, he showed no sign. Neither did he show any inclination to follow the other man's directions, although it was clear enough that he understood them.

Gabriel couldn't see Marshall's face from where he stood, but he could tell the man's eyes were locked on Caleb's. He ordered

him once more to shoot the couple, his voice a loud rasp that
managed to express his meaning through the rage of the sound
alone. But again Caleb stared as if he'd heard no such command.
Finally Marshall cursed the black man and pulled his pistol away
from Gabriel to shoot the others himself.

Only then did Caleb move. He lifted the rifle up to sight.
From Gabriel's angle, it looked as if the man were aiming at him.
When Caleb pulled the trigger, the boy even felt the impact of
the bullet against the side of his head. The arm gripping him
moved away, and he fell free, into space. He hit the ground with a
thud that released him from the sensation, and his body sprang
up of its own accord. He spun in a sharp half-circle and realized
then that it was not he who had been shot.

Marshall lay sprawled on his back, arms wide and pistol thrown
some distance away. The boy stared at him, disbelieving. He tore
his eyes away to search out Caleb, who was slowly lowering the
rifle. The black man's eyes were dark pinpoints in his face, like
stones embedded in him, rock-hard objects whose function was
uncertain. He shifted them from the fallen body, up to the boy,
then over to the kneeling couple. They all stared back at him, sharing a moment of silence louder than any they'd ever heard.

*THE TWO MEN RODE as if the entire world depended on their
speed. Their horses ran neck and neck, pushing through the high
prairie grass, sending up a flock of doves before them, and leaving
behind them that strange silence that is the wake of bodies slicing
the air. The horses were lathered and exhausted and cried within
themselves for this to stop. But it didn't. It couldn't. The Scot felt
his horse throw a shoe, and he thanked the horse for being all and
completely the beautiful creature that she was. The Mexican only
rode, knowing that each second passing here was a second passing
there as well.*

Both men knew where they were as they approached a gently sloping rise. It was a subtle feature on an expanse of similar features. They knew that they should slow here and think this through. But they didn't, and the distance closed. The momentum they had already created, which was many weeks old now, carried them on. They crested the rise, and the homestead came into view. Only then did they rein in their mounts.

They could barely make out the players' identities from this distance, but they knew immediately that the scene was not one they could have predicted. They took it all in within the space of a few seconds: the wounded in the field, those bound beside the soddy, the two standing, and the dead form laid out motionless in the short grass. Before the Scot could converse with him, the Mexican had spurred his horse forward. He swept down the slope at a mad run, a confusion of hooves and flapping arms and a sound that the Scot realized only later was some sort of war cry.

The black man saw him coming. He looked from one to the other of the party around him, lingering on the dead man, and then he walked to his horse. He mounted, again surveyed the carnage that he had helped create, and moved his horse forward. First at a walk, then into a canter, and finally, as if gaining strength as he moved out of the orbit of the homestead, up to a gallop. He moved to the east, away from his pursuer. He didn't look back. He managed to make his way out of the shallow depression that was the homestead, to rise up and watch as the sky opened before him in all of its magnificent breadth.

But he got little farther than this. He felt his horse shudder before he heard the rifle's report. The beast paused in midstride, trembled, and lost step, then regained its footing and ran on as if it were mistaken about its own injury and could gallop away from it. It couldn't. Within fifty yards it went down, falling onto its rear and spilling the man off its backside. The man rolled away, found his footing, and dodged as the horse's hind legs flared out at

*the air. It tried to rise but couldn't, and the man saw the wound
and knew it was one of death. His rifle was trapped beneath the
horse. He had a pistol in a hip holster. He touched it once, almost
unconsciously, but he did not draw, and soon let his hand relax at
his side.*

*The Mexican rode toward him, now unhurried, his rifle point-
ing to the sky. He stopped before him. There was much the
Mexican had thought he would say at this moment. He had
rehearsed his words in quiet hours both waking and sleeping, and
he didn't forget them now. Neither did he speak. The black man
stood before him, but it was clear that words had little meaning at
a time like this. In fact, words might simply defile the sanctity of
what was to come. Instead, the Mexican lowered his rifle and shot
the other through the chest. The blast blew the black man backward and laid him out flat, heart-shot and spine-broken. His fingers twitched at his side for a few seconds, but this was his last
motion. The Mexican looked down only long enough to verify his
death. Then he let his gaze rise up and float across the plains.*

*The sky was a deepening gray. The clouds lay like the underside
of a great cotton blanket, with all its softness and ripples and
curves and weight. The black man's horse still breathed slow,
labored breaths, and the wind rushed across the prairie, rippling
the grass like the ghosts of the great herds. But these were the only
sounds. In all the world, these were the only sounds. The labored
breathing of the living. The whispers of ghosts.*

EPILOGUE

IN THE EVENING, THE BELOVED UNCLE SPEAKS. He tells a tale that all around him have heard before. It is the story of a young man loose in the world. The boy wanders through the land and looks upon things with his own eyes, as he trusts little the words of others. He sees the glory of God, sees his creations as they go about their loves and hates, sees them make a confusion of that which could be so divine. He sees them struggle with the petty things that they believe to be their souls but that are not. This boy becomes a man, and he speaks to the people in words he hopes they'll understand, but few do. These few are a blessing to him. He holds them as close as he can while beckoning to the others, to the mass of souls who will not listen, they who fuel the turmoil of the world. These tortured souls must be won over one at a time, sometimes with joy, other times through great suffering. For some, suffering is the only way.

The uncle takes a seat gingerly, for his wounds heal slowly. He looks around at those he calls family. They sit quietly. The father and the mother, the two sons whose faces so mirror each other, the foreigner who will stay awhile in these people's quiet company: they all listen. Each is reverent in his own way, each saddened and joyful in his own way. The uncle sees a question unspoken on the eldest son's lips. And he answers it.

Sometimes the trials the children face go beyond any their parents imagined, and yet it is not for them to reason with divinity. There are moments when even the angels of God must do battle. Did not Raphael do battle with Asmodeus? Did not Elijah smite the prophets of Baal? And was it not Michael, who sits at God's right hand, who threw down Satan and his legions? He tells them that a battle won in the name of good, for protection of family and against the devil's agents, is a blessed thing. Remember that the angel Uriel, who guarded the gates of Eden, stood with a fiery sword in his hand. No, the uncle says. There is no sin in this. Not even the angels live in peace. At least, not yet.

ACKNOWLEDGMENTS

First, of course, I thank my wife, Gudrun, whose faith carried me
through the lean days and pushed me into territory I would not
have dared tread alone.

My mother, Joan Scurlock. You are the beginning of all my
stories. Thank you for creating this kid and then letting him find
his strange way in the world.

My agent, Sloan Harris. Thanks for stepping into the fray
with such enthusiasm.

And a most heartfelt thanks to my editor, Deborah Cowell.
You felt my writing from the early days, when few others did, and
your patient efforts and faith have truly been a blessing.

I'd also like to thank everyone in the clans Johnston, Durham,
and Scurlock. One way or another, pieces of you all live in everything I write.

This novel is a work of the imagination. All the characters and events and many of the central settings, such as Crownsville, McKutcheon's Station, and the Three Bars Ranch, are completely fictional. While I've done my best to ensure the accuracy of all historical details, I also accept full responsibility for any errors. And although my landscapes may occasionally vary from those of geographical fact, they are certainly true to my intention to convey the diverse majesty that is the real American West.